Also by Sue Moorcroft:

The Christmas Promise
Just For the Holidays
The Little Village Christmas
One Summer in Italy

A CHRISTMAS GIFT

Sue Moorcroft writes award-winning contemporary fiction of life and love. *The Little Village Christmas* was a *Sunday Times* bestseller and *The Christmas Promise* went to #1 in the Kindle chart. She also writes short stories, serials, articles, columns, courses and writing 'how to'.

An army child, Sue was born in Germany then lived in Cyprus, Malta and the UK and still loves to travel. Her other loves include writing (the best job in the world), reading, watching Formula 1 on TV and hanging out with friends, dancing, yoga, wine and chocolate.

If you're interested in being part of #TeamSueMoorcroft you can find more information at www.suemoorcroft.com/street-team. If you prefer to sign up to receive news of Sue and her books, go to www.suemoorcroft.com and click on 'Newsletter'. You can follow @SueMoorcroft on Twitter, @SueMoorcroftAuthor on Instagram, or Facebook.com/sue.moorcroft.3 and Facebook.com/SueMoorcroftAuthor.

A Christmas Gift

Sue Moorcroft

avon.

AVON

A division of HarperCollins*Publishers*
1 London Bridge Street,
London SE1 9GF

www.harpercollins.co.uk

A hardback original 2018

1

A catalogue record for this book is
available from the British Library

ISBN-13: 978-0-00-826007-1

Typeset by Palimpsest Book Production Ltd, Falkirk, Stirlingshire

Printed and bound in Great Britain by CPI Group (UK) Ltd, Croydon CR0 4YY

MIX
Paper from
responsible sources
FSC www.fsc.org **FSC™ C007454**

To every wonderful member of my street team
Team Sue Moorcroft
with grateful thanks for your support.
You rock!

Chapter One

Georgine tied the laces of her running shoes, keeping one anxious eye on the patterned glass in her front door and the two manly shapes silhouetted by November sunlight.

One of them knocked with measured movements. 'Miss France? Miss France? Come to the door, please.' Then he muttered something to his companion.

The companion answered clearly, 'Not giving up yet,' and leant on the doorbell, raising his voice above the sound. 'If you could just open the door, Miss France, we won't keep you long.'

Everything about the men and their insistence said 'debt collectors'. Even though she knew they weren't as bad as bailiffs, who could lawfully gain entry, they raised too many horrible memories for her to open the door, even just to say that Aidan no longer lived with her. She wouldn't have expected to be believed, anyway.

Heart tumbling, she fumbled herself into her running jacket and gloves, then checked her backpack for the Christmas student show production file. Yep, there was its pretty Christmassy cover, nestling on top of her distinctly less-Christmassy work clothes. Quietly, she swung the backpack onto her shoulders and let herself silently out of the back door, heaving a sigh of relief as she turned the key. The debt collectors would have to come up the footpath behind the terraced houses on Top Farm Road and climb her six-foot fence to see her here. She hoped they wouldn't, because that was the route she was about to use to escape.

Breath forming a white cloud, she loped across the lawn, every grass blade rimed with frost and squeaking beneath her feet. A run and jump onto a garden chair and her gloves found enough purchase on the top of the ice-beaded fence to allow her to swing a leg over the top, then she was up, over and jogging along the footpath.

When she reached the point where Scott Road met Top Farm Road she lengthened her stride. She'd intended to drive to work until her unwanted callers had planted themselves between her and her elderly hatchback, but it was exhilarating to race through the zing of frost on the morning air. Any number of men could bang on her door all day long without bothering her.

Her breath came easily as she found her rhythm, legs carrying her out of the Bankside estate, soon reaching the last houses of Middledip village. The pavement petered out and her comfortably worn running shoes began slapping the road. She tried to concentrate on thinking about props for the Christmas show, but every time a car whooshed past she hopped onto the verge and held her breath in case it was the debt collectors and they'd somehow guess she was the Miss France they'd been trying to speak to.

It was a relief, when she'd covered a mile or so, to swing left beneath an iron arch bearing a white sign with black writing:

ACTING INSTRUMENTAL

Performing Arts College

Sanctuary. A place where she could leave reality behind. Her running feet ate up the final few hundred yards as she wove through students ambling along the drive, chatting or heads down over their phones.

One called, 'Good mawnin', Mizz Jaw-Jean,' in a pretty fair Midwest American accent.

Laughing breathlessly, she raised a gloved hand. The student, Isla, was not only a drama student at Acting Instrumental, but the daughter of Sian from Georgine's own schooldays. Her schoolmates in the huge comprehensive school in the nearby town of Bettsbrough had loved to rib her with awful parodies of her American father's soft Georgia drawl. She wished she had a pound for every time her teenaged self had heard it. It might pay off the scary men at her door – if it had been her debt they were trying to collect. Which it wasn't.

She'd honestly thought she'd finally be OK for money when she landed the job of events director at Acting Instrumental three years ago, but what with Georgine's dad and her sister, Blair, needing support at different times, and Aidan falling apart upon being made redundant, which had led to the current financial mess . . . Still, never a day passed without her thanking her stars that she hadn't been daunted by the formal language in the ad for an events director of student productions. What her role actually required her to be was stage manager, producer, handholder, bridge-builder and breach-filler.

Georgine specialised in that kind of role.

She veered towards the main building. Barely slowing as

3

she yanked off her backpack, she touched her pass to the card reader. The door clicked a greeting and glided aside.

The first person her gaze fell on was Norman Ogden, the principal of Acting Instrumental, strolling past the as yet naked Christmas tree in the foyer at his usual deceptive pace. Peering from under his fringe, he reminded Georgine of an enormous schoolboy who'd found an adult set of clothes and tried them on. 'Cold enough for snow,' she panted, to draw her boss's attention away from the fact that she only had a few minutes in which to change out of her running gear before work.

'A snow day to keep us at home would probably suit the students,' he responded good-naturedly. 'Need a catch-up. Quick meeting, you and me, ten minutes, my room?'

'Great,' she replied as she jogged towards the staff area, suppressing the urge to point out that she was busy, busy, busy as it was just six weeks until opening night of *A Very Kerry Christmas, Uncle Jones,* this year's Christmas show by the top year students. It would be her sixth show since she'd come to the college.

And she had to phone Aidan to give him a giant bollocking about responsibility dodging. It was more than time for him to man up. She sighed as she reached the female staff locker room. Left over from when the house had been a luxury private residence, the locker room had a sumptuous pale grey marble shower room attached.

Queen of the lightning-fast shower, she switched on the water, wriggled out of her running kit and hung it on the radiator so it wouldn't be clammy for the run home, and jumped into the spray. Soon she was dressing in the clean clothes she unrolled from her backpack. Two further minutes with hairbrush, tinted moisturiser and mascara wand and she was ready to start her day.

As she emerged into the corridor, students were streaming towards rehearsal rooms or first sessions, crowding her with their backpacks and instrument cases and confining her pace to what she thought of as 'the student shuffle'.

Chatter and laughter rippled through the air. Georgine smiled. She loved this time of year. Halloween and bonfire night had passed and now the students were looking towards the main event of the term: Christmas. Already posters advertising *A Very Kerry Christmas, Uncle Jones* were appearing in Middledip, Bettsbrough and even as far afield as Peterborough.

Some of the students called, 'Hey, Georgine!' and she returned their greetings, only pausing when a tall, solemn youth with a guitar-shaped gig bag on one shoulder fixed his gaze on her and announced sternly, 'Got me grade seven acoustic guitar.'

Not fooled by the unsmiling delivery from Tomasz, a student generally held to be 'challenging', she raised her hand for a high-five. 'Fantastic, Tomasz! That's awesome!'

'I'll get a stiffycut.' Tomasz's heritage might be Polish but his accent was pure Bettsbrough. He performed his part in the high-five as if obliged to humour her, but triumph shone in his eyes before he turned away.

Georgine was still grinning at his pronunciation of 'certificate' when she reached the office suite, calling 'Morning!' to Fern as she passed through the admin office and reached the door marked *Norman Ogden* at 8.30 a.m. precisely.

'C'mon in,' Oggie called genially and gestured towards one of the tub chairs that stood around his desk. 'Tell me all the news.'

Georgine settled herself in the brown chair. She was long past hunting for hidden meaning in Oggie's habit of opening meetings with informal questions, knowing he'd listen with apparently equal interest to progress reports, student concerns, personal news or downright gossip. Previous years working in mainstream schools as a teaching assistant or arts support staff had made Georgine deeply appreciative of a head like Oggie.

She knew if she told him about the men banging on her door he'd instantly offer any support he could, but she felt sick just at the idea of sharing such shaming information, so she got straight down to business. 'Tomasz has passed grade seven acoustic guitar. He's waiting for his certificate.'

Oggie gave several claps of his big hearty hands. 'I'll find him later to offer congratulations. He seems to have settled a bit this term.'

Georgine nodded. 'Because it's his second year, maybe.' Knowing Oggie would want an update on the progress of the show, she opened her file and reported speedily on music, dance and drama rehearsals, winding up with finance. 'I've negotiated a better discount with the Raised Curtain by supplying our own lighting and sound crews from the theatre-tech students. It'll be great experience.' *Experience* was a buzzword at Acting Instrumental.

She closed the file and shifted to the edge of her chair ready to get on with her day. A Christmas musical-theatre piece was a fantastic showcase of student abilities and evidence for their courses, but it meant a lot of sweat from the events director.

Oggie stretched and settled more comfortably. 'A new guy's joining us today and I'd like to introduce you.'

Georgine sat back in her chair again. 'A staff member? I didn't know you were recruiting.'

Oggie made a vague cycling motion of his hands. 'Not

formally. But when the right person comes up . . . I know Joe will make a valuable contribution.'

'I'm sure,' she replied politely. 'What's his role?'

Oggie's eyebrows lifted as he considered her question. 'To be defined. He has broad experience with contemporary bands – road manager and drum technician, and so forth. He could be helpful with lighting rigs and sound desk. I'll call him in. He'll have to be accompanied everywhere he might encounter students until his DBS comes through, so I'm landing him on you for a bit.'

Georgine didn't protest, not just because Oggie was the boss, but because he was the best boss in the world and must have good reason to bring in someone who hadn't got his Disclosure and Barring Service certificate in order, so she didn't even look at her watch as he made a call. 'Joe? Ready for you. Come to reception and Fern will see you to my room.'

It was typical of Oggie to say 'room' rather than 'office'. Georgine had never heard him refer to himself as 'principal' and he expected students to address staff by first names. Staff and students alike called him Oggie.

She was roused from these reflections as Oggie's gaze shifted to the doorway. He smiled. 'C'mon in, Joe.'

Georgine turned in her seat to offer a friendly greeting. 'Hi. I'm Georgine France.'

The tall, clean-shaven man with a brutally short haircut blinked at her through thin-rimmed glasses. His expression froze. Then he cleared his throat and muttered, 'Pleased to meet you. I'm Joe Blackthorn,' before nodding politely and seating himself in one of the other chairs.

Oggie embarked on outlining to Joe the role Georgine held at Acting Instrumental. Though Georgine played her part in the conversation, warm and welcoming, she was intrigued by the strained behaviour of her new colleague. Somehow, she expected tall, handsome men to be bursting with confidence, yet this one was behaving as if he was suffering severe anxiety. It might explain why Oggie would choose a low-key and unorthodox induction to their establishment.

'So, Joe,' Oggie wound up. 'Stick with Georgine for now. She'll give you a quick tour and an idea of how we do things.' Oggie raised his dark eyebrows. 'That OK? Great.'

Joe evidently understood they were being dismissed and rose, murmuring, 'Thanks for giving up your time,' in Georgine's direction.

Swooping up her file, Georgine replied, 'Not a problem,' though having to keep him with her or pass him like a baton to another staff member just added to her load. 'If we start in the new block, we can finish in this building.'

'Sure.' He stood back to let her lead him out to the glass corridor that linked the buildings and gave them a view of a paved area currently empty of anything but benches, flower tubs and twinkling frost.

At the end of the corridor, Georgine turned to her near-silent companion, noticing the way he kept one step behind, as if it was uncomfortable to let his soulful brown eyes meet her gaze. Lifting her voice over a sudden burst of drumming, she said, 'This block holds sound studios and rehearsal rooms.' The drumming paused, and the sound of an argument took its place, culminating in a snarled, 'Tosser! You knew that was mine.'

'Whoops!' Georgine quickly followed the sound through a doorway and found a group of teenagers surrounding two gangly lads squaring up to each other, faces red and eyes glittering. One of them was Tomasz, whose good mood over his 'stiffycut' appeared not to have lasted.

'No tutor here yet, guys?' she asked calmly.

Both heads swivelled her way, faces wearing matching expressions of dismay. Tomasz rubbed his ear sheepishly. 'Not yet.'

'We're waiting for Errol for Music Industry,' volunteered the other, backing away as if the field of battle had nothing to do with him.

Georgine treated each to a keen stare. 'I'm sure he'll be here any time. You don't need me to wait with you. Do you?'

Both lads flushed and shook their heads.

Georgine beamed. The other students had fallen back to sit on tables or rummage through backpacks. 'Everybody OK? See you later, then.' She returned to Joe in the corridor.

He glanced towards the now subdued room they were leaving behind. 'Do you need to wait for their tutor?'

'It's not how we generally do things. The tallest one, Tomasz, can't always afford things like guitar strings and he gets protective of his possessions, but Oggie likes to treat the students like adults as far as possible. I think they'll be OK now they've let off steam.' She opened a pair of doors.

'Oggie was always good at treating kids as if each one mattered.' Joe stepped into the lofty hall beyond the doors.

Georgine followed him in. 'Did you work at Oggie's last place? I know he was head of a big academy in Kent.'

Joe looked away. 'He taught at my school in Surrey when I was a teen. He put on the plays and concerts and I did scenery shifting and stuff. It took me a while to fit in, but Oggie helped. I kept in touch with him through college and we became friends over the years.'

'Wow, you've known him for ages,' she said encouragingly. She did the maths in her head, knowing Oggie to be in his mid-forties. 'The Surrey school must have been one of his first jobs.'

He shrugged.

Nobody could accuse him of drawing things out with his chat, chat, chat, she thought. 'This is the studio theatre. We're incredibly lucky to have it. Some rehearsals take place here but we put performances on at the Raised Curtain, a theatre attached to a local academy.' She cast her satisfied gaze over a drum kit standing near mic stands, amplifiers and equalisers. The front rows of the retractable seating were out but the rest were tidily away like a giant set of drawers ready for rehearsals.

She speeded up as she led the way back up the corridor. 'The main building used to be a house called Lie Low, the bolthole of a *Carry On* star and then a shady businessman.' They passed dance studios, Joe glancing in on students and giving the brief nods he seemed to consider sufficient interaction as Georgine continued to provide background information. 'Acting Instrumental's a small independent further education college. Our current roll is eighty-four students across two year-groups. The cafeteria's through here. Oggie got funding to subsidise lunches so the take-up is high.' She turned right. 'This is my room.' She laughed to see a garland of turquoise tinsel hanging from the handle. 'I'm collecting Christmas props so people are bringing me their cast offs.' She whisked past, heading straight for dance rehearsal.

She paused at the door. 'This is the big rehearsal room. Maddie's working with dance students on our Christmas show, *A Very Kerry Christmas, Uncle Jones*. The students are Level 3, which is the same as A Level.' She stepped inside. At one end of the room a stage space was denoted by yellow gaffer tape on the floor where a small dance troupe was learning a routine.

Maddie glanced round without pausing in her dance. Tall and willowy, her fair hair pulled back in a plait, she flashed a smile before returning her attention to the teenagers who were mirroring her movements. The shuffles and thumps marking the rhythm of their feet made Georgine's heart lift.

'Forward, back,' Maddie called, 'step-two-three, change, step-two-three, back, leg lift, and chassé . . . and then we're ready for the last part of act one, scene two. Let's try it to music.' She clicked a small remote in her hand and a lively jive tune burst onto the air.

'Here we go . . . two, three *and* forward, back . . .' The troupe moved as one, girls in leggings and boys in jogging pants, all eyes on Maddie unless a head turn was required with a step.

'Wonderful! Concentrate but don't frown, chassé, back, leg lift,' Maddie sang gently. Frowns vanished, limbs moved in time.

Georgine's toes were already tapping. She whispered to Joe, 'Each student will keep a progress log: how their creative journey's developed, decisions made and the effect on the audience. We make rehearsal and show-night videos too.'

'Great.' His nod definitely looked approving.

Encouraged by this slight sign of engagement, she went on. 'We're extraordinarily proud that we're open to students' choices, nurturing them, cheering them on, proactively helping them make whatever they can out of music, dance or drama. A kid can come here without a single GCSE and try vocational qualifications from entry level up to Level 3. The "can do" attitude here is awesome.' She laughed at her own enthusiasm. 'I love how amazing, how fantastic Acting Instrumental is.'

Joe actually smiled. 'I'm sure you're proud of helping it happen.' It probably counted as gushing from Mr Chat and Personality.

Georgine turned back to the dancers, jigging on the spot to the catchy number. 'I need to watch the rest of this rehearsal and get involved. You OK to look on?'

'Yep.' But Joe, to Georgine's surprise, moved further into the room with her to continue the conversation. 'Will they dance to recordings on the night?' His hands were stuffed in the pockets of his jeans.

'No, this is a rehearsal track. The show's composed by Jasmine, an alumna who went on to university and won a scholarship that paid her final year's tuition fees. She's provided rehearsal recordings that her music student mates have played on. We have two bands of our own, but they're still rehearsing separately at this stage.'

She half expected Joe to look bamboozled by so much detail, but his deep brown eyes were aglow with what looked like satisfaction. 'Ace.'

Georgine could only agree.

Before them, Maddie was still mirroring the troupe's routine, occasionally calling out the steps, gaze moving back and forth to monitor each student. Unable to contain her impatient feet, Georgine thrust her shiny Christmas show file at Joe and moved up behind Maddie, picking up the steps to dance along.

A couple of the students grinned her way and Maddie, seeing Georgine in the mirror, implemented an impressively smooth about face to dance opposite Georgine. Forgetting all her pressures and worries, Georgine laughed aloud as the troupe moved forwards and she had to reverse. It was a bit like being Ginger Rogers to a bunch of Fred Astaires . . . apart from wearing jeans and trainers instead of a swirly dress and heels.

At the close of the segment Maddie called, 'Three, two, one, cha-cha-cha, and sliiiiiide, jazz hands. Fan*tas*tic everybody! Quick break. Grab a drink if you want one.'

Back down to earth now the dancing was done, Georgine caught her breath and approached her colleague. 'Maddie, I'd better introduce you to the new guy, Joe. Oggie was one of his teachers, apparently, and he has technical experience.'

Maddie sipped from a bottle of water and winked. 'The cutie rocking the designer specs? What's he like?'

'Nice to look at,' Georgine admitted, 'but flippin' hard work. Hardly speaks.'

Yet when she took Maddie over to Joe and made the introductions, Joe flashed a smile, showing no signs of shyness. 'I've really enjoyed watching,' he told Maddie, and went on for a whole minute about how great the dancers had looked and what a shame it was that there weren't more male dance students.

Then he turned back to Georgine and returned to using only necessary words. 'Oggie's texted. I need to go to Fern's office and apply for my DBS online.'

'OK, I'll show you there.' Georgine turned back to the dancers. 'You're doing brilliantly! I'll be back shortly.' Then Georgine delivered Joe to the capable hands of Fern, with her bouffant silver hair and air of unflappable calm.

She skipped back to dance rehearsal trying not to mind that Joe had turned to Fern's computer with such an obvious expression of relief.

Chapter Two

After filling in all the necessary boxes on-screen and watching Fern check his application before it went off, Joe thanked her and made for Oggie's room. Pretending not to see the look of reproach in Fern's eyes because he hadn't cleared his destination with her, he shut the door.

He flopped into the same brown chair he'd occupied earlier, threw off his glasses and covered his eyes.

Oggie laughed at his theatrics. 'What?'

Joe didn't move. Mortification was easier to deal with from behind eyelids. 'Georgine France. I was at school with her. Here, not in Surrey. I'm behaving like a teenage doofus around her.'

Oggie stopped laughing. 'Oh! Will it be a problem?'

Joe pressed his palms harder against his face, the short, freshly cut ends of his hair and his close-shaved cheeks feeling weird to his touch. Since he'd gone clean-cut he felt a stranger to himself. 'I don't know.'

'Did she recognise you?'

'No sign of it. Everyone changes a lot between fourteen

and thirty-four. When I knew her I was blond and scrawny and looked as if I lived in a skip.'

Oggie's voice dropped sympathetically. 'You're not that person now. Did you know her well?'

Slowly, Joe slid his hands down from his eyes, blinking at the raw winter light streaming through the window. 'Reasonably.' Then, because he'd never wanted to bullshit Oggie, corrected himself. 'We were friends from age eleven to fourteen.' He sucked in a huge calming breath. 'I had *the* most gigantic, painful crush on her. She was one of the popular girls. Her dad had money and she went on holidays abroad and had dancing and singing lessons after school. The princess to my pauper.'

'A monied princess?' Oggie looked slightly surprised.

'Compared to me. She came to Bettsbrough Comp on the bus from Middledip or in a posh car. I lived on the crappiest estate in Bettsbrough with a couple of alcoholics masquerading as parents. The Shetland estate was known as "Shitland" back then and I was part of the infamous Shitland gang, but she was always nice to me.' He swallowed. 'I recognised her instantly. Not even Georgine's sister had the same unusual colouring.' Her hair was what she'd used to tell him was 'cool strawberry blonde', her skin golden and spangled with faint freckles like a blonde photographed through the palest sepia filter. Except for her eyes. Not green, nor grey or blue, but a mix of the three, like a winter sea.

He'd had to paint her portrait once in art class and the teacher had said, 'Good effort!' Some of his moron mates from the Shitland gang had jeered and so he'd painted the ends of her hair like worms, because clowning around was a good way to distract them from how he'd felt about Georgine. He was the fool, the kid who never had the

15

right shoes or uniform or PE kit. The one whose stepdad was known throughout the town by just his surname, Garrit, and ridiculed, along with Joe's mum, for being drunk on cheap lager almost every day.

Garrit hadn't been funny to live with.

In fact, not much about Joe's life had been funny. If he hadn't developed strategies to make people laugh with him instead of at him he would have punched their stupid heads in for not using their stupid eyes to see how stupidly unfunny it was to be him.

He rose on what felt like hollow legs to get a drink from the small cooler in the corner. 'She doesn't know me as Joe Blackthorn, or by my full first names, John Joseph.' He kept his back to his friend as he sipped from the flimsy disposable cup. 'You probably remember me telling you I had my stepdad's surname from the age of two or three. Then all the Shitland gang got nicknames and mine was "Rich" because I wasn't. Everybody called me Rich Garrit.'

He dropped back into his chair and sent Oggie a rueful smile. 'Sorry to be a diva. It was a shock to see Georgine and after the crap that's happened with the band lately . . .'

Oggie nodded, not rushing in with platitudes or questions, but letting Joe work through things in his own time, just as he had all those years ago. His Uncle Shaun had rescued Joe from Cambridgeshire and put him in the school in Surrey with, for the first time, *all* the right uniform and *all* the right PE kit. Even the right haircut. If he hadn't had the right accent to begin with, well, he'd soon changed that. He'd claimed the name on his birth certificate, but chosen to be Joe instead of Johnjoe, which his mother had called him, another way of disassociating himself from what he'd used to be.

He still remembered the pleasure and relief of blending in.

Freed of the expectation of clowning, he'd worked at the subjects he liked, such as music and art. Oggie had noticed him spending break times alone and got him painting scenery for school plays. He'd made friends.

It was to Oggie that he'd admitted his uncle was teaching him piano and drums. Oggie who talked to Shaun about weekend sessions at a local stage school; Oggie who'd arranged extra music lessons so Joe got the GCSE he needed for a place at music college. There he'd got together with Billy, Liam, Nathan and Raf and his life had changed again . . .

'If you're going to stay here, you're going to encounter Georgine a lot,' Oggie said, jerking Joe back to the present. 'She's at the heart of Acting Instrumental. We did talk about the possibility, even probability, of you meeting your past head-on if you came.'

'Yeah.' Joe drummed his fingertips on his leg. 'I could have coped with anyone better than her.'

Oggie grunted. 'Perhaps you should consider how you'll feel if she remembers you. It might be easier if you remind her first. Get it over with.'

'Yeah.' He tried to envisage it. Those green eyes had gazed at him with zero recognition, as if Rich Garrit had never existed, which made him both glad and sorry. 'It could be a tactical lack of memory on her part. We parted on bad terms.'

Because he'd acted like a moron on the last day of term before Christmas. Made her the object of ridicule because he knew that baring his young heart in front of the Shitland gang would have set her up for cruel teasing. But the hurt in her eyes had sent him home hating himself,

17

vowing to apologise at the school Christmas party that evening.

But Georgine hadn't shown up. He'd waited outside because he didn't have the entrance money – or anything to wear or a gift for the Secret Santa.

Eventually, he'd trailed home to find waiting for him an uncle he hadn't known he had, ready to transform his life.

Joe's Christmas miracle, fairy godfather and Secret Santa rolled into one. He'd gone to live with Shaun in Surrey and rarely looked back.

When he did, it was to think about Georgine France.

Chapter Three

At lunchtime, Georgine knew she had to let life outside Acting Instrumental intrude, so held back from the rush to the cafeteria. Zipping herself into her jacket, which was an inadequate defence against the sharp wind unless you were running, she slipped outside. She rounded the jut of the big rehearsal room to huddle behind the main building. The garden there was frequented mostly in summer sunshine when the grassy area held more attraction.

She hunched her shoulders against the wind blowing from Siberia, took a deep breath and rang Aidan, knowing that the man who answered would be a lot different to the one she'd met a couple of years ago on a rare visit to a nightclub with Blair. She'd been attracted to his happy-go-lucky nature, maybe because she felt she always had to be so sensible and together. Unfortunately, the happy-go-luckyness later proved to be hugely dependent on the 'happy' part. When the going got tough Aidan had retreated into bad moods and deception. He'd even begun taking money from her purse with the excuse that 'couples share'. When she discovered he'd been unable to pay his share of the household bills and had continually lied that he had savings to cover them, it was the last straw. It was months since she'd called time on their relationship and asked him to move out of her house, yet still she was suffering the repercussions of being involved with him.

He answered, ''Lo, Georgine.' His voice was just as smooth and deep as it had been when it used to curl her toes, but he also sounded down and defeated.

He wasn't the only one having a hard time. She dived in. 'Please sort your debts out. I had collection agents knocking at the door while I was eating my porridge this morning.'

'No money,' he replied listlessly.

'Well, tell them that! You've been gone for three months. Stop them coming to my house or give me an address I can pass on.' She waited. 'Aidan?' She checked her phone screen and glared at it. *Call ended.*

She counted slowly to ten, annoyed with herself for venting. Since being made redundant from his job as a commercial executive for a huge car manufacturer Aidan didn't really handle anger.

After three minutes of pacing and huddling into her jacket, Georgine rang back. 'Look, Ade,' she said, pouring syrup on her voice. 'I understand you got in a muddle with money and didn't feel you could tell me.'

'Because you're funny with money. I was protecting you,' he put in morosely.

Georgine closed her eyes and tilted her face to the sky. 'OK, because I'm scared of financial pressure.'

'Yet you give Blair money. And your dad.'

Her nails dug into her palms. 'You know I feel an obligation.'

20

'Yeah, I know the whole sad story, even if I don't understand it.'

Georgine refused to let herself be sidetracked into explaining yet again why she helped her dad and sister, but didn't have a pot of gold handy for Aidan. 'I understand that, in law, I'm as liable as you are for the unpaid utility bills, even if those were your agreed responsibility. I sold the jewellery you gave me to offset some, and the rest I'm paying off as I can manage it. But I can't cover whatever other liabilities you took on unbeknownst to me while you lived at my place, even if I wanted to. So please contact the organisations concerned and tell them not to come knocking at the door of 27 Top Farm Road. Explain you no longer live there.'

Aidan sighed. 'But you can tell them.'

Revulsion shivered through her. 'I don't want to speak to debt collectors! It's your responsibility . . .' She recognised the futility of talking to Aidan about responsibility and changed tack. 'I'm only asking you to stop them turning up at my door.'

'There are websites that tell you what to do when that happens,' he said with irritating calm. 'They say *don't panic*. Don't let them in; complain to their company if they intimidate you.'

'I don't want to talk to them to *find out* which company they're from! And I can't help panicking.' If she clenched her eyes shut any harder she'd bring on a migraine. Her voice rose, despite her best efforts. 'If I lose my house because of you—'

He sighed. 'Did I ever ask to use the house as security? No. Then how can you lose it because of me?'

Sleepless nights worrying through all the worst possible outcomes had provided the answer to this one. 'If I can't meet my mortgage because I'm catching up on all the bills you left unpaid! Or I miss a catch-up payment and the utility company takes me to court.'

It was Georgine who ended the call this time. How could Aidan have changed so much? Until last year he'd held down a good job, worn an expensive suit and driven a late-model car. But when the job went as the company restructured, everything good about him had followed.

In the early days, she'd loved his joy in life, not realising until everything went wrong how heavily he'd depended not only on a fresh pile of money hitting his bank account each month but bonuses coming along twice a year to wipe clean his credit card excesses. It became obvious that saving up had never been in his psyche.

With a sigh that matched any of the pitiful ones Aidan had been heaving down the phone, she blinked open her eyes, unclenched her fists and used the fingers of her gloves to wipe stray tears from beneath her eyes, then looked up and saw Joe standing motionless on the outside staircase that rose up the side of the building. Watching her.

She jumped, then, hoping he'd been too far away to overhear her conversation, forced herself to smile and call up to him. 'Hello. Are you lost? Those stairs lead to some kind of private apartment. The landlord keeps it separate and Oggie says it's not in our lease.'

He glanced down at the staircase beneath his feet. 'Right. Thanks. That would explain why up here wasn't included in your tour.' He ran lightly down to ground level. 'Oggie said to talk to you about the Christmas show. He thinks you might like lighting and sound taken off your hands.' Joe looked much more self-possessed than he had this morning, even if he talked slowly, quietly, as if he were testing every word before letting it loose.

'Would I ever. I'll take you through what you need to know,' she said promptly. She didn't bother reminding him he wasn't supposed to be wandering around unaccompanied, because she hadn't given any thought to his whereabouts after he'd gone off to the admin office during dance rehearsal and probably she should have. Georgine gave a last sniff and pushed Aidan and his troubles into a mental 'worry about this when I'm not at work' box. 'I'm going for lunch. Shall we walk over together?'

'That would be great.' Joe flashed a smile. It was so unexpectedly warm that she grinned back as if she'd known him for much longer than a few hours.

Lunch break was half over and tables were freeing up when they reached the cafeteria, though the noise level was only a couple of decibels below deafening. Georgine was convinced that some students sat two tables away from their friends just so they could shout conversations like, 'Have you done any of your Christmas shopping yet? No, me neither. Got to get some money first.'

Three lads were picking at guitars, apparently trying to master a tricky bit of fingerwork. It wasn't unusual to see students turning any spare spot in the college into a rehearsal room.

She went ahead of Joe in the queue in case he wasn't sure of the system – not that it was hard. You chose your food and drink and paid by scanning your pass, having already credited the cafeteria account linked to it. Accounts could be topped up online, pleasing parents who suspected their kids would use meal money to buy cigarettes or sweets if the actual cash was put in their hands.

Even at staff rates it was an economy to eat a hot meal in the cafeteria at lunchtime. Georgine would content herself with a sandwich or a bowl of soup at home in the evening.

'Oh,' said Joe, ruefully, when they got to the head of the queue and he saw Georgine hold out her pass card to be scanned by Celine, who was on the till today. 'I was supposed to collect my pass from Fern before lunch and I forgot.' He turned to Celine who, in her blue smock, was waiting patiently. 'Can I pay in cash today?'

Regretfully, Celine shook her head, complete with hat and hairnet. 'I'm sorry, darlin', it's not a cash till. We don't have actual money.'

'Oh.' Joe dropped his gaze to the contents of his tray: pasta and the biggest latte on offer, garlic bread he'd already taken a bite from and a cereal bar. His face reddened. 'Erm, I can't really put this back.'

Celine turned to Georgine. 'Shall I put it on your card? Then he can give you the cash.'

'Would you mind?' Joe switched his gaze to Georgine too, expression hopeful and relieved.

From the scalding in her cheeks Georgine was pretty sure she'd turned every bit as red as him. She didn't have much choice but to say, 'Not a bit,' and proffer her card again, but her heart began a slow descent to her chilly toes.

Celine passed the card beneath the scanner. It beeped angrily. She flashed Georgine a look of surprise, then returned the pass with a shake of her head. 'I bet it won't go through twice in a row as some safety precaution.' She tapped at the till's screen then said to Joe, 'I've voided your bill for now. Get your card and account sorted and you can pay us tomorrow. You look the honest sort.' She scribbled down £6.38 on a torn-off receipt, gave it to him with a big smile and moved on to the next in the queue.

Hurrying off towards a half-empty table, Georgine felt as if she'd just missed being hit by a speeding car. She knew very well that the card hadn't scanned because there wasn't enough in her cafeteria account after paying for her own lunch. The balance of about four pounds was barely enough for a meal tomorrow, Wednesday, without coffee. The account would top up on payday, Thursday.

For a horrible moment she'd feared Celine would shame her by saying, 'Not enough money on your card, darlin'.' But the woman's eyes had held an apology. She'd realised she'd dropped Georgine in it. Georgine had swung from dread to gratitude in a heartbeat at the way Celine had covered up.

She made a mental note to add her to the 'gets chocolate brownies at Christmas' list. She baked a lot of Christmas presents rather than buying them.

Joe cleared his throat as they took seats at a table. 'Thanks for trying to save my blushes. I feel as if I'm wearing a big sign saying "can't pay for his own lunch".'

Seeing that he was genuinely upset, and completely empathising because she hadn't been able to raise the small sum to pay it for him, Georgine tried to shrug it off. 'It makes you feel conspicuous, but it's only an admin issue. Induction days are usually better organised than yours seems to have been.'

Georgine had chosen a vegetable frittata with salad. It was one of her favourite lunches, but today the subject of money was under glaring spotlights in her mind.

Two more paydays till Christmas. She was only able to claim mileage and other show-related expenses retrospectively so she hoped she could afford the extra trips back and forth to Bettsbrough. She was having Dad, Blair and Blair's boyfriend, Warren, for Christmas dinner. Luckily

Mum and her husband, Terrence, would spend Christmas in their French holiday home, so she wouldn't have to drive to their posh house on the Northumberland coast for a festive visit, but buying Christmas gifts for them was a trial. Terrence was careful with his fortune. He released money for Christmas gifts, but he expected something worthwhile in return. Last year Georgine had bought their presents from charity shops then parcelled them up in dark red tissue paper and stencilled on 'The Vintage Shop' in gold, because calling stuff 'vintage' increased its value to the power of ten. They'd actually been impressed and Terrence had displayed his wooden letter rack behind glass in their vast sitting room. Luckily, Georgine's mum, Barbara, never now set foot in Middledip, Bettsbrough or even Peterborough, so couldn't demand to be taken to the non-existent 'Vintage Shop'.

Mum and Terrence had bought Georgine cashmere jumpers. She'd run her fingertips over them admiringly, but she'd rather have had winter boots with fleece inside, or a couple of pairs of jeans. She didn't live a cashmere kind of life.

Joe's voice jolted her out of her reverie. 'Do you live in Middledip?'

She blinked, realised her frittata was getting cold and hastily dug into it, nodding while she chewed and swallowed. 'I did a year at the University of Manchester, but I've always lived here otherwise. I rented for a while, but then managed to buy a starter home in the new bit of the Bankside estate.' And it represented security, at least for so long as she could afford the mortgage.

'What did you do at uni?' Joe picked up his mug of latte.

'A foundation year in performing arts. I would've

specialised in dance with some singing if I'd stayed, so I could do musical theatre.' She paused. 'My parents split up and it was hard for Dad to keep me at uni so I opted to become independent. It's difficult enough to make a living in the performing arts with a degree so, without one, I didn't even try. Far too perilous financially! I did lots of teaching assistant stuff, and am dram and open mic in my free time, and then I got this job. I love it so much that I'm just happy I got here, whatever my route. For a long time I regretted not getting the chance to finish uni, but I'm lucky that the qualifications for this role are more about enthusiasm and ability than a degree.'

Joe looked as if he were paying close attention, his brown-eyed gaze steady through his glasses, a perplexed frown puckering the skin at the bridge of his nose.

'What about you?' she asked politely, keen to change the subject from the various messes she'd made of her life.

He dropped his eyes to his lunch. 'I lived in Surrey and London for a lot of the time.'

'Which part of London?'

'Various. Camden for the last few years.' He put a forkful of pasta in his mouth.

She watched him eat it, noticing the firm line of his jaw. 'Isn't London crucifyingly expensive?'

He shrugged. 'If you can shoehorn enough people into one house the rent becomes manageable between you.' He loaded his fork again. 'Tell me about the theatre where you'll put on the Christmas show.'

Georgine was happy to talk about Acting Instrumental and everything attached to it. 'The Raised Curtain? It's part of the Sir John Browne Academy, but it's put to a lot of community use outside school hours. We're lucky that they let us hire it the week before Christmas. It's unusual

27

for a student run to last for six shows but we're ambitious here.' She went on, Joe asking an occasional question. He was so relaxed and normal now, Georgine felt as if she must have been towing a cardboard cut out of him around this morning. Who would have thought that in a few short hours they'd be well on the way to establishing a rapport?

Chapter Four

Georgine ran home that evening, her backpack bumping in rhythm with her stride and the winter chill nipping at her ears. A hot shower was her first priority. She'd just finished getting dried and dressed when her doorbell rang.

She paused.

When the bell rang again she crept to the head of the stairs, heart jumping. A silhouette at the glass wrapped its arms around itself and hopped from foot to foot. Georgine waited. The silhouette was unmistakably female and none of the collection agents who'd harassed her to date had been, but was this some new gambit to see if she'd be less cautious with one of her own sex?

The silhouette raised her arm, the fist appearing hazily against the glass as she knocked. 'Georgine! Are you there? George*ine*!'

Georgine let out her breath with a whoosh, almost laughing at hearing the impatient tones of her sister, Blair. 'I'm coming!' After hurrying down to the hall, she fumbled with the lock and chain and threw open the door.

'Brrrrr!' Hunching theatrically, Blair scurried in. 'It's like a fridge out there!' She paused to give Georgine a big chilly hug. 'Lovely to see you, sis! What are your plans tonight? I'm hoping you don't have any and we can order a pizza or something. Isn't your heating on?' She paused at the thermostat on the hall wall to turn it up.

Georgine, following, turned the thermostat down again. It gave a disappointed click. 'No money for takeaway.' She made a mental inventory of the contents of her kitchen. 'I could make pasta with cheese sauce and a few bits of veg, if you're not feeling ultra-fussy.'

'Hmm.' Blair had reached the kitchen and was already filling the kettle. She turned and gave Georgine one of her beautiful smiles. She took after their dad's mum, Patty France – pronounced 'Paddy' by the American side of the family. Both possessed the same high-wattage smile that made others feel almost lucky to be smiled upon, and melting brown eyes to keep the world under their spell. Patty's hair had long since turned white, but had once been brown and curly like Blair's. 'Got any wine?' Leaving the kettle to boil, Blair opened the fridge and inspected its contents. Or lack of.

Slowly, she closed the door and turned around to gently run her hands up and down Georgine's arm, her expression dismayed. 'You're not still broke?'

Georgine made a face. 'I'd be OK if Aidan hadn't left me in the poo. I get paid on Thursday so I'll be able to stock up then.'

Blair switched the kettle off. 'Pop your coat on. Let's nip to Booze & News for a bottle of wine. My treat,' she added, picking up her bag.

'Are you sure? Melanie's prices are a lot steeper than a supermarket.' As Blair merely rolled her eyes in reply, Georgine fetched her coat from its usual home on the newel post and zipped it up as they stepped out under the street lights. Top Farm Road was edged by the parked cars of villagers home from work.

'So you still haven't paid off the mess sodding Aidan left behind?' Blair slipped her hands into the pockets of her coat, a colourfully embroidered Joe Brown number. Temperatures had plummeted in Cambridgeshire the moment the calendar flipped to November.

For Blair, Georgine usually made light of her problems, financial or otherwise. Neither of them had ended up with the life they'd expected and the knowledge that Georgine had played a part in their change of fortunes lay between them like a dozing dragon, liable to breathe fire when disturbed.

But fatigue swept over her. She was tired from running to and from work, tired of hiding from creditors she hadn't wronged, tired of an empty fridge two days before payday. And tired of pretending everything was fine.

'I've made inroads into the outstanding utility bills. The utility companies are only too used to this carry on and they're letting me catch up the arrears over time,' she admitted wearily, making for the turn onto Great Park Road and the footpath to Ladies Lane. 'But now I'm being hunted by debt collectors.' The final sentence was out before she could run the words through her inner censor. Realising from Blair's stunned stare how dramatic she sounded, she tried to soften it by adding a laugh.

But the laugh wavered.

By sheer will she forced the tears to the back of her eyes, her throat tightening until it hurt, her fists clenching in her pockets. As the ground was firm and frosty she chose the route over the playing fields instead of turning the corner onto Main Road. There was enough light from surrounding houses to light their way. 'I try,' she croaked. 'I really try not to let the financial situation get to me, but anything to do with debt makes me panic. I relive that implacable lack of sympathy and it makes me feel alone and frightened.'

'Oh, Georgine!' Blair gasped, tugging on Georgine's arm to bring her to a halt. 'That's awful! Can't you report them to someone? They can't harass you for Aidan's debts. Tell them to piss off!'

Glad that there was nobody about on the playing fields on this wintry early evening, Georgine buried her face in her sister's shoulder, the fabric of the stylish coat warm against her cheek. 'I'm scared to talk to them. Scared that if I say he doesn't live here now they won't believe I don't know his current address – which he won't tell me! And it's such a freezing November. The inside of my house feels like Narnia but I daren't turn the heating on. I su-suppose pipes will begin to burst next. And that can't happen because I couldn't afford the payments for the contents insurance so if my carpets get ruined, they stay ruined.'

Blair's arms tightened around her as she said, 'Shh,' comfortingly and 'Oh, shit, Georgine,' less comfortingly.

Georgine recovered enough to disengage herself from Blair's sisterly hug and find a screwed-up tissue in her jeans pocket to trumpet into. 'Sorry. Things are getting on top of me.' She made another attempt to laugh, finding it hard to meet her sister's troubled gaze. 'You don't have to worry. I'll get through this.'

'Right.' Blair sounded unconvinced.

'Honestly, I'm all right,' Georgine insisted as they resumed their march towards Booze & News. Except for a bone-deep fear – despite Aidan's probably well-meant but actually empty assurances – that somehow she'd be pulled deeper into his problems and lose her little house. She couldn't! It was just a modest inner terrace with two bedrooms, one bathroom, a lounge-diner and a kitchen, but it represented the tiny amount of progress she'd made.

She linked arms with her sister, nodding to a dog-walker passing the other way with a snuffly pug. 'Don't know what's wrong with me today. I'm being a wuss.'

'You're never a wuss. You're so brave and resourceful that I suppose anxiety is something I generally think is reserved for other people,' Blair said quietly. They passed the Angel Community Café, tinsel at the window and lights still showing.

'Usually is.' Georgine pushed open the door to Booze & News with a *ting*!

'Hello, folks,' said Melanie from behind the counter. Her eyes fell on Georgine's face like a missile homing in on its target. 'What's the matter?'

Instantly, Georgine wished she'd made Blair come in on her own. Melanie was good-hearted but also uncomfort-ably inquisitive and red eyes would instantly attract her attention. 'Nothing,' Georgine said defensively.

'We need wine!' Blair declared dramatically. 'What's on promo?'

With a last look at Georgine, Melanie allowed herself to be drawn into a conversation about merlot and Chianti while Georgine pretended to be fascinated by the display of tinned goods near the door. Blair chose the Chianti and paid.

Georgine called, 'Bye, Melanie!' and turned for the door.

'I've won a cake,' Melanie called out, halting her.

When Georgine reluctantly turned back she saw Melanie was holding out an orange raffle ticket, her expression sympathetic. 'Here,' Melanie said gruffly. 'I won it in one of Carola's everlasting raffles and I'm doing Slimming World so you'd better eat it instead of me. You need to take this to the Angel Community Café. If you go now you might get them before they close.'

Warmth washed through Georgine. She'd known Melanie for over five years and was well aware how much she loved her cake. 'That's so nice of you—'

'Just grab it before she changes her mind,' Blair joked, twitching the ticket from Melanie's fingers. 'Thanks, Mel. You're a sweetie. C'mon, sis.'

Heart soothed by this gesture from such an unexpected quarter, Georgine followed Blair back to the Angel, pushing open the door to find blonde Carola who ran the café busy mopping the floor.

'Sorry, ladies, I'm shutting up.' Carola dipped the mop in the bucket and worked a noisy lever with her foot to squeeze the excess water out.

Blair brandished the raffle ticket and, with a keen glance at Georgine, who, despite her experiences at Booze & News, had been too cold to wait outside, Carola went off to the fridge to fetch a boxed cake.

'Chocolate and pear gateau,' she announced. 'I'll sell you tickets for the Christmas hamper raffle another time. Have a happy evening.'

They stepped back into the dark evening again, Blair carefully bearing the cake box. 'I must look pathetic,' Georgine sighed. 'Melanie gave up cake for me and Carola let me get away without buying a raffle ticket.'

Blair shifted the box so she could give Georgine a one-armed hug as they stepped back into the playing fields. 'It's the village. They take care of their own.'

Once home, they dined on Chianti and large slices of

gateau. Blair became quieter and quieter. A frown lodged itself on her brow and stayed there.

After a while, Georgine ventured: 'Is something wrong?'

Blair's forehead smoothed straight away. 'Should there be?' But then, while Georgine was clearing up, she announced abruptly, 'Just popping to the bathroom,' and quit the little kitchen.

The sound of Blair's footsteps diminished as she walked up the stairs. Georgine, wiping surfaces, kept one ear on the sounds from overhead. Blair seemed to be meandering about. Maybe she was peering out of each window, worried about lurking debt collection agents.

Georgine sighed. She hoped she hadn't put the wind up Blair so much that now her sister was feeling anxious.

Blair reappeared eventually, frowning heavily and looking pale, though she managed to smile at the storyboards Georgine had just pulled out of her backpack. 'I can imagine all those funky students plastered in sequins and glitter for a Christmas show.'

Attuned to Blair's moods and reading the signs of misery in her dark eyes, Georgine put down the board she'd been considering. 'What's the matter?'

Blair made an attempt at a carefree smile. 'What do you mean?' Then abruptly clamped a hand over her eyes. 'Oh, *shit*,' she breathed, her voice squeaking in her throat.

Alarmed, Georgine guided her sister to one of the dining chairs. 'So something *is* wrong,' she exclaimed.

Blair allowed her head to drop onto Georgine's shoulder. 'I wish I didn't have to tell you this right now. I've been racking my brains for alternatives but I've come up empty.' She heaved a sigh that stirred the ends of Georgine's hair, and Georgine's heart fluttered unpleasantly, all kinds of unwelcome scenarios of illness flashing through her imagination.

'Please tell me,' she breathed.

Blair groaned. Then she sat up straight with the air of one who was pulling herself together, though her eyes still brimmed. 'It's over between Warren and me. We've had a humongous row and he told me to leave.'

Georgine stared, searching her sister's tear-streaked face. 'No! He adores you. His eyes follow you round like a spaniel—'

Blair scrubbed her cheeks with her palms. 'Not any more. He's tired of what he calls my "money-pit ways". We've been having problems. You've had enough to worry about so I haven't let on, but it's all been building and –' her voice began to wobble '– last night he told me he was throwing me out of the last chance saloon. I took today off work to pack my things.'

'But surely . . .' Georgine broke off, unable to categorically deny that Blair was bad with money. She threw it at anything that took her fancy. Automatically stroking her sister's hand, Georgine thought of the mini-break she and Blair had shared in October half-term – Warren hadn't been able to take the time off work so Blair had invited Georgine to the smart barn conversion in the country in his stead. They'd each had a king-sized bedroom and sumptuous en-suite, and it had still left a bedroom empty. Georgine had thought at the time that it was pretty extravagant for two people.

Since then, she'd been sucked into the whirl of putting on the Christmas show, more concerned with how to evoke Christmas with a black curtain and a twist of tinsel than how things were going in her sister's life. 'Oh, Blair,' she breathed remorsefully. 'I didn't realise.' She blinked hard.

Blair's attempt to laugh caught and broke. 'All we've done tonight is say "oh, Blair" or "oh, Georgine". What a pair.' She found a tissue in her pocket and blew her nose, then tossed back her hair. 'You won't believe this but I came here to ask you to put me up until I sorted myself out. What timing, eh? Just what you don't need.' She propped her elbow on the table dispiritedly.

Georgine gazed at her sister, having an idea of what was coming next and knowing she'd be incapable of refusing.

'Unless . . .' Blair went on tentatively. 'Unless it's actually exactly what you do need? What if I did move in here? A rent-paying lodger would help you out too. You'd be able to have the heating on and catch up the arrears on the utilities much sooner.'

Georgine tried to compose her features into an expression of neutrality, but it was hard to fall on the suggestion with a cry of joy. 'Are you sure you'd really like it, Blair? My second bedroom is *tiny*. Teeny-tiny.' The sound of Blair's footsteps tracking restlessly from room to room upstairs made sense now. She must have been assessing the space, trying to envisage herself moving from Warren's spacious four-bedroomed house in Peterborough to a small share of Georgine's bijou abode. That she even saw it as an option spoke volumes for her situation.

Blair must be desperate.

'Of course, it goes without saying that you can stay,' Georgine said quickly. 'It's just that you'd have to be tidy because the house is so small that you can't move if you just dump stuff all over the place. It's a far cry from Warren's big, bay-fronted detached.'

Blair made a face. 'You make it sound like a palace.'

'It might be, compared to this,' Georgine pointed out. 'Big rooms, high ceilings, an attic conversion.' Mostly full of the detritus of either Warren's life or Blair's.

Blair inspected her nail varnish, lower lip jutting. 'That attic conversion was tiny really.'

'But bigger than I could offer you here.' Georgine tried a joke. 'The box you keep your Christmas decorations in is probably bigger than my spare room.' Then, gently, Georgine reached out and stroked Blair's shining hair. 'You're welcome to come. It's just that you'll have to be really, really realistic about two things.'

Tipping her head back, Blair closed her eyes with a mock groan. 'Don't come all big sister on me!'

Georgine pressed on remorselessly. 'You do have to pay rent, I can't afford to feed you or face an increase in household bills. And you'd have to respect my space.'

'Because you freak if there's a thing out of place.' Blair sighed.

It seemed an unnecessarily harsh description, but Georgine accepted that her sister was emotional and anxious. 'I don't like to live in chaos, that's true.' Whereas Blair, smiling and sunny, expansive and generous, lived as if she truly didn't notice when she put something down and never touched it again. Magazines, make-up, shoes, clothes seemed to whirl into new and unexpected resting places in her wake. Doors and drawers opened themselves and never shut. A mountain of unwashed dishes had usually ornamented the worktop in the vague vicinity of Warren's dishwasher – and there was no such thing as a dishwasher at Georgine's.

Blair blew out her cheeks and gazed at the ceiling as if looking for inspiration there. 'I can't move in with Dad.'

'No. You'd affect his benefits,' Georgine agreed, which happened to be true. More importantly, she'd give her own room up to Blair rather than let her burst in and disrupt their dad's already difficult existence.

'It's not fair on him since he had his stroke,' Blair insisted, as if Georgine had disagreed with her. 'He needs his space and his routine.' She paused and sighed, her eyes once again bright with tears. 'I hate to see him living on sickness benefits but he's never going to be able to work himself into a better income bracket now, is he?'

Guilt and regret lurched into Georgine's gut. 'No.'

Blair's gaze flew to Georgine's face. 'Sorry, I didn't mean to sound . . . It's just that he used to be so different. We all were.'

'It's OK.' Georgine didn't need to be told everything her sister wasn't saying about the spacious home Randall France once provided for his family via Randall France Construction. She also had vivid memories of fab holidays in Malta and Italy, the indulgent Christmases that had seemed to begin weeks in advance of December the 25th, sometimes involving extended trips to America to visit their grandparents, Earl and Patty, when relatives both close and distant had crowded in to join the fun.

Randall France had been so vital then, pushing his business to new heights through hard work, vision and ambition – though a little caution and consolidation wouldn't have gone amiss, it later turned out when Georgine had been nineteen and Blair nearly seventeen.

'Maybe I should give Mum a call and ask to move in with them,' Blair mused caustically. 'Good old Terrence might give me money to go away.'

Glad of this small break in the tension, Georgine rolled her eyes. 'And you think I'm a neat freak? Compared to Terrence I'm a slattern.' She suppressed a sigh as she got up, knowing herself to be the best option for her sister, at least for a month or two. Though Blair was too nice to actually say 'you owe me', Georgine did, in fact, owe her, so she'd shove aside her misgivings and welcome the additional income.

'You can move in whatever you need to.'

Instantly, Blair's dazzling smile flashed out as she leapt to her feet. 'I'll be a model lodger, I promise.'

'I know. You might be right that this could work for both of us.' Georgine accepted her sister's effusive hug. Crossing her fingers behind Blair's back, she wondered whether Blair was doing the same behind hers.

Chapter Five

The next morning sped by for Georgine. Joe had been co-opted into something by Oggie and she was glad to be able to focus on her job.

After lunch, she made contact with Joe and took him to her room to give him a flavour of the show and what he'd need to know to take on the lighting. 'Come in,' she said, opening the door. 'It looks more chaotic than it is. And sorry about the huge Christmas tree in the corner. It's a prop. I'll move it – oh, damn, hang on.' Her phone had begun to ring.

While she talked, Joe wandered about the room, running his eyes over rehearsal schedules stuck to the wall and sequins and glitter gracing the table.

'Sorry,' she said when the call finally ended. 'But that was exciting! A local small theatre company, the Bettsbrough Players, is folding and they're offering us their costumes and props. How brilliant is that? For us, not them, obviously,' she added with a wince.

'Brilliant,' he agreed.

She glanced at her watch. The afternoon was running

away and she still had to go through things with Joe. He must be bored to tears. 'Just need to email Oggie to get his OK to collect the stuff.' She opened her laptop and rushed through the email.

Then she grinned. 'Right. Event orientation. This' – she tapped her shiny folder lying on the table – 'is the production file – my bible.' She opened the ring binder and flicked through a few pages, halting at a table. 'This might look like a cross between word search and twister, but to me it represents who'll be on stage in act one, scene one.'

Joe took the chair beside hers as she explained the initials and arrows. She soon became over-aware of his proximity; even a nod seemed to disturb the air that surrounded them both. It was distracting.

She turned a page. 'I'll try and give you a feel for the show. Two acts: three scenes in the first and four in the second. Eleven songs. Rehearsals going well but work still to do on transitions, which is the way people move on and off between scenes or songs.' She paused to glance at his profile. Perhaps he felt the air move between them, too, because he turned slightly and made eye contact. He'd evidently got over his shyness. She went on, 'The first and last scenes are full-company musical. We have forty-two students to give stage space to. The show's the backbone of this module and crucial to their courses.'

She flipped to the cast list. 'Kerry Christmas is the female lead and Uncle Jones, the male. Other major characters are Kerry's parents, Mr and Mrs Christmas, brother, Casper Christmas, Auntie Jones and Jones kids, plus a TV presenter. Then there are the minor roles – gang members, police officers and neighbourhood kids.'

She turned to look at him again. His eyes were dark

but lit by tiny glints of gold. His gaze flickered to her mouth for an instant, making her concentration waver. 'The storyline,' she went on, 'is that rich Uncle Jones always invites the Christmases to join the Joneses for the festive season. Then Kerry sees one of those *Crimewatch*-type TV programmes and recognises Uncle Jones as the leader of a gang of crooks. She realises where all his money comes from and has to decide whether to dob him in.'

'Presumably she's got to,' Joe observed. 'Or else the message is that crime pays. That gangs are OK.'

Georgine was pleased at his understanding of the world of fiction. 'Absolutely! But apart from turning against this man she's always thought is a generous uncle, Kerry has the problem of how to tell her mum, who loves her brother. The trigger is when Kerry discovers her own brother, Casper, is to work with Uncle Jones.'

Joe frowned. 'Poor Casper's being sucked into a gang?'

Georgine nodded, charmed at how quickly he'd become caught up in the story. 'Jasmine's done a great job with offering the audience food for thought. It's a colourful storyline, but we have to remember it was written for Level 3 students to perform. It makes imaginative use of a dual stage. We hope for a lot of bums on seats.'

Joe propped his chin on his fist. 'Dual stage?'

'We split the stage and have different things going on. Like, take act one, scene two, Kerry's bedroom in the Jones household.' Quickly, she explained how one side of the stage would carry the TV-programme action while Kerry 'watched it on TV' from the other side.

She reached out for a pile of large cards. 'I've story-boarded the show, in a scribbly sort of way. There's a board for every scene or segment and when I get them done there will be one for every transition.'

Joe drew a couple of the large white cards towards him and examined them. 'Who's responsible for set design?'

Georgine rubbed her nose. 'Ultimately, I am. We don't have a big budget for it but minimal's fine, a backdrop and a few sparkly props, because we need a lot of stage space for song-and-dance numbers. Scene changes take place under dimmed lights, props whisked away or repositioned by scene shifters dressed in black.'

He smiled reminiscently. 'I used to be responsible for props for school productions sometimes.'

She grabbed his arm. 'If you can look after props I'm going to eat you up.'

Catching his eyebrows shooting up, she blushed, hurriedly removing her hand from his arm. 'Eat you up' was *not* the right phrase to use when you'd only just met a man. Colleague. She made her voice more businesslike. 'Sorry. I wanted to give you an overview so you could begin thinking about lighting and suddenly I'm twisting your arm about props! We've six weeks to the first night, so plenty of time to pull things together.'

'If I can borrow the storyboards I can start thinking about the tech.' Joe stood up, reaching out.

Instinctively, Georgine put her hand on the boards. Then felt stupid as she saw his astounded expression, and laughed. 'Sorry, I'm like a tiger with my storyboards and production file.'

Joe's eyes danced with amusement behind his glasses. 'How about I take photos of each with my phone? If you're certain I can't borrow them even for so long as it takes to pass them through a photocopier.'

Reluctantly, Georgine grinned back, pushing the boards towards him. 'I'm being an idiot. The students should have all left, so take the boards to Fern's office and get them copied. But I do need them back for the four o'clock meeting,' she added.

He took the stack, backing towards her door. 'You'll have them.' He smiled and she found herself smiling back. Even if he'd spent the first morning with her tongue-tied, it somehow felt as if she'd known Joe Blackthorn for more than a day.

Outside the door, Joe smacked his forehead, hissing, 'Get a grip, you sad sack of shit!' to himself as he strode down the corridor. A couple of female cafeteria staff coming the other way grinned, obviously having overheard. He nodded to them gravely and stood aside to let them pass.

As they rounded the corner he heard them dissolve into gales of laughter. Fantastic. He managed the fifty yards to admin without making a further prat of himself and asked Fern if he could use the photocopier.

Instantly, she jumped up, pushing up her glasses. 'I can do that for you.'

'That's really kind.' He gave her a smile, making her smile back and blush. 'But don't disturb yourself. As I'm so new I'm sure I have nowhere near as much to occupy me as you do.'

'Well, if you're sure . . .' She fluttered back to her seat at the computer.

'And Georgine will have a nervous breakdown if I let anybody touch these without her permission.'

Fern giggled. 'Dear Georgine. She does get invested.'

'I'm beginning to realise.' It took only ten minutes for Joe to complete his task, feeding the copier while it sighed *bzzzzzzzzzzclunk*, freeing his mind to reflect on the scalding wave of lust that had surged through him when Georgine said *I'm going to eat you up*. Ohhhhhh mannnnnn, if she only knew what boyhood fantasies she'd awoken. He really hoped she hadn't seen him look at her mouth. Then when she'd likened herself to a tiger it had swept him back to a long-ago drama lesson.

He'd had to stop himself from blurting, 'Do you remember when we were all given a character and location prompt? I got "tiger" and "party" and stalked around the room tripping drunkenly over my "paws". When I roared at the same time as getting the hiccups you laughed so hard you had to lie down.'

But he hadn't said it.

Because he couldn't bring himself to remind her of the shitty way he'd let that long ago friendship end.

Not knowing whether to be glad or sorry that she showed no signs of recognising him, he sighed as he closed the photocopier lid on the last card and the machine thanked him with another *bzzzzzzzzzzzclunk*. Maybe he should get it over with and tell her who he was. But what if, despite them being all grown up now, he saw dislike in her eyes before she was able to put on a let's-keep-it-professional face? What if his betrayal, even stemming from teenage clumsiness and desperation as it had, had stuck with her? It was only day two but he was enjoying his escape to Acting Instrumental, seeing Oggie again. And working with Georgine . . . The weeks before he came here had been so shitty that—

From behind him, Fern queried, 'Everything all right, dear?'

He jumped, realising that he was standing still and gazing at his completed copying. 'Yes, thanks for letting me use the machine.' He gave her another smile.

'Joe?' Oggie's voice floated out of his room. 'Just hang on and I'll walk along with you to the production meeting.'

'So will I,' confided Fern. 'I'm the performance prompter, you know,' she added importantly.

'OK.' Joe settled down to wait politely. Perhaps he could use the time to coach himself into not turning into a buffoon every time Georgine France smiled. Or said things like *eat you up*.

Instead, he spent the time wondering who Georgine had been talking to on the phone yesterday lunchtime as he'd paused on the steps in the freezing air. He'd heard enough to learn that the conversation had been about money. Or lack of – and that so wasn't the Georgine France he remembered.

Chapter Six

Georgine so loved everything about putting on a show that even production meetings felt like fun.

Errol, head of music, arrived first, checking out the refreshments. 'What, no biccies? No milk?'

Errol wasn't Georgine's favourite amongst the staff. When she thought of him the word 'weasel' often popped into her head, not just because of his sharp features but because he was the world's best at weaselling out of work. Being head of music automatically made him Assistant Director (Music) in the show but he frequently forgot or dodged his tasks.

'There's whitener,' Georgine pointed out. 'Sorry about the biscuits but you're like a plague of biscuit locusts and can munch through a packet on your own.' Also, she hadn't got to Aldi in Bettsbrough where she could get three packs for the price she'd pay for one at the village shop.

Errol grinned and let it go.

People arrived in a constant stream after that.

She waited patiently for the queue for the hot water

dispenser to disperse and shuffling to subside. Her ears pricked up as she heard a familiar, good-humoured voice in the corridor and Oggie strolled in, filling the doorway with his bulk for a moment as he exhibited the coffee mug he held. 'Hope nobody minds me bringing my own.' He glanced behind him then stepped aside. 'And here's Joe Blackthorn, our new staff member. Some of you have met him already.'

Georgine was surprised when her stomach gave a little hop as Joe stepped into the room and, with a flourish, placed her storyboards in front of her. She pushed the puzzling reaction aside. 'Are there enough seats?'

She knew there were. She was good at detail. It was part of her armoury if anyone – like Errol – tried to pretend they hadn't agreed to something, because she could usually produce the relevant note and the date on which it was made. She lifted her voice. 'Shall we begin?'

'But I can smell Oggie's proper coffee and it's giving me coffee-envy,' Errol complained, gazing with dissatisfaction at his cup of instant.

'Oggie brought his own. Nothing to stop you doing the same in the future.' Georgine glanced at her agenda. 'Oggie's already introduced new recruit Joe, who's agreed to head up the tech work and help look after props.' She paused to allow for an exchange of greetings. 'Are we off book with any scenes yet, Keeley?'

Keeley, pushing back her mousey hair, looked apologetic. 'They're still using scripts. It's a bit early to be off book.'

Georgine turned to Errol before he could begin checking his watch or heaving sighs. 'So, Errol. How's the music going?'

Errol folded his arms and made a sorrowful face. 'Just not enough hours in the working day to keep up with your schedule, Georgine. I've got teaching hours, planning, marking—'

'Can you give me some idea of where you're at?' Georgine interrupted sweetly. Errol loved to paint himself as put upon. She made an effort not to let her irritation come through in her voice as she typed *Errol behind schedule* on her meeting notes. Then Errol got down to his report and actually wasn't behind schedule at all so she overwrote her last note with *Errol is an attention-seeking drama queen* instead.

The meeting progressed. Georgine's list of tasks grew. With one eye on the clock, remembering she had to change for the run home, she dealt briskly with the remaining items on the agenda.

'Any other business?' she asked at length, glancing round. A couple of people began to lever themselves from their chairs, evidently keen to get away.

Oggie raised his hand. He sent her one of his most cherubic smiles, as if divining her disappointment that she couldn't wrap things up yet. 'A little more on Joe's role.'

Georgine glanced at Joe, who looked bemused to find himself popped into the meeting spotlight.

'As Georgine said, Joe's already taken responsibility for tech and props,' Oggie continued. 'So – and sorry I haven't had a moment to speak to you about this first, Georgine – I propose to give him the title of assistant events director. For those of you who don't know, Joe's been a road manager and drum tech with commercial bands so has the experience to make himself useful.'

'Oh,' said Georgine, surprised that ultra-courteous and professional Oggie would spring it on her that Joe's role was to concern her quite that comprehensively. 'I mean yes, of course. Great.'

She switched her gaze to Joe, meaning to send him a welcoming smile, but was brought up short by the astonished look Joe was sending Oggie, who merely smiled gently and cocked a quizzical eyebrow. 'Erm . . .' she added, discomfited. 'So long as Joe's happy with it.'

Joe's expression switched to neutral. 'Delighted.'

Georgine wouldn't have minded knowing why he actually looked shocked rather than 'delighted'.

Chapter Seven

A debt-collector-free doorstep for eight days! Yay! Blair's boxes and bags lying everywhere in the house apart from Georgine's bedroom? Not so yay.

Georgine made a big effort to focus on the relief of having no looming silhouettes at her front door this week and kept her thoughts on Blair's encroaching possessions to herself. Blair, after all, was making the best of having barely enough space to stand up in.

'If I get the loft ladder down this evening we could put some of your stuff up there.' Georgine tried to make it more of a statement than a question.

Blair grimaced from in front of the bathroom mirror, where she was applying her third coat of mascara. 'Not if there are spiders.'

'I had it de-spidered only last week,' Georgine coaxed.

'Yeah, right.' Blair laughed. 'Gotta get to work. Sales executives have to look willing.' Blair spent her days selling products to the hospitality industry. She threw her mascara down beside her make-up bag and whirled from the mirror, performing a little shuffle to pass Georgine in the bathroom doorway. 'Laters, sis! Mwah!'

'Laters,' Georgine echoed, watching Blair trot downstairs, step elegantly into the navy metallic kitten-heeled shoes she'd left beside the front door and breeze from the house. In her wake, silence reigned.

Before doing her own eyeliner and mascara, Georgine moved the make-up Blair had left balanced behind the taps to one side of the shelf above. Her own stuff had already been shunted to the right to make room. *I'm not a neat freak*, she assured an imaginary Blair in her head. She grinned at her reflection. *Much*. Her eyes took about two minutes to Blair's ten, then she hurried to grab her backpack, glad there was nothing to prevent her from jumping into her trusty old Ford Fiesta to drive to work.

She was soon absorbed in her day at Acting Instrumental. Joe didn't make an appearance in her room so she worked through her inbox before tucking her laptop beneath her arm and rushing off to watch Errol's music students rehearse for the Christmas show in one of the smaller practice rooms.

The second and third scenes in act one included one song each, rehearsed together because they were both sung by female lead Samantha, who played Kerry Christmas, with Band One backing her. 'That Baddy is My Uncle!' covered Kerry learning her beloved uncle had a Godfatherlike role in local organised crime. In 'Dilemma/Don't Put it All on Me' she agonised over the consequences of doing the 'right' thing. About disillusionment and the death of childhood dreams, it was a haunting song and Kerry would wring the hearts of the audience.

When she joined the rehearsal, the band and Kerry Christmas were in full swing. Georgine's heart flipped the way it did whenever she saw the kids perform. Laptop deposited on a chair, she tiptoed to the back of the room to watch and listen.

The band was made up of two guitars, bass, piano, drums and saxophone. The student on saxophone was Isla, whose mum, Sian, had been at school with Georgine. Sian was already down as a volunteer to sell programmes or tear tickets on performance nights, along with several other parents.

Sections of Isla's black hair were gathered into knobs, one either side of her head, the rest falling down around her shoulders. Her eyeliner was so lavish that her eyes almost disappeared when she grinned at Georgine. The rhythm guitarist/vocalist was also female, her hands looking far too small to span the strings. The rest of the band was male, all with hair in fairly uniform trendy cuts on heads that nodded to the beat – apart from Tomasz, on lead guitar, whose hair was scraped back in a man bun.

'Dilemma' drew to its end on a long, perfect C, and Georgine bounced to her feet to clap enthusiastically. The band members and Samantha smiled in acknowledgement then looked expectantly at Errol. He stood at the side of the rehearsal room, one elbow propped on his other arm so he could finger his chin, on which had lately sprouted a thin black beard. He gazed thoughtfully at the leading lady. 'OK, Sam. Has Hannalee talked to you about posture at all?'

Samantha, face falling, coloured violently. She was a pretty but fey girl, given to hiding behind her hair. Until she sang. Then she shook back her dark auburn locks and straightened her spine, joy and talent shining out of her. In Georgine's view she was a star student. To question a singer of her calibre about something so fundamental as posture was a typical undermining tactic on Errol's part. Samantha came under the singing tutelage of Hannalee rather than being directly his student and, evidently, he didn't want her to twinkle too brightly.

Restraining herself from asking when demoralising outstanding students had ever been an effective teaching technique, Georgine cut in: 'That number's really coming on! Samantha, you'll have half the audience in tears. Band One: playing really tightly – well done.' Her voice full of warmth and enthusiasm, she flicked a look Errol's way.

Errol gave a wintry smile. 'Oh, yes, it was very good.' He made it sound as if he'd had a *but* to add, then thought better of it.

'It was awesome,' Tomasz muttered, slapping Samantha on her shoulder and sending Errol a black look.

Abandoning her laptop, Georgine tried to move swiftly on from Errol's lukewarm reaction, striding further into the room to beam round. 'You're doing so well! I'm working on the transitions between scenes and we're well on schedule to include them in rehearsals.'

Errol broke in. 'Just to let you know, we've only got Sam for another couple of minutes. Hannalee's expecting her back.'

'Thanks,' said Georgine without looking his way. Errol was full of stupid power plays like interrupting because she'd made a small announcement with no accounting for the accepted hierarchy of first apprising him. Whoever had coined the term 'passive-aggressive' must have been thinking of Errol.

'Georgine could sing with us if Sam's got to go,' Tomasz broke in, resting his arms on the top of the guitar around his neck.

'Thanks Tomasz, but not this time.' Georgine scotched the idea before Errol had a chance to object. He wasn't a fan of Georgine joining in with the students.

Errol sent her a flinty, unsmiling look as he resumed control. He was one of the members of the teaching staff who saw interaction with support staff as an opportunity to establish who was more important. 'Thank you, Band One,' he called. 'Samantha, thank you. You'd better go and rejoin your own group. Band Two, you're up.' Three girls and four lads, all significantly grungier than the members of Band One, rose with alacrity, grabbing instruments and heading for the performance space. Trent, the singing student who played the male lead, Uncle Jones, ran in, throwing his bag under a chair and taking position at a mic for a song from act two, scene four: 'Uninvited guests'.

Down the line, Maddie's Troupe One would be performing a street dance front and centre, which Troupe Two would join in the guise of police officers and gangsters. It was the one scene costume decisions had already been made on because both dancers and band would dress in combinations of black and white to allow for the gradual infiltration of police uniforms and detectives in suits into the party.

Georgine planned to get hold of plenty of sports whitener for shoes. Many of the dance students wore Converse or Vans for street dance, taking pride in their grubbiness.

She backed up to lean on a wall while Band Two finished setting up. A murmured conversation took her attention and she glanced around to see Joe Blackthorn crouching beside the chair of the bass player from Band One. A little shock darted through her. It shouldn't have, because she'd sent him a copy of the rehearsal schedules spreadsheet marked with those she intended to attend and the comment that he might like to sit in on a few as time and his DBS status allowed.

The bass player – Nolan, she thought he was called – was poring over whatever Joe was showing him on his phone.

She hovered casually closer.

'Don't just keep your metronome for when your music teacher's listening,' Joe was suggesting. 'Download a free metronome app for your phone. The bassist and the drummer are the backbone of the band. Practise with a click track at home and it'll pay off in spades. Tell your drummer, too.'

Georgine was fascinated. She'd heard it said that 'techs' had to be as competent as the players they supported but Joe hadn't until now displayed his experience. Professional skill was gold dust to students.

Her attention was drawn to Band Two, who made a couple of false starts because lead guitarist Sammy was clearly flustered, probably by the presence of Georgine and Joe. Band One didn't help the situation by catcalling gleefully.

Errol, to give him his due, made time for his own students. 'Freestyle for a bit, Sammy,' he suggested. Sammy nodded and, head down over his instrument in embarrass-ment, began to improvise. The drummer and bassist soon picked up his tempo and the rhythm guitarist positioned himself where he could see Sammy's fingers and select the right chords to back him.

After a couple of minutes Errol said casually, 'OK, let's go again.' Sammy proved to have settled. The band kept it tight for the whole number. Errol gave them a wide smile and raised his hands above his head to applaud. 'Great stuff!'

'Really great! Thanks,' Georgine called, moving back towards the door and swooping up her laptop en route. Out in the corridor she made a note to make sure that Sammy was kept calm and comfortable, especially for live shows. Hopefully Errol would be on top of it. But, if not, Georgine would be.

The rest of the morning went by on wings. First she telephoned Ian, box office manager at the Raised Curtain. He gave her the news that they'd already sold more than a hundred seats over the six performances. She pulled a face because they had over a thousand to sell, but said, 'That's a great start!' Declaring it a so-so start wasn't going to do anything for her business relationship with the box office.

'And I was about to ring you,' Ian continued, with the air of pulling a rabbit from a hat, 'because I've just heard from Girlguiding Cambridgeshire West. They want to select the Saturday matinee for their Christmas outing and I've been asked to hold a provisional hundred and thirty seats.'

This time Georgine didn't have to struggle to sound happy. 'Wow! That's brilliant!'

They spent a few minutes discussing the discount, Georgine refusing to be drawn into being overgenerous. The more each show made, the more Acting Instrumental could pour into other productions or resources. They were a comparatively rich college, thanks to Oggie being a whizz at securing funding from all the relevant bodies, but couldn't run at a loss.

Girl Guides dealt with, she turned to a fresh subject. 'By the way, a new member of staff, Joe' – she had to grope for Joe's surname – 'Blackthorn will be handling the tech crew so he'll probably want to check out your space. Will that be OK? Great, thanks very much.' She ended the call, glad Joe hadn't been here to witness her almost forgetting his name, but just for an instant something had got in the way of her memory function. Joe just didn't seem like a Blackthorn somehow.

At lunchtime, she went to the cafeteria, selected lamb ragu with rice, then looked around for somewhere to sit. At a table in the corner she spotted Joe with some of this morning's music students and dance tutor Avril and headed their way. 'Hi, everyone,' she said as she deposited her plate and drink on the table.

Avril beamed, 'Hiya!' Her blonde hair was coiled at the back, the fringe left to frame her face.

Joe said, 'Hi.' His plate was empty and he was lounging back in his chair, coffee mug cradled in his hands.

With only a minuscule pause to acknowledge her arrival, the students continued with their own conversation. Georgine savoured her first mouthful of lamb with an appreciative murmur. Acting Instrumental was the only education establishment she'd worked in with catering of this standard.

Avril finished her meal and put aside her knife and fork. 'How's your stressometer?' she demanded of Georgine. 'Climbing nicely as you pull everything together for the show?'

'I thrive on it.' Georgine grinned. 'The buzz and thrill of seeing progress at rehearsals.'

Lowering her voice, Avril enquired, 'Nothing new on the Aidan front? No resolution?'

Conscious that the students could be listening, Georgine was circumspect. 'One to put down to experience.'

'Awwwww.' Avril pulled a sympathetic face. 'So you'll be living alone at Christmas?'

Georgine laughed. 'Except my sister's moved in for a bit.' And had come through with the first month's rent,

59

which had allowed Georgine to pay extra to the water authority's outstanding bill.

Joe joined the conversation. 'Is your sister moving in a good thing?' A smile lurked in his eyes.

She made a face. 'Time will tell. I love her to bits but we're very different. Do you have siblings?' She took another mouthful.

The smile in Joe's eyes changed to something more wistful. 'I had a stepsister or, at least, my mother and her father lived together for a while. I lost track of her.'

'That's a shame, you must have been close if you were brought up in the same house.' Then, seeing Joe's gaze drop as if he were becoming uncomfortable with the subject, she tried to change it to Ian at the Raised Curtain.

'What's your sister's name?' Avril asked Joe at the same time as Georgine opened her mouth.

Joe glanced at her. 'Chrissy.'

Avril, who could out-talk an auctioneer, opened her mouth with, no doubt, yet another question, but a student paused at the table. 'Oggie's looking for you, Rich.'

Joe looked up at the student and opened his mouth as if to reply. Then a student called Richard jumped up from his place further along the table. 'I asked him to sign my passport form. Thanks. I'll go to his room.'

Joe closed his mouth again, his gaze flicking towards Georgine.

Avril asked Joe something else.

Georgine couldn't make herself listen. Her senses were locked on the man across the table, the room around them receding to hiss and blur, almost obscured by the sudden acceleration of her heartbeat. Now she knew why the name Blackthorn hadn't seemed quite right, and, probably, why 'Joe' seemed to watch Georgine a lot.

Maybe because she'd just heard his sister Chrissy's name again, and when he'd almost answered to the name of Rich a moment ago it had spun the tumblers of her memory. His face and voice clicked into place, like one of those optical illusions where you thought you were looking at one thing but suddenly realised there was another picture there all along.

Rich Garrit.

Joe Blackthorn was *Rich Garrit*. How the hell had she missed it till now? It was so obvious! The face shape had matured, he was tall instead of small and spindly, the hair was completely different, but the eyes were the same, and the shape of his mouth.

Rich Garrit had been the most underprivileged kid in their school with horribly outdated or unsuitable clothes in a mishmash of sizes. The wrong shoes. A PE bag that was a supermarket carrier bag with his name written on it in marker pen. The kind of parents that no kid would choose.

Dumb with shock, vaguely she registered Avril checking her watch and making 'back to work' noises, the students moving off in a body to whatever awaited them next.

And Joe gazing ruefully back at her.

Through the soulful brown eyes of Rich Garrit.

Chapter Eight

If he hadn't been cursing himself so bitterly, Joe could almost have laughed at Georgine's flabbergasted expression. Lips parted, sea-green eyes wide, sandy eyebrows almost vanishing into her hair.

But, shit. Even if he'd known the chances were high that this day would dawn, he'd hoped to find his feet in his new life before being obliged to embark on the emotional journey back to the infinitely crappier one.

He cleared his throat. 'Why don't I get us both a coffee—'

'Have you got an extended lunch hour or something? My watch tells me it's time to get back to work,' Avril put in, giving him a tiny prod in his shoulder as she got to her feet. 'Crack the whip over your new assistant, Georgine!' She giggled.

Wrenching her gaze from Joe, Georgine stumbled to her feet, backing away. 'I have to get back to work too.' Dispensing with farewells, she rushed to join the line straggling out through the cafeteria doors.

With a rapid, 'Bye!' tossed back to Avril, Joe hopped up and charged after her. Georgine's amber hair made it a cinch for a tall person to keep her in view as the flow of students carried her along until she forked off right towards her room. He watched to check she went inside, then headed left for Oggie's quarters.

Finding the principal of the institution at his desk he whipped over to the coffee machine and helped himself to two cups of coffee with a breathless, 'Sorry, Oggie. Explain later.'

Oggie, who rarely looked anything other than serene, actually frowned. 'Joe, you're supposed to be—' was all he got out as Joe, heart beating surprisingly hard and high up in his chest, set off in pursuit of Georgine.

At her door, he paused, then stepped inside. 'I brought you coffee.'

From the other side of the large table, she gazed at him, her expression frozen into unfriendly lines. 'You're supposed to be—'

'Accompanied, yeah. So sue me.' He closed her door with an impatient foot. 'You've obviously realised who I am. I'd like to explain.' He put one of the coffee cups down on the table and pushed it across to her. It felt like he was creeping up on a wild creature and trying to gain its trust with food.

Georgine's eyes moved over his face. 'This is beyond weird. Like a time warp crossed with the hall of mirrors.'

He offered a smile. 'I had a few reasons for not reminding you who I was straight away.'

'You had planned to come clean at some time, then?' She glanced at the cup of coffee but didn't touch it.

Her words rankled but he didn't let his irritation filter into his voice as he pointed out, 'I haven't done anything wrong to "come clean" about. I recognised you. I can't help it if you didn't recognise me.'

63

The green eyes were wary. 'You've changed so much. I kept getting a strange feeling about you, but not knowing why. The penny dropped when you almost answered that kid when he said "Rich".'

'I was a ragged arse runt when you knew me. Becoming healthy after being underfed for most of your life is bound to prompt changes,' he said with a hint of bitterness.

'Your hair's a lot darker now. You wear glasses. And, crucially, unlike me, you've changed your name.' She took a few steps around the table, then paused as if not wanting to venture too close.

He remained where he was, willing to stay out of her personal space but not by backing up. 'Why don't we sit down and I'll tell you the story over coffee?'

'Because I have to start ringing around the parents who are volunteering to act as house managers or to run the bar and refreshments counter during show week. Six shows means a lot of volunteers.'

'Right.' For an instant he'd forgotten he was in a 'normal' job. Maybe because he hadn't had too much experience of normal. He spent a lot of his life on the road or rehearsing or recording. He didn't think he'd ever had a reason to be in the same building five days a week since he'd left college.

'I feel odd,' she said, before he could speak again. 'I'm supposed to be looking after you, but I actually don't want to, not this afternoon. I want to concentrate on what I'm doing, not trying to solve the puzzle that's you.'

'I'm not a—' he began.

She held up her hands. Impatience seemed to be taking the place of shock. 'No, don't. I've got most of the notes together for you so I'll walk you to the staff room. If you have your copy of the *Very Kerry Christmas* script you can begin adding your tech notes.'

'OK,' he said. 'But it's important we clear the air.'

She nodded, though her heavy sigh suggested she regretted the necessity. 'Could it be away from here? Maybe tonight, if you're free. If we're to work together a talk would be . . . enlightening.'

'I can be free this evening.' Until he made a decision or two, every evening on his calendar was free, with a question mark over Christmas week. His uncle and aunt, Shaun and Louise, usually invited him, but this year Shaun was working with a band in Australia and Louise had gone along for the whole Christmas-on-the-beach experience. 'Here in the village? Is there a coffee shop?'

'The Angel, but it's only open in the evenings in summer or when there's something on in the village. It'll have to be the pub. Give me your phone number and I'll text you details.'

He shifted awkwardly. 'I don't have a phone I can use right now. Just tell me where and when and I'll be there.' His phone was off and as he'd no intention of switching it on any time soon it wasn't a lie to say he couldn't use it.

She frowned, as if the fact that he didn't have a working mobile phone made her even more wary. As if to show him what he was missing, her phone began to burble. Reaching for a notepad, she tore out a page and scribbled *The Three Fishes, Main Street, 8 p.m.* on it, shoving it towards him as she answered the call.

'I'll be there,' he murmured.

'OK.' Then, into her phone, 'Hello, Maddie. Yes . . . no, I wasn't going to, but I can come along if you want me to.' She reached for her production file and laptop,

65

pausing to grab the cup of coffee he'd brought her then waiting for him at the door. He followed as she walked briskly up the corridor to the staff room and saw him inside with a nod and what passed for a smile.

The door swung closed.

He'd been dismissed.

Irritated, Joe opened his locker to get the laptop Fern had issued to him, a battered old hand-me-down 'from the pool', though he would have thought 'the shit heap' a more accurate description. It was a far cry from his own state-of-the-art Mac Pro, but he supposed Acting Instrumental had a policy on what computers they made available to which staff and he was a very new, lowly volunteer who could be temporary. A shit-heap computer was evidently his level.

Also, he wasn't turning on his own laptop, to avoid the siren call of his inbox at present. Raf, Nathan and Liam from the band were probably trying to contact him, not to mention Billy, but, though he felt slightly ashamed for ducking them, he hadn't formulated answers to what he knew would be their very real concerns.

He cast a jaundiced eye over the overheated staff room. It boasted the kind of low chairs that seemed designed to make a tall person uncomfortable. A peek out of the door revealed not a single student, so for the second time since lunch, he broke the unbreakable rule that he shouldn't be alone until his DBS checked out, and left. Soon he was unlocking a door that led him out of the building directly beneath the outside stairs that clung to the side of the building. From either side, the door looked to be the kind that led to a cupboard or some utility and had presumably been used to access staff accommodation in the days when the building had been a private residence. The flight of stairs was obscured by the bulk of the big rehearsal room and it had only been by chance that Georgine had caught him there on his first day. Wrong-footed at her presence, he'd hovered indecisively as she'd turned and spotted him. Letting her think he had no business being where he was had seemed the easiest way out.

But now he ran up the steps, tapped a number into the keypad and let himself into a corridor with three doors, two on the left and one on the right. He opened and went through the one on the right, kicking off his shoes and hanging up his jacket.

The apartment, apart from being as big as the other two put together, had appealed to him because it was so white and clean looking. Its impressive kitchen area held a battery of built-in equipment, making him appreciate why whoever had planned the apartment had gone with open plan. That kitchen was a work of art and shouldn't be hidden behind a door.

He crossed to the fridge and helped himself to a bottle of water, then moved into the living area and dropped onto the sofa, taking off his glasses and swinging his feet up onto the coffee table. Opening the shit-heap laptop, he emailed Oggie to let him know Georgine had recognised him, then fetched the photocopies of her storyboards from where he'd left them on the table by the window last night. Her notes had already dropped into his inbox so he searched out a notebook and a pen – he thought better with a pen in his hand. Then he settled down to work.

Interrupting himself, once in a while he tried a couple of lines of lyrics, as the songwriting habit, imbued in him at college, had never left. Something about an old crush being the reason he'd been wary of seriously long-term relationships . . . ? Sounded ridiculous. An immature get-pregnant-to-get-him-to-marry-me scheme a few years ago had been responsible for any wariness he had in that direction, and the woman who'd followed had been so incredibly indiscreet on social media about the details of their relationship that he hadn't even felt obliged to end things face-to-face. She'd got her revenge by revealing the details of that phone conversation in a Twitter storm that had made him feel sick.

He got up once to make coffee, standing at the kitchen window and staring out at the new block, which replaced what had once been a wonderful view over gardens and paddocks. He felt charged, restless, but made himself return to the work. He kind of wanted to show Georgine what he could do.

His long ago alter ego Rich Garrit continued to invade his thoughts. At nearly fourteen, he would have almost wet himself with excitement to know he was going to meet Georgine France in a pub tonight. She was the prettiest and most popular girl in their school year, and to him an unlikely but highly prized friend. She'd lived in a big house in Middledip village and her parents had a car each: a Jaguar XKR and limo-like black Mercedes.

Young Rich Garrit would have pretended to himself that they were actually going on a date. He'd never asked to start seeing her of course, knowing he'd be destroyed if she'd said no, and, in all probability, so would their friendship. And enough money for an actual date? In his dreams.

Present-day Joe Blackthorn had to explain what Georgine obviously considered strange, if not downright suspicious, behaviour. He closed his eyes and tipped his head back to come to terms with that uncomfortable thought.

Rich Garrit had been an odd kid.

But Georgine probably thought Joe Blackthorn odder still. Fucksake. Why wasn't his life ever simple?

Chapter Nine

After work, Georgine drove to Bettsbrough. Gold Street, on the left just before the town proper, led her to the sheltered housing where her father lived without her being sucked into the one-way system.

She used her key to let herself in through the main door. There was no sense in using the entry system, which would oblige her dad to ease himself out of his high-seat chair and shuffle across to press the 'open door' button. She would have tried to get him some kind of mobile phone-based system so he could remain in his chair while he talked to callers at the door, but his speech was now so unclear that he wasn't keen. At least that saved her from having to find the money.

Money. Who said it was the root of all evil? To her it was the root of all sodding hassle and disappointment.

No trace of that kind of frustration showed in her face though as she let herself into the flat, past the bathroom and into the sitting room. 'It's me, Dad.'

Randall twisted in his chair. 'Hi, honey!' It came out more as: 'Ha unny' but he'd said 'Hi, honey' every time he saw her for as long as she could remember so the imperfect diction didn't matter.

Cheered just to be with her dad, who seldom complained, no matter what life threw at him, Georgine stooped to hug him as he groped for the TV remote with his good hand to switch off the late-afternoon news. He was bulkier than he used to be and she couldn't make her arms meet around him. 'I called in at the supermarket and got the stuff for a full English as promised. Hungry?'

'Oh, yes. Favourite.' Randall gurgled a laugh. As his speech had deteriorated he'd compensated by developing a kind of verbal shorthand and making greater use of laughs, groans, nods and headshakes.

Georgine chatted for a few minutes, satisfying herself there was no fresh reason to worry about him, then moved into the kitchenette, switching on the grill to warm up as she unpacked sausages, bacon, eggs and mushrooms. 'How'd you like your eggs today, Dad?'

''Amble, p'ease.'

'Scrambled it is.' She pricked the sausages and put them under the grill, letting them get a head start while she cut the rind off the bacon, wiped the mushrooms and mixed the eggs. As she worked, she updated Randall on the Blair-moving-in situation. She knew Blair had visited Randall and told him in person about Warren ending things.

'Poor Bear.' Randall couldn't get his mouth to form the L in Blair very well. He asked a question, which, on the second attempt, Georgine got as, 'Is she very upset?'

She paused to consider, cooking tongs dangling from her fingers. 'Putting a brave face on, but I think it's rocked her. She wasn't expecting it and she still loves him.'

'Gi' her a 'ug.'

71

Georgine grinned. 'I will. I'll tell her it's from you.' She turned the sausages and took a tin of tomatoes from the cupboard. 'By the way, a new guy at Acting Instrumental turns out to be someone I went to school with, Rich Garrit. I didn't immediately recognise him. He's changed his name to Joe Blackthorn for some reason.' It made her stomach drop to remember the shock of the realisation.

Randall made a puffing noise, trying to get a word out. Georgine gave him time as she opened the tomato tin. Finally, he managed, 'Criminal?'

'Blimey. Hope not.' At school, she reminded herself with an unpleasant thrill, he *had* hung with all the rough guys and it had been really weird the way he'd turned on her one day and then disappeared. Nobody had known where. Georgine had even put aside her hurt and anger to ask his sister, Chrissy, but Chrissy had just shrugged and turned away. Then, in a matter of weeks, Chrissy had gone too. Unnerving rumours of Garrit doing away with both children had swirled around the school until the teachers had heard and said that Rich and Chrissy had each transferred to schools out of the area.

Starved of oxygen, the flames of rumour went out, but Georgine had struggled to cope with the loss of a friend. It had been like a bereavement. For the first time in her life she'd become moody and difficult, which had led, eventually, to that truculent moment of stupidity that had changed everything for everybody she loved.

Her family became a distorted thing. Dad lost everything. Mum left. Blair developed an awkward relationship with money. It had all stemmed from *Georgine* and those moods, and it seemed as if she'd spent her life since then battling the fallout. It was probably why now she liked everything to be neat and controlled.

'Careful with him.' Randall groped for his hankie to wipe his mouth before he finished. 'Ve'y careful, p'ease.'

Georgine's heart warmed at the love in her father's gaze. 'I'm meeting him at The Three Fishes at eight. It's nice and public.'

''Kay.' Randall nodded. 'Tex me later?'

'I will. Now, I'm just putting the bacon under. I'll give you three rashers.' She moved on to tell him how the Christmas show was going. He loved to hear about her job and she loved to talk about it, so the subject lasted them through dinner and the washing up. Then Georgine checked Randall's bank account for him, exhibiting her phone screen so he could nod in satisfaction that his benefit was coming in OK and his rent going out.

Then she said goodnight and drove home, grateful that her car, small and middle-aged as it was, remained reliable in the face of increasingly cold weather.

Despite her assurances to her dad, when the time came to meet Joe, she wasn't sure she should have agreed to it. Blair was out or Georgine might have asked her to come along. And why had she suggested the pub? She didn't have money to spare on non-essentials. She resolved that if Joe bought her a drink and she bought him one back, that would provide ample time to hear what he had to say. She could squeeze that much out of her budget now she had Blair's contribution to the household.

The hood of her coat protected her hair from the worst of the swirling wind as she strode along the footpath that brought her out of the Bankside estate where Great Hill Road joined Main Road. A few strides from the village pub, her footsteps slowed. Last time she'd spoken to Rich Garrit she'd been struggling to hold back hurt tears and he and his scruffy mates had been hooting with laughter

73

at her. OK, they'd been fourteen, but it had felt like a betrayal because Georgine had stuck up for Rich when others had poked fun at him and said unkind things. They hadn't been 'seeing each other', but they'd done art, drama and music together and their friendship had seemed enough for them both. Once away from his braying mates he'd dropped his naughty-boy persona and shown his intelligence, discussing unexpected subjects like karma and whether good people really did return to more enjoyable lives, as a TV programme about Buddhism had said.

Though the intervening years had been enough for her to shuck off a schoolyard gripe, Rich Garrit had once proved himself to be unreliable.

His reappearance with a completely different name didn't encourage her to trust him now.

She crossed the road towards The Three Fishes. Built of the local russet-coloured stone and presently festooned with a blinding cat's cradle of Christmas lights, it was at the heart of Middledip both literally and figuratively. M.A.R. Motors, Booze & News and the Angel Community Café were all a short walk away down Main Road. Nearby stood the playing fields and the village hall. The latter was currently closed and rather than its own Christmas decorations sparkling from its windows, a car park full of building machinery and skips indicated that work had begun on replacing the roof.

The wind more or less blew Georgine in through the door of The Three Fishes, bringing her to the attention of the landlord behind the polished wooden bar. Known in Middledip as 'Tubb from the pub', opinion was divided as to whether or not his sometimes-uncertain temper hid a heart of gold, but you certainly didn't get through the door to his pub – in either direction – without him noticing.

'Evening,' he said, his eyes flitting over his bar as if wondering what Georgine would buy.

When the France family had lived in The Gatehouse, a three-storey stone property near The Cross, they hadn't frequented The Three Fishes much. Randall had been a member of Bettsbrough Golf Club and their mum, Barbara, of Port Manor Hotel's country club, and one of those polished establishments had usually won the France family's custom. Tubb never seemed to hold that against Georgine.

She was the only member of her family remaining in the village – not counting Blair, who was really just using Middledip as a safe harbour while she recovered from her most recent emotional storm. Randall's assisted living flat was in Bettsbrough and Barbara flitted between a big house on a beach in Northumberland and a big house in the hills of central France.

Not put off by Tubb's boot-face, Georgine shoved back her hood and offered him a friendly grin. 'Phew, blowing a hooley out there.' Unwinding her long aubergine scarf she swapped greetings with a few villagers she knew then, unzipping her coat, glanced about the busy bar for Joe.

Rich.

Whoever the hell he was.

Then she glimpsed him. He'd bagged a table by the fire and was lounging in a chair and watching the goings on of the pub through his specs with a half smile. His dark grey jeans and leather cowboy boots looked expensive, as did the thick black jacket lying over a nearby chair.

She weaved her way towards him, the boots making her think roadies must be 'music biz' enough to dress a bit alternatively. When he noticed her, he rose, giving her the smile that *now* she recognised perfectly clearly from the days it had flashed from the face of the boy who'd been the class joker. 'Well, howdy, Mizz Jaw-Jean.'

The delivery of the well-worn joke was deadpan, but his eyes laughed. Despite having spent the afternoon brooding on why he hadn't mentioned their old connection as soon as he recognised her, Georgine felt the corners of her mouth twitch. It was reassuring to be reminded of his clowning, the days when Rich would try to make her giggle in class. Once he'd pretended to take out his eyeballs to polish them. Next time he'd opened his eyelids he'd been cross-eyed, as if he'd replaced them in the wrong sockets. She'd had to look away to prevent herself from laughing out loud. Pretending had been OK then.

But now?

'Hello . . .' She hesitated.

'Joe,' he finished for her. 'What can I get you?'

'A glass of chardonnay, please.'

While he went to the bar she took a seat, noticing a couple of the younger Acting Instrumental students in a coterie of teenagers in the corner. All had soft drinks on their table. Tubb knew better than to serve the underage youth with alcohol. Apart from the threat to his licence, their parents, aunts and uncles could well be knocking back a merlot somewhere in the pub.

On the bar, tiny white lights sparkled on a small Christmas tree – Tubb wouldn't waste space he could fill with customers by putting up a larger, floor-standing tree – and a colourful range of notices about Christmas raffles and hampers was tacked to the wooden posts around the bar.

Georgine combed her hair with her fingers before flicking it back over her shoulders.

When she looked up, Joe was watching her. Then Janice

the barmaid arrived to serve him. 'Yes, duck, what can I get you?' she said, and he turned to give his order.

When he rejoined Georgine, he placed the drinks on the table as he took his seat. She became uncomfortably aware of her heartbeat. The time had come to hear what he had to say, and there was a part of her that didn't want to. It was unsettling that he'd had the opportunity to observe her and absorb the memories of twenty years ago, while she hadn't recognised him at all.

She took a sip of wine, unwilling to be the one to start the conversation.

Joe's own drink was fruit juice and he took a long draught of it, then rubbed his palms down his jeans. 'I've been obsessing over where to start. Or even how much you want to know. I'm sorry I wasn't transparent with you.'

Georgine nodded.

He glanced around. 'I'm not sure this is the right venue for this conversation. I suppose I thought a village pub on a weeknight would have a quiet corner.'

She said nothing. The only quieter venue within easy reach was her home, and she was not going to invite him there. Blair might be in by now, and anyway, home was her safe place.

Joe cleared his throat as her silence continued. 'OK. I'll approach this as chronologically as I can. There are still things I don't know and probably never will.' He took another gulp from his drink. 'I was born John Joseph Blackthorn.'

Georgine felt her eyebrows flip up. She'd presumed the name she'd known him under to be his birth name and that Joe Blackthorn was an identity he'd assumed, the reasons behind which had been at the heart of her unease today.

He gave a small, wry smile. 'Yes, it's my real name. My mother called me Johnjoe and sometimes it got shortened to Joe. I don't remember my father, Tim Blackthorn. He died when I was two. They'd taken me to a beach on the east coast and he'd had a few beers. He went for a swim, got caught in a current and drowned.'

Georgine felt a shiver run through her, not just of compassion for such a tiny tot losing his dad but because he'd never told her such significant things about his life. 'I'm sorry. I didn't know.'

He gave a low laugh. 'I didn't know about my dad myself for ages. For the few years before he died, he didn't speak to his upper middle-class parents. They'd made their feelings known when Dad, a student at Cambridge, took up with Mum, an under-educated local girl with the wrong accent, who, in their opinion, encouraged him to drink too much and work too little.'

'Were they harsh?' Despite her earlier reservations, Georgine was beginning to get caught up in the story.

Joe sipped his fruit juice and shrugged. 'I think my parents were as bad as each other. They moved in together and Dad flunked out of uni in his second year. I came along – by accident, I expect – and he never told my grandparents about me. Not long before he died, he did ring his brother, Shaun, and ask if they could meet. Said he had someone to introduce to him. At the time Shaun thought he'd maybe got a new girlfriend and was hoping Shaun's approval might pave the way to him talking to their parents again. Now, of course, he thinks the "someone" was me. But Dad died before he could set up the meeting.'

Georgine found it hard to even imagine the situation. She'd had such a golden childhood, brought up by loving parents whose marriage gave at least the illusion of security. 'But when your dad died, didn't your mum contact his family? Tell them about you?'

His eyes grew shadowed. 'She took it into her head that if they knew about me they'd try and get me off her. Do you remember Garrit?'

Georgine nodded. She had known the man Rich had lived with was not his natural father. He'd always referred to him as Garrit, like everyone else, as if Garrit hadn't been worthy of a first name, let alone a title like 'dad'.

'Mum hooked up with him. He was a shit but a kindred spirit so far as booze was concerned.' Joe paused to give a little shake of his head as if finding the workings of his mother's mind hard to comprehend. 'When I began infant school she registered me as John Joseph Garrit. She told the school she didn't want my real father knowing where I was, but she meant Dad's family, if they ever discovered I existed.'

'Do you think the Blackthorns would have wanted to take you off her if they had?' Georgine took a gulp of her wine to free the lump that had risen to her throat at the way the child Joe had been helpless to influence his own fate.

'They would have been heartless bastards if they didn't, considering the life I was living.' Joe smiled bitterly. 'The years went on. Mum and Garrit sank lower, neither of them holding down a job, Garrit doing bits and pieces on the side and claiming every benefit he could think of. Once I reached my teens he used me as a runner for whatever he was mixed up in – obviously dodgy. He used to send me off with packages or envelopes with promises of dire retribution if I peeked at the contents or didn't bring the payment straight back to him. We ended up in the worst house on the worst council estate in Bettsbrough, filthy curtains at the windows and a garden that was a rubbish heap. I used to have actual nightmares that you'd somehow find out where I lived and turn up.'

Georgine took another glug of wine. Of all the horrible aspects of the life Joe had lived as Rich Garrit, *that* was what had given him bad dreams?

He carried on, the evenness of his voice making the bite of his words all the deeper. 'I hated Garrit. He knocked us all around and was verbally abusive. When I was about nine I found my birth certificate in a case on top of a wardrobe. It took me a few minutes to realise from the date of birth that John Joseph Blackthorn was me and that I'd once had a dad called Tim. I asked my mum about him. She was economical with the truth and said he hadn't stuck around. I used to fantasise he'd come back for me, that he'd be a good man I could live with. In my head, I tried my real name on for size. "I am John Joseph Blackthorn". I used to write it on bits of paper and then rip them up so nobody found them.'

Tears pricking in the backs of her eyes, Georgine murmured, 'I had no idea.'

His smile was bleak. 'I probably should have been an actor, I covered up so well.' He glanced up as if checking no one was listening in. 'It got worse when I went to senior school. My primary school had been in the crappy area we lived in, but Bettsbrough Comp was fed by several other primaries and I finally saw how shit my life was when I met kids from comfortable homes.' He took a slow breath. 'Apart from you, they either laughed at me or ignored me. I think that's why the kids from the Shetland estate formed their rat pack. Stuck with their own. We called the Shetland estate "Shitland", do you remember?

I was unwillingly absorbed by the definitely dodgy Shitland gang. They all had nicknames and with stupid teenage humour they called me "Rich" because I wasn't.'

Georgine swore under her breath. His smile flashed at hearing her curse but she couldn't smile back. 'You made people laugh. You were perpetually clowning around.'

'Sometimes they laughed because I meant to make them laugh,' he acknowledged. 'Sometimes they laughed because I had to wear wellies to school that were so small my heels stuck halfway up the leg part and I had to walk around on my toes. You should try that some time . . . all day.' Beneath the table he shifted his legs, as if his feet, tonight in tooled leather, remembered those wellies. 'I found that if I laughed at myself then at least they were laughing with me more than at me, but I hate to even remember those old humiliations.' He fell silent, propping his chin on his hand and gazing across the room, perhaps seeing not villagers chatting but long ago insensitive teenagers sneering and pointing.

Allowing him time to gather his thoughts, Georgine fidgeted with her wine glass on the table. If she positioned it correctly the Christmas lights on the bar were reflected, as if the last mouthful of wine was joyfully twinkling.

But it was an illusion.

So much of life was.

Quietly, she waited.

Finally, he heaved a great sigh. For the first time this evening, he seemed reluctant to meet her eyes. 'Remember the Christmas card?'

Georgine nodded. The shiny blue front had been hand sewn painstakingly with gold beads, the careful lettering inside. *To Georgine, Merry Christmas, Rich*. How could she forget?

'I'm really sorry about how I behaved.' He groaned, closing his eyes for an instant. 'You'd always made me feel . . . well, as if I was just like everybody else.' He held up a hand as if she'd tried to interrupt. 'We both know I wasn't. "Neglected" I heard Miss Penfold call me, the one who looked after the sale of second-hand school uniform, which she gave me free if I was looking particularly desperate. "Neglected" was a sanitised term for not enough food or adequate clothing.'

'Are you sure you want to tell me all this?' Georgine's hands had begun to sweat at the way Joe was exposing himself with this bald recounting of his early life.

The expression in his eyes altered, became wary. 'Aren't you sure you want to hear it?'

It sounded like a test: *Are you strong enough to listen to my story?*

'Listening's hard,' she admitted, 'knowing that all this was going on right under my nose. But it's a lot easier than living it. Would you like another drink before you go on?' She reached for her bag. But when she turned back, purse in hand, she saw he was already up and threading his way through the drinkers that filled the area in front of the bar.

He was served quickly this time. He dropped back into his seat and slid her glass of wine across the table to her before taking a gulp from his fruit juice, waving away her attempt to pay for the round. It seemed that all his attention was focused on telling his story now he'd begun. He rested his elbows on the table and leant closer. 'I made that Christmas card at lunch times in the art room. I wanted to show you what your friendship meant to me.'

'Why did you sign it "Rich", not "Joe"?' she asked, frowning as she tried to put herself in his place.

He gave a mirthless laugh. 'Would you have known who Joe was?'

'No,' she admitted. 'Because you hadn't told me. I don't understand why even the teachers called you Rich.'

The hint of a smile flashed in his eyes. 'I brought that on myself with silly boy bravado. When I first joined Bettsbrough Comp my form teacher called me John, as I was on the register as John Joseph Garrit. I said I was called Joe and he got me a form to fill out to tell the school what I wanted to be known as. Bettsbrough Comp was trying to be forward-thinking over that kind of thing. But I was sitting with my Shitland mates when I completed the form and one of them snatched it off me and in the box "What would you like everyone to call you?" he wrote in my nickname, "Rich". Everyone thought it was hilarious. We all laughed. So I handed it in like that.' Slowly, he sat back, folding his arms as if putting up a barrier. 'The deputy head called me in.'

'Mr Jenson,' she supplied.

He nodded. 'He gave me this little talk about it being up to me what I was known as in school, but my medical letters and exam entries would always be in my full name. And if I ever went on a school trip abroad my proper name would be on the passport.' He gave a short laugh. 'I was too busy thinking that as I didn't have lunch money the passport question was unlikely to arise to take the opportunity to say "I don't want to be Rich, I want to be Joe," let alone sussing out that this was a perfect time to let someone in authority know that it said Blackthorn on my birth certificate.

'Letting my proper identity slip away – it was all part of the powerlessness I felt back then. I was different to the other kids – but the Shitland rat pack shared more experiences with me than the rest of you. A gang . . . you have a love/hate relationship with it. Sometimes it's your best friend and sometimes it's a tyrant. The gang pushed me into doing shit I didn't want to do, just as Garrit did. I identified with the other members, though, and let them influence me.'

'And you were standing with the gang when I came up to thank you for the card . . .' Georgine broke in, the scene suddenly shockingly clear.

He nodded. 'I'd slipped it into your bag at the end of art, the last lesson in the afternoon. You were meant to open it on your way home on the school bus. You weren't meant to turn around and gallop back to find me to thank me, showing everybody the card.'

She screwed up her eyes in pain at viewing the scene from a new perspective. 'It was so pretty. You probably thought it made you look soft. So you said it wasn't from you, snatched it off me and ripped it up.'

'I had to,' he said hoarsely. 'I didn't care for myself but a lot of us in Shitland would wake up on Christmas morning to nothing. It made us angry at the rich kids who had nice parents to supply a sack of presents. Those guys in the gang would've enjoyed ridiculing you; and considered it a victory if they could have made you cry. Some of them had even begun to look specifically for rich kids to bully out of their money and designer kit. And there was you, wearing your gold watch, with Nike trainers in your school bag, pointing out that we were friends! I'd already told them we weren't really friends but just happened to be in the same lessons because I was terrified they'd start pressuring me to steal your stuff. Acting like a moron and denying any knowledge of the card was the best way to protect you.'

'Wow,' she breathed. It had never once occurred to her that their friendship could have made things uncomfortable for him.

Then he lightened his morose expression with a comical eye-roll. 'I can't imagine why people visit psychologists to confess all the stuff that festers inside them. It's plain awkward.'

She found herself half laughing, though her heart ached to see that even now he mocked himself as a defence mechanism. 'Stop if you want. We were four*teen*—'

But he shook his head. 'Let me get it over with. I wanted to apologise. I thought I'd be able to talk to you at the Christmas party that night. I waited outside for you all evening. But you didn't turn up.'

She felt her cheeks burn. 'You'd shredded my feelings. I told my mum I felt ill so I didn't have to go. And then . . .' She breathed in deeply, surprised that she still remembered the hurt so clearly after two decades. 'You just vanished.'

Chapter Ten

He smiled. And it wasn't any of the strained, bitter, wry or self-deprecating smiles of the last hour. It was a proper smile that warmed his eyes and softened the hard line of his mouth.

'It was the most amazing, unbelievable thing,' he replied obliquely. 'At the time, I didn't much care who or what I left behind, just so long as I could escape my crap life. It was only when I reached my twenties that I began to wonder how it played out for others, and to have a couple of regrets.'

Georgine was impatient to have two decades worth of curiosity satisfied. 'But where did you go? Nobody seemed to know. The teachers said you'd changed schools. Your mates said Garrit had killed you and hidden the body.'

He tipped his head back and laughed. 'I never knew that! It was more like a fairy tale than a horror story. I came home from the Christmas party and my Uncle Shaun was waiting for me. I didn't even know he existed, but there he was – my real father's brother. Garrit was looking smug. Mum and Chrissy seemed bewildered. To cut a long story short, Shaun had chanced across someone Dad had known at uni and stayed in touch with after. She'd asked what had happened to me after Dad drowned. Once Shaun got over the shock of discovering he had a mystery nephew, he set people on trying to find me.

'Mum making me use Garrit instead of Blackthorn turned out to be a giant waste of effort,' he continued wryly, 'because she'd kept her name of Deborah Leonard and Shaun simply had her traced, reasoning that I was likely to be in the same place. He turned up, took one look at the conditions I existed in and said he wanted to take me away to live with him in Surrey. Money changed hands, which accounted for Garrit's good mood, but I didn't care. It's amazing when you think of it but I didn't hesitate for a nanosecond. Didn't question a thing. I didn't even ask if we ought to do things in a more official way. It was a Christmas miracle and I just went up to my room and grabbed the few things I wanted. Shaun said, "Leave the rest. We'll get you sorted with new clothes." I suddenly identified with Cinderella.' Joe rocked back in his chair, eyes glowing at the memory.

He went on. 'Shaun's wife, Louise, took me in as if I was all she needed to make her life complete, saying she'd been too busy to have kids so loved it that Shaun had brought her a readymade one. They'd discussed the possibility of giving me a home before Shaun had ever turned up at Garrit's house, of course, but at the time I didn't make that connection. I just thought they'd taken one look at me and wanted me. I can't tell you . . .' His voice caught.

Georgine couldn't speak either. Her throat felt as if it had been closed with a drawstring.

Joe took several seconds, sipping his drink and fastening

his gaze on a notice advertising a Christmas Tree Festival until his voice returned. 'It was like I'd stepped into someone else's life – someone like you, with adults who cared about meals and clothes and haircuts and school trips and presents.'

It wasn't the right time to explain that the life he painted had only lasted for her until she was nineteen. 'I'm so glad,' she murmured instead, realising that every last vestige of wariness towards him had melted away now she knew the truth. 'Thank you for explaining. It's an astonishing story.'

The door opened to admit a group of six people, laughing and chattering as they made for the dining area, pulling off the coats and scarves they'd worn as a defence against the wintry evening. A couple detached themselves, a woman with dark curls and a fairer man, and made a beeline for Georgine, who hopped up to accept their hugs and make introductions.

'These are my friends, Alexia and Ben—'

'And I'm Joe,' Joe put in with a smile. 'I'm doing a bit of work at Acting Instrumental, giving Georgine a hand.'

'How fab. Great to meet you.' Alexia sent Georgine a less-than-subtle approving look.

Feeling herself blush, Georgine hurriedly steered Alexia into a conversation about how the Angel Community Café was doing now it was approaching its first year of existence, exclaiming over the deliciousness of the cake Melanie had gifted to them, explaining to Joe how Alexia had led the team that last year transformed the café from a neglected old pub.

When Alexia and Ben moved off to catch up with their party, Georgine turned back to discover Joe had somehow conjured up cups brimming with delicious coffee while she'd been chatting.

Once more he waved away her offer of payment. 'I want to tell you a bit more of my story, if you don't mind. There's a reason.'

Although she was surprised, as she'd thought he'd finished and spilling his history had looked as much fun as having fillings without anaesthetic, she nodded. 'Of course. Go ahead.'

'I became Joe Blackthorn, the name I all at once felt entitled to.'

'Your birthright,' she agreed, sniffing appreciatively as she picked up her cup and coffee-fragranced steam rose to tantalise her taste buds. Tubb had recently installed a frothy coffee machine behind the bar, presumably so he didn't lose more customers than he must to the Angel Community Café.

He inclined his head. 'Sean got me into a decent school. I learned a bit about fitting in, partly because of Oggie, as I mentioned. After school, I went to a music college.' He raised a finger. 'I forgot to tell you, Shaun's a musician and a music producer. He was the keys man with a couple of bands and I loved the world he moved in.'

'Oggie said you'd been a roadie and a drum tech.' She sipped her coffee, savouring the rich flavour. Was it her imagination, or did Joe's expression suddenly close down?

He took his time opening a sachet of brown sugar and stirring the contents into his drink. Then he looked up and smiled and she thought she must have been imagining things. 'Musicians tend to take personal recommendations for that kind of position and, through Shaun, I was nicely placed. He was able to get me the kind of work experience the other students could only dream about. I'd made loads of contacts by the time I needed a full-time job.'

'Which bands have you worked with?' Georgine had

very early lost sight of the glittering career in musical theatre she'd once dreamed of and loved to hear about how others made their way.

Joe looked guarded. 'Crew for big name-bands draw journalists like flies to honey if they go around boasting about who they've worked for.'

'Disappointing!' Georgine joked. 'I thought you could get me lots of autographs to auction on specialist sites.'

He grinned. 'You've just highlighted another reason that a band's crew don't talk about their work.'

She wrinkled her nose at him. 'How über uncool of me. But what brings you to Acting Instrumental? Are you tired of the high life?'

Something flickered in his eyes. 'I can't tell you how much I want a more low-key and peaceful existence. At least for a while.'

'Oh.' Georgine was taken aback by his obvious relief. 'So why are you telling me all this if you can't actually tell me anything?'

'Because . . .' He paused, brow creased in concentration, 'the most immediate thing cropped up as you introduced me to your friends. Alexia went to our school, didn't she?'

Georgine shrugged defensively. 'Not in our year, but just about everyone in Middledip who was a teenager at the same time went to Bettsbrough Comp.'

'Of course. And you didn't know whether to introduce me as Joe or remind her that she might have known me as Rich Garrit.' His voice dropped as he said the final two words.

'Oh.' Georgine began to see where he might be going with this. 'You'd prefer not?'

He dragged in a deep breath, letting it out only slowly. 'I would *infinitely* prefer not. I've tried my utmost to leave behind the sad kid Rich Garrit used to be and all the old humiliations. I can't emphasise that enough. When I first went to live with Shaun and Louise they said, "We can't change the past but let's get you the very best future we can." I only shared the story with you because of you recognising me.' He gave a faint smile. 'And because of the long-overdue apology.'

She frowned as she turned his words over. 'There seems a big flaw in your story. Why the hell have you come back to the area?'

He gave a half laugh. 'That's actually the other thing I wanted to tell you. Again, though, I have to ask for your discretion.'

'Hm,' she mused doubtfully. 'I suppose that depends what it is.'

'It's nothing that will hurt anybody else,' he put in. 'I know you guys in education are always wary about anything that might affect safeguarding the students. It's simply that it makes sense of what I'm doing back in the area that I thought I'd left forever.'

He paused, frowning. 'Mum's still local. She and Garrit split up eventually and once I could emotionally afford to forgive her and financially afford to be generous, I began to help her out. She lives in a flat in Bettsbrough and seems content with a quiet life. What I totally don't want is Garrit crawling out of the woodwork. It's not that I'm scared of him,' he added quickly. 'The undernourished kid he used to shove around is all grown up and can adequately defend himself. But I don't want to see him, and I *really* don't want to jeopardise the better life I have by grabbing the creep by the throat and banging his head against the wall until his brain splats out. I'm pretty sure prison food wouldn't suit me.'

'Wow, fierce!' Georgine sat further into her chair, taken aback by the icy anger in his voice. 'OK, I understand. I won't say a word.'

As if trying to bring himself back to the present, Joe glanced around the pub. Then he lowered his voice. 'What I'm leading up to is . . . I own Acting Instrumental.'

Chapter Eleven

Georgine stared at him, confused. 'How can you own Acting Instrumental?' Did he mean 'own' in the sense of stamping his personality on it? Judges on *The X Factor* irritated her with proclamations such as 'You need to really *own* that song' when they wanted the contestant to throw themselves into a performance.

A nearby couple paused their conversation as if they'd like to know the answer to her question. Georgine waited until they'd resumed their chat then dropped her voice. 'Sorry. But what on earth do you mean?'

He leant on the table, bringing their heads closer together and making it harder for anyone to overhear. 'I only own the property, obviously. Oggie had this ambition to begin a further education institution dedicated to the performing arts. When education became compulsory for sixteen to eighteen year olds and all kinds of further education places started springing up to cater to the kids whose strengths are vocational, he saw his opportunity. I wanted an investment, so I bought the property and had the new block built, with help from the bank. He implemented Acting Instrumental. We share the philosophy of not turning a student away for not having already gained qualifications. It's about their futures, not the past.'

Stunned, Georgine just stared. Joe looked perfectly serious but it was hard for her to grasp that this wasn't a joke. 'Oggie's only ever spoken of "the landlord" in the vaguest of terms. It's way above my pay grade to get mixed up in leases and tenancies and things, but I suppose I thought the landlord would be a property investment company or something.' That it would be not only an individual but the one she'd known when he existed below the poverty line was almost too much to take in. 'You call it an investment but I see what you've described as pretty philanthropic. Whatever band you worked for must have paid you pretty damned well.'

He shrugged off her comments. 'I've developed a few minor properties along the way, which all made money. What I want to emphasise is how much I value being at Acting Instrumental right now, working with musicians and performers of the future instead of coping with the egos of the stars of the moment. When someone I thought I could trust disappointed me in a big way, I wanted to do something more –' he circled his hand as if he could scoop the words he wanted from the air '– more worthwhile. Less superficial, but, at the same time, where less rested on my shoulders. Maybe helping kids to realise their vocation in the areas that I found success somehow reassures me that I'm never going back to being Rich Garrit.'

He returned to the subject of his landlord status. 'When I was looking for a suitable property the agent found several likely prospects. When she said one was just outside

Middledip I had an emotional reaction. I used to imagine living here. Every kid from the village seemed to have a nice home.'

'I suppose so,' Georgine acknowledged. 'Middledip's lovely and safe and property's sought after. I could have bought somewhere bigger in Bettsbrough, but I didn't want to live anywhere but Middledip.'

He nodded as if he wouldn't have expected anything else. 'Once I saw that the property looked a sensible investment I went for it. I'm not sure what a psychologist would make of my desire to enter, in some way, a world that used to be closed to me.'

'It seems perfectly understandable.' Georgine took a moment to try to see The Three Fishes through his eyes, the exposed stone walls and wooden beams, the solidly middle-class clientele. 'When I first arrived you were looking around and smiling,' she ventured. 'Were you enjoying being part of that "world", as you called it?'

He looked abashed. 'I was savouring the moment, yes. Maybe it's stupid to get a buzz from being in a simple village pub, considering the places I've stayed in around the world. But it's a pub in Middledip.'

'I can see where you're coming from,' she admitted. She was intrigued about the 'around the world' comment and wished he'd say more about the mysterious band or bands he'd crewed for. She'd noticed how selective he was being with which of her comments he responded to, but she couldn't oblige him to talk about his wealth and what he did with it. Fancy *Rich Garrit* having the kind of money Joe must have.

She suddenly remembered seeing him on the outside stairs on his first day. 'Are you living in the apartment up in the eaves?' And, when he admitted that he was, she added: 'When I saw you on the stairs that day, you acted as if you were lost.'

He nodded. 'Sorry. Oggie agrees that it would muddy the waters if staff and students see me as the landlord, and it doesn't gel with my wish to be a part of things, so I try not to be caught going in and out. I've spent a few days here and there in the apartment during college holidays. It's a good place to decompress and I generally get an invitation to Oggie's for dinner. His wife and kids are as good and kind as he is.'

'I've met them,' Georgine said faintly, freshly rocked that her vanishing teenage friend had occasionally been pretty close to her in the recent past. She studied him. As an adult he was much cleaner cut than she would've expected, hair cropped so short it laid bare the planes of his face. Rich's blond hair had masked his forehead and ears in a mass of untidy rat's tails – not a style choice on his part, she knew, but veiling the trouble in his eyes. Or maybe the young Georgine had simply not seen it? Had she even been capable of appreciating what his home life had been like? She'd thought she'd known him but . . . maybe she'd spent too much time polishing her inner halo just for being friends with the underprivileged kid. It was an uncomfortable thought.

She wondered whether it was a woman responsible for the disappointment Joe had mentioned. If so, she must be picky. Joe Blackthorn was, by any standards, a handsome man, whether watching the world through dark expressive eyes and designer specs or flashing his killer smile. And, because he was wearing a T-shirt tonight she'd noticed the size and strength of his arms and shoulders and the grey-blue shadow of a tattoo peeping from beneath his left sleeve. Realising he was returning her regard, she flushed, glad he couldn't read her mind.

He smiled. 'It was an experience on my first day to be shown around my own property. And by you, of all people.'

She made a face. 'I probably made a complete idiot of myself, gabbling away as if you knew nothing. And you hardly said a word.'

'I was struck dumb by the surreal experience of meeting Georgine France, the all-grown-up version.'

She regarded him steadily. 'I feel disadvantaged that you realised who I was but I didn't recognise you – it seems so obvious now.' It was in the tilt of his head, the way his eyes smiled before his mouth caught up. 'I'm glad you came back.' Then, as his eyebrows arched she added, 'Because it's nice to see you're doing OK, after not knowing what had happened to you.'

A long moment. His gaze didn't falter. 'Did it bother you?'

'Of course,' she said. 'I asked Chrissy but she played dumb. Then she moved away too. Did you say today in the canteen that you'd lost track of her?'

His face fell into lines of sadness. 'It's one of my big regrets. Caught up in the euphoria of Shaun arriving to sort my life out, we barely said goodbye. She was only two years older and we used to try and protect each other from Garrit – lying our heads off or creating distractions when he was throwing his weight around. I worried about her when I went to live with Shaun but he didn't see how he could help her, apart from trying to get the authorities involved, which I knew Chrissy was conditioned not to want. Shaun pointed out that I could see Mum if I wanted to, which would bring me news of Chrissy, but I hadn't forgiven Mum for making me live with Garrit. Once I knew she'd carried me off to a shit life out of spite towards the Blackthorns rather than because she couldn't bear to be parted from me, I blamed her for everything.

'At first, I took at face value that it would be impossible to keep in touch with Chrissy if I wasn't speaking to Mum. Then I got hold of one of Chrissy's friends on MSN. Chrissy didn't have access to a computer and I knew if I wrote to the house Garrit would open or destroy the letter, so I asked the friend if it was OK to send a letter to her to pass on. But she told me Chrissy had already gone.' He slapped the table top as if still angry with himself. 'I was out of options so I got on with my new life. I had these amazing things called holidays and friends who didn't turn on me if I showed weakness. Nobody sent me out on hooky errands. I loved being Joe Blackthorn and not Rich Garrit.'

He paused, gazing around the comfortable pub with its twinkling Christmas tree as if he needed to reassure himself where he was now.

'When I was older and I finally located Mum again I asked about Chrissy, but apparently the three of them moved to Peterborough when they got the dosh from Shaun – Garrit was probably nervous Shaun would find some way of getting it back so he did a moonlight flit. Later, Garrit and Chrissy disappeared while Mum was asleep, after a bottle or two of wine I expect. I assume Garrit decided the money would go further without Mum on board. Mum hasn't told me too much about what happened to her after that and I'm not sure I want to know.'

The pub was emptying rapidly now and Janice came to clear their coffee cups, saying, 'Hello, duck, how's the family?' to Georgine. When they'd had a quick catch up and Janice had moved on, Georgine glanced at her watch and saw it was nearly ten thirty, later than she'd planned to stay. She reached behind her for her coat. 'I can tell Chrissy you'd like to get in touch, if you like. I speak to her on Facebook. She found my profile and friended me a couple of years ago.' She didn't tell him she'd searched for Rich Garrit on Facebook a few times too. Knowing what she now knew, it wasn't surprising she'd drawn a blank.

'*What?*' Joe looked completely thunderstruck. 'But I've combed social media for her!' he protested. 'Even a tracing agency came up blank.'

Georgine frowned. 'Really? Maybe because she's married to an American serviceman and lives on a base in Germany. Do they keep a low profile for security reasons, do you think? I think her husband—' Then she halted. It wasn't good etiquette to over-share personal details without permission, whoever you were. More guardedly she offered, 'Why don't I send her a private message? Give me your phone number and I'll give it to her.'

He hesitated. 'I need to get a new phone.'

'Oh, yes.' Georgine remembered being almost shocked when he'd alluded to this earlier. Even she had a functioning phone, albeit an elderly and crotchety one. 'OK.' She shrugged. 'I can tell her I've met you and you'd like to get in touch.'

'That would be fantastic.' His smile flashed. 'Thank you, Georgine. *Thank* you. It would mean a lot to me to be able to talk to Chrissy again. Is she OK? Does she have an OK life?'

'Seems to.' Georgine slipped her arms into her coat. 'I think it's time I got home. I never got to the end of those transition boards.'

'I'll help you tomorrow,' he replied absently, picking up his own coat. A shadow fell across his face. 'But the next day, Friday the twenty-third, I have to go to London for a meeting, and I don't know when I'll get back.'

Georgine halted, noticing the way he was disposing of his own time, almost assuming the leadership role although 'assistant' was in his title, not hers. 'So, tell me, Joe,' she said, lowering her voice and moving closer to him. 'Are you actually on the payroll at Acting Instrumental?'

He shrugged. 'No. I suppose you could say I'm a volunteer.'

Zipping up her coat, she began to move towards the door. 'Which explains why you turned up out of the blue, why Oggie didn't have a real role for you, why you didn't have a DBS . . . all kinds of things.'

He reached past her to hold the door open so she could move ahead of him to step into the night, where fine sleet was swirling in the wind. 'Structured employment's new to me.' He paused outside, yanking up his collar and pulling a black beanie hat out of his pocket. 'I'd offer you a lift home, but I don't have a car right now.' He paused. 'Shall I walk you home?'

Georgine shook her head. 'Thanks, but it's only a few minutes for me. See you tomorrow.'

He raised his hand in farewell and pulled on the hat.

'Oh!' Georgine halted before she'd taken two steps. 'What about my sister, Blair? She's living with me at the moment. Is she included in the information embargo?'

He quirked an eyebrow. 'I think we can trust her with my murky secrets. Give her my regards, if she remembers me.'

'Will do. Bye.' Georgine put her hood up against the sleet and headed off alone for the footpath into the

Bankside estate. Her head was spinning as if she'd had eight glasses of wine, not two. Almost everything she'd heard from Joe this evening had shocked or surprised her. Even his position in Acting Instrumental was unsettling. Her 'assistant' owned the whole place? Interesting state of affairs.

Blair arrived home a little after Georgine and they shared a cup of hot chocolate to warm them up before bed. 'Do you remember Rich Garrit?' Georgine asked, pulling her dressing gown snugly around her.

'Your friend who did a disappearing act?' Blair blew across the surface of her drink. She favoured a white fleece onesie with a pink satin tail and she looked young and sweet with her make-up removed and her dark curls tousled. 'You went round like a raincloud for weeks after.'

Georgine flushed. 'He's reappeared now,' she said, not attempting to justify her teenage moodiness. 'You know I told you about my new assistant, Joe Blackthorn? Same person.'

Blair nearly choked on her hot drink. 'Why isn't he called Rich Garrit any more?'

'It's a really freaky story.' She related the whole tale and Blair's eyes got rounder and rounder as she listened.

'That's awful,' Blair breathed. 'He was always scruffy but I never suspected he had such a horrible home life. But how amazing that his uncle found him and put it all right. Good on him!'

'Definitely,' Georgine agreed, yawning but reluctant to end this cosy chat with her sister by heading up to bed. To recount everything Joe had told her was . . . what? Comforting? A way of processing?

'Soooooooooo,' Blair sing-songed mischievously, breaking into her thoughts, 'do you still like him? Are you hanging out with him again at lunch break? Does he carry your bag? Is he hot?'

After a moment of trying to look reproving, Georgine giggled. 'Hotter than you in that onesie. He's very respectable and clean-cut these days, though some of his clothes are a bit edgy.' She thought about the expensive-looking leather boots. She went on to tell Blair the astonishing fact of Acting Instrumental's ownership until she finally had to give in to her fatigue and go yawning up to bed.

It was only as she flopped into bed that she realised . . .

Joe had told her a hell of a lot about his past.

But very little about his present.

Chapter Twelve

The summons of Joe's other life had to be answered – at least temporarily – on Friday morning.

He sat in the back of the taxi that drove him into a London where giant Christmas decorations of silver and gold, red and green, trembled in the wind above every major street. Dropped off just before ten at his house in Clarence Way, trendy Camden, he paused on the pavement newly aware of the sound of the city. Traffic. A nearby siren. Shouting. The grumble of a train. All very different to a happy little village in Cambridgeshire.

If his sojourn in the country lasted he'd have to get his own car, he decided, as he unlocked the front door of his compact Victorian end terrace. Calling for a minicab was fine when you were based in London but not having a vehicle in Middledip was inhibiting. He'd have to turn his mind to what kind of thing Joe Blackthorn would drive. Something not too boring but not too flash.

He was still enjoying working at Acting Instrumental and his all-important DBS certificate had arrived yesterday, prompting Oggie to suggest he pick out music students to mentor, one-to-one or in small groups. It was remarkable how much he was looking forward to working with musicians who hadn't spent half their lives in the biz under all kinds of pressure. He envisaged a jam-session approach, letting the students relax and innovate, helping them develop. He had his eye on that kid Tomasz, the one Georgine said didn't always have the money for guitar strings. He played with passion. The passion was undisciplined sometimes but Joe could help him there.

If he was honest with himself, working closely with Georgine France was a big draw too. The teenage crush had reignited. He didn't know what that said about him . . . but he was interested to see where it led. Georgine wasn't, so far as he could see, attached, so why not? She seemed interested in him too, but whether that was actual attraction or just her satisfying her curiosity over what had happened to him, he couldn't guess.

He'd shied away from telling her the whole truth.

Two personas seemed almost too much for her, let alone introducing a third by explaining why his days of being a drum tech or roadie had been few and were long over.

He pushed open the sturdy front door and stepped straight into the lounge, pausing to gather from the doormat the untidy heap of mail displaying pretty Christmas postage stamps. When the band had been on tour he'd frequently been away for much longer than the two and a half weeks he'd spent at Acting Instrumental, but now he felt disconnected from his life in London. Maybe it was because he'd been on so many emotional journeys lately.

Today he'd embark on another, one with a big fork in the road. He couldn't delay that journey indefinitely. That wouldn't be fair to the rest of the band.

After the apartment at Acting Instrumental, the house felt cramped. There were three rooms downstairs and three up: none were spacious. Yet for under twice the house's worth he'd been able to buy the whole of his Middledip property: the house then known as Lie Low with its gardens and paddocks.

Yawning, he made automatically for the kitchen and its coffee supply, glancing out of the French doors into the tiny rear courtyard. This morning's hoar frost hadn't melted out there; it was almost entirely in shade in winter. The main outdoor space of the house, and one of the reasons he'd bought it, was a roof terrace behind a small parapet. In summer he loved to sit up there, part of the London skyline in a tiny way, surrounded by the noise from the nearby elevated train line. In winter it felt like Siberia and he left it to the pigeons.

Not bothering to switch on the filter machine, he made a cup of instant coffee and carried it and the mail into the lounge, deliberately avoiding entering the last room downstairs, the one that contained his drum kit and piano. He threw himself down on the cream corner sofa, kicking off his boots so he could swing his feet up. He had a couple of hours before he was due in Holborn to meet Jerome.

Joe liked the fact that Jerome Rumer still worked out of his legal firm's modest Holborn address rather than the upmarket Rumer Thornton offices in Kensington, Mayfair and the City of London. Jerome was as unassuming and unpretentious as his office, but that didn't stop him being highly effective.

Joe took his first gulp of almost-too-hot coffee as he flicked through the small stack of envelopes, opening a couple of credit card statements and putting them aside, sorting rapidly through the junk to filter out a few early Christmas cards.

Lastly, he turned to a long white envelope addressed in handwriting he recognised.

Billy's.

He brushed it back and forth across his fingers. Should he shred it unopened? He dropped the envelope in his lap and drank his coffee, taking both phones out of his pocket to study them; two iPhones, one coloured silver, one gold. They seemed symbolic of the two parts of his life at the moment.

His original phone he'd deliberately left switched off during his sojourn at Acting Instrumental. The second, bought in Bettsbrough after work just yesterday, was stubbornly silent. He'd texted its number to Georgine to pass to Chrissy, which Georgine had done, but his stepsister had neither called nor texted him. His intention to send his own Facebook friendship request had been frustrated by Georgine's apologetic refusal to supply Chrissy's current surname unless Chrissy sanctioned it. A few minutes with Google had shown him that there was an unexpected number of US bases and military installations in Germany, so he'd abandoned any attempt to get a lead on her himself.

Turning to his original phone, he weighed it thoughtfully in his hand. Maybe he should have kept it on in case his mum or Shaun wanted to contact him, but Shaun could reach him through Acting Instrumental. He was one of the few people who knew about Joe's benevolent involvement with it and the only one apart from Oggie who knew he was hiding out there.

The situation with Debs, Joe's mother, was different. She had his number, but she'd never yet called him, although she always seemed pleased when he called her.

He'd long ago made peace with his conscience about how he related to Debs. The flat she lived in for a peppercorn rent was his. Her cousin Mari lived with her as a companion and, earlier this year, Debs had fallen in love – with a black-and-white Jack Russell called Bernie. Joe hadn't been callous enough to mention that Debs showed a lot more responsibility and love to Bernie than she ever had towards Joe.

The pragmatic truth was that Debs had been too young, too weak, too addicted, too scared to perform well when motherhood had sought her out. Joe accepted it, but Debs wasn't the person he looked to when he was feeling vulnerable.

She'd been the first person to let Joe down but not, he thought as he returned his attention to Billy's unopened letter, the last.

Puffing out a sigh, he snatched up the letter, ripped it open and unfolded a sheet of A4 ruled paper, the kind Billy usually used for songwriting.

Dear JJ,

As you're not answering phone or email, I'm sending this to your house for when you come back. Seriously, man, we can't even talk now? Where the fuck are you? What are you doing? You're hurting the band. You need to grow up and smell the roses – yeah, some roses do have shit around the roots. It makes the roses better and more beautiful. Concentrate on that.

A typically self-conscious metaphor, Joe thought sourly, wondering whether Billy had immediately dashed off a song called 'Roses and Shit'. He moved on to the next paragraph.

We need to all get round the table with Pete and sort this out.

Yeah, because that had worked so well three weeks ago. After a volatile band meeting in their manager Pete's office, Billy had got right in Joe's face and shoved him, a move that resulted in Billy finding himself on the end of Joe's flying fist and seeing all four walls and the ceiling before he crashed to the floor.

Maybe if Billy had accepted Joe's hand to help him to his feet the apologies would have been said there and then. Instead, Billy had not only slapped the hand away but spat at it, climbing slowly from the floor as the rest watched, stunned into silence by a flash of violence that had solved nothing but changed everything.

'Hey, you can't act like that!' Pete had shouted, the only one to put into words what the others were probably thinking.

'One of us is going to have to leave the band,' Billy had growled, gingerly touching his rapidly swelling lips.

Joe hadn't been in a fight since he left Bettsbrough and, no matter the provocation, he was bitterly ashamed of how that mechanism of meeting violence with violence had clicked into rapier-quick action. His anger turned inwards and the way forward had shone blindingly clear. 'Me,' he'd said bleakly. 'It's me who has to leave.' And, as the others all seemed to want him to do, he signed off on Billy's lyrics for the song that had begun as his, 'Running on Empty', and walked out on everything he'd known all his adult life. The band that had represented his friendship group as well as his living.

Yet now Billy wanted to talk and was, in typical Billy fashion, trying to make everything Joe's fault. Billy always wanted to be the centre of attention and get his own way but, until now, had always been sensible enough not to divide the band. Now Joe was on one side of a chasm and Billy had managed to get Raf, Nathan and Liam with him on the other.

How much was Joe's own fault? He was relying on today's meeting with Jerome for perspective before talking to anyone else.

He couldn't imagine not being with the band. He let his head tip against the sofa back and closed his eyes. Most winters he managed to grab a spot of sun in the Middle East or Australia and it would have made good sense to do that again when he'd wanted time to clear his head and re-evaluate. Instead, he'd gone to a village in north Cambridgeshire as the British winter gained hold, wanting a project, a way of giving something back to the music industry that had provided him with all he had. He had a special interest in Acting Instrumental. It had been his brainchild as much as Oggie's. Now he was relishing the almost peace that had come with just being Joe Blackthorn, volunteer and assistant events director.

Yes, he'd wondered whether Georgine still lived in the Middledip area and if he'd hear word of her, but, recruitment being Oggie's end of things, Joe hadn't known she worked actually at Acting Instrumental.

His old feelings had roared back and seized him in their jaws. He thought about her all the time. He'd told her his story. He'd admitted he was Acting Instrumental's landlord.

But he'd let her continue to believe he was still a drum tech and roadie.

A long way from the scruffiest, poorest boy in the school now, yet still some insecurity or instinct had made him uncomfortable at the notion of his worlds colliding.

Maybe he'd tell her soon, but it was peaceful just being Joe.

He opened his eyes and stretched, then took himself upstairs to shower. In his bedroom, he pulled clean jeans, shirt and jacket from the wardrobe. As he was about to push his arms into the shirt's sleeves he caught sight of himself in the mirror. His tattoo encircled his left shoulder, extending from the bottom of his neck and over much of his upper arm. It was cleverly designed, a circlet of features that made up different faces depending on how you looked at it. Women in his past had been intrigued, tracing individual details or counting how many faces they could make out.

The tattooist had specialised in optical illusions. He'd created the design from Joe's own sketches, expounding confidently about it being an expression of the many moods and facets of one person. It had been a close enough interpretation that Joe hadn't bothered to explain that it was actually more about identity.

One person with many personas.

He'd made sure it remained covered up all the time he'd been in Middledip, as well as having worn those stupid fashion glasses with plain lenses and returned his hair to the natural golden brown it had become in adulthood. The tattoo was part of his band persona, along with his messy-crop dyed-red hair – which he still felt odd without – and exaggerated sideburns shaved to points in the hollow of his cheeks.

The tattoo would be instantly recognisable to a lot of students. It had appeared on stage at rock venues everywhere, in promo shots and selfies – on the shoulder of JJ Blacker.

JJ Blacker.

He stared at himself again in the mirror. JJ Blacker: that's who he was today. Musician. Songwriter. JJ Blacker lived in trendy Camden, rode prestige cars, gave interviews to the music press, spent long days in the pressure cooker of expensive studios creating albums put out by a big record label.

JJ Blacker who had to sort out his life.

His eyes were drawn to a framed promo shot the record company had presented to each of them. Blond Billy Langridge, grasping a mic, Liam Willson and Nathan O'Brien with guitars slung around their necks, Raf Radkov with his bass nearly down at his knees. And JJ Blacker, drumsticks crossed in one hand. *The Hungry Years* was inscribed in a gothic-looking white font on a black name-plate. 'The Hungry Years' was the title of a mega-hit by legendary singer-songwriter Neil Sedaka, a past pub in Brighton . . . and the name of the highly successful British rock band of which he was the drummer.

He finished dressing and jogged downstairs to pull on a thick coat before leaving the house, sliding on his glasses, which would automatically darken in the harsh winter sun, and his black beanie hat. Lifting his collar, he turned into Hartland Road for the walk into Chalk Farm Road then Camden High Street to the tube station. He could have easily called a cab but it was great to see Camden, never short of ornamentation at any time, blazing with every colour of Christmas light.

The two stops on the Northern Line to King's Cross, and two more east on the Piccadilly Line to Holborn, passed quickly and uneventfully. Nobody shouted, 'There's JJ Blacker, clean shaven in glasses and a beanie!' or tried to take a crafty photo. It was no surprise that clean-cut him blended in so successfully as his new image seemed

111

to have passed completely beneath the radar of eighty-odd performing arts students for the past two and a half weeks.

He walked up Southampton Row to Theobald's Road and in a few more minutes he was sticking his glasses in his pocket and announcing himself to the young guy on the front desk at Rumer Thornton, pulling off his coat as he was shown straight into Jerome's panelled office where the paintwork was yellowing, the carpet fading, and the wooden edge of the capacious desk bare where Jerome had worn the varnish off as he worked. He claimed he couldn't spare the time to clear his office for redecoration.

Small and wiry, Jerome was in his mid-fifties and had smooth dark skin. As he'd been Shaun's friend and lawyer for years, Joe hadn't hesitated in going to him whenever the need arose. Jerome's cherubic smile sometimes fooled people into thinking he wouldn't go for their throats in court. He would. In fact, he probably kept a file in his desk drawer to sharpen his teeth.

'Hey, JJ.' Jerome came around the desk to offer a hearty handshake. 'You're looking mainstream. What's happened to your red hair and sideburns?'

Joe settled himself in a cracked leather chair as Jerome seated himself again behind the desk. 'I needed a change.'

Jerome nodded. 'It sounded like it from our phone conversations at the beginning of the month. No sign of a reconciliation since then, I suppose? Tempers cooled and all that?'

'Tempers have cooled,' Joe acknowledged. 'And it looks like second thoughts are being had.' He showed Jerome Billy's letter.

Jerome read, one corner of his mouth lifting. 'Perhaps those second thoughts aren't particularly comfortable ones.' He turned on his chair to face the big computer monitor protruding from the wall on an articulated arm and pulled out a keyboard. He called up a page of notes then glanced at Joe. 'As discussed on the phone, I don't see grounds to make a stink about the band deciding to go with Billy's lyrics rather than yours. Billy and you wrote different lyrics for the same song and the band voted to go with his version.'

'Because he manipulated them and our manager Pete supported him,' Joe couldn't resist putting in, the hairs on his neck prickling just thinking of that day. 'We were going with my lyrics until Billy came in rubbing his chin and saying he was worried that my version would be too much of a departure, hinting someone, presumably from the label, had given him the nod that we should stick with his. Pete and the others took his vague rumblings as gospel and said they might as well go with his version. But the band's put out plenty of my songs with equally socially aware lyrics on singles and albums. It was all BS.'

Jerome shrugged. 'From that description of events, he hasn't broken the law. He's just managed to manoeuvre himself into the lion's share of the publishing royalty.' He grinned, looking more like fifteen than fifty. 'Would it be a horrible pun to say musicians have a "record" for professional differences?'

'Yep.' Joe slid down more comfortably in his chair. 'But I'm not expecting you to advise me to take legal action against Billy for being more of a motor mouth than I am. It's the other stuff that could be tricky. Is he going to bring a suit against me?'

Jerome's smile faded. 'I'd say that if neither of us has heard anything yet it's a good sign. According to my notes . . . well, you say you struck him?'

'Afraid so. I suppose the fact that it was in reaction to

him shoving me wouldn't dissuade him? A "he hit me first" sort of thing?'

Swivelling gently on his chair, Jerome raised his eyebrows to meet his neat hairline. 'It's some mitigation. However, your words were that he gave you a feeble shove and you nearly smashed his teeth down his throat. If that's true, his legal team would feel in a strong position.'

'That is pretty much what happened,' Joe acknowledged with a sigh. 'I'm ashamed I hit him but I did it. Thanks for being honest. I suppose we just have to wait and see if he starts anything.'

'Perhaps in anticipating legal action we're being hasty. The letter did say Billy's willing to talk . . .' Jerome let the thought hang in the air.

For several moments the two men gazed at each other, Joe thinking, Jerome giving him time to.

It was Joe who broke the silence. 'I suppose I'll have to talk to him. Things can't be left in limbo. I need to talk to them all.'

Jerome nodded. 'Have you decided whether to leave the band?'

Joe propped his elbow on the chair and let his head tilt onto his hand. 'Part of me wonders how in the hell it's come to this. The other part feels that the explosion's been coming for a while. I seem constantly to be at loggerheads in situations like this. Pete says my ethics, whatever he means by that, are holding the band back from even greater commercial success. *Is* it me? Am I idealistic? Or scared of our increasing success? I don't know. Since the band demonstrated such a lack of confidence in me I'm not sure I particularly feel like touring, working in the studio, or even writing.' Briefly, he explained where he'd been for the past weeks and what he'd been doing. 'Working with those kids, helping the events director pull the show together, it feels as if I'm doing something important. I'm not on the payroll but it's satisfying and honest.'

Slowly, Jerome nodded. 'You wouldn't be the first musician to leave a band, JJ.'

Joe rubbed his temples, every beat of his pulse tightening the tension above his eyes. 'I need to start a conversation with the guys, I suppose.'

'And your manager?'

Joe thought for quite a long time before answering. Pete 'the Beat' Betterby had been a drummer in a prog rock band in the seventies and had turned eventually to management. 'Until recently, I trusted Pete. He's been mumbling about the agreement between him and the band but I don't think he'll really do anything to rock the boat. He's doing too well out of us.'

Jerome raised his eyebrows. 'Nevertheless, run it past me if he does more than mumble about it.'

'Of course.' Impatiently, Joe returned to the subject of the quarrel. 'Pete's entitled to like Billy's lyrics more than mine, but I resent the way he dismissed me. It was as if he expected me to say "Oh, OK, Billy's taken a song that was really important to me, substituted his cheap, crappy lyrics and covered up an amateur rhyme scheme with repeated obscenities, lining himself up a heap of cash as lyricist in the process. And you guys have all been manipulated into saying it's 'safer' to take that to the record company, without even recording my version to get the record company's reaction. That's OK then, I can see it's easier all round." Pete shouldn't do things the easy way. He should do them the right way.' He could feel his hands clenching at the remembered injustice.

Jerome nodded. Outside, the traffic rumbled up Theobald's

Road. The hum of conversation from the outer office was punctuated by the ringing of a phone. 'Are the royalties the main issue?'

'No, you know they're not,' Joe replied morosely. 'The main issues are about betrayal and integrity. Or lack of integrity. But royalties are easier to measure.'

Jerome pulled his keyboard closer and typed a note. 'I agree, but you've signed off on Billy's version of –' he checked his notes '– "Running on Empty". I can only support your decision to enter a new conversation with your manager and the other members of The Hungry Years and suggest you let me know what transpires, especially if you decide to part ways with the band. I think we can leave dealing with the prospect of a suit against you for if and when it materialises.'

'Right.' Joe passed a weary hand over his eyes. 'I need to think. If I stick by what I said and go, the ramifications will be huge – like divorcing four people. Being the man who broke up the band.'

Jerome made a tiny movement of his shoulders. 'But we can make it happen, if that's what you decide.'

The clock on the wall moved on nearly an hour while they talked through the various legalities, Jerome making notes as they planned for the aftermath if Joe left The Hungry Years. Eventually, Joe's brain protested at the overload of information about things like future royalties on past work. 'I'll talk to the boys and get back to you,' he said abruptly, it suddenly hitting home that he'd just moved a step closer to leaving not just Billy, but Raf, Nathan and Liam.

'Understood.' Jerome typed another note with an air of finality.

Rather than stirring from the chair and leaving Jerome

to get on with his working day, Joe scratched self-consciously behind his ear. 'As I'm here, do you know where I can get information about debt and the powers of debt collectors? For a friend?'

Slowly, Jerome sat back and pushed aside his keyboard. He folded his hands behind his head, regarding Joe narrowly for a moment. 'It's not my field. I can dig you out some general information, but your friend would be as well going along to a debt charity. They're pretty good, I understand.'

'Cheers.' Joe rose. 'I'll be in touch.'

Jerome came around the desk to clap Joe on the shoulder. 'Just remember, JJ, you haven't done anything you can't undo.'

'Yet,' Joe supplemented.

'Yet,' Jerome agreed, and Joe left via the busy outer office, carrying along with him a mental image of Jerome's confident, astute smile. He'd always appreciated that it was better to have Jerome with him than against him.

Outside again, fastening his coat against the raw winter day, instead of turning left to the tube station he turned right up Gray's Inn Road and ambled all the way back to Camden, absorbed in his thoughts as London went about its busy day. With a pause to buy a calzone from the takeaway window of a little Italian place near to his home, he let himself back into his house an hour later.

He plugged in and turned on his phone and fired up his laptop, eating the calzone slowly at his small kitchen table while a host of texts, missed calls and voicemails indicated their presence on his phone screen and his email client populated his inbox with messages that had things like '*WTF????*' or '*Where the hell are you?*' in their subject line.

He began by listening to the voice messages. Nathan, Liam and Raf had initially left sympathetic messages like, 'Hey, can see why you're upset. Are you OK?' and progressed through, 'We need to talk. This affects us all,' to, 'Where the fuck are you, JJ? What are we supposed to tell the record company? This isn't cool!' He winced. They were right.

Towards the end there were a couple of abrupt messages from Billy too, saying they couldn't leave everything up in the air. Finally, he said gruffly, 'Maybe we can sort something out.' Not exactly an apology but at least a hint he accepted the existence of an issue.

The emails and texts followed a similar pattern. Manager Pete had emailed on a daily basis; smooth requests to get in touch, there were matters to be resolved. Joe smiled cynically. Maybe Pete the Beat had realised that he'd handled things badly and was belatedly worrying about damage to his own career if popularity of The Hungry Years took a dive as a result of JJ leaving. Feedback from the fan club and the record company had always been that Joe was a popular and recognisable member of the line-up often referred to as 'the Hungries'. Girls wrote *We love you JJ!* on their skin. Unofficial merchandise depicted his tattoo. A girl had had the letter J tattooed on each breast, then pulled her top off at a gig to show him. The music press and social media alike had gone crazy.

All signs of popularity that had dimmed Billy's smile a bit.

Joe scratched his head through his shorn hair. The blow up with Billy had awoken a pretty pissed-off kraken.

He sank his head into his hands and for a full half hour chased his thoughts in circles. He could ring each of the guys individually, but that would be messy and inefficient.

On the other hand, meeting with Liam, Nathan and Raf without Billy and/or Pete stank of collusion. But he couldn't talk to Billy and/or Pete until he'd got together with Liam, Nathan and Raf . . . He still couldn't believe they'd voted not to even record a demo of his version of the song.

Mess. It was a mess.

The only 'conclusion' he came to was that possibly he wanted both to stay with the band and with Acting Instrumental. Or maybe he didn't.

After a few minutes' more thought, he texted Georgine: *Just to confirm that I'll be back on Monday. Looking forward to visiting the theatre as we discussed.*

It felt important to set a limit on the time he bubbled in the present cauldron of discontent, but if the boys from the band could see him sending that they'd be miffed. The Hungry Years had been his life for fourteen or more years. He'd lived the band. Endured the period of five men sharing crappy rooms meant for two and supporting bigger bands. Found success.

He pulled his laptop towards him and began to compose an email.

To: Raf, Nathan, Liam
From: JJ Blacker
Subject: I'm in London

Sorry to have been out of contact but I needed to get my head together. We need to talk but I'm not sure of the best approach. What do you think?
JJ

Then he took himself off into the tiny room behind the kitchen, just large enough for his practice drum kit and digital piano, set Green Day's *International Superhits* playing, picked up a pair of drumsticks and relieved his feelings by drumming along, arms flying while his right foot set the pounding rhythm on the bass drum and the left brought in the hi-hat cymbals, the music thrumming through him like his heartbeat. Then he switched it off and let the sweat dry while he messed around with an eight-beat sequence using bass, floor tom, snare and crash cymbal, which had come into his head in the car. He thought about writing a song advising everyone never to join a band, but Reel Big Fish had done it already. Finally, reluctantly, he laid down his sticks and went back to the laptop.

Three emails had pinged into his inbox, so the boys must have been hanging around waiting for him to show signs of life. All three replies were some variation of *About time! Yes, we have to talk.* And all three of them suggested that Billy and Pete be excluded from the first meeting. *After all,* as Nathan said bluntly, *they've had their say while you've been out of contact, JJ.*

The time was set for the next evening and the venue Joe's house. He closed his laptop with an unfamiliar reluctance to meet up with the guys. He wasn't sure there was any way back from where they were . . . which would make it easier to leave the band.

If that was what he wanted.

If.

He went back to his drum room to think as he practised, head swinging, limbs flying. Becoming the beat.

Chapter Thirteen

On Saturday morning, Georgine decided on a run through the frosty village to clear her head.

Despite gloves and two long-sleeved base layers under her running jacket, she shivered as she stepped outside and began to jog. Left right, left right, her feet slapped the tarmac along Top Farm Road and the cut-through to Port Road. She was nicely warmed up by the time she reached the bridleway through Church Close to the Carlysle estate and the winter skeletons of hawthorn edged her route past greensward and coppices.

As she ran, she pondered the text she'd received from Joe last night confirming arrangements for Monday. It was a courtesy she wasn't sure she had a right to expect as she now knew Joe to be an odd kind of assistant, not only a volunteer but landowner of the very place she went to work every day. When he'd left for London she'd suspected his life there would call him back, yet he'd deliberately flagged up that he intended to return to Middledip.

Funny to think he'd been living in the apartment in the roof of the building for the last couple of weeks. He'd obviously done a good job of coming and going discreetly, and she understood why: without knowing he was the landowner she, and probably most of the staff, would've asked questions about someone joining Acting Instrumental and instantly beginning to live on site.

Her feet slowed as she approached a stile, scrambled over it – cautious of the slipperiness of the wood – and then re-established their rhythm again on the other side. Away from the road, there wasn't much to hear but her breathing and the thump of her feet carrying her along. Her cheeks stung with cold and she was glad of the head-band that protected her ears.

As it had so many times since Joe had shone a light on his past, her mind turned back the clock to the days when she and Rich had been gawky teenagers. Who would have thought the kid with such low prospects would return with such personal wealth?

He'd been in her heart a little bit, Rich Garrit. At four-teen, she'd been old enough that she and her friends had teased each other about boys they liked, but none of them had teased her about Rich, perhaps because he'd never occurred to them as being boyfriend material. Secretly, she'd thought friendship was about to become something more when she'd received that handmade Christmas card signed *Rich* – which, of course, was why she'd made such a fool of herself racing back to thank him for it . . .

At the fork in the path, she swung left towards Little Lane, not wanting to enter the trees around the little lake and lose what warmth there was in the wintry sun. Her throat rasped and she wished she'd brought water.

That day when Rich had switched from friend to jeering enemy had shaken her to her young core. She remembered gaping at the scorn on his face, shocked into immobility as he'd crowed, 'Ooh-er, as if I'd waste my time on a pretty card for *you*.' His hoots of derision had invited the others to join in.

Horrified, mortified, betrayal like acid in her throat, she'd turned and fled. For the next couple of weeks she vowed never to speak to Rich Garrit ever again. By the start of the January term she'd calmed down enough to realise there might be an explanation for Rich's turncoat behaviour. But by then it was too late.

Amazing how these memories had the power to tighten her chest. She slowed her pace until she could drop her breathing back into the correct rhythm and tried to think about preparations for the Christmas show. If Joe kept on handling the tech then it was going to enhance the production because he was really creative.

The Christmas show made her think of Christmas presents and that, however much she loved the festive season, it had to be budgeted for. She wasn't a greedy person but it would be nice to think that one day she wouldn't have to worry about money. Like Joe . . .

Every thought seeming to come around to him one way or another, she concentrated on picking up speed, moving out of the bridleway and onto the grass verge beside Little Lane, legs protesting as they carried her past Honeybun Cottage. She shouted a breathless hello as she overtook Tess and Ratty Arnott-Rattenbury as they set out for a walk with their youngster in his buggy. At the Cross, she had to slow for traffic, jogging on the spot before crossing. Passing Booze & News she was just in time to catch sight of her sister in a fetching red woollen cloche hat, turning up the path to the Angel Community Café.

'Blair!' Georgine called hoarsely, coughing because her throat was dry.

Blair grinned and waved. 'I've decided to splash out on one of Alexia's cappuccinos. Join me?'

'Thanks,' Georgine wheezed, and let Blair make an elaborate performance of putting her arm around her as if she needed help to cover the distance to the warm and fragrant interior of the café. While Blair ordered, Georgine did some half-hearted stretches hanging on to the back of a chair, more interested in exchanging greetings with those she knew – tiny blonde Carola behind the counter with Gabe, his grey hair gathered in a ponytail, and darkly pretty Alexia who replied, 'Mawnin' Mizz Jaw-Jean,' with a wink and a grin.

Two students slurped shakes while their mothers drank coffee and they all looked up to say hi too.

When Blair arrived with their drinks and two double-choc cookies, Georgine gladly fell into a chair and prepared to refuel. Alexia, Gabe and the two students instantly joined the table and as the laughter and chatter gathered pace and volume Georgine sipped her frothy coffee and laughed along. She might have a lot in her life to worry over, but everything she had to enjoy more than made up for it.

Nathan was first to arrive at Joe's on Saturday evening, peering from beneath his blond combed-forward hair as if he'd walked from his place in Chalk Farm in a tornado rather than the chilly breezes of late November.

'Hey,' he said glumly, when Joe opened the door. His eyes widened. 'Where's all your crazy red hair?'

'Haircut, natural colour,' Joe replied economically.

Nathan stepped inside and flopped onto the sofa without removing the long black coat that nearly reached the top of his boots. An illuminated stick pin in the shape of a

Christmas pudding flashed from his lapel. He studied Joe. 'You OK?'

A car door slammed outside and the bell rang before Joe could reply so he rose to let Liam and Raf in. Liam's hair was long enough to be pulled back in a man bun. Raf's quiff was in relaxed mode, lying to one side instead of gelled up. They both stared at Joe and echoed Nathan's words of a moment earlier. 'Where's your hair?'

'It's shit-awful short,' Nathan answered for him, still sounding as if he was at a funeral. 'And where are your sideburns? Man, you look all . . . tidy.'

Somehow it relaxed Joe to be gently ribbed about his new look. 'I'm trying tidy out to see if it suits me.' He went to the kitchen where he'd left a jug of coffee on the hot plate.

'It doesn't,' Liam called after him.

He didn't have to be told the boys' individual coffee preferences so he soon returned, handing out the mugs.

Then he took a seat on the very end of the L of the sofa and glanced around at the guys. He couldn't recall a single other occasion on which he'd felt so jittery in their presence. 'So? What are you thinking?'

The others exchanged glances, obviously feeling their way. 'We should have sent both versions of the track to the record company,' Nathan began. 'But you overreacted. We've never had violence in the band. You were out of order.'

Joe nodded, though he pointed out, 'If the entire band turned on you, Nathe, you might get cross too.'

A further exchange of glances. Liam, often the peace-maker, sat forward. 'If you want an apology, JJ, it's yours. We let Billy and Pete panic us into backing Billy's song by listening when they said the record company talked about it being "more challenging" or whatever this week's buzz phrase is. Your song's better and no one seems to know who it was at the record company that made this mysterious pronouncement anyway.'

'But why did you disappear?' Raf butted in, chin jutting. 'And where have you been? Why not answer your phone?'

With a sigh, Joe sank back into the sofa. 'I took time out. Billy pulling a fast one made me reassess. It's not just the publishing royalty on the lyrics; his lyrics poked fun at being hungry, and I don't think being hungry is funny.'

Liam tried a feeble joke. 'But your song's about a pie. Pies are always funny.'

For a second, Joe thought rage might rupture a vein in his temple, and something of his fury must have shown on his face, judging from Liam's startled expression. Joe took a breath, letting it out slowly so he could reply calmly. 'It's a song about hunger. Our freakin' band name's about hunger. You know these things. And you know why I find it unacceptable to joke about it.'

'Being irreverent is part of being a rock band,' Raf murmured, 'but we accept we might have stepped over the line. We know your background.'

Joe had told them his story when, straight out of college, they took the band to Tenerife to play in the bars of Playa de las Américas. One day Billy had referred to a down-at-heel teenager hanging around the beach as 'feral'. Joe had jumped in to tell him fiercely that the kid's problems probably stemmed from neglect, and exactly what neglect could mean.

His story had all come pouring out. Their horror, mixed with pity and compassion, had made him vow not to talk about it in future, a vow that had held good until he'd seen Georgine again and his younger self had suddenly come at him out of the past.

Joe cleared his throat. 'If we need to be insensitive arseholes in order to succeed then you can see why I needed time to think. I went to hang out at Acting Instrumental. It's been good just to be with people only just getting started, untarnished by the bullshit.'

Raf fiddled with the ends of his hair. 'And all the thinking turned your phone off?' He glanced at Liam and Nathan. Nobody cracked a smile.

Joe's stomach clenched with an uncomfortable mixture of anger and remorse. 'I didn't want to talk to Billy or Pete mainly, but I was in no rush to talk to you either. I felt fucking betrayed and so I had a diva moment.'

'For three weeks? Long moment.' Nathan looked at Joe with puppy-dog eyes. 'We didn't even know if you were alive. Then Liam rang your uncle and he said you were OK.'

Joe hadn't known that. It moved his guilt up a gear. 'Thank you for worrying about me, Liam.' He took a couple of quick gulps of coffee to swallow down the lump that had jumped to his throat. 'I'm OK.'

'You're not OK,' Raf contradicted him softly. 'You've been like our brother since college so if you blew us off you're not OK; if you ignored our messages, you're not OK, and it's not OK to do that no matter how pissed off you were.'

Liam glared at him. 'We've been proper scared for you.'

Unexpectedly, Joe's eyes prickled. 'That's confusing. One minute you're ganging up on me and the next you think I owe you explanations?'

Nobody chose to tackle that. After a silence, Liam leant forward and offered Joe his hand, thumb uppermost as if they were about to arm-wrestle. 'Good to see you in one piece.'

'Despite that hair,' Nathan put in as Joe shook Nathan's hand and then Liam and Raf's in turn.

Even such a feeble joke defused some of the tension and Raf volunteered an update on happenings in Joe's absence. 'Billy's backtracked and says maybe we should go with your version of the song. Pete doesn't agree but has said grudgingly that it might be less incendiary if "Running on Empty" is replaced on the album with "Worthy", which you and Billy at least wrote together so you get fair shares.' Liam pulled a face. 'The Hungry Years has never had problems like this. You hear it with other bands, but never with us. It's shit. I hate it.'

Sombrely, Joe agreed.

Nathan's eyes bored into Joe. 'So, what next? We all heard you say you were leaving the band. And you haven't taken it back.'

Silence.

Emotion closed up Joe's throat. 'I suppose I don't feel sure you want me,' he managed in a low growl. 'Certainly not Billy.'

'That's shit, so we've got to freakin' sort it,' Liam said bitterly. 'Talk to Billy, JJ. He was a thoughtless twat, but we've got second from top of the bill on the Pyramid Stage at Glastonbury next year. We're supposed to be pushing the new album by then. If you can clear the air now we can all enjoy Christmas and start pulling together our tour material in the New Year.'

Joe had to clear his throat before he vocalised what he'd been forced to think about. 'You can get another drummer.'

Raf's eyebrows almost jumped off his head in horror. 'But that won't be you! Even the fans who are excited by your big tattoo flexing to the beat know you do loads more than the drumming.' Raf leant forward and gripped

Joe's forearms as if he could physically prevent him from drifting away. 'You've written over half our material, you sing leads on some tracks and your voice is part of the sound of the band. Come *on*, man. Sort it out. It's like the end of the freakin' world. If the music press gets hold of this . . . !'

It wasn't quite doomsday, but the idea of what could be made of The Hungry Years suffering infighting was scary. They talked for the remainder of the evening, ordering in pizza and drinking Joe's coffee.

'What's with Acting Instrumental, anyway?' Raf demanded, trying to stand his hair up by pulling it hard through his fingers. 'I thought you were only involved as an investor.'

'I was.' Joe felt an urge to share his joy in his odyssey. 'We've got such great facilities: a studio theatre with a lighting rig and sound equipment, a sprung-floor dance studio and rehearsal rooms.' He halted, seeing only astonishment and dismay on their faces, conscious that he'd sounded like Georgine during his first-day tour. He went for a simpler sell. 'It feels good to decompress at Acting Instrumental and we've got this amazing Christmas show, *A Very Kerry Christmas, Uncle Jones.*'

Nathan snorted in amusement. 'Wacky title.'

'It's written for students by a student who was one of the many who got enough UCAS points at Acting Instrumental to do a music degree.'

'Since when do you need a degree to get in a band?' Raf demanded blankly.

'Maybe not to be in a band, but there are lots of other careers in the performing arts.' But Joe could tell by the sceptical expressions that he wasn't convincing his audience.

At midnight, Liam suggested they call a halt to discussions. 'We're not doing any good here. What we need to know is: are you ready to get the band stable again, JJ?'

Joe was back to facing the questioning stares of the guys who had been his best mates for so long. 'I wish I knew. I'm getting a kick out of doing something else for a while – but I hate the idea of never working with you guys again.'

Silence.

It was Raf who eventually suggested, 'Let's decide not to decide while JJ puts in time at his rock school. Pete can tell the record company we want the album launch put back – yeah, I know they'll freak out, but Pete will just have to earn his money and deal with them because none of us is feeling like doing the promo. Let's talk again after Christmas.'

Joe turned the idea over in his mind. There seemed no downside. 'If you don't mind hanging on for a bit, OK. For now, I won't formally leave the band.'

But that was when Joe's phone rang. Raf craned his neck to read the screen before Joe could retrieve the handset from the table. 'It's Billy!'

Three pairs of eyes swivelled Joe's way, daring him not to pick up.

His hand hovered. Billy had to be faced sooner or later. So, sooner? Or later? Joe snatched up the phone on the sixth ring. 'Billy.'

Billy sounded astonished. 'Hey, JJ. Hey, man.' Then he went silent, as if actually reaching Joe rather than his voicemail had stymied him.

Joe decided to take the initiative. 'I was about to ring you,' he lied smoothly, because he didn't want Billy to leap onto his high horse and begin another unproductive row. 'I've just told the others that I want more time to think. They've agreed we're going to talk in the New Year.'

'Oh. Surely we can get past this?' Billy sounded uncertain, but he didn't query why or how Joe had talked to the rest of the band without him. 'We'll put your version of the song on the album,' he added in a rush.

'We can't flip-flop about over an issue that stems from something so fundamental to the band, Billy. If the album launch can be delayed—'

'No!' Billy interrupted, sounding panicky. 'We won't get money from the tour for ages. We need the album to go out on time. I apologise for trying to bulldoze you. I was just in a shitty mood that day and spoiling for a fight. Let's just get this fucking album out.'

Eyebrows raised around the room as, presumably, Liam, Raf and Nathan heard every word.

Joe tried to read between Billy's lines. 'Thing is,' he said experimentally, 'I'm sort of committed to a volunteer project for a while. And we make such peanuts from album sales now and the initial payment's split five ways—'

'But it's something,' Billy muttered.

Slowly Joe closed his eyes. 'So, Billy, it's about money?'

After a pause, Billy laughed. 'Isn't everything?'

'Not really. OK, we do need to talk.' Fatigue swept over Joe. 'I'll email Pete to set it up. I don't want to meet without him. It exerts some kind of control to have someone to keep us on topic.'

'Pete's in Spain till Friday. Taken his wife and grandkids to his villa,' Liam said, raising his voice so Billy would hear.

'Shit, that's right,' Billy said in Joe's ear. 'I'll email him and ask for a meeting as soon as he gets back.'

'I'll do it.' Joe leant forward to reach under the coffee

table where he'd stowed his laptop. Ignoring Billy's, 'No, I'll do it,' he went to his email client and put his phone on speaker, leaving both hands free to type. 'Right,' he said after a minute of tapping. 'I've asked for a round-table meeting with him ASAP to decide where we go from here. I've copied you all in. OK?'

Liam, Nathan and Raf all said it was so Billy said, 'Great. Yeah,' though he didn't sound super thrilled.

As the call ended, Joe mentally bet himself a thousand pounds that Billy was now sending another email to Pete suggesting he come back to the UK for the meeting rather than making them all wait a week.

Billy obviously felt the need to have everything back on track as soon as, but he'd be wasting his time. Joe would be returning to Middledip tomorrow.

Chapter Fourteen

Georgine faced Blair across the landing, trying not to plant her hands on her hips and be drawn into a sisterly spat. But failing. 'If you dump your shoes on the landing then how is it my fault if I trip over them and hit my head on your door?'

Blair stood in her doorway, face creased from sleep and eyebrows knitted. Her pyjamas were dotted with cute cartoon snakes wiggling forked tongues. 'It's not even eight on a Sunday morning! FFS, Georgine! I'm really, really tired. How can you not see red shoes?'

Georgine, dressed for a run, rubbed her stinging forehead. 'It's barely light at eight in winter so what difference does colour make? And anyway, who woke who up at one this morning?' Georgine had lain awake listening to Blair readying herself for bed with no apparent regard for noise level.

Blair gave an exaggerated sigh as she folded her arms – with difficulty as she clutched a red satin peep-toe stiletto in each hand. 'I get that you're my landlady now, but I don't think it says anywhere in our agreement that I have to be in by ten.'

'What agreement?' Georgine demanded hotly. 'The one where you turn up with nowhere to go so I let you move in?'

Blair glowered. 'I'm sorry if helping your sister is inconvenient. At least it should help soothe your guilty conscience.'

Georgine experienced a lurch of exactly the guilt Blair alluded to, rapidly followed by a tide of shame. 'Blair! I know you're not good if you don't get your sleep but you don't have to use that against me. I live every day with what happened that summer.' The summer she'd been nineteen and had condemned her family – well, most of it – to living on a shoestring.

Contrition flitted across Blair's face, but before she could reply the air was shattered by a prolonged peal of the doorbell followed by a loud knock. A familiar voice called, 'Miss France? Miss France? Can we speak to you, please, Miss France?'

Georgine peered down the stairs in consternation at two familiar-looking burly silhouettes visible at the front door in the glow of the street lights. 'Debt collectors on a *Sunday*?' Then the doorbell gave another *riiiiiiiiiiiiiiiing* and her hold on her temper snapped. 'Right! I've just about had e-sodding-nough of this!' Without giving herself time to reconsider, she flew down the stairs and snatched open the door just as one of the debt collection agents leant on her doorbell again. '*What?*' she bellowed into his startled face.

The agent, a balding and bulky man in his forties wearing a white shirt and a black stab vest as if hoping people would think he was a police officer or bailiff, blinked. 'Miss France? Sorry to disturb you—'

'You so aren't,' Georgine snapped, the red mist so hot that it made her cheeks sweat.

He blinked again. The other agent, smaller and thinner, was the one to chirp up. 'We're looking for Aidan Rustington—'

'And he doesn't live here, which you know, or you wouldn't be shouting my name through my door, you'd be shouting his, wouldn't you? He hasn't lived here for months and you're here to intimidate me into paying his debts or giving you his address. But he refuses to let me have an address because he's scared of you *gentlemen* giving him as shitty a time as you're giving me. I'll give you his phone number though,' she added, the idea occurring to her for the first time.

Georgine snatched her phone from her pocket, pulled Aidan up on her contacts list and read the number out, repeating it for good measure while the agents fumbled to tap it into their own handsets. 'And I'll tell you his mum's address too. He might easily be hiding out there,' she said, wondering why she'd feared this confrontation so much as she reeled the information off. She was almost enjoying an opportunity to vent the wrath that had built with every visit from the debt collectors. Sorry as she might be for Aidan, she'd given him an opportunity to deal with this a better way and he hadn't taken it.

She shoved her phone away, allowing no opportunity for the agents to take control of the conversation. 'That's all the information I have. Now go away and don't come back or I'll call the police.'

The thin agent ignored her threat with a placatory smile. 'Now, Miss France, maybe you could tell me whether you have a Find My Friends app? Perhaps Mr Rustington—'

Furious that he wasn't creeping off with his tail between his legs as intended, Georgine whipped out her phone again. 'Nine,' she said, beginning to dial. 'Nine—'

The bigger agent began backing away. 'We'll try Mr Rustington's number.'

Georgine held up her phone to show her finger was hovering over the nine for the final time.

The thin agent rolled his eyes. 'Now, now, I really don't think—'

Georgine's finger moved and he turned and hurried off in the wake of his colleague.

'And stay away,' Georgine bawled as they reached their white van. She stepped back into the house and slammed the door so hard she was surprised the glass didn't break.

Then she began to tremble as she deleted the nines from her screen. Holy crap. She'd just chased debt collectors away from her door!

Blair's voice, high and frightened, came from the top of the stairs. 'When did you get so scary?' And Georgine burst into tears.

In an instant Blair was beside her, drawing her into a warm hug. 'I'm sorry, Georgine. I'm sorry I was horrible and provoked you into facing them.'

Sobs racking her, Georgine let Blair cuddle her, glad for the sisterly embrace and the cessation of hostilities. 'You know how sorry I am for what happened—'

'The past is past,' Blair said firmly, as if she wasn't the one who'd just raked it up. 'Everything's going to be fine. We're going to get on with our lives and some day we'll have all the money we need. I'll buy my own house like you and we'll both have new cars and go on four holidays a year.'

Georgine sniffed, wiping her face with the heels of her hands. 'How?' she croaked.

Blair gave her a squeeze. 'Rich men? It's worked OK for Mum with Terrence, hasn't it? She's always swanning off somewhere.'

Knowing her sister wasn't serious, Georgine managed a watery smile. 'She gets holidays and new cars, but Terrence rules her. I'd rather work for every penny and know it's mine to control.'

Though Blair nodded, she sighed. 'Not sure there are enough hours in the day to allow me to work hard enough. Anyway, sorry again. I'm cranky through lack of sleep. I'll go back to bed.'

After a final hug, Blair trailed up the stairs and closed her door. Georgine decided she was no longer in the mood for a run and headed for the kitchen. Coffee and her favourite breakfast of porridge with chopped nuts comforted her while she waited for her laptop to whirr through its start-up routine. She wished she could Skype Grandma Patty but it was five hours earlier in Georgia, America than in England.

Leaving her bowl in the sink, she turned to her emails and a message from the Bettsbrough Players wardrobe person, Ralph, who was looking to get rid of all the group's costumes and props. The morning began to pass in an absorbing exchange of emails and images to show Georgine what was available.

I'm particularly interested in the pantomime stuff like the oversized foil Christmas decorations that collapse so ingeniously for storage. That black backdrop twinkling with glittery stars positively makes my mouth water, she typed rapidly. *I don't want to miss this opportunity so could come today, if the weekend isn't inconvenient to you.*

Ralph's reply pinged straight back:

Weekend is just the job, but I'm on my way out to my grandson's birthday party. Next weekend any good?

She replied, *Absolutely!*, made arrangements for Saturday December 1st and signed off. The show was really coming together. Her schedule for the coming week was full of rehearsals, and production meetings.

Even Errol had been enthused at the Friday meeting, joining in the buzz without any of his customary snark or sneers. It had been a pity Joe had been off on some mysterious meeting in London because a few nice things had been said about the value of his contribution. She'd already typed up the meeting notes and emailed them to him with a couple of thoughts about lighting. After a moment's consideration, she forwarded this morning's conversation with Ralph to him too.

Just forwarding FYI. If that backdrop's any good we could use it in Very Kerry Christmas.

She found plenty more in her inbox or on her 'to-do list' to keep her occupied for the rest of the morning. Then, noticing her stomach grumbling, she checked the clock and paused for lunch. Thinking back over the debt collection agents' visit and feeling sorry for the way things had ended up with her and Aidan, she texted Grandma Patty.

Are you up? Can we Skype today sometime? xxx :-)

She opened Skype ready for Grandma Patty's call while she washed up and commenced a blitz on the kitchen. The call came in just before two in the afternoon and she hurried to seat herself at her laptop as a window opened up and her grandmother materialised, smiling, on the screen.

'Hello, Grandma! How are you?' It was common in north Georgia to call grandparents grandmommy and granddaddy, but with the children growing up in England, Grandma Patty and Grandpa Earl had been chosen instead.

All Grandma Patty's laughter lines creased, her silver hair piled up untidily on her head, dark eyes brimming with life. 'Well now, isn't this a lovely way to begin the day?' Her voice was soft and slow. 'I'm looking forward to hearing all your news, dear.'

Georgine beamed back, loving the opportunity to chat with this emotionally close, if geographically distant, member of her family. As usual, knowing Grandma Patty was always anxious to hear it, she began with her father's health, which had been static for some time now, reassuring her grandmother that she usually saw her dad a couple of times a week. Once she thought Patty's mind was put to rest, she moved on to her own doings. 'The Christmas show's really getting into gear. The students are working hard. It's only just over three weeks to opening night.' She rolled her eyes. 'And I just frightened myself to death saying that out loud!'

Grandma Patty laughed. 'I have every faith in you. I wish I could see the show myself.'

Sadness made Georgine's chest heavy. 'I wish you could too. Do you still feel travel would be unwise?'

Patty's smile faded. 'I just haven't felt like it since your Grandpa Earl died, Georgine. My lung condition makes it tricky and you know I had to have oxygen once, so now my doctor doesn't recommend air travel, which invalidates my health insurance.'

Not wanting to make an elderly lady feel guilty about her quite understandable limitations, Georgine answered cheerfully. 'I understand, although it would have been lovely to have you.' Then she remembered her little sister, who still hadn't emerged from the only spare bedroom. 'Blair's here for a while, but I would've sent her to camp out at Dad's if you visited.'

Patty's eyebrows flew up, making her forehead divide into soft lines and furrows. 'What happened to Warren?'

Georgine explained, dropping her voice in case Blair had woken and could overhear. 'We're still in what I think we should call "a period of adjustment",' she concluded wryly.

Her grandmother gurgled with laughter. 'I'll just bet. The two of you have quite different personalities.' Then she brightened. 'Say, why don't you come here soon? It's been way too long since we saw you. How about on your spring break?'

'Um—' Georgine felt her heart getting ready to leap for joy, but reality chained it in place. 'Maybe.' She'd *love* to see America again but was totally unable to envisage it unless she won the lottery. And she knew Dad would love to 'go home' for a visit. Easter provided her with more than two weeks off. Maybe she could get casual work to earn a little extra and begin a holiday fund? Her dad wasn't walking well since his last stroke, but she could ask his doctor's advice.

At that moment, the sitting room door opened and Blair wandered in, still in her cute-snake pyjamas, but wearing a much cheerier expression. 'I heard you say "Grandma" – are you Skyping her?' She hurried around to stoop over Georgine's shoulder. 'Hi, Grandma Patty!'

Georgine shifted to one side of the chair so Blair could perch on the other, making a three-way chat possible. Blair was always excited by 'getting in touch with her American side' as she termed it, demanding details of what was going on in Georgia and letting little Americanisms creep into her speech.

Patty tried to draw Blair out about Warren. 'And is there someone else?' she asked when Blair had given her a brief summary. Grandma Patty had a talent for sounding like a fun confidante rather than a nosy older relative. 'If not, it won't be long. You're so pretty, dear.'

Blair blossomed under compliments so Georgine let her have the whole chair while she drifted off to put the finishing touches to the weekend clean up in the kitchen, where she could still hear the conversation, returning to the laptop only to bid farewell to Grandma Patty, who had a coffee date with girlfriends to prepare for.

After the Skype call, Blair proved she was over her morning-grouch mood by making coffee for them both and they curled up on the sofa to chatter about how well Grandma Patty looked. Georgine was happy to let their irritation with each other drift away on the joys of a lazy Sunday afternoon. She was getting used to having her little sister living with her.

Chapter Fifteen

Joe was now used to getting himself out of bed at seven a.m. on weekdays, but on Monday he was glad he only had to jog down the outside stairs from his apartment. The icy morning caught his breath as he unlocked the door and gained admittance to the college building.

It felt great to be back at Acting Instrumental. He hurried along the corridor, encountering Oggie coming the other way, a pen behind one ear. 'Are you too old to be told to walk instead of run?' Oggie asked, eyes twinkling. 'Or are you trying to impress Georgine with punctuality?'

'Both.' Joe grinned.

'I saw her heading for her room a few minutes ago,' Oggie called after him, just as Joe swung around the door-frame into Georgine's room to discover that fact for himself – or, at least, it looked like her jeans-clad rear end sticking out from under an enormous toppled Christmas tree.

He juddered to a halt. 'Um . . . are you OK under there?' She looked more than OK from his angle but, judging by the tuts and squeaks coming from within the prickly branches, she wasn't happy.

142

'I'm stuck!' she wailed. 'This stupid thing's fallen on me and it's hooked in my hair and my collar.' She shook like a dog, presumably trying to dislodge whatever held her fast. Strands of silver foil attached to the tree trailed over her left buttock.

Pretty, Joe thought, though what he said was, 'Shall I help you out?' He watched her top edging up as she struggled, the silver strands now trying to find their way into the waistband of her jeans.

'That would be lovely,' she said sweetly. 'I'm sure you wouldn't want to just stand there watching me struggle.'

Actually he did, but it'd probably turn out to be against some rule or other. Education was full of them. 'Keep still,' he suggested, coming alongside the tree to inspect the problem, training his gaze on the dark green tree limbs rather than the skin showing above her waistband. But then, oops, he looked after all. If her waistband was dragged down any further he'd start to physically sweat.

Training his mind on the job in hand, first he got his shoulder underneath the tree to relieve Georgine of its weight, then he pulled a couple of Christmas tree limbs gently aside. 'A branch has skewered your ponytail.' The mass of strawberry blonde hair was half bunched up and half dragged loose. 'Hang on.'

He pulled locks of her hair free one at a time until it was all out of the elastic band. 'Don't wriggle,' he muttered, distracted. Her top, a cream-coloured sweatshirt, was riding right up to reveal the small knots of her spine that bisected the smoothness of her back.

'Is something the matter?' she queried. 'Why have you stopped?'

'Just looking for the best approach,' he fibbed. Switching his gaze to her neck, he followed with one finger the tiny

143

Christmas tree branch that vanished into her collar, concentrating on feeling for what it was hooked around rather than letting his knuckles explore the nape of her neck. 'It's caught up around a label. Hold still . . . there. Sorted.'

He eased the tree upright, a few flakes of glitter floating down around them as Georgine sat back on her heels, shoving back her tangled mass of hair and breathing a big sigh of relief and laughing. 'Thank you.' For a few seconds, before she gathered it back up, her hair lay loose around her shoulders, gleaming amber in the overhead light. 'I must have looked stupid. I don't know what you must have thought.'

What he'd thought when he'd slipped his fingers into her collar and felt her skin was that he'd never wanted to undress a woman more, but he smiled blandly. 'I would never say you looked stupid.'

'Not out loud,' she agreed, eyes dancing. 'We should move the tree and this other stuff to the props room. But, first, I need to get along to a rehearsal.'

'Act one, scene one, full company,' he agreed, having brought himself up to speed from the notes she'd sent him over the weekend. 'You're heading for trouble between Band One and Band Two though.'

Georgine, having climbed to her feet, grabbed her production file. 'How so?' Her eyes were bright, looking up at him as if she valued his opinion. A memory hit him like a blow just below his heart of when they'd been fourteen and she'd been about the only person to give him that kind of respect.

His voice emerged more croakily than he'd anticipated. 'One drum kit, two drummers. You can easily add guitarists and vocalists to the mix because their instruments are portable and every student has their own. But you can't

144

condemn one of the drummers to standing around like a spare part, bashing a tambourine. You're going to have to have a double set-up. A single set-up isn't working well anyway because Wayne, the drummer from Band One, is right handed and Dilip from Band Two is left, which means changing the kit around at scene change.'

She swept out into the corridor, then paused to wait for him to follow. 'It would mean a double set on the band platform for the whole production.'

He easily kept pace with her to the foyer and into the corridor to the new block. 'And it'll look awesome, because the two kits will mirror each other. Working on the stage space dimensions you gave me, we could extend the band platform by a couple of feet, which would help. I'll take a tape and look at that this afternoon when we go to the Raised Curtain.' When she shoved at a door he put his hand up above hers to hold it open as they stepped through.

'OK,' she said, still sounding doubtful. But when they got to the studio theatre he watched over her shoulder as she made a note under today's date. *Two drum sets??*

'Double drum set-up,' he corrected her. 'And it will look awesome.'

As if taking dictation, she wrote *It will look awesome*, mouthing the words as she wrote, making him chuckle when she added two question marks after that too. Their gentle teasing of each other gave him the sensation of returning to something good.

The rest of the day flashed past. Suddenly it was three thirty, their appointment at the Raised Curtain theatre was scheduled for four. 'My car?' Georgine called, dragging on her coat.

'Have to be,' Joe replied. He'd supplied himself with a

145

big pad and a few pens. 'I bought one yesterday in Bettsbrough, but I'm not picking it up till Saturday.'

It was twilight, verging on darkness outside. Joe settled into the passenger seat of Georgine's little hatchback. The interior was distressed in high-pressure areas like a pair of jeans. His jeans, anyway.

Georgine talked as she drove, her ponytail swinging as she checked for oncoming traffic at junctions. 'So, what you need to know about the Raised Curtain is . . .' And she kept up a steady information stream as they barrelled along the lanes to the outskirts of Bettsbrough where the roads became lined with respectable residences of red brick or the copper-coloured stone common to the area.

They passed the top of a triangular green that marked the entry onto the one-way system. Joe, on familiar turf now, looked left, half-expecting to encounter his younger self scuffing along from the Shetland estate in too-small shoes.

'Is this the first time you've been back to Bettsbrough for a while?' Georgine asked. Her voice was neutral but the glance she flicked his way was full of compassion.

'Mum's here. I visit her.'

'Of course.' She nodded, slowing for traffic lights. 'Whereabouts does she live?'

'Manor Road. A couple of big houses were gutted and converted. She shares an apartment with her cousin Mari and a yappy dog.'

'Nice area.' There was a hint of a question in her tone.

Inbuilt caution made him hesitate, but Georgine knew the worst of him already. There was a certain relief in not having to hide anything. 'I wanted distance between her and the Shetland estate and her old drinking cronies, but it would have been mean to uproot her from Bettsbrough altogether.'

Georgine drove on, around the one-way system to the other side of town and in through a pair of gates and over a series of speed humps to the Sir John Browne Academy. She parked at the far end of the hardstanding, close to a glass-fronted building with *Raised Curtain* in black metal lettering bolted into the brickwork. Light beamed out into the car park. Although she switched off the engine, she didn't immediately leap out. Instead, she swivelled in her seat to face him. 'My dad lives on the Shetland estate.'

For a moment, he just stared. Randall France of Randall France Construction with his big black cars and fleet of white vans, living in Shitland? 'Really?' he managed.

She sighed. 'It's not as you knew it. There was a big clean up; the police cracked down on the gangs and a lot of nice new houses and flats were built. But, yes, that's where he lives.'

Then she jumped out of the car and closed the door on the conversation while he was still assimilating her words. Added to the desperate-sounding telephone conversation about money he'd overheard it painted a picture that was hard to believe.

Georgine turned and hurried towards the double doors of the theatre. As he was beginning to grasp that being her assistant meant tracking her shooting star of energy, he followed, Randall France still churning in his mind as they crossed the foyer. Then he was distracted by a frisson of excitement. It was a tiny venue compared to some of those he'd played, but the lighting rigs, the tiers of seats, even the smell from a floor-buffing machine being guided by a cleaner in overalls, they were all familiar.

He half expected to see Billy pacing nervously at the front of the stage, getting irritable with the techs because, having no instrument to set up, he wanted to get on with the sound check. Beyond Billy, the rest of the band materialised in Joe's imagination, talking too much and laughing too loudly as anticipation built.

He glanced behind him. At the back of the theatre, above the highest tier of seats, was the room from where sound and light would be controlled, always referred to, in his experience, as 'the box'. Even the sight of that made his heart beat harder.

'Joe!'

He jumped.

Georgine laughed, eyes dancing. 'Where were you? Cloud cuckoo land? This is Ian, box office manager. We have to be very nice to him because he tells us what we can and can't do with the theatre.'

Joe summoned up a smile as he shook hands with a middle-aged man with black-framed glasses and a quiff. 'Just admiring your set-up.' He gestured about the theatre's interior.

Ian looked pleased. 'Small but beautifully formed. Being a recent build, we're above average regarding tech. All the lights and sound can be controlled remotely. Shall I give you the tour?'

They began with the props room, where yards of silver tinsel and crates of baubles were everywhere, because the students of Sir John Browne Academy had their own seasonal shows in rehearsal ready for the week before *A Very Kerry Christmas, Uncle Jones*.

'Changing rooms: one male, one female, nice big signs on the door in the hopes the little darlings don't accidentally-on-purpose barge in on each other.' Ian shoved open doors and let them swing shut, giving Joe a glimpse of benches with hooks above. 'We usually have our prompt in this area of the wings, tucked behind this curtain. None of the curtains are the expensive kind that actually move, I'm afraid.'

'Understand,' Joe said, as some response seemed to be expected.

'Right. Let's get you up to the box, then I'll leave you to it. Just shout if you want anything and I won't be far away. Have to have you out by five forty-five 'cos a male choir will be in here this evening.'

'On the phone he said six thirty,' Georgine muttered, once Ian had departed. Out came her precious storyboards and they worked through them, discussing, redrawing, making notes.

Then they went down onto the stage area, fine tuning and taking it in turns to run up to various points in the seating to view from there. Deploying Joe's tape measure satisfied Georgine that they could afford a slightly larger dais for the band at the back. 'The double drum set-up better work,' she grumbled at Joe as Ian arrived to tell them their time was up.

But she did book the platform with Ian before they left.

Chapter Sixteen

A wintry shower had begun when they stepped outside; stinging sleet flying into their eyes in the wind.

As they drove from the car park, Georgine's headlights turned the sleet to glitter in the darkness, as if they were driving through a snow globe. They headed back into town where colourful illuminations in the shapes of stars and bells, snowflakes and Christmas trees hung over the shopping area.

They made slow progress through the home-time traffic. Joe didn't mind. Georgine's company made him feel buzzy and he could do no more about The Hungry Years until Pete responded. He felt more at peace than he had at any time in the past four weeks.

Impulsively, he turned to Georgine, whose face was changing colour beneath the festive lights as the car inched up Sheep Street. 'Do you have plans this evening?'

Surprise flickered in her eyes as she glanced his way. 'Only to go home. I might redo a couple of the messier boards.'

'How about we find a pub?' he suggested. 'When we

met in The Three Fishes that night I rudely talked about myself all evening. I'd like to hear your story from 1998 till now.'

Her eyebrows rose as she took the left lane that would eventually lead them out of the one-way system. She shrugged, not replying until they finally left Sheep Street for Silver Street and the Peterborough traffic peeled off. 'If you like. There's a chain pub down by the river called the Boatman. That OK?'

'Sure,' he returned, half-expecting her to 'remember' a pressing engagement before they reached the Boatman.

She drove straight there, however, and pulled up her hood to brave the thickening sleet. 'It's nice to eat outside in summer,' she said as she made a beeline for the well-lit pub decked in lights of the kind of blue usually seen on emergency vehicles, the occasional red star providing the only relief.

'I think I'll give the beer garden a miss this evening.' He lengthened his stride to keep up.

In the bright warmth of the pub he bought her a glass of wine and himself a pint of cranberry juice and soda water while she chose a table. There were plenty vacant. Despite a mouth-watering smell of cooking, a pub on the outskirts of Bettsbrough obviously failed to attract the after-work crowd he was used to in London bars. Over the mantel, a red wire reindeer pulled a green sleigh and nearby a Christmas tree hung, interestingly, upside down from the ceiling. More upside down Christmas trees, small silver ones, hung above the bar.

When he joined her at a table near the fire she took a swig of wine as if needing the bolstering effects of alcohol. 'So, what do you want to know?'

Joe gave what he hoped was a reassuring smile. 'I'd

love to hear about your life since we last met. But we can talk about the show, if you'd be more comfortable with that. Acting Instrumental. The price of eggs.'

A sudden smile. 'Egg-spensive?'

If puns would relax her, he could provide them all night. 'Don't yolk about it.'

'A-fried I'll beat you at your own game?'

He pulled a mock-gloomy face. 'Eggs-actly what it boils down to.'

She laughed, sinking a little more comfortably into her chair. 'Eggs-traordinary. Your sense of humour hasn't matured at all.' Then she sobered. 'OK. I told you I went to uni for a year. I left because Dad's business went to the wall.'

'Shit.'

She nodded. 'I know. It was . . .' She fidgeted with a beer mat. 'Dad missed out on a contract he'd been counting on to get over a downturn – a downturn he'd kept to himself. To the family, everything had seemed the same. When he didn't get the contract the bank called time. Don't you drink alcohol at all?' she asked, changing the subject, her gaze on his glass.

He shook his head. 'Not except for a swallow of champagne at celebrations.'

'Because of your mum and Garrit?'

'Yeah. And Dad. Would he have drowned, if he'd had one pint instead of ten?'

'Right.' She picked up a beermat and contemplated it while he wondered if she'd told him everything she was going to. But then she took up the story again. 'I think I told you Mum and Dad split up. Mum didn't want to be poor and made no bones about the situation not being her fault. The house had to be sold and the legal situation

152

was a nightmare – creditors wanting blood and Mum trying to keep hold of equity for herself. But banks are good at securing their borrowing, so Mum got angrier and angrier. Blair was bewildered and cried all the time. Then Dad started having strokes. Blair had to at least get her A Levels so there was only me who could bring in a wage.'

'I'm so sorry,' he said inadequately.

Georgine paused to watch what looked like a small busload of people come in wearing illuminating antlers or Christmas jumpers. Laughing and chattering, they settled at a long table at the end of the room. The volume of noise increased ten-fold.

Georgine began folding the beermat into quarters. 'It took a long time for the dust to settle and for us to discover what we had left,' she went on. 'And that proved to be not much. A tiny rented house in Middledip because Ratty, the guy at the garage who owns a few properties around the village, felt sorry for us and gave Dad a deal. Dad was no longer medically fit to drive, so Blair and I went to Bettsbrough each day on the bus.' The beermat broke raggedly and she dropped the bits on the table. 'Blair went on to uni after sixth form because by then she could get the full loan, as Dad's circumstances were dire. It was hard to keep her there, because she hadn't exactly learned economy in her formative years.'

Listening, Joe felt cold. Part of him wanted to tell her not to say any more. But another part was desperate to know. 'What about your mum? She wasn't in a position to contribute?'

Georgine laughed, but her eyes were sad. 'Mum went into survival mode and did whatever the upmarket term is for sofa-surfing, living in a succession of her friends' guest rooms or holiday homes. Granddad, her father, made her an allowance, I think. He gave Blair pocket money too, which helped a bit. After a couple of years Mum found a new man, one with a few quid. I don't see much of her, partly because she lives in Northumberland.'

With a blind instinct to comfort, he reached out and took one of her hands. 'I don't know what to say.'

She looked at their clasped hands. 'Shit happens, and it certainly happened to us. Financially, there always seems to be something to drag us down – car repairs or broken boilers. Blair's had a job since leaving uni, but she's not good with money. Dad struggles on benefits.'

Before Joe could comment, Georgine's phone began to ring. She freed her hand to answer, groaning when she saw the name on the screen. 'Here's one of the disasters now.' She put the handset to her ear. 'Hello, Aidan.'

As she didn't move away to take the call, Joe remained seated, recognising the name as the one she'd used when he'd overheard her phone conversation on his first day.

The unseen Aidan, who Joe could hear quite clearly, demanded, 'How could you give the debt people my number?'

Georgine sighed feelingly. 'I am sorry I had to do that, but they're your debts so they're your debt collectors. I couldn't just carry on being hounded at my own front door.'

She listened as Aidan vented, using her free hand to pick at the tatty remains of the beermat, lifting her eyebrows at phrases like 'in view of everything we had' and 'you gave them my mum's address! She went mad!' This last was delivered at such volume Joe thought people three tables away would hear.

Most of the colour had leached from Georgine's face.

'I'm sorry we've ended up so disappointed in each other,' she said. 'Two people who once thought enough of each other to live together shouldn't have to have this kind of conversation.'

Aidan continued at unabated volume. 'You've really changed!'

Georgine heaved a sigh. 'I think you'll find you're the one who's changed, Aidan. All traces of the nice man I felt a lot for have gone.'

Apparently, the latter observation was enough to prompt Aidan to end the call and Georgine put her phone away. Sweeping up the remains of the beermat she'd been systematically destroying, she discarded it on the fire, her smile brittle. 'Ex-boyfriend. He got me in a right fix, not paying his share of the household bills and then doing a runner. And that pretty much brings us up to date on the whole sorry story of how I went from princess to pauper. Improbable as it seems, I now count every penny. And I'm not especially trusting of the man-plus-money combination.'

He touched her arm. 'But not all men are Aidan.'

''Course not,' she agreed, though without real conviction. 'Are you hungry yet? I'll grab some menus.' She got up and set off for the bar.

Left alone, he tried to absorb everything she'd just told him. Then, as she talked to the lady behind the bar, he found himself noticing the way her jeans and cream top skimmed her curves. He had to consciously refocus his gaze when she turned to make the return journey, weaving her way between the tables with a drink in each hand and menus tucked beneath her arm. Somehow, he felt the relationship they were slowly building – rebuilding? – wouldn't profit from her catching him watching the way she moved.

They spent the next few minutes studying the laminated menus of budget-venue staples like fish 'n' chips and pie 'n' mash, with a paper insert offering traditional turkey roast and classic Christmas pud.

'I know it's not December until Saturday but the idea of a turkey dinner is making my mouth water,' Georgine confessed. Then she sighed. 'I had a meal at lunchtime, though. I'd better go for a jacket spud.'

Joe compared the festive menu to the jacket potato option. Turkey dinner was £9.99 and the potato £4.99. He wanted her to have turkey if that's what she wanted, but he remembered how it felt to watch every penny or even have no pennies to watch.

He gathered up both menus. 'I'll order.'

'OK, thanks.' Georgine fished around in her bag and handed him a fiver. He wove his way to the bar, idly watching the members of the large party fighting over paper hats and bottles of wine. Judging from their raucous laughter, they were keen to embrace early Christmas spirit.

The server met Joe at the bar. 'Any special offers on the festive menu?' he asked. 'Buy one, get one half price, for instance?'

She smiled regretfully. 'Sorry, love, no. Offers would be printed on the menu.'

'OK. Two turkey dinners then.' If Georgine said she'd rather have the potato anyway he'd just come back and change the order. He tucked her fiver in his wallet and extracted two tens and allowed himself a wry smile as he carried cutlery rolled in napkins back to the table. All the times he'd lied to get food, now here he was lying to give it away. But he remembered a certain girl at school sharing her lunch with him sometimes. It was time he repaid the favour.

Back at the table he set the cutlery down. 'There's a buy one, get one half price deal so I ordered you turkey.'

'Really? I love Christmas food.' She beamed, but then reached for her purse. 'We can split the difference—'

He waved her offer away. 'No need. I pay the same whatever you have.' As she looked unconvinced, he flipped to a subject he felt was guaranteed to distract her. 'Tell me if I'm sticking my nose in,' he said, lowering his voice. 'But a friend I saw in London's a lawyer and happened to say some interesting things about debt.'

'Oh?' Georgine said guardedly. She was drinking fizzy water now and began to turn the glass in its ring of condensation on the table while she waited for him to go on.

'He mentioned debt charities like Step Change and how much they help people whose finances are out of hand.'

'Oh,' she repeated, though with more interest this time. A moment's frowning reflection, then she took out her phone and set her thumbs dancing over the screen. When she'd finished she said, 'I've texted the name of that debt charity to Aidan. Hopefully he might see it as a bit of an olive branch.'

Joe nodded. That wasn't exactly what he'd expected her to do with the information, but he could see how it worked for her.

Within a minute her phone chirped and she picked it up to read the message. She shook her head sadly. 'Aidan says: "I wouldn't need that if my ex-gf hadn't sneaked to the debt collection people."' She began tapping again, this time, voicing the message slowly as she typed. '"Can only repeat. You . . . have to . . . deal with . . . your . . . debts. I think . . . it's best if . . . I block . . . your number. I . . . wish you well."' Then she tapped at her phone for a few moments more before stowing it in her pocket. 'There.'

A few minutes later, two steaming plates of turkey and roast potatoes arrived courtesy of a young man who said, 'Hey, guys!' when he saw them. Joe wouldn't have recognised him but Georgine answered, 'Hey, Marcus! This is what you get up to when you're not at Acting Instrumental, is it?' Joe gathered from the following conversation that Marcus had joined the college in September and was a dance student.

'Mmm, this smells lovely.' Georgine thrust her face into the fragrant steam and sniffed like a Bisto kid. 'And look at all the goodies! Stuffing, pigs in blankets and Yorkshire pud.'

They spent the rest of the evening discussing Christmas meals, and almost anything that wasn't the past, except when Georgine said, 'Did you ever hear from Chrissy?'

'Afraid not. Maybe I never will,' he admitted, feeling his stomach tipping with disappointment.

'I haven't either. Maybe she doesn't feel she knows you in your new persona.' Georgine ran a piece of roast potato through her gravy and popped it into her mouth.

'Maybe.' The mention of persona made him wonder briefly whether it was a good idea to tell Georgine that he was also JJ Blacker, drummer with The Hungry Years, a successful rock band. But he felt reluctant to let JJ Blacker join the party. It was so much easier to be Joe Blackthorn and, as she'd been upfront about her trust issues, he hoped she'd understand his. It was more enjoyable to join in her enthusiasm for the Christmas show and, when their plates were wiped clean, help her make notes about today's visit to the Raised Curtain.

After coffee, Georgine checked the time. 'Better be getting home. Everything connected with *A Very Kerry Christmas* is ramping up. I've arranged to pick up the costumes and props we've been offered by Bettsbrough Players on Saturday.'

'I could help you with that if it's the afternoon,' he offered. 'I pick up my car in the morning.' Pete hadn't got back to him about meeting at the weekend so he felt free to dispose of his time.

She cocked an eyebrow. 'The wardrobe guy, Ralph, lives on the Shetland estate.'

'Ooh, scary.' He smiled, but it looked a bit of an effort. 'Let's see if I can cope with being back there.'

Her eyes twinkled. 'I'll hold your hand if you get frightened. The afternoon works for me – I'll take lunch to my dad first.'

They pushed their way through the heavy front doors to the car park and then halted. 'Fairy snow!' Georgine exclaimed, looking up into a halo around a light.

'Never heard of it.' Joe pulled up his collar and buttoned his coat as he watched the tiny flakes of snow that seemed to dance in mid-air instead of floating down to the ground.

'It's what I used to call it when I was little.' Dreamily, she gazed up at the sparkles in the darkness. 'I used to pretend that each flake was a fairy playing on the wind.'

'Sweet.' He hadn't known her before the age of eleven but he could easily imagine her as the kind of little girl for whom snow meant getting caught up in imaginary worlds. For him snow had meant a whole world of shivering misery. He was glad to erase the memory by jumping into her car and turning on the heaters.

It wasn't until he got home, still thinking about the evening as he drew his day to a close, that he glanced at his email and saw a message from Pete. He clicked on it to open it up. Pete had said: *OK, can make Sat. Noon at my office?*

Nobody else had replied yet so Joe jumped in. *Sorry, not available Sat now. How about Sun?*

Before he switched off the lamp beside his bed he saw a couple of terse messages from the others saying they could make Sunday if JJ was sure he couldn't put whatever it was aside and make Saturday, as already pencilled in.

He knew he was stoking the mood of irritation they were all struggling with. Lying in the darkness, he asked himself whether he was doing it deliberately, trying to provoke another explosion of such magnitude that staying with the band would no longer be an option.

He didn't think so. When he'd first entered the Raised Curtain this afternoon he'd wanted to be on stage with the band again so badly he had almost tasted it.

But he wanted to do what he was doing as well.

Chapter Seventeen

By the last Wednesday in November Georgine felt as if there simply were not enough hours in the days to accommodate everything to be done.

Joe had provided her with sketchy lighting plans. 'But everything's subject to change,' he said, when she tried to pin him down to something more definite. 'We'll do trial runs in the studio theatre. Better ideas may emerge.'

Georgine wasn't used to such a fluid approach but soon began to appreciate his apparent lack of ego, especially when he found ways of defusing tensions between Errol, Maddie and Keeley, creative directors of music, drama and dance respectively. When Errol dissed an idea, Joe simply asked him what he, Errol, would do. Flattered, Errol proposed things often spookily similar to whatever he'd just dismissed, happy because it now seemed to come from him.

Maddie could be stubborn, but Joe would say, 'Break it down for me,' and Maddie would begin to move her dug-in toes slowly towards new solutions.

Keeley, a ditherer, reacted positively to, 'I have faith in your decision. Why don't we give it a try?'

When Georgine remarked on his skill at 'influencing negotiations' he winked. 'Easy compared to keeping the peace amongst a bunch of blokes who've been on the road so long they're sick of the sight of each other.'

'Your peace-keeping skills are going to be at full stretch this afternoon,' she observed, loading her arms up with everything she'd need. 'Everyone gets edgy when we try to "top and tail" a whole act, only performing the beginning and end of each song or scene to see if it flows. Tempers can fray, especially if we realise we've gone badly wrong.'

They hurried up the corridor towards the other building. Through the glass they could see a few hardy students taking the outside route, hunched in their coats. The forecast was for snow at the weekend and the wind was so icy that Georgine could quite believe it.

Soon they joined the students funnelling into the studio theatre, noisier and more excited than usual with the anticipation of a run-through, probably forgetting the stop-start nature of topping and tailing, when 'let's try that again' would vie for unpopularity with 'try this instead . . .'

The studio theatre was already well populated when they arrived. The lower third of the retractable seating was out and Errol, Keeley and Maddie were gently herding students in that direction. Instrument cases stood along the side of the room under very temporary-looking signs for *Band One* and *Band Two*. The stage space and band stage had been marked out with gaffer tape by Joe earlier and the double drum kit was already in situ. A dotted line of tape through the middle of the main stage space divided it into stage left and stage right for the dual-stage scenes.

The Christmas tree prop was in place at the back of

the stage as a reference point. Eventually, one side of it would be decorated in red and gold with white lights and the other multicoloured so that, by turning it around, it could be the tree of Uncle Jones, or one in a neighbour's house.

Joe had added a broader base to ensure the damned thing wouldn't fall on anyone today. Georgine touched the scrape on her neck from when Joe had rescued her from its scratchy clutches, his fingers warm on the nape of her neck and voice full of laughter.

'Where in the room are you basing yourself?' he asked her now, jumping her out of her thoughts. 'Do you want the storyboards laid out? I could put a few tables together.'

'I usually grab myself a piece of floor,' she said. 'If you put tables up in the middle the students on the seating can't see well. They'll get restive enough when they're watching, without putting up a barrier.'

'OK.' In moments he'd co-opted Tomasz to help mark out an area between the seating and stage with gaffer tape, storyboards, pad and file stacked neatly in the centre. Students chattered, Keeley talked about props, but Georgine gave them only half her attention as she watched Joe write on a piece of paper with a marker pen. When he taped it to the floor she could see it said *Events Director*. Tomasz said something and Joe nodded, causing Tomasz to grab his guitar and hurry back to show it to Joe. They bent over it together, Joe's golden brown head and Tomasz's fair one.

Then Joe handed the instrument back and Georgine caught him saying, 'Try that.'

Tomasz slung the guitar around his neck and played something with the smothered notes of an electric instrument being played with no amplifier. It seemed to be the

163

tremolo bar that had been the issue, but now his face cleared as he tried it and he gave Joe a thumbs-up.

Then Joe hared off to talk to Errol, who was stroking his beard and pacing at the front of the stage. It seemed to Georgine that Errol unwound just through being in conversation with Joe. He'd stopped pacing and was smiling and nodding instead.

She shook herself. They had a busy afternoon before them and she'd no time to zone out while she thought about her assistant which, she'd noticed, was happening a lot. Their evening at the Boatman had felt like a return to their past easy friendship, until he'd asked about how the France family had lost their money. Then panic had pulsed through her veins at the prospect of confessing to Joe what she'd done.

She'd thought about it later, in bed. She hadn't wanted to look bad in his eyes by admitting she'd been the spark that exploded Randall France Construction. She could empathise with Joe's wish to distance himself from the Rich Garrit of the past, because the memory of Georgine France at nineteen made her ashamed.

She gave herself a mental shake and marched over to her designated area to begin laying out the boards. Errol, Keeley, Maddie and Joe gravitated towards her and the last few student stragglers found seats. Wiping her palms on her trousers, Georgine smiled around her colleagues. 'Ready to go? Great!'

She turned to the assembly of students. 'Hey! How's everybody doing?'

Her question brought forth a chorus of 'OK!' and 'Good!' with even the occasional, 'Let's do this!' Then silence as several rows of expectant eyes fixed on her.

A little fizz of excitement shuddered up her back.

Everybody was as ready to get things underway as she was. 'As you know, we're going to run through act one this afternoon,' she began, 'topping and tailing every scene, song or dance to check out the transitions and smooth out inconsistencies. You're all experienced so you know we have to be a bit patient. When you're not on stage you might feel at a loose end. Entertain yourself with your phone by all means, so long as it's on silent. Just don't talk your heads off because then nobody can concentrate. OK?'

A chorus of OKs.

Georgine moved over to a lectern at the side of the room, which she'd set up before lunch. There her laptop waited, hooked up to the electronic white board, and she woke it up to show a slide of the day's running order. 'We'll start with singing all of "Everyone Loves Uncle Jones" to get warmed up. From then we'll top and tail "Thank you for making Christmas, Uncle Jones", "A Very Kerry Christmas" and then "Family is Everything". To avoid a stampede, I'm going to bring you up to take your starting places in groups. Bands, please collect your instruments and find your places on the band stage. Kerry Christmas and Uncle Jones, off stage right; rest of the Christmas and Jones families off stage left, ready to come on. Dance Troupe One, off stage left; Two, off stage right, ready to take up your cues. And, remember, everyone – it's Christmas! So sparkle!'

The run-through began amidst laughter and good humour.

By the time it ended the students were over an hour late going home and the atmosphere spoke of fatigue. Errol was irritable, and Maddie and Keeley were casting longing glances at the door. The start-stop and the boredom of delays and discussions had got to everyone, but Georgine was now happy with every transition in act one.

'That's it for today! Thank you all, you were brilliant!' she called over the clatter and chatter of forty-odd seventeen and eighteen year olds getting the hell out. She too was ready for the day to be over and a headache lurked behind her eyes.

Then Fern hurried in, swimming against the tide of departing students until she arrived at Georgine's side. 'Sorry to barge in,' she muttered, eyes anxious behind her oval glasses. 'Aidan came to reception asking for you and seems reluctant to leave. Mr Ogden's invited him into his room for now.' She only called Oggie Mr Ogden when she was being particularly official. 'He asked me to ask you whether you wished to speak to Mr Rustington. Or not.'

Not, if she were honest. Why the hell would Aidan come to Acting Instrumental? Then mortification swept through her. It couldn't be for a good reason. 'I suppose I should see what he wants,' she muttered ungraciously, all her artistic satisfaction in what they'd achieved this afternoon fading away.

Fern squeezed her arm. 'I'll tell him you'll be along when you're ready, shall I?'

'Thanks.' Heart bumping uncomfortably, Georgine tried to relocate her place in the proceedings. Errol was making sure the amps were switched off and Maddie and Keeley were threading their arms into the sleeves of their coats as they made for the door. Joe was hovering, storyboards under one arm and her laptop under the other, the production file at his feet. Waiting for her. His gaze was sympathetic.

Nothing like an ex-boyfriend showing up at her place of work unannounced had ever happened to her. She had no idea what Aidan wanted, but her sense of foreboding was strong as she picked up the production file. Stomach like lead, she followed the corridor towards the main building, conscious of Joe behind her as they passed a volunteer crew of Level 2 students in the foyer giggling over decorating the Christmas tree.

Finally, Georgine reached the admin office, cringing to already be able to hear Aidan through the open door to Oggie's room, pugnacious and angry. 'I'm not going till I've seen her!'

'Oh, shit,' Georgine muttered. She had to force her feet to carry her the final few steps into the room. She found Aidan standing one side of the desk, Oggie sitting in his usual position behind it. Oggie saw her first and gave a reassuring smile. 'Mr Rustington—'

But Aidan was obviously in no mood to let anyone else have the first word. 'Georgine!' he snapped, spinning to face her. 'What the fuck? I'm no sooner out the door—'

'Mr *Rustington*,' Oggie repeated, a note of warning in his voice this time.

Georgine shut the door with a snap, her own anger suddenly rising. 'Why are you here, Aidan?'

'Because I went to your house—'

'When you knew I'd be at work?'

'And I find your fucking sister there!'

Oggie cut in again. He'd come to his feet now. 'Mr Rustington, I must ask you—'

'I'm hardly out of the door,' Aidan raged.

'You've been gone months. And why shouldn't I have my sister at my house?' Georgine kept her tone moderate with difficulty.

'You've always, always treated her better than me,' Aidan raged, spittle gathering at the corners of his mouth.

167

Georgine was astonished. 'She's my *sister.*'

'I suppose you've been giving her money?'

'That's my business!' Georgine snapped.

Then Joe's voice came from behind Georgine, making her jump because she'd lost track of him and hadn't realised he'd slipped into the room behind her. Now his voice was low and steely. 'I think it's time you went, mate.'

Oggie intervened more conventionally. 'I must request you leave the premises immediately, Mr Rustington, or the police will be called.' He rounded the desk, his arm outstretched to herd Aidan from the room.

Aidan glared, seeming to deliberate for a moment whether or not to stand his ground. Then he spun on his heel, shouldered past Georgine, and strode from the office.

Joe followed, casting back over his shoulder, 'I'll make sure he can get out of the main doors.'

Sudden silence rang in Georgine's ears. Face boiling, she turned to her boss. 'I am so sorry. I can't imagine what he thinks he's doing these days. He's always been so civilised. I've hardly even seen him angry, let alone make an incomprehensible scene.' She gulped in a breath. 'I shouldn't have engaged with him, should I? It just made him angrier.'

Oggie guided her to a chair. 'It's not necessary to apologise for him, Georgine. You're not responsible for his behaviour. Let's have a cup of coffee and give ourselves a moment for the adrenalin to subside.'

Silently, Georgine watched her boss's measured movements at the coffee machine. She was pretty sure her adrenalin was quite a way from subsiding because her head felt like a balloon about to burst.

Then Joe returned. 'He's just taken off down the drive in a red Vauxhall. I've told Don the site supervisor to watch out for it and let someone know if he turns up again. I'm not having this behaviour,' he added, which reminded Georgine of his status of landlord.

'I'm sorry he turned up on your property,' she began, thinking that if Aidan was driving a Vauxhall he must have had to sell his beloved BMW.

Joe frowned. 'You didn't invite or encourage him.' He reached over and added another cup to the two beside the coffee machine, taking one Oggie had already filled and passing it to Georgine.

Her hand trembled slightly as she reached for it.

Oggie and Joe seated themselves. Georgine felt two inches tall for somehow being the cause of the unprofessional upset that had just taken place.

'Now,' Oggie began, 'I'm sorry that happened, Georgine. Evidently, I made an error in judgement in asking Fern to show him in here. Having only known the civilised Aidan, as you call him, I thought I could quiet him down while Fern found you, rather than inflame him by ordering him straight off the premises. In hindsight, I achieved the opposite of what I intended and the delay just stoked his anger.'

Georgine blinked downcast eyes. 'I can't imagine what makes him think he has a right to be angry with me.' Her face, if anything, grew hotter. 'Debt collectors came to my home looking for him – about *his* debts,' she emphasised, in case Oggie thought she was in debt. 'After giving him a chance to contact them himself, I gave them his phone number and his mum's address.'

'And it's gone down like a rat sandwich,' Joe put in grimly.

'Quite.' Oggie smiled. 'I think we can agree that, for whatever reason, whatever he found at your house this afternoon lit his blue touch paper.'

Slowly, Georgine extended her hand for her coffee,

taking several sips before she could trust her voice. 'But what on earth is he thinking of? Visiting me at home when he knew I'd be at work, then getting in a snit because my sister's living with me, and coming *here*?'

'Quite,' Oggie said again. 'The question is what happens from here. Would you like to involve the police? Or consider it a one-off and keep it in-house? Fern will no doubt keep her own counsel if we request it. I leave the decision to you. Should it be repeated, however . . .' He let the thought trail away but Georgine was in little doubt that if Aidan repeated his behaviour then Oggie would take steps. He had the wellbeing of a lot of young people in his hands, as well as that of his staff.

Her shoulders hunched. The police? She cringed from the idea. 'I've never known him behave this way. I'd just like to forget it.'

'People do act out of character if you put them under enough stress,' Oggie told her kindly. 'How are you feeling? Your wellbeing's a primary concern.'

'Stunned and shaken, I suppose.' Georgine drained her cup and replaced it on its saucer. Absently, she wondered if the phrase 'rattled' came from being incapable of placing a cup on a saucer without one chattering against the other.

'Will someone be there if I send you home?' Though it had rung with authority when trying to deal with Aidan, Oggie's voice was as soothing as a relaxation tape. 'Are you fit to drive?'

Georgine nodded. 'I will be in a few minutes.'

'I'll come with you,' Joe said instantly. 'Just in case.'

'Of what?' Georgine began to say. Then, 'Oh,' as she realised Joe thought that if Aidan would behave as he had today, it wasn't out of the question that he'd wait for her at home. The thought made her shiver.

170

'That sounds a very good idea.' Oggie got up and came around the desk to crouch his large frame in front of Georgine and regard her keenly. 'You can stay here for as long as you need to, if you're not ready to go home.'

From the corner of her eye, Georgine saw Joe move restlessly, as if he wanted to say something. She took a couple of deep breaths, feeling her heart rate steady. 'Thanks, but I want to get home and check on my sister. She must have come home from work early if she was there when Aidan called.' She paused, forehead gathering in a frown. 'It was crazy of Aidan to think I might be at home before four on a term-time weekday.' She rose to her feet, glad her legs didn't feel too much like washed string.

Oggie rose too. 'As long as you're sure you're good to go. I'll check back with you in the morning. Let's have a chat then.'

Georgine nodded. 'Of course,' but her heart sank. As well as checking she was OK, Oggie, as principal of Acting Instrumental, would want to hear more about what led to Aidan's tantrum. She understood he had the welfare of both students and staff to think of, but the prospect of him having to assure himself Aidan wasn't a threat to anyone under his wing made her feel hollow.

After saying goodnight, Georgine went to the staff area. Joe paced along at her elbow and, deciding she couldn't face work this evening despite the show looming in less than three weeks, she relieved him of the storyboards, production file and laptop and shut them in her locker. When she emerged from the women's locker room she found him leaning on a wall in the main staff room.

He straightened when he saw her. 'OK?'

She was struck by the unfairness of him being put out

on her account. 'Are you sure you don't mind being dragged off to my place?'

'I'm not being dragged,' he returned easily.

She demurred no more. Aidan's anger had been unsettling.

Then Joe's expression changed. 'Of course, if letting me see where you live makes you uncomfortable—' he began stiffly.

Georgine groaned, digging her gloves out of her coat pocket. 'Of course not. Don't let's have more drama. If you're sure you don't mind riding shotgun then I'm very grateful.'

His expression softened. 'Happy to help.' He fell in step beside her for the short walk through a light mist that hung over the car park, then, in silence, she drove them the few minutes to Top Farm Road.

Chapter Eighteen

'That's Blair's car.' Georgine nodded at Blair's sporty silver Renault Megane as she pulled up behind it. Thankfully, there was no sign of the red Vauxhall Joe had reported Aidan to be driving earlier.

Joe got out of the car and leant against it. 'I'll hang on while you check your sister's OK, shall I?'

Georgine paused, remembering how he'd leapt to the conclusion that she was reluctant to let him see where she lived when she'd only been trying to avoid putting him out. 'You could come in for a cuppa and say hi to Blair.'

In an instant, his features relaxed. 'That would be great. I just about remember her.'

'She was in Year Seven when we were in Year Nine.' Georgine led the way up the short front path and unlocked the door, jumping when her sister bounded up to meet her in the hall like a dog relieved to see its owner safely home.

'That arse Aidan,' Blair began hotly, 'you won't believe what he did today.' She stopped short when she caught sight of Joe. Eyes widening, she dropped her voice to a lower, more breathy, key. 'Well, hello.'

Georgine made introductions, or re-introductions really. 'I told you about meeting Joe again after not seeing each other since school. He used his nickname Rich Garrit then,' she added, so Joe would know Blair was up to speed. 'Tell me what Aidan's been up to. Are you OK?' She pulled off her coat and gloves, leaving Joe to shut the front door on the chilly evening.

Blair tossed her hair dramatically as she led the way into the lounge diner, where the sofa was ornamented with a sunny yellow duvet. 'I came home at lunchtime with a dodgy stomach. I was lying here reading when someone unlocked the front door and walked in. I shouted to ask what you were doing home, thinking it was you, Georgine, obviously. Then Aidan waltzed in – with his stuff! I couldn't believe my eyes.'

'Stuff? What stuff?' Georgine's stomach performed a slow, unpleasant flip.

'A backpack and a suitcase!' Blair's eyes flashed with indignation. 'I think he was all set to move back in. We had one of those "What are *you* doing here?" "Me? What about *you*?" conversations. He looked furious when I said I was living here. Started spouting about you treating me like a princess.' Blair's eyes gleamed. 'So I told him I could see exactly why you'd dumped his sorry arse and he told me to do something anatomically impossible and slammed out. He was *seething*,' she added impressively.

Georgine collapsed into a chair. 'He came to Acting Instrumental. He's gone barmy.' She found herself turning to Joe. 'Do you honestly think his behaviour could be all about pressure?'

His eyebrows rose. 'I'm no expert, but he's behaving erratically. You need your locks changed.'

'I suppose so.' Georgine buried her head in her hands.

'His decision-making seems to have gone crackers. He obviously feels betrayed and thinks our past relationship should mean I'd protect him.'

Joe snorted. 'Your past relationship should mean him not expecting you to stand in the line of fire.'

'What on earth was his end goal in coming here?' Georgine wondered aloud, heavy and sad that Aidan, who not so many months ago had told her he loved her, was now seeing her as the enemy. However unreasonable that was, it wasn't a comfortable thought.

'I was wondering the same,' Joe agreed. He hadn't sat down, although Blair had made room for him on the sofa by shoving her duvet onto the floor. Instead, he stepped closer to Georgine's chair, crouching to bring their eyes level. 'I don't think you should feel guilty. He's not coping so he's playing the blame game.'

Blair hunched forward. 'I think he thought the debt collectors would never look here because you've already chased them off.'

Georgine's eyes burned with tears. 'I feel sorry for him. He used to be a nice guy with a nice life.'

'You aren't thinking of letting him move back in, are you?' demanded Blair, sounding alarmed.

'Of course not.' Georgine blinked hard. 'It's not nice to see someone I once cared for so down, that's all.'

'I feel sorry for him too, but it doesn't make me assume responsibility for his situation.' Joe touched her hand. 'Do you want a drink or something?'

Blair jumped up. 'I'll make coffee.' She gave Georgine a consoling hug, then disappeared into the kitchen.

One of the tears that had been gathering in Georgine's eyes slithered down her cheek.

'You've acted perfectly reasonably,' Joe reassured her

quietly. 'You even sent him the information on the debt charity.' His hand had ended up on top of hers, warm and comforting.

She wiped her cheek on her sleeve. 'Maybe I should have carried on stonewalling the debt collectors instead of pushing him into a corner.' In the kitchen, the noise of the kettle boiling rose to a crescendo. Blair clattered around, calling through to ask Joe how he took his coffee.

Georgine continued drearily. 'When he was made redundant he changed. Then the rot set into our relationship when the truth about the unpaid bills came out. I admit I'm scared of bad financial situations and I raged at him. He said I made too much of it.'

Joe rose to take two coffee mugs from Blair as she bustled in, passing one to Georgine. 'It sounds as if he sees it as your job to sort things out for him,' he said.

Blair arrived to resume her seat on the sofa, cradling her coffee mug. 'That's his mum's fault, and all those older sisters. He thinks women ought to look after him.'

Georgine didn't comment because Aidan had never liked Blair, and Blair had returned the antagonism with interest.

Each had expected Georgine to prefer them.

Each thought they had most right to her helping hand when finances got tight.

Wearily, she let her head fall against the back of the chair. 'Money, money, always sodding money.' People were more important than money but it could be tricky to separate people from their financial situation.

Her mind circled around the Aidan issue as she half-listened to Blair trying to draw Joe out. Joe telling her about this afternoon's run-through. It seemed days ago, rather than a couple of hours. Georgine only roused from her thoughts when she realised Joe was preparing to leave and Blair was offering him a lift.

'I'll drive you,' Georgine said. 'It's my fault you're here.'

He smiled faintly. 'It's not your "fault", I offered to come with you, and I don't need to trouble either of you for a lift, thanks. It's a twenty-minute walk, that's all.' His gaze narrowed. 'As long as you feel safe enough for me to go.'

Georgine hauled herself to her feet. 'I'm sure I'll be fine.'

'I'll be in all evening,' added Blair.

Joe buttoned up his coat. 'You've got my number. Don't hesitate to ring me if . . . well, if you need to.'

'Thank you.' Georgine felt a little blossoming of warmth at his thoughtfulness. 'Hopefully he's got it out of his system now.'

Joe nodded, opening the front door. 'See you tomorrow, Georgine.'

She smiled, hearing the echo of their younger selves. *See you tomorrow at school.* 'Yes. We have a day to work on whatever we've learned from today's run-through, then on to act two on Friday. Thanks again.'

She directed him to where he could cut through on foot to Port Road and he lifted a hand in farewell as he strode away.

Closing and locking the door, she attached the chain for good measure.

It was much later in the evening, when she'd eaten a sandwich and watched a couple of episodes of *Strictly* that it occurred to her that turning up unannounced, like Aidan, was pretty much what Blair had done. No phone call to sound Georgine out, not even a text to say she was on her way.

Blair had thrown herself on Georgine's mercy and she'd

taken her in. Aidan had tried a similar thing. Did it mean Georgine was easy to manipulate?

Gnawing on this conundrum, she made two mugs of hot chocolate, checked the back door, then carried both mugs upstairs with the intention of talking to Blair. But when she got to the bedroom door she had to pause to balance one cup on the flat cap of the newel post so she could lift her hand to knock, and she clearly heard Blair's voice saying, 'Thanks for taking my shift tonight. My tum's calmed down so shall I work yours tomorrow night in exchange?'

Though conscious of eavesdropping, the moment she heard Blair end the call, she knocked on the door and went in.

Blair glanced up from where she was lying on the bed.

'Sorry to barge in,' Georgine breezed. 'I've brought you hot choccie. Couldn't help overhearing . . . Have you taken an evening job? I thought you'd been out a lot.'

Blair flushed. 'Yes. A few evenings in a bar.'

Georgine perched on one corner of the bed, conscious that her sister living in her house didn't entitle Georgine to intrude on her privacy. 'Can you cope with two jobs? It's no wonder you get tired.'

Blair sipped her chocolate. 'Yes. I'm trying to stand on my own two feet financially. I thought you'd be pleased.' She peeped at Georgine under her lashes.

Slowly, Georgine nodded. 'I suppose I am.' She paused, wanting to say, 'I might be able to help if . . .' But this was the first time Blair had made any attempt to save herself from her overspending. It may have arisen from Georgine being more-than-usually potless, but it was a positive development. So she said, 'What did you think of Joe?' instead.

Blair's eyebrows gave a waggle. 'He's grown up hot, hasn't he? I remember Rich as being a scraggy little thing.' The eyebrows gave another waggle, more suggestive this time. 'More importantly, what do you think of him, taking care of you and suggesting you get new locks? Bit protective, eh? Have you done anything you want to tell me about?'

Georgine flushed but couldn't help the smile that tugged at the corners of her mouth. 'No.'

'But . . .?' Blair grinned, reaching out to dig Georgine in the ribs.

'But nothing.' Georgine moved out of poking range and sipped her hot chocolate so the steam gave her face an excuse to pinken. ''Night.' In her head, a little voice said, *But you never know . . .*

In her own room, throwing herself on her bed, she opened WhatsApp on her phone. She brought up *Grandma Patty* on her contacts and tapped in, *Fancy a chat, Grandma?* Grandma Patty evidently did, as her WhatsApp call came straight in, and Georgine spent a happy half hour chatting about the run-through of the Christmas show, a safe and happy subject and one where she felt in control.

Grandma Patty declared, 'You must send me some of the video. Oh, my, I so love Christmas!'

'Having visited you in Christmases past and witnessed the house positively blazing with decorations, I know that!' Georgine laughed. 'But I love it too.'

Her grandmother giggled. 'I paid a neighbour kid ten dollars to set up my illuminated reindeer and sleigh on the lawn already. I wish you could come and see it, dear.'

'Take a picture and send it over,' Georgine suggested, not wanting to get into the 'Why don't you come for

Christmas?' conversation again. 'Do you have snow? We've had flurries.'

'Wouldn't a white Christmas be lovely?' Grandma Patty breathed. Georgine could picture her clasping her hands beneath her chin as she did when excited.

'Yes – unless it stops people turning up to my show!' Georgine exclaimed in mock horror. 'Good news, by the way – we're being given a load of costumes and stuff. I'm picking it up at the weekend. The wardrobe guy lives not far from Dad so I'll be able to pop in and make him lunch first.'

Grandma Patty sighed. 'I wish my boy would get better, Georgine.'

Georgine agreed, though, personally, she'd settle for him not getting worse. There was no point upsetting her grandmother with the implications of that thought though, so before much longer she wound up the conversation.

But when she did turn out the light she spent a long time staring into the darkness as if her worries had grown wings and were circling overhead.

Aidan's bizarre and embarrassing behaviour.

Blair splitting up with Warren.

Dad needing care.

Money.

Not having begun a single Christmas present yet, or written a card.

She tried to turn her mind to *A Very Kerry Christmas* instead but then found she was thinking about Joe. After an uncertain moment, she let those thoughts continue. Despite his past, he'd matured into a self-confident man and a good human being. And he was definitely pleasant to think on. Eventually, she calmed enough to sleep.

Chapter Nineteen

Saturday was the first day of December and the weather celebrated with an iron frost, coating everything in what looked like fine white fur. Christmas trees had sprouted in many Middledip windows overnight. Joe noticed them from the taxi taking him to pick up his new car from a dealership on the edge of Bettsbrough.

They drove through the nice part of town with its grey-and-brown stone buildings alongside the occasional mock Tudor. It wasn't much like the shabby brick of the Shetland estate of his memories, with its layers of graffiti, where the policy had seemed to be to dump all the problem people in one place. When you were one of those problems, or their powerless offspring, the policy had condemned you to low expectations and provided few positive role models.

When the taxi dropped him at the gleaming Mercedes showroom, he submerged the bad memories in the satisfying formalities of taking possession of a recent-model sporty black Mercedes GLA. Maybe it was because of his mood, but having time to kill before meeting Georgine, he drove to Manor Road where his mother, Debs, lived. He found a parking space at the rear of the fancifully named Whispering Court, which had been converted from two Victorian houses, The Court and Whispering Leaves. The drive and car park were edged with flowerbeds, the first three floors contained four apartments each and the attic floor two. The rear apartments, except for the ground floor, looked out over a park called Providence Fields and Debs and Mari occupied one of those.

Joe played with a few of the buttons on the car's dash before he finally left his new toy. It was a temptation to put it through its paces instead of going through with this visit, but that could wait until he hit the motorway en route for the meeting at Pete's tomorrow. Three and a half weeks he'd been staying in his apartment at Acting Instrumental but he'd yet to tell Debs he was living nearby.

Unfortunately, his conscience knew.

Their relationship would never be warm but he understood now that alcoholism was a disease. Could you blame someone for suffering from a disease? He'd discovered he could at least forgive her . . . now she could no longer hurt him.

He used his key to access the back way in to Whispering Court and took the stairs to the fourth floor, pausing on each landing to look out over Providence Fields. The bandstand's domed lead roof was a paler grey on the shady side, where the frost had yet to melt. Horse chestnut trees stretched their branches as if to shake off the final few brown leaves. Although it was hidden from his view, he knew that the Shetland estate was less than a mile beyond Providence Fields.

He carried on up the stairs. Time enough to face Shitland when he met Georgine there at two.

Soon he reached the apartment where a brass number fourteen shone on the door. He rang the bell, triggering a volley of excited barking from behind the door. As it was Debs and Mari's home, he never let himself in, though he'd retained ownership of the place to prevent it ever being exchanged for a lifetime's supply of lager.

The door opened to reveal Mari's beaming face and silver curls atop her plump body. At her feet, Bernie the black-and-white Jack Russell abandoned his enthusiastic yapping in favour of his friendship dance, pirouetting with excitement, ears back and tail a blur.

'It is you!' exclaimed Mari. 'We were looking out of the window and thought we saw you getting out of a car.' She stepped back to welcome him in, opening her arms.

Joe gave her a hug. 'Hi, good to see you.' Mari had lived in Scotland all through his childhood, her husband's career having taken them there. When the husband moved on in favour of, as Mari put it wrathfully, 'a thinner woman!' she was happy to move to Bettsbrough and be Debs' stabilising influence. She also notified Joe if Debs sparked rows. It had been three years since Debs had been on a bender, but sobriety brought occasional mood swings when encountering certain neighbours or almost any sign of authority – from police officers to doormen.

'How is she?' he murmured, pulling off his coat then giving in to Bernie's desperate pleas for attention and crouching down to pet him.

Mari replied in an under-voice. 'Bit emotional. No lapses, though.'

Joe nodded. 'Lapses' was the term Mari used to indicate Debs drinking alcohol. Mari and Joe did their best to help avoid 'lapses' by controlling Debs' finances and keeping out of her orbit small items of value that might easily be sold for ready cash. Luckily, Debs saw Mari as her dear friend and ally, and far from resenting Mari's company, was happy for them to spend most of their time together. Joe thought Debs would probably be dead by now if not for the benevolent guidance of her cousin.

'Is that you, Johnjoe?' called an uncertain voice from the sitting room.

With a last pat for Bernie, who bounded ahead as if it was his job to announce visitors, Joe made his way down the hall. 'Yes, it's me. How are you doing?'

'All right.' Debs was curled at one end of the sofa. She didn't get up to embrace Joe. If he really scoured his memory he thought she'd probably last cuddled him when he was five. Joe could still hear Garrit snapping, 'Don't coddle the boy, he'll grow up soft.' Joe had grown up hard enough not to stoop down and hug her either.

He sat down on a chair instead, accepting with thanks Mari's offer of a cup of tea, not because he wanted one but because drinking it would give him a reason to stay for a worthwhile period. 'Bernie looks well,' he observed.

Debs brightened. 'He's a lovely little boy. Aren't you, Bern?' Her voice became a coo. 'Who's my ickle boy?'

Bernie jumped up on her lap, waggling his entire rear end in joy at his human's sugary tone. Obviously, Joe thought idly, he should have been born a Jack Russell. Debs fed Bernie twice a day and hardly ever lost her temper with him. Lucky Bernie. 'I suppose walking him gets you out most days?'

Debs' smile broadened. 'Yes, we take him to the park, don't we, Mari? Or we go out in Mari's car and take him with us. We went to Hunstanton in September. He loved the beach.'

Joe accepted a bright blue mug from Mari and took

several sips of tea, the sting of the scalding liquid prefer-
able to voicing his thoughts. If he hadn't known that he
was on the beach when his father drowned, he'd believe
he'd never seen the sea for his first fourteen years.

Deep breath. Quell the bitterness. *She's an alcoholic.
She probably feels safe expressing love for a dog. Dogs
are uncomplicated. They offer unconditional love. You
don't offer her love at all.* 'I'm working up here for a bit,'
he said, and talked about Acting Instrumental and the
Christmas show. Debs didn't express interest in attending
and he didn't invite her.

'What about The Hungry Years?' Her hands moved
constantly, caressing Bernie's silky ears.

'Tricky stuff to sort out there,' he said briefly.

Mari joined in the conversation. 'We've got nice fresh
ham, if you fancy lunch.'

Probably because the band's name made him think of
hunger, and hunger reminded him of how Debs had let
him down, he was a touch too hasty in his refusal. 'Thanks,
but I have plans.' A shadow passed over Debs' face. Her
hands changed their rhythm, stroking Bernie with long
movements from his head to haunches, faster and faster.
Bernie dipped his back as if not certain he liked it.

Joe recognised the signs of agitation but didn't alter his
decision. It wasn't that Debs really wanted Joe to stay for
lunch. Reading a slight into his refusal was a sign that
she was feeling combative. 'Do you hate me because I let
Shaun Blackthorn take you away?' she demanded suddenly.

'No,' he replied frankly. She occasionally confronted
their joint past like this and he'd never skirt the issue,
even if she seemed to be spoiling for an argument. That
would be protecting her from her failures to protect him.
'It was the best thing you could have done for me.'

185

Bernie wriggled out from beneath Debs' stroking hands, jumping to the floor and giving himself a good shake before trotting off to his bed beside the radiator.

Debs regarded Joe fiercely. 'Before I met Garrit I was reduced to living in a car. With you. Life wasn't easy.'

Joe nodded. 'Perhaps you could have told the Blackthorns about me? They might have paid you an allowance to enable you to bring me up.'

'Or they might have taken you away!' Her eyes began to redden.

Joe kept his voice even. 'Which they did in the end, so you could have saved us all a lot of trouble. This isn't a new conversation, Mum.' He watched her pick up a sofa cushion and squeeze it. Maybe Bernie knew what he was doing when he jumped down before she reached the squeezing stage.

'I was too young when I had you. I was scared of the Blackthorns. They didn't like me.'

'I know.' That was the truth. 'It doesn't matter how many times we go over it, we can't change the past, Mum. At least my childhood taught me to be self-sufficient and to appreciate life when it was good. And we're both in a better place now.' He drained his cup and rose, relieved that he'd been there for nearly half an hour and could leave. 'See you in a while. Take care.'

'Bye,' she said, heaving a sigh and tucking the cushion between her cheek and the wing of the sofa.

Mari and Bernie both got up to see Joe to the door, Mari looking uncomfortable. 'In some ways it's easier when she pretends that part of your lives never existed,' she said softly.

'Easier on her state of mind, maybe,' he agreed. After saying he'd be at the end of a phone if Mari needed him, he ran lightly down the four flights to ground level and into the car park. He jumped into the car and pressed the button that made the engine burst into life, then he bowled out of the car park. Perhaps it made him a horrible person but he felt relieved his duty was done.

The clock on the dash said it was nearly one, which left an hour before he was to meet Georgine. He drove to a new retail park he'd noticed near the town football ground. There he had a choice of a pub, McDonald's and Pizza Hut. He chose the pub because, it being Saturday, the other two would be overrun with kids getting over-excited at the Christmas decorations festooning every shop and shouting optimistic Christmas lists to each other.

In the pub he took a small table in the restaurant and ordered the Christmas panini, which proved to be chopped turkey and sausage with stuffing, and fries. It wasn't the healthiest option on the menu but, hey. Christmas spirit. He even drank cranberry juice.

While he ate, he read *Kerrang!*'s website on his phone, checking out who was headlining at Reading and Leeds next year. The Hungry Years had headlined at Leeds last year as Fall Out Boy and Panic! at the Disco were this year—

His mind jumped tracks. Shit. The Hungry Years would know those triumphs again, but would he be part of the line-up?

He examined his feelings. For a moment there he'd almost known his mind, known he wanted to sort things out with Billy, Nathan, Raf and Liam, even with Pete the Beat. Then he thought of tomorrow's meeting leading to him leaving Acting Instrumental, not seeing *A Very Kerry Christmas* through to opening night.

Not seeing Georgine . . .

Georgine! He looked at his watch, waved at the waitress to show he was leaving twenty pounds on the table for his meal, acknowledging her delighted smile at his over-paying by more than eight pounds. An early Christmas tip.

He was soon on his way to the Shetland estate and even the sight of two familiar water tanks on familiar blocks of flats didn't blacken his mood.

Here it was, he thought as he pulled into a car park and switched off his engine. Shitland. He got out and locked his car, looking around. Everything looked better than he remembered. There was hardly any graffiti deco-rating the walls and he couldn't see a single burned-out car. Several of the old blocks of flats had been replaced with long rows of terraces or maisonettes with their own garages underneath.

A hundred yards away he could see a children's play-ground and a grassy area currently home to a noisy bat-and-ball game. He didn't realise Georgine had arrived until she spoke from behind him. 'Nostalgic?'

He spun around. She wore a green knitted hat and it brought out the colour of her eyes. 'No!' he said. 'But the estate looks a lot better these days. I didn't hear your car.'

She pushed her hands up the sleeves of her coat, a sort of bronzy, puffy thing with fur around the hood. Her hair blazed in the winter sun. 'I've just cooked Dad lunch. He lives in one of the blocks of flats for over sixties. They're on the edge of the estate, but not far enough away to make it worth moving my car yet.'

His eyes followed her pointing finger. At the top of a flight of concrete steps stood some newer blocks with their own parking area, heavily decorated with disabled notices. It looked pretty OK, but he still had trouble imagining the Randall France he remembered living on the Shetland estate.

'Nobody would have guessed how things would end up,' Georgine said, as if reading his mind. 'After several strokes, he has a crooked arm, a crooked smile, but a battling heart. His flat has a pull-cord if he needs assistance and he has a cleaner and other help.'

He nodded, almost embarrassed to realise he was glad his mum didn't still live here, feeling a curious mixture of relief for his parent and pity for Georgine's. Was that the way she'd felt all those years ago? Sort of self-conscious at having so much when some people had so little?

Maybe he'd become too pleased with himself over his bit of philanthropy in shoring up funding at Acting Instrumental. He'd made sure there was a sturdy community programme for weekends and holidays with big discounts for kids from poorer backgrounds, but Middledip was four or five miles away from the Shetland estate. He should have provided transport. He'd talk to Oggie about it.

'What?' Georgine said, interrupting his uncomfortable thoughts. 'You look like you've just eaten a pin.'

He shivered in the wind. 'Just thinking.'

'Not particularly pleasant thoughts, judging by your expression.' She nodded in the direction of a yellow-brick building. 'Ralph's place is in Swallow House over there. I'm hoping he'll know how we can get a vehicle closer. It's not clear on Google Earth.'

He fell into step as she set off down a concrete path cast in a brick-like pattern. 'I don't remember a Swallow House.'

'It's new. Much lower rise than what it replaced.' She glanced his way. 'Has your old home survived?'

He'd wondered the same. 'Can't see from here. It's no loss, if not. It was the scruffiest place on a scruffy estate.'

They passed the grassy area, where children still shrieked over their game. In Joe's day – or Rich Garrit's day – the only greenery had grown through the cracks in the concrete area designed for washing lines and dustbins, but also used as a hang out.

Swallow House was the other side of the green. Ralph's flat was on the first floor but there was a lift. 'Good news,' Georgine observed, when she'd pressed the button and the lift arrived.

Ralph, who looked to be in his late sixties, opened his door with a smile on his seamed face. He sported two cardigans, one over the other. 'Come in, come in! If you can,' he added, grinning at a mountain of cardboard boxes and black bin bags. 'I'll be glad to get this lot out of my little flat. I've tried to put all the Christmas stuff together.'

'Thanks,' Georgine said, surveying the pile with wide eyes.

Ralph told them to bring their cars up on the grass outside. 'Everybody does. How would we pack our cars up for holidays, otherwise?' There followed a couple of hours of strenuous work as they filled first Georgine's Fiesta and then Joe's GLA to bursting.

Even with both sets of rear seats folded down Joe wasn't convinced they were going to get everything in, especially with Ralph puffing instructions such as, 'Don't squash that! It's a big bleedin' bauble and you'll dent it.'

Several passers-by spoke to Ralph as they worked. Joe was uneasy, half-expecting to know one of them. Ralph was old enough to have known Garrit. Might know him yet. He didn't tell Ralph he'd used to live on the Shetland estate, though he took a quiet satisfaction in seeing from the windows of the flat that the row of pale brick, flat-roofed houses he'd lived in had been replaced by maisonettes.

As the short winter day began to wane, lights came on over the walkways. It reminded Joe of when hardly a lamp had been left whole and mothers kept their kids indoors as the local miscreants slunk out of the shadows. He stepped up his pace, keen to load up and get the hell out.

'You're very quiet. Are you OK?' Georgine whispered to him as they squashed sacks of costumes into the front passenger seat of his car, now beginning to bear a resemblance to the vehicles the band had half lived in before they began to make money.

'Sure,' he answered briefly.

When every sack and box was crammed in somewhere, they took their leave of Ralph then clattered downstairs, feeling no need to take the lift without a burden to transport.

Georgine fished out her car keys. 'I'll meet you back at Acting Instrumental.'

'Yep.' He placed his hand onto his door handle.

She hovered closer. 'Have you been battling ghosts all afternoon?'

He managed a smile at her perceptiveness. 'I'm a big boy now but it's uncomfortable to remember the old gang. The fights.' The thumps from Garrit.

Compassion shone from her eyes. 'I suppose I didn't see much of that side of you.'

'Good. I didn't want you to.' Just as he didn't want her to know about him landing one on Billy. 'I'm glad there's an improvement to the standard of living for the kids now. I'd forgotten how hopeless I felt here, seeing no way out.'

'Thank you for facing your ghosts so you could help

me this afternoon.' Georgine gave him a quick hug, then broke away, flushing as if embarrassed at her impulsiveness. Or as if she too had felt the heat that had flashed between them.

Joe couldn't speak.

As JJ Blacker he was used to being on view on stage, in the music press, even on TV.

What he wasn't used to was the sensation of someone really seeing him, clear through to his heart and soul.

Someone who knew the worst of him and didn't mind.

Chapter Twenty

On Sunday morning, Joe jumped awake as if anxiety had bounced on the end of his bed.

He forced his eyes to remain closed, trying to kid himself that he didn't feel twitchy about meeting the band at Pete's today. He'd see Billy for the first time since his explosion of temper. Shame was like a slimy area in his heart. Whatever the meeting brought, however tense it got, even if everyone aligned themselves with Billy to oust Joe from The Hungry Years, he would not stoop to violence again. It was never the solution.

Sleep having deserted him, he got up and dressed in his tattiest jeans and a sleeveless T-shirt with a thick sweatshirt on top. Then he left the apartment, jogging through the thin winter air down the steps and around to the main entrance to the new building where he knew he could switch off the alarm. Then he found the nearest rehearsal room with a drum kit, threw off the practice pads, grabbed the heaviest drumsticks from a nearby box and on seeing the sound system had airplay, paired it with his phone. Seating himself on the stool, he pulled the snare drum a smidgen closer, then located his favourite playlist on his phone.

One spin of his sticks as the first track hit the air, Green Day's '16', and he hit the skins, throwing himself into the boom-catta-cha-cha rhythm. The track ended and he threw off his sweatshirt, warmed by the physical effort of beating the drums and cymbals, calming a bit for the quieter passages of 'Nicotine' by Panic! at the Disco then getting completely taken over by the manic, train-like rhythm of My Chemical Romance's 'I'm Not OK (I Promise)'.

By the time it had finished, he was beginning to relax. He switched off the sound system and dropped the sticks back in the box, restoring the practice pads to the snare and toms.

Then he moved on to the piano and idled away half an hour on the strict tempo exercises Shaun used to give him – legato quavers in the left hand and staccato crotchets in the right, not that hard for someone who knew the limb independence of a drummer. He stopped, absently using the hem of his T-shirt to wipe fingerprints from the black keys.

A slow, deep breath, then he returned his fingers to the keys and began the introduction to – his version of – 'Running on Empty'.

> *Inside I'm pinched*
> *My skin is chill*
> *I don't need the nurse*
> *I'm not ill*
> *Dizzy and stupid*
> *But not thick*
> *I don't need the nurse*
> *I'm not sick*

He moved into the chorus.

> *I'm sorry, lady*
> *I'm sorry I stole*
> *Have you ever been hungry?*
> *Ashamed?*
> *Alone?*

He stopped. Closed his eyes, remembering that day in Tesco. He'd been eleven. Someone in the gang said it was time he 'showed he wouldn't put up with starving' and stood outside while Joe went in with his heart banging around in his chest. A woman caught him sliding a pork pie into his pocket and set up a fuss. His voice had squeaked out. 'I'm sorry, lady, but I'm ever so hungry.' Suspicion and pity had warred in her eyes until he couldn't stand it.

Then it had been too late to take advantage of her moment of indecision because the sweaty security man in a blue shirt and a peaked cap had hauled him into the manager's room. They'd rung the police. He'd sat frozen on an orange plastic chair, dizzy and scarcely breathing, like a bird caught in a snare.

All he knew about the police had been learned from his fellow gang members. The police locked you up, treated you with contempt. The instant the office door had opened to let the two police officers in he'd thrown himself at the gap between their legs and the door, hardly feeling the bumps and scratches as they tried to stop him.

His shirt tore and he was free. He'd raced through the store, dodging another security guy at the big glass doors, then across the car park – from where the older gang member was now conspicuously absent – and flown through the streets until he came to a grassy patch where two roads met. There, he'd dropped to the ground, his legs giving out from lack of food. Or from shame.

Shame that had never left him.

Luckily, there had been food at home that night and he'd eaten as much as he could fit in without feeling the back of Garrit's hand or depriving Chrissy.

The next time his mother's chaos or Garrit's bullying caused food to be withdrawn, he'd returned to Tesco in a jacket with pockets big enough to supply him and Chrissy. But he'd made sure nobody caught him. Humiliated he might be, but at least now he had a full stomach.

His fingers moved over the keys again, taking comfort from the easy, well-known tunes that Shaun used to teach him: 'Für Elise' and 'Hallelujah!'. Finally, calmer, he pulled his sweatshirt back on, made sure everything was as he'd found it, set the alarm and left.

Back in his apartment he showered and dressed in black jeans and a favourite shirt. Then he did what he probably should have done more often. He rang Shaun, connecting his ear buds so he could drop the phone in a pocket and make himself toast while they talked.

'Hey, kid.' Shaun sounded pleased to hear from him. It was evening in Sydney and he and Louise were chilling after dinner.

His uncle was one of the most unflappable people Joe knew though, so now he'd decided to make contact, he didn't hold back. 'Can I run something by you? I'm at a bit of a crossroads with the band.'

'Go for it,' Shaun said easily.

So Joe, between mouthfuls of hot buttered toast,

recounted the whole story, not glossing over the moment he'd lost control of his fists. What Jerome had said, and Nathan, Raf and Liam. How he'd enjoyed stepping away from the madness and losing himself at Acting Instrumental. What he did there.

Shaun listened. Asked questions like, 'What do you want most?'

'If I knew that . . .' Joe laughed. 'All I've decided at the moment is not to decide.'

'Good decision.' Shaun's voice was soothing. 'Don't rush into anything, Joe. The rest of the guys will have their agendas, but keep your eye on your own. If you need more time, say so.' He paused. 'Maybe you could go into the meeting with a game plan. Some compromise you could offer to move things in the direction you'd like.'

Struck by this good sense, Joe poured himself coffee. 'Thanks. Great thought.'

'Hang on.' Shaun's end of the conversation became muffled, then he came back on. 'Louise says come and spend Christmas in Oz with us.'

A warm feeling settled in Joe's chest and he found himself smiling. 'I'd love it, but I need to be here for the show. I'm to go through a ton of old costumes and props tomorrow to inventory anything to do with Christmas or gangsters.'

Shaun grunted a laugh. 'I hope the kids and the staff know what they're getting in you.'

'They don't. That's the pleasure of it. I'm Joe Blackthorn, I can set up lights and sound. I'm assistant to the events director.' Never dissembling when it came to Shaun, he added, 'The events director is someone I used to know at school. The posh kid who was my friend.'

'I remember you telling me about her.' Shaun sounded interested. 'Has she grown up into a posh woman?'

'She's grown up differently than I'd have expected,' Joe admitted. 'Her dad lost all his money so she's had to make her own way. It hasn't stopped her being a good person though.' They chatted for a few moments more about Joe's role at Acting Instrumental, and when the call ended Joe felt grounded by his uncle's quiet good sense and more prepared to face whatever the day brought.

It wasn't until he was driving down the M11 and mulling over Shaun's words about having a game plan that he realised he'd committed, at least mentally, to being around for *A Very Kerry Christmas* in show week.

A couple of hours later, having enjoyed putting his car and its sat nav through their paces on the journey to Blackheath, he turned onto the drive of Pete's big, ivory-coloured Georgian detached house on the gated Cator estate, with its fascinating mix of traditional houses and grand designs. Pete had moved his wife, Luanne, and their two boys there from a smaller place in Putney and brought his office under the same roof from Hammersmith. Blackheath was a gorgeous place to live, he could get from the station to London Bridge in half an hour and it was a cinch to get his acts into the On Blackheath festival. The house had come with the kind of price tag it could be hard to distinguish from the estate agent's phone number.

Joe had barely locked the car when the glossy red front door opened and Pete emerged, closing the door behind him before strolling down the steps. 'Joe. Great to see you.'

'How are you?' Joe replied, not quite able to pretend it was great to see Pete. In fact, the chilly climate affecting him had more to do with Pete than the winter.

Pete scratched where his steel-grey quiff dangled over his forehead. 'I'll be better when we've got this situation sorted. Anything you want to ask me before we go in? Or say?'

Joe shook his head and Pete ushered him up the steps, taking his coat, complimenting his new car and being affable as he ushered him along the hall and beneath the staircase, then through a door to what had once been a coach house but was now Pete's workspace. A door in the far corner led to a smaller office with a couple of desks, but the main office reminded Joe of a lounge-diner, boasting sofas and armchairs around a coffee table in one half and a rectangular meeting table with eight chairs around it in the other.

Currently decorating one sofa were Liam and Raf; Nathan and Billy had taken the other. Joe paused just inside the door.

For a frozen moment it seemed as if everybody was waiting for a lead. Then all four band members jumped up; Liam, Raf and Nathan tripping over each other as they hugged Joe or shook his hand and slapped his shoulder.

Last came Billy. His platinum-blond dead-straight hair fell into his eyes and his skinny jeans made his legs look like liquorice sticks, shiny and thin. He halted in front of Joe and they eyed one another. Then Billy offered his hand. 'Friends, man? Didn't mean to piss you off.' A ghost of a smile crossed his face. 'Had a few problems to take care of and I got unreasonable.'

Whatever was to happen from here on, Joe knew acting on the olive branch was key. He took Billy's hand and let himself be pulled into a man-hug. 'Sorry I hit you. The red mist descended.'

Billy rolled his eyes. 'Luckily, there was no lasting damage to my amazing good looks.'

Everyone laughed and the atmosphere warmed a degree or two. Joe took an armchair. Pete's assistant, Marek, a squat man with a jutting beard, got everybody coffee, placing a plate of biscuits on the coffee table before vanishing into the other office and closing the door.

'OK,' Pete began. He whooshed out a breath as if he were a weightlifter preparing to lift. 'In a nutshell . . .' Then he proceeded to set out the areas of acrimony, taking a good fifteen minutes longer than needed, which would have made even a coconut shell burst at the seams.

Joe listened, nodding occasionally.

'I think everyone with an apology to make has made it,' Pete concluded, not looking at either Joe or Billy. 'So let's take things forward. My first concern is that we stick to the March launch date for the album, to support the tour. The label wants to get into production, obviously.'

'That's my first concern, too,' Billy put in, leaning forward as if he wanted to rush off and launch the album with his bare hands.

'My first concern is the content of the album,' Joe said quietly.

Nathan played with a button on his shirt. 'I want it settled whether Joe's still with us. It affects the tour, the promo, everything.'

'Me, too,' chorused Liam and Raf.

Joe nodded in acknowledgement, though as he didn't know what he wanted, resolving that particular concern might be tricky.

'OK, good.' Pete wrote several notes on a pad balanced

on his knee. 'So would it be fair to say that if we can sort out Joe's concern, the content of the album, the other two items would fall into place?'

'Yeah,' agreed Billy, Nathan, Liam and Raf.

'Not necessarily,' said Joe.

Five pairs of eyes swivelled in his direction.

'But it's a good starting point,' he added.

Pete tapped his pen, regarding Joe with a frown. 'Then maybe you'd like to say what would need to happen for you to be in accord with the rest of the band?'

'I don't have a ready answer.' Joe looked around at the faces he knew almost as well as his own. 'Sorry. I've given it loads of thought but I can't say, "If you want me in the band, I'll stay". Album content was only part of what led up to the argument, and it's bothering me.'

One by one, gazes were lowered, until there was only Pete who could meet Joe's eyes. 'Can you explain your view of the circumstances?'.

Just thinking about it made a chill slither unpleasantly down Joe's spine. 'It's not being outvoted,' he said, carefully. 'That happens. It was the *way* it happened.

'We'd agreed on my version of "Running on Empty",' he went on, 'and then suddenly Billy was going around the band lobbying to change to his version. OK, it's not much fun to be on the wrong end of it, but that can happen too. But that song was important to me, and Billy's version ridiculed what I'd been trying to recognise. I couldn't believe you were all willing to put out a song laughing at hunger. The kids – our target market! – call us "The Hungries". Giving them the message that hunger's a joke would just be *wrong*. Not to mention the way my feelings were shat upon – by you all,' he added, for the avoidance of doubt. 'Which is why

201

when Billy said one of us had to leave the band, I volunteered.'

Billy shot in: 'I completely take that back. I was out of order.'

The others shifted on their sofas and murmured uncomfortably about insensitivity and hasty reactions.

Joe studied the way Billy, literally on the edge of his seat, had clasped his hands, thumbs beating time against one another. Billy was where the key to everything lay, Joe decided. Now was the time to follow the game plan he'd devised on the drive down. 'How about you and me chat one on one, Billy?'

Everyone switched their gazes to Billy, whose twitching thumbs paused. 'OK by me,' he declared, though his Adam's apple jumped noticeably.

'Let's find you a quiet corner.' Pete jumped up to lead Joe and Billy back through the house, leaving Nathan, Raf and Liam behind. The voice of Pete's American wife, Luanne, drifted from upstairs, bubbling over with enthusiasm for something. Pete showed the way to a sunny sitting room with an encouraging, 'Take your time, guys,' and shut them in.

Joe glanced at the door and wondered whether Pete was listening behind it. They moved right up the other end of the room to where they could look through a window at a long lawn, autumn's leaves dancing on winter's wind.

Joe wasted no time. 'From what you said on the phone last week, wanting to go with your lyrics instead of mine was motivated by a need for money.'

Billy flicked his hair back. 'You could look at it like that.'

Heart sinking and irritation rising, Joe frowned. 'What

does that mean? The only way to sort things out is by being straight with one another.'

Billy grinned wryly. 'Have to point out that you generally keep your cards close to your chest, JJ.'

'OK,' Joe agreed, because the truth was hard to argue with. 'I promise to be transparent. Go.'

Billy's shoulders dropped. He stared glumly outside at the bare trees shaking twiggy fingers at the sky. 'Yeah, I need the money. Like, now.'

Joe picked his words. 'It's bad manners to delve into other people's money matters, but I'm going to say something. The Hungry Years isn't stratospheric, though we're getting there. None of the rest of us lives in such a huge gaff in Primrose Hill or buys new prestige cars every year. And that's without funding any habits you might have – you party friggin' hard, Billy.'

Billy hunched a defensive shoulder. 'I like a certain lifestyle, yeah.'

'Sorry to be blunt,' said Joe, without being sorry at all. 'But if you need money so much that you're prepared to stamp on me, or any of the boys, to get it, it's an issue. You and me, we out-earn the others because we write the songs, but I'd rather go solo or find a new band than accept you finding underhand ways to get a still more favourable split.'

A sudden gust outside hurled something at the window. Joe stared at Billy and Billy gazed out at the garden. Finally, he shrugged. 'OK, I'll abide by that.'

Joe's heart lifted at this glimmer of light at the end of the tunnel. 'I have a suggestion, but it has to be made in front of the others.'

They trailed back to Pete's office like kids let out after detention. The others fell silent as they arrived, apart from Raf munching noisily on a biscuit.

As Joe resumed his seat he took the lead before Pete or Billy could. 'I have a suggestion.' All eyes swivelled to him and he took silence as a signal to carry on. 'I want to keep my version of "Running on Empty" for myself. I might put it out solo at some time and I don't want the band to use it. Neither do I want Billy's version to be released by The Hungry Years, because it pokes fun at hunger.'

'For fuck's sake!' Billy broke in angrily.

Raf raised a peremptory hand. 'Hear him out.'

'In return,' Joe continued, 'I'll sign over to Billy all rights to another song that we wrote together to recompense him financially. I think the record company's amenable to "Worthy" making the album, aren't they? So instead of us jointly owning writing royalties for two songs, we'd entirely own one song each. Billy doesn't lose and I get what I want. On that basis, I'd be happy for the album to go out in March as planned.'

Slowly, Billy sat back, anger replaced by an almost comical expression of relief and disbelief. 'I'd be up for that.'

'I imagine you would,' Raf said, sending Billy a hard look. 'A lot of people would expect you to have been the one to make concessions here, Billy. Like let him keep his version of "Running on Empty" as it means so much to him and you acted like a prick over it, and just substitute "Worthy" with the usual split.'

The relief faded from Billy's face. 'But he offered—'

'You're being distracted by numbers,' Liam broke in impatiently. 'The most important question remains to be answered. Are you staying with the band, JJ?'

Once again, it was all eyes on Joe. And whether he stayed was the vital detail he'd omitted from his game plan. His heart felt as if it were galloping around inside his chest as the silence stretched.

'Let's stick to talking after Christmas,' he said in the end, because *still* the only thing he could decide was not to decide.

Chapter Twenty-One

On Tuesday, to avoid being interrupted in the delicate task of creating the programme to be sold at each *A Very Kerry Christmas* performance, Georgine had gained permission from Oggie to work at home until lunchtime.

Handily, this allowed her to wait in for the locksmith to change her front and back door locks, just in case Aidan turned up again. She couldn't completely put it past him to stew until he'd convinced himself he needn't be put off by Blair's presence because he could just take up his old place in Georgine's room.

The locksmith was ready to go by ten, leaving her a collection of shiny new keys. 'Let me show you,' he said, one of the keys in his hand. 'You need a key to open it from the outside whether the deadlock's on or not, but not to open it from the inside if the deadlock's not on.'

She thanked him and paid the bill with her credit card, mentally squeezing Christmas shopping into an even smaller financial package than already planned. The rest of the morning she spent hunched over her laptop, creating programme covers and six pages. She'd sold advertising to local dancewear outfitters and a music shop, and they'd sent over text, photos and a logo, and left her to display it. It seemed a task fraught with opportunities to make mistakes.

Once happy, she began on the laborious task of cast listing. Major roles, minor roles, members of Band One, Band Two, Troupe One and Troupe Two. She moved on to the tech crew.

Another couple of hours and she was on the brink of converting her document into a pdf and circulating it amongst tutors/directors, Joe and Oggie for feedback and proofing when her doorbell rang.

When she reached the hallway, she stopped dead.

Two familiar-looking dark silhouettes showed at the glass in the door.

Her heart began to thump, her palms to sweat. More debt collectors? Well, if it was, she'd dealt with them once and she'd deal with them again. Squaring her shoulders she took up one of the shiny new keys, marched to the door, unlocked it and wrenched it open.

Sure enough, on the front path stood two men in black trousers and stab jackets. Two different men, one with a goatee and the other with glasses. 'Aidan Rustington has not lived here for months,' she began stiffly.

'Blair France?' asked the one with a goatee.

Blair? All at once a lot less sure of her ground, Georgine gripped the doorframe. 'No. I'm her sister.'

'But she does live here, yes?' asked the man with glasses.

Both the men wore body cameras, Georgine realised belatedly. One was clutching a thin sheaf of papers.

She licked her lips. 'What do you want?'

Goatee man spoke again. 'We're high court enforcement agents. Do you have ID, madam? It would help us considerably to be able to confirm your identity.'

Her thoughts whirled but she could see no option but to do as asked. 'All right.' Slowly, heart racing so hard she felt giddy, Georgine closed the door and crept on rubbery legs to where her bag rested on a chair. When she returned to the front door with her driving licence, neither man appeared to have moved.

The man with glasses took the licence, photographed it with his phone, noted something on his clipboard and gave it back with a word of thanks. 'Are you able to contact your sister? We need to talk to her. We have a high court writ here.'

Georgine began to shake. The man's voice seemed to come from very far away as he repeated his request for her to contact Blair.

Fifteen years ago men like these had turned up at The Gatehouse and taken away the family's cars, which, it turned out, had all belonged to Randall France Construction. At nearly twenty she'd been an adult in their eyes, although a particularly easy one to ride rough-shod over. She could still remember the congratulatory looks they'd exchanged as she'd fallen back and they'd walked into the house to gather up keys and documents. The process had changed a bit, and the script, but the bailiffs on her doorstep still had the power to terrify her.

'This is my house,' she whispered as she fumbled her phone out of her pocket and dropped it.

Glasses man picked the phone up and handed it back. Impassive. Just doing his job.

Blair answered on the second ring. 'I'm at work,' she murmured. She wasn't supposed to take calls during office hours.

Georgine had to swallow before she spoke. 'Blair, there

are high court enforcement agents at the door. They're looking for you. They have a writ.'

Silence. Then Blair hissed, 'Shit.'

The man with the goatee held out his hand. 'Mind if I talk to her?'

Blindly, Georgine let him take the phone, shaking so much she almost dropped it again. 'Miss Blair France?' he said into the phone. 'I'm at your address and I have a high court writ in the sum of £4,741.55. I and my colleague are here to collect payment today.'

Whatever Blair might have answered, the man repeated the same information implacably, adding that if they couldn't secure payment they'd look to remove assets to settle the debt.

Georgine whispered to the other man, 'But this is my house.'

In an even voice he returned, 'But she lives here.'

Almost before she knew it her phone was placed back in her sweating hand with Blair alternately apologising and pleading, 'Don't let them take any of my stuff. Give me a chance to sort this out. I think I can get the money. Hang on, Georgine. I'm on my way.'

At the same time the men informed her of their right to enter the house and begin to assess assets. Then they politely but firmly moved past her and she once again fell back to let them, unable to summon enough breath even to burst into tears.

'We'd rather get paid and leave,' the one with glasses told her smoothly. 'But I'm not sure that that's what's going to happen here today.'

'Most of the stuff's mine,' Georgine protested shakily, following the men into the lounge diner.

'Yours? OK, that's fine. Anything that does not belong

to Blair France will be left alone,' Mr Goatee said in the same polite but inexorable tone.

The bailiffs moved further into the house, not unkind, but unstoppable. 'Does anything in this room belong to Blair France? How about this one? Which is her bedroom?' one asked while, in counterpoint, the other droned, 'This is going to happen. I know it's not pleasant but we're here to secure payment of a debt or seize property to satisfy that debt.'

Georgine could no more imagine them backing down than putting on pink tutus and doing ballet.

As if in a dream, she led the way up to her sister's bedroom, forcing words past numb lips. 'The furniture's mine – bed, dressing table and wardrobe. All the moveable stuff's Blair's.'

Both men hesitated in the doorway as if the mountain of bags and boxes was the first thing they'd seen to daunt them. Then, 'Thank you, madam.' They waded in and cast around for a place to start. The TV set Blair had managed to perch on the dressing table attracted their attention and they began making notes and photographing it.

Georgine felt like Judas as she stood by while bailiffs crawled over Blair's possessions like termites, discovering a white wooden box of jewellery and checking for hall-marks before taking photos. At the same time, she was filled with black rage with Blair for, like Aidan, leaving Georgine to cope with the consequences of her financial disaster. Heart racing, fingers tingling, skin prickling, she wasn't sure whether it was sweat or tears trickling down her cheeks.

'I know it's stressful,' said the man with the goatee. 'You're doing the right thing by keeping calm.'

Georgine gazed at him. Calm? Her ears were buzzing. Her lungs had seized. Definitely not calm.

Then her phone rang in her hand. *Joe Blackthorn* blinked on the screen. Trembling, she accepted the call.

'Hi, Georgine,' Joe's voice said. 'Just wanted you to know that the resident tech at the Raised Curtain has invited me to go through the equipment in the box this afternoon.' He paused. 'OK?'

Georgine opened her mouth to answer but it was a harsh, wrenching sob that emerged. Shocked, she slapped her hand over her mouth. Even the steely bailiffs turned to look at her.

'Georgine? Georgine!' Joe's voice echoed in her ear as the sobs refused to be corralled by her hand and burst out, punctuated by throat-scouring gasps. 'HAH! *Urrrrrurgh.*' Her vision narrowed. She tottered until her back encountered wall, and she slid down to sag against the skirting board as if hurled there by a giant hand.

Joe was shouting in her ear. 'Where are you?' Then the bailiff with glasses was beside her, taking the phone from her unresisting hand and speaking to Joe, giving an explanation Georgine didn't take in.

Then he slid the phone back into her hand. 'Your friend's coming to be with you, madam, OK? He'll be a few minutes. I'm going to get you a glass of water. Would you be better downstairs?'

Georgine shook her head wildly, suddenly rediscovering her ability to make words when she saw his carefully neutral expression, as if this was all *so* much in a day's work for him. 'Just fuck off!' she shrieked up at him. 'Get out of my house!'

He ignored the abuse with aplomb. 'As soon as we can, madam, we will.'

While his colleague with the goatee went methodically through Blair's jewellery, he trod downstairs, reappearing with a glass of water. Georgine wanted nothing more than to fling it in his face, but she forced herself to take it, though she was shaking so violently that the glass chattered against her teeth.

When the doorbell shrilled again she almost blacked out in panic, but one of the bailiffs went down to open the door and then Joe came pounding upstairs, falling to his knees beside her and pulling her into his arms.

'It's OK, it's OK,' he murmured against her hair. 'You're going to be OK, Georgine.'

Georgine laid her face against the heat of his neck and cried big shocked sobs until she heard the front door open and close and Blair's voice, hostile but composed. '*Really*? You couldn't wait *half an hour* for me, you had to start this distressing process? Oh, shut up with your sanctimonious bullshit. Yes, I can pay it. Yes, right now. The money's in my current account and I can transfer it by Internet banking. There was no need to cause my sister anxiety. I told you I'd get the money and I have. Give me the numbers I need.'

The bailiffs didn't react any differently to Blair's scolding than they had to Georgine's panic. They continued in smooth, controlled voices, polite but implacable to the last.

'Here's your receipt, Miss France. Thank you. We'll leave now. We appreciate your co-operation.'

Their feet clumped on the carpeted stairs, the front door opened and shut. And then there was silence.

'Look at the state of my room,' Blair grumbled, although with a distinct air of bravado, as if aware she didn't exactly hold the moral high ground. When met with only silence, she eased herself down onto the floor and stroked Georgine's hair. 'I'm so sorry. Those morons!'

Georgine had somehow found herself on Joe's lap on the floor, curled up like a frightened mouse. 'How did they get this address?' Her voice seemed to scratch her throat.

Blair gave a bitter laugh. 'I was trying to do the right thing, believe it or not. There was this county court judgement against me and I was making payments so I thought if I just moved address without telling the court, I might be in trouble. So I gave them my new address.'

'Why did they come if you were making payments?' Georgine kept her eyes closed, her cheek against Joe's coat. He must be boiling, she thought distantly, scrunched uncomfortably on the floor in his outdoor things with a soggy woman on top of him.

Blair hesitated. 'I had to pay you rent. Not that I'm saying it's your fault,' she tacked on hastily.

Georgine recoiled, despite Blair's denial of blame. 'But you owed over four thousand pounds. You gave me £250.' When Blair didn't seem to have an immediate reply, she pressed on. 'You must have missed a deadline.'

Blair sniffed. 'Not exactly sure.' Then, reluctantly, 'I suppose so. I didn't realise they'd be so quick off the mark—'

Georgine's breathing had calmed. It wasn't hurting her chest now. 'How could you put us through this again?' she whispered.

Blair's voice shrank to a squeak. 'I didn't mean to.'

Joe's warmth still surrounded Georgine. He didn't join the conversation but his embrace said *You're not on your own*. For the first time in what seemed like forever, someone was letting her use them as a shield, instead of the other way around. She couldn't open her eyes and

213

look at Blair. 'Is this the debt that came between you and Warren?'

'Yes,' Blair admitted, still in a tiny voice. 'He said he was sick of it.'

'So am I,' Georgine rejoined. 'Go back to work.'

'I told them I felt ill.' Blair sniffled – softly, not with huge snotty sobs as Georgine had.

Slowly, Georgine uncurled, sliding inelegantly off Joe's lap. 'Let's go to Acting Instrumental,' she said to him.

Joe uncoiled from his cramped position. 'Sure? Then I'll drive you.' It was the first sound he'd uttered since Blair catapulted onto the scene.

'Yes, please.' On shivering limbs, Georgine eased to her knees and let Joe help her to her feet. At the foot of the stairs they collected her coat and he left her sitting on the bottom step while he gathered her laptop and everything she wanted to take to work. Then he helped her up as if she was really ill, slipped his arm around her once more and opened the front door.

'Georgine?' Blair quavered from the top of the stairs.

Georgine didn't pause. She stepped out, then reached back to shut the front door. She didn't bother deadlocking it with Blair inside. At that moment she didn't much care if someone got in.

'We don't have to go to work,' he murmured, opening the passenger door of his car for her.

'I want to feel normal.' She let her head fall back against the headrest and sat, eyes closed, as Joe drove. Despite it being her choice to go to work, she fantasised for a few minutes that he was driving her somewhere wonderful. A luxurious spa hotel on a clifftop, perhaps, where she could loll about an overheated pool in a fluffy robe and the wintry weather, like the harsh realities of life, couldn't get at her.

214

When, after a few minutes, the car stopped and the engine died, she opened her eyelids, feeling as if her eyeballs had been rolled in desiccated coconut like truffles, to find Joe's car not at a clifftop hotel – she hadn't really held out much hope of that – but at the foot of the stairs to his apartment, shielded from the view of the rest of the property by the jut of the big rehearsal room. 'You've parked on the grass,' she said stupidly.

'My grass.' He hopped out and came round to open her door. 'I think maybe you'll want to clean up before going in.'

She felt as she had the only time she'd had flu, almost too weak to climb to her feet. 'Right. Thanks.' She toiled up the steps as if climbing Everest and entered his apartment, following his example when he kicked off his shoes inside the door. He pointed out the bathroom and she trailed into what proved to be a luxuriously appointed room. There, she caught sight of herself in the mirror and gave a little shriek of horror.

Mascara rivers had solidified on her cheeks like lava flow. Her face was covered in red blotches. 'I'm hideous,' she groaned.

Joe, diplomatically, didn't confirm or deny it, just produced a clean flannel and a wrapped bar of soap. 'The soap's not a girly scent, I'm afraid.'

The picture on the packet was of a pair of male hands and crystal clear water. 'It's OK. I don't look feminine.' She ran water in the hand basin and began, gingerly, to wash. Her skin felt too sensitive to rub, so she sat on the loo lid pressing a soapy flannel on her face until her misplaced make-up softened and disappeared. She repeated the exercise with clear cold water and the reddest of the blotches had calmed when she left the bathroom.

'I'm afraid the flannel will never be the same,' she confessed when she found him on a tan sofa in what was obviously his main living area. Two steaming mugs stood on the table. 'Is one of those hot chocolates for me? Thank you.' She dropped down beside him, inhaling the smell appreciatively, realising there was nothing she wanted more in the aftermath of the emotional storm.

Joe watched as she sipped. He'd discarded his glasses and his eyes looked brighter, more intense. 'The flannel's no loss. It came as some kind of free gift.'

She blew across the surface of her drink before taking a gulp, appreciating the immediate sugar hit. 'Odd free gift.'

'Bands attract all kinds of stuff. Probably supplied by someone hoping for an endorsement.'

'I'd forgotten about your exciting previous life.' Vaguely, she imagined him hauling instruments about as the glamorous rock stars who owned them discarded unwanted gifts and slid into sleek limousines. 'I don't suppose there was freebie moisturiser and make-up?'

He uncrossed his legs and rose. 'Moisturiser I can do, if you don't mind it being aimed towards men. But I'm afraid I left my guyliner and mascara in my other home.'

She laughed as he padded off down the short hall. 'Pity.' She drank the chocolate, which made her feel stronger by the mouthful, until he returned with a dark grey tube. She uncapped it and began to smooth on the thin white cream, closing her eyes, letting it relax the tightness caused by tears and soap. 'Thank you. Sorry if I'm being a bit lavish with it, but it feels as if it's giving my skin a drink.'

'You're welcome.' When she opened her eyes he was smiling at her. 'I'll get you a sandwich. It's nearly two o'clock.'

'Wow.' She felt a wriggle of alarm. 'I can't even think what I'm supposed to have been doing this afternoon.' He got up and moved into the kitchen area while she found her phone, quickly opening her calendar app and studying it. 'Not too bad, thank goodness. I was supposed to be watching rehearsals with Band Two and Troupe One. The rehearsal tape for "That Baddie is My Uncle" and "Dilemma" is quicker than Band Two have been playing it. It needs sorting out.'

He glanced at his watch. 'You'll catch some of the rehearsal, if you really feel you should. Or I could just report to Oggie that you're under the weather.'

Inside her, warmth stirred. Joe Blackthorn was nice, just as he'd been in his youth, though it had been deeper down then. 'Thank you,' she said quietly. 'For coming to support me and looking after me. It was horrible . . .' A shudder gripped her. 'I don't even want to think about it.'

'Then don't.' He took down plates from a cupboard.

She laughed shakily. 'You probably thought you were seeing the old Princess Georgine.'

'No.' He gave a decisive headshake. 'I've never known you have hysterics – unless of laughter – so it had to be something really frightening or upsetting.' He turned to the fridge. 'Chicken, ham, cheese, lettuce, tomato, marmite or Nutella.'

She got up to join him in inspecting the contents of the big fridge. 'May I have Nutella on toast? I'm in the mood for comfort food.'

'Sounds good.' He dropped bread into the toaster and filled glasses with fruit juice.

Georgine began to pay attention to her surroundings. 'Nice place,' she said, running her fingertips over the granite worktop. 'Brave to have cream carpet everywhere. I see why you took your shoes off at the door.'

He unscrewed the lid of the Nutella. 'It was already here. The other two apartments are more sensible colours, but this is the biggest.'

'You could put your mum in one of the other apartments.' She grinned, glancing back in time to catch his eyes-wide expression.

'I came out in a sweat when you said that. Did you ever meet my mother?' The toast popped and he began to give it a lavish coat of Nutella.

Noticing his dropped gaze, she felt small. She had no business making jokey remarks about the woman who, at best, had been an embarrassment. 'I knew who she was,' she said carefully.

His mouth tightened. 'One of these days I'll take you to meet her. She's a more stable person now, but we still have our moments. Here's your comfort food.'

'Thanks.' She took the plate, the delicious smells of hot toast and Nutella mingling on the air as she seated herself beside him on a stool at the breakfast bar. She took the first bite, relishing the sweetness. 'I suppose the past will always be between you and your mum.'

He shrugged. 'True. But you can't choose your family.'

'No.' She thought of Blair and heaved a sigh. She'd no idea how to sort things out with her little sister. She definitely needed time to calm down first. Maybe she'd go and see her dad after work. She wouldn't 'tell on' Blair about what had happened, but she really could do with hearing his, 'Hi, honey,' as she walked in the door.

When she'd eaten her toast and drained her juice glass, Georgine glanced at her watch. 'Right. Now I can face real life. I'd better get to that rehearsal.'

'You get your afternoon back on track. I'll catch you up.' He cleared the counter and began to stack the crockery in the dishwasher.

Georgine put her hand on his arm. It was warm and firm beneath her fingers. 'Thank you. It can't have been nice for you to wade into that scene. I really lost it,' she added, flushing at the memory.

He put the plates down to give her a quick hug. 'You were terrified. Don't apologise.'

The strength and broadness of his upper body hit her. His heat scorched her cheek, his stubble gently scratching. When she'd given him a spontaneous hug on Saturday at the Shetland estate, and when he'd held her protectively today as she crumbled, coats had provided padding between them and she hadn't been so . . . aware. Thrown, she pulled back, trying to pin on a smile. 'See you there, then.'

She grabbed her things, hurrying out into the inhospitable winter afternoon, clutching her coat closed against the slicing wind. Before long, she'd taken up station at the back of the big rehearsal room as Errol and Maddie conferred on the subject of the band having rehearsed a song at a considerably slower tempo than the dancers. Maddie was pointing out, reasonably, that as the composer had provided the rehearsal track, it had to be correct.

'But surely the dancers can just follow—' Errol was insisting, probably because he should have been aware the band had misread an instruction or not listened to the rehearsal track properly. Or both.

Georgine cut across him, not feeling in the mood to put up with his posturing. 'Let's show our belief in the band's talents and ask them to play at the proper speed. It's pretty basic stuff.'

The door to the rehearsal room squeaked open and Joe slipped in. His eyes sought her out and he mouthed, 'OK?'

She smiled and nodded. The heat of the moment when they'd pressed together in his apartment hit her anew. It was Joe. The skin-tingling, breath-snatching response had been to Joe.

As the thoughts chased one another through her mind she continued to look at him, and his eyes narrowed. Then he smiled, as if divining her thoughts and saying: *Noticed that moment we shared, did you? Me, too . . .*

She felt herself blush.

Chapter Twenty-Two

The last half hour of rehearsal seemed endless. The band tried the new tempo and, under pressure, were ragged. Sammy, on lead guitar, flushed a dull red and seemed to lose the ability to play altogether.

Errol sidled up to Joe, smoothing his beard so he could mutter behind his hand. Georgine could see him out of the corner of her eye. Guessing he was trying to enlist Joe as an ally, she had to smother a smile when Joe replied at normal volume, 'But playing at the requested tempo is within the capabilities of your students.'

Errol frowned, caught out by Joe disagreeing with him but at the same time complimenting his students.

By now the members of Band Two were beginning to look mutinous. Joe moved further into the room. 'OK, guys, let's do this. Mind if I take the drums, Dilip?'

Dilip looked relieved to quit his stool and hand over his sticks. 'Go for it.'

'Right, guys, I'll give you the beat,' Joe called.

The rest of the band angled themselves so they could

see him, looking as thankful as Dilip had that someone was moving things forward.

'One-two-three and . . .' Joe brought his sticks down on the snare and the tom and everyone hit the first note of the introduction, the vocalist's head keeping time as he waited to come in.

Crash-crash chakka-chakka, bang-bang, bang-bang, bang-bang chakka-chakka went the drums, Joe's sticks flying, upper body swivelling to allow his arms to range around the full kit, thighs moving as his feet worked the bass drum and hi-hat cymbals.

'*Don't tell me, don't tell me! Uncle Jones is a baddie,*' the vocalist came in, rocking out the lyrics to match the up-tempo mood.

Halfway through the song Joe stopped and the band faltered to a halt. 'Let's hold it there. Dilip, come back in on the drums. Can I borrow your spare sticks?' Joe took up position in front of the band, waving the dancers into position. 'Band, you can record this on your phones so you'll have it for practice if you want.' Phones were instantly set up and placed on the floor by feet.

Then Joe brought the band in again, this time using the sticks on one another above his head. 'One-two-three and . . .' He kept time and Dilip picked up the tempo effortlessly, along with the rest of the band.

Georgine watched the rhythmic motion of Joe's arms, beginning to get an idea of where he got his upper body strength. Drum techs had to be drummers, of course. Why did Joe never perform? He was like a human metronome. Surely nobody learned to play an instrument so well just for their own entertainment? Musicians she'd known seemed to be always forming themselves into bands. Even if they didn't gig, they jammed, or took part in open-mic nights.

Then she forced herself to concentrate on the rehearsal, ready to clap like mad at the end and give the students loads of encouragement, hoping heaped praise for Errol's students would take the sour look off his face. She really could only deal with so much hysteria in one day.

Three o'clock arrived and rehearsal ended. Everyone clapped, then Georgine, exhausted, trailed back to her room. Joe followed.

She checked her phone and saw several texts from Blair and, though her finger hovered over the first, she decided to wait until she'd finished for the day. Her laptop was waiting for her to update her rehearsal notes, but she was flagging. She was also jumpily aware of Joe sorting through a box of props in the corner of the room and every time she thought about that quick hug in his apartment her spine shivered.

'So,' she said casually, 'you really know your way around a drum kit. The students were awestruck.'

He glanced up. 'Shaun taught me drums and a bit of piano, then drums were my instrument for my diploma.' He hesitated. 'Actually, my college band became—'

Fern popped her head around the door. 'Your sister's here, Georgine, so I brought her along.'

A small shock travelled through Georgine and she rubbed her forehead, which had begun to ache. 'Blair's here?' Then seeing her sister step out from behind Fern, wearing her embroidered coat and a contrite expression, had little option but to reply, 'OK, thanks.'

Joe cleared his throat. His military-short haircut had grown out a bit and was spiking at the front. 'Shall I find somewhere else to work?'

'No need,' Georgine was quick to say. She waited until she heard Fern's footsteps tapping back the way she'd come before speaking to her sister. 'What's up?'

Blair stepped into the room, closing the door behind her. 'Do you hate me?' Now she was nearer, her eyes looked red-rimmed.

Georgine's heart thought about thawing, but then she remembered the awfulness of the bailiffs and it froze again. Her voice emerged stilted and odd. 'I can be upset without hating you.'

'I know how you feel about bailiffs and everything. I wouldn't blame you if you hated me,' Blair added piteously, 'but I don't have to clear out, do I?'

'I haven't said that,' Georgine objected. 'We need to talk. But now's not the time.'

Joe closed the box he'd been working on and hoisted it into his arms. 'I'll stick this back in the props room.'

But Blair was blocking his exit and she didn't seem to see or hear him. Her focus was on Georgine. 'I am sorry. I know it was my fault, but you can't blame me for last time.'

Stung, Georgine jumped to her feet. 'I'm *well* aware.'

Paling, Blair said no more but turned suddenly and left the room. Weakly, Georgine sank back into her chair. 'I should have dealt with that better,' she muttered remorsefully.

Joe shot after Blair to see her to the main doors, while Georgine sat with her head in her hands. Blair had never forgiven her. The knowledge filled her with ice.

Then she felt the air in the room change and Joe was back, his hand on her arm. 'How about coming to my place for a few hours? Give yourself time to chill. I make a mean Spanish omelette.'

'Oh, really?' she choked. 'Haven't you had enough of me and my dramas for today?'

He laughed softly. 'I have a few hours left in me. Come on.'

Georgine scrabbled her possessions together haphazardly and they slipped quietly out by a door Joe unlocked at the end of the corridor near the big rehearsal room. She'd barely registered the door, but its presence explained how Joe came and went to his apartment. Outside, the winter's afternoon was almost dark and the wind harried them with its chilly breath as they traversed the back of the building to access the stairs.

When they were inside, past the unoccupied apartments, and closing Joe's door on the world, Georgine had to gulp hard not to bawl all over again with relief.

He rested a hand on her shoulder briefly, ushering her into the lounge area to sink down wearily onto the sofa while he went around the apartment switching on lights and turning up the heating. Georgine felt cold right through and not from the moments they'd spent in the raw December weather. It was more like being the little boy with the frozen heart in *The Snow Queen*. Cold on the inside.

She tipped back her head to gaze through the skylight. There were no stars to lighten the darkness. 'It's true what Blair said: it's not her to blame for my family not having enough money. Because it's me.'

The rustlings that had been accompanying Joe's movements around the flat paused. Then suddenly he was sinking down to sit beside her. 'That's hard to believe.' His warmth was right next to her. Not quite touching.

But when his arm curled tentatively around her, she gave in to temptation and huddled into him like a shivering kitten. 'It wasn't deliberate.'

He laughed softly. 'That I *can* believe.'

'I had no idea how business really worked.'

For once she found herself actually wanting to drag out the shame that had festered for so long.

'I knew someone Dad contracted to had gone bust owing him a lot of money, but not that Dad was holding on by his finger ends as a consequence. He hid that he was pinning everything on one big job to stave off creditors and keep the workforce in employment. It was a job for local millionaires, Martin and Emma Luck. People used to call them the Lucky Lucks, but they'd accumulated their money through hard work, rising to partners in a London ad agency. They'd cashed in and bought Bellthorpe Hall, between Peterborough and Cambridge, for a less pressured lifestyle.

'My family had a nice life too, as you know,' she continued, settling her cheek more comfortably against his shoulder. 'We were invited to a barbecue at Bellthorpe Hall one Sunday. I knew Martin and Emma were Dad's clients, but I never had to worry about what that meant. I was home for the summer. The sun was shining and there was lots of lovely food. And drink. Have you ever drunk punch?'

'One of those bowls of fruit floating in alcohol?' he asked. 'I don't think so.'

'They look innocuous. But they're not.' She groaned, the memory feeling cold and clammy inside her. 'I had about four glasses and got tipsy. I was a nineteen-year-old university student, I'd been drunk before but I'd always been able to gauge the potency of what I was drinking. This time it snuck up and turned me into a loud-mouthed show off. I'm surprised I've never sworn off alcohol like you.'

His voice rumbled in her ear. 'I've never sworn off through high ideals. I've just never had the compulsion to try much. The smell reminds me of being deeply miserable.'

'Right.' She let herself be sidetracked for a few moments.

'So if you liked a girl, but she'd been drinking, you'd be repelled because you could smell wine on her?'

He burst out laughing. It was so sudden and loud that Georgine jumped. 'You've got me there,' he admitted. 'I've never let a woman drinking alcohol deter me – unless she was actually drunk.'

Not examining too closely why she felt a twinge of relief that he wasn't religious about the smell of alcohol, she returned to her story. 'Martin and Emma Luck had two daughters, Chelsea and Bex. Bex was OK, I got on well with her, but Chelsea was a couple of years older than me and she and I didn't warm to each other. She had her boyfriend with her that day and they disappeared off on their own into the house.'

She wriggled self-consciously. 'After a while I began to feel rather ill.'

'Oh, dear,' he said drily.

'I didn't want Mum and Dad to know I'd drunk too much so I sidled into the house too. I'd visited once before, but I didn't know the layout very well. There was a loo on the ground floor, but that was being used by other barbecue guests, so I thought it would be a good idea to creep upstairs and get a little privacy. I knew where the family bedrooms were so I went to the other end of the house.'

'I have a horrible feeling that I know where this is heading,' he murmured, his voice full of sympathy but also holding a tiny thread of amusement.

She groaned again, feeling as if she ought to be inspecting this memory through her fingers. 'I opened what I thought would be a guest room, looking for an en-suite I could hide away in,' she confessed miserably. 'It was a guest room all right – Chelsea's boyfriend's room. He and Chelsea were stark naked, right in front of my eyes.'

227

'Oops.' His arm tightened.

Georgine took a deep breath. 'Chelsea was *incandescent*. She called me all kinds of names and because I was tipsy, instead of apologising and making myself scarce, I piled into the argument. Her boyfriend was standing there, clutching a pillow to hide his man parts, and I was standing my ground, telling Chelsea she couldn't speak to me like that. Didn't she have any manners? I was a guest. It was all drunken bravado of course. I was mortified, but I didn't know how to make my mouth sober up enough to get me out of there. It was horrible.'

'I'll bet.'

'And then Emma arrived, having heard the commotion. She instantly took her daughter's side, of course. She told me exactly how she felt about my behaviour.'

'So you finally apologised and all was forgiven?' Joe asked, not very hopefully.

'That would have been too sensible,' Georgine responded bitterly. 'I marched downstairs, barrelling up to Mum and Dad in the garden to announce that Emma had shouted at me and they had to take me home.' She cringed at her younger self. 'It was a totally spoiled-princess moment. Emma arrived hot on my heels and explained to my parents that I'd invaded her daughter's privacy and abused their hospitality. Indoors, she would have accepted a private apology and said no more about it, but now I'd made things twenty times worse by making a public scene, she was afraid she had to ask for my apology in public too. And I refused.

'Dad was horrified. Mum kept trying to placate Emma, but she probably didn't realise these clients held the fate of Randall France Construction in their hands either. Martin asked us to leave. On Monday morning the Lucks got in touch with their architect and said he had to line up another construction company, or cancel the whole thing. Sober and ashamed, I rushed round to apologise, but they didn't even allow me over the doorstep. They said it was a bit late now and shut the door.'

'Wow.' He tried to look into her face. 'Seriously? They didn't make allowance for you being a bit drunk and big for your boots?'

'Maybe they'd got on in business by not budging an inch. What came next was hideous. Dad's company went to the wall. Thirty people lost their jobs and we lost our house, cars and the boat. Dad started selling things to stave off the bank foreclosing, but it was like trying to hold back the tide with a bucket. The day –' she swallowed hard '– the bailiffs came and took the cars, I was there alone. Crying.' Her voice wobbled.

'You poor thing,' he muttered hoarsely, pulling her closer. 'And you were only nineteen? Somebody should have tried to protect you.'

'Dad did,' she admitted, feeling calmer now. 'He said I shouldn't blame myself too much because he was the one who'd pinned his escape plan on one job. Then Mum left. She couldn't cope with the penury and certainly not with the shame. Blair just wept all the time. I feel as if I've been simultaneously trying to make amends and make ends meet ever since.'

'And Blair and your dad still blame you?' he sounded incredulous.

'I don't think Dad ever did. After he had his first stroke he'd moved us into the rented house in the village and we managed to live there on my earnings and his benefits. Blair just can't seem to help bringing it up in moments of stress. She had this lovely life and I lit the fuse that blew it up.' She tried to laugh. 'Sorry. I didn't mean this to be a pity party. I just felt . . . I didn't want you to think I was the kind of person who'd get the family in a mess and not care.'

Joe's hand stroked her upper arm. His voice deepened. 'Does it matter what I think of you?'

'Yes,' she replied unguardedly. Then, embarrassed at being so direct, glanced around for distraction. She noticed patterns on the skylight above. 'Wow, is that snow?' It was quite wet snow, judging by the way the flakes made star shapes on the glass, but it was beginning to settle.

Joe glanced up. 'Pretty. I've never been here when it's snowed,' he said. 'I care what you think of me too. When I was a teenager and part of the Shitland gang, stuff happened. The kind that could get me sent to naughty kids' school.' He smiled crookedly. 'I used to lie awake worrying what you'd think about me if I got caught.'

'Oh,' Georgine breathed, disarmed by this frank confession, amazed to think she'd had this unexpected and unknown influence.

'I took things,' he admitted suddenly. 'There was gang pressure and Chrissy and me were really hungry.'

'You had to steal *to eat*?' Suddenly her story was reduced to 'the princess got her comeuppance and deserved it'.

'Yeah.' He looked away. 'I was caught by this woman once when I was stealing a pork pie. The police were involved, but I ran. Then I got better at it.' He looked straight into her eyes. 'I found ways to blag food too. Once, a teacher took me to casualty because I had a huge egg on my head. The nurse asked if I was dizzy and I said yes. She asked if I'd eaten breakfast. I said no, which was the truth, and she gave me a sandwich. It was a revelation! I repeated it as often as it would work, bashing my head on a wall and going into casualty on my own, saying I felt dizzy. Then, at what seemed the right moment, I'd add that I hadn't eaten that day.'

He withdrew his arm from around her and turned in his seat so he could take both her hands. His brown eyes regarded her levelly. 'I never stole once I lived with Shaun. It was only when I was desperate.' A faint smile. 'Only a few people know. The reason I've told you now is that I don't want to do . . . *this* . . . without you knowing the worst of me.' He leant in and brushed his lips across hers.

Heat flooded through Georgine. It felt so good to feel the softness of his lips, caressing so slowly, so gently that it seemed to sensitise her whole body.

She almost stopped breathing as she kissed him back. Never, with any other man, had she felt so hot, so shocked, so wanting.

His mouth moved to her throat. 'Georgine,' he murmured against her skin. He lifted her onto his lap to be cradled by his body, firm against hers. 'I feel as if I've wanted you in my arms for most of my life. I can't quite believe it.'

Her hands stroked his shoulders as she let out a quavering laugh. 'Whatever happened to each of us in the past, here and now feels right.'

And that's when her phone began to ring.

She groaned. 'If it's important, they'll call back,' she said breathlessly.

'Sure?' Joe settled her so snugly against him that she could feel the pounding of his heart.

The ringing stopped.

'Positive.' Georgine nibbled her way along Joe's jawline as his hand rose to cup her breast and she pressed against him, loving the heat building inside her.

The ringing began again.

Joe's embrace slackened.

'Hell.' Reluctantly, Georgine forced her arms to unwind themselves from around his neck. Breathing unsteadily, she slid off his lap and searched around for her bag. Crouching beside it and pulling her phone from one of its zipped pockets, she answered, 'Blair?' aware she sounded irritable. But for goodness sake! To be yanked out of that tingly, heart-rushing moment with Joe was just too much – and then she realised her sister was crying. 'What? What's up?' she demanded, alarm returning her brutally to real life.

'It's Dad,' Blair sniffed. 'I called to see him and he's really poorly. I can't rouse him properly. I'm worried about another stroke.'

Georgine jumped to her feet. 'I'm on my way. Pull the red cord and do whatever the emergency centre staff tell you. They'll probably call an ambulance.

'Dad's ill,' she told Joe briefly as she ended the call and grabbed her bag. She stopped. 'Damn, my car's at home,' she said, remembering Joe had driven her back to work after the episode with the bailiffs.

Joe was already on his feet. 'I'll take you to collect it.'

'Oh, *thank* you,' she said fervently, shoving her phone away with trembling fingers and racing up the hall. 'Blair thinks Dad's had another stroke.'

He was right behind her, dragging her jacket off its hook and holding it so she could scramble her arms into the sleeves.

'I can take you into Bettsbrough from here, if it's better,' he offered.

Grateful at the way he'd switched to crisis mode when only minutes ago they'd been hot and heavy on his sofa, she gave him a hard hug. 'Thanks, but I want my car in case I have to follow the ambulance to hospital or something.'

'Then let's get to it.'

Collars and hoods up, Joe wearing his beanie hat, they dashed out into the sleet and snow, which was much nicer to watch through a skylight than to feel flying on the wind into their faces, and ran down to Joe's car.

Strapped into the passenger seat, Georgine stared at the snow driven against the windshield in the cold early evening, willing the journey to pass quickly so she could get to her father. Perhaps he was on the way to hospital already. She hoped so if it was a stroke, because time was of the essence. The prospect that Randall might now be further incapacitated and need different care, even a different place to live, seemed frighteningly real.

When Joe pulled up behind her car she wanted to thank him and fly to her dad's side, but she hesitated, one hand on the door handle. Her heart set up a pitter-patter but she didn't shy from voicing the facts, though her voice emerged thick with tears. 'Joe, I'm not sure if this is the wrong or right time to say it, but my life's often like this. Things go wrong. I'm not the golden girl you used to know. I'm sorry if I'm being clumsy or rude. I'm too frightened to think straight.'

His eyebrows flicked up. Then down. 'I see.' But his smile returned and he reached out to give her arm a reassuring pat. 'Go then. Your dad's your priority.'

'That's kind of my point.' She opened the door and hopped out, the snow lying in wait to sting her face and slither down her neck.

'Are you sure you don't want me—?' she heard Joe begin to say as she flung the door shut. But her focus was all on getting to Randall. Finding her keys, she fumbled with the ignition, jumping to see a figure loom over the driver's window, then she realised it was Joe clearing snow with his hands. She cleared the front and back screens with the wipers and he stood back as, arms rubbery, she found first gear and released the handbrake. Joe was a good man, she thought as she roared off up the road. But now she had to get to her dad.

Joe drove back to Acting Instrumental, thoughts whirling. Georgine had seemed to be warning him about not jumping into a relationship. For a split second he'd felt hurt that she'd pause in her headlong flight solely to warn him off. Then it had hit home that she was actually trying to protect him.

It had felt as if she'd reached inside him and stroked his heart.

He pulled up at the electric gates to Acting Instrumental and whirred down the window. The black iron gates swung open in response to him tapping the out-of-hours access code into the keypad, and he drove into the car park.

When he'd switched off the engine he sat thinking, the only sound that of the occasional whisper of snow blowing against the windscreen. Apart from the site supervisor's car parked close by, everything he could see, edged with snow and occasionally sparkling in the glow from the security lighting, was his. This patch of the planet, these buildings, this car, even those trees.

Real and tangible, things he could touch and trust.

Both he and Georgine had stuff in their pasts that made it hard for them to trust. But she'd trusted him for a few all-too-brief minutes this evening, her body soft and exciting, her emotional guard down. Georgine was real and definitely something he could touch – a shiver ran through him at the memory of doing exactly that. Being on the brink of acting out his fantasy had left him feeling slightly shocked. But so hot.

Next time, he'd explain about The Hungry Years and the reasons he'd been reticent about his real place in the music industry till now. He'd been going to do it at the end of his confession tonight but then he'd looked at her lips and his scrambled brain had told him that then was the right time for a kiss. Now he was away from her and could think properly, he knew that he could trust her with his secrets.

And, maybe, one day, his heart. And a heart wasn't a Christmas gift you could return intact, even if you kept the receipt.

Chapter Twenty-Three

Georgine half expected to see an ambulance in the car park when she pulled up outside her father's block. As there was no sign of one, she locked the car and ran to the main door and up the stairs. There was only one lift and it was slow.

Outside Randall's door she paused, trying to control her breathing. Her dad's condition wouldn't be improved by her running in like a headless chicken. Several moments later she let herself in quietly. 'Hello, it's me.'

'Hi, honey,' croaked a familiar voice. And there was Randall in his chair as usual.

'Hey, Dad.' Georgine hurried across the hall to the sitting room.

Blair rose warily from the seat opposite him. 'He's awake now,' she said unnecessarily.

Georgine kissed Randall's forehead. It was hot and clammy. 'So, what's been going on?' she asked gently.

'Inhection, pobbly,' he croaked, lifting his right hand to his left ear.

'Another of those ear infections, do you think?'

Randall nodded. Then he smiled his one-sided smile and patted her hand. 'Cold.'

'Yes, it's snowing. Very wet stuff. I don't think it's settling much. You're very hot to the touch.'

He nodded, then winced and said something that sounded as if it might be 'earache'. He was pale except for pink patches on his cheeks.

'Do you feel as if you have a temperature? Hot and cold shivers?'

Randall nodded again.

'Pain anywhere but in your ear?'

He shrugged, then shook his head and tried to say something that didn't come out properly.

Georgine began to run through possibilities. 'Throat?'

'Bit.'

'Head?'

He nodded. Sweat glistened on his forehead. He closed his eyes and let his head rest against the wing of his chair.

Georgine rose, pulling off her coat and dropping it on a chair. She glanced at her sister. 'What made you think he was having a stroke?'

Blair looked sheepish. 'He was difficult to rouse and felt clammy.'

'But no worsening of the damage to his left side? Was he confused? Having more trouble with his speech than usual?'

'Definitely confused.' Blair lifted her chin.

'Bear oke nee uck,' Randall put in.

'Blair woke you up?' Georgine asked, to clarify. 'Is that why you were confused?' When Randall nodded, she turned back to Blair. 'Did you call the ambulance? Or pull one of the red cords?'

Blair looked uncomfortable. 'No. He – I realised he

wasn't as bad as I first thought, once he came round a bit. But he has a headache.'

'Bit,' Randall put in.

'Right.' Georgine frowned down at Randall, who definitely looked under the weather. 'What do you think, Dad? Do you think you might have had another stroke? Even a minor one?'

Randall shook his head, but winced again and stopped. It didn't seem anything like the crippling pain in his head that had accompanied his strokes, but she was unwilling to put him in any danger. 'I think I ought to ring the NHS helpline for advice.'

Randall shrugged.

Georgine looked at Blair. Blair shrugged too, her eyes on Randall.

As usual, it was left to Georgine to make the decisions. She pulled out her phone then went through the protracted procedure of logging her request and waiting for a return call. When it came, it was from a GP. Georgine explained, being clear about her father's communication limitations. Blair had got up to busy herself in the kitchenette making a hot drink. She answered when Georgine passed on questions but made no move to take the phone and speak to the GP herself.

Eventually, it was decided that a GP would come out to visit Randall, providing a prescription if one was needed.

Randall dozed through most of the process, his breathing noisier than usual. Georgine got him a rug for his legs and he alternated between huddling beneath it or pushing it off in a sweat.

Georgine and Blair spoke to each only as necessary. Randall roused enough to point his finger between the two of them and rasp, 'Ot's up?'

Georgine glanced at Blair. Neither of them would want to give Randall stress by telling him about the bailiffs. Though his memory had been affected to some extent by his strokes, she was pretty certain he had sufficient recall of his own insolvency nightmare to be upset. She summoned up a smile. 'It's nothing to worry about. Let's just get you better.'

She felt Blair relax from right across the room.

Later in the evening, the GP arrived: Dr Bauer, a drawn and harassed-looking man in a checked jacket, carrying a doctor's bag that looked as if it had seen as much service as he had. By then it was past Randall's usual bedtime. He was tired and tetchy and disinclined to make the massive effort needed to communicate.

Georgine did her best and Blair chimed in to explain that Randall had been difficult to rouse.

'Understandable with a severe ear infection,' Dr Bauer observed. And added, 'Taking the "better safe than sorry" route given your dad's medical history is no bad thing, I suppose.' The 'I suppose' hinted that Dr Bauer thought the call could have waited until morning. Once he'd written a prescription, he didn't linger.

As the door closed behind him, Georgine glanced at her sister. 'The prescription needs taking to the nearest out-of-hours pharmacy and Dad could probably use a hand to get to bed tonight. Which do you take?'

'I'll do the prescription.' But then Blair hesitated, withdrawing her hand before actually taking the piece of paper from Georgine's hand. 'Will you be here when I get back?'

'Yes. But if I'd gone home you'd be capable of getting Dad a drink of water and seeing he took the first pill, wouldn't you?' Georgine began to feel exasperated.

Blair dropped her gaze. 'Yes,' she muttered, taking out

her phone to check which pharmacy was on duty in Bettsbrough.

Randall was capable of putting himself to bed, albeit taking his time over washing and undressing, so Georgine really only had to check that he had everything he wanted and text the scheme manager to tell her Randall was under the weather. When Blair returned with the pills Randall took one and firmly closed his eyes. 'Night.'

Georgine was happy to take the hint, yawning as she and Blair left the flat, so tired that she even waited for the lift instead of taking the stairs.

It was in the lift that Blair said tentatively, 'Are we talking?'

'Yes,' Georgine said tiredly. 'But I can't wait to get in bed, and for this day to be over.'

'Am I still living with you?' Blair's voice thickened.

Georgine realised having her house to herself again would now feel slightly odd. 'Of course. Until you can get yourself sorted.'

The lift doors sighed open and both women pulled their coats close around themselves as they crossed to the outer door. The snow had stopped and Jack Frost had followed along to cast his glittering mantle over the world.

Shivering, Georgine made straight for her car. Blair's voice floated after her. 'So why have you locked me out?' She sounded hurt and confused.

'Locked you out?' Georgine stopped, car key in hand. It took a few seconds for the penny to drop. 'Do you mean the new locks?' It seemed much longer ago than this morning that the locksmith had visited. 'I told you both locks were being changed to stop Aidan—'

'I couldn't get in when I went back,' Blair said in the same hurt tone.

240

Georgine gazed at her little sister, the pretty face, the defensive expression. 'The new keys are on the dining table. I suppose I forgot to tell you when I left . . . after everything that had happened.' Exasperation warred with pity and guilt inside her as things began to click into place. Blair must have gone home after the confrontation at Acting Instrumental, found she couldn't get in so had gone to Randall's flat. Then she'd seized on his being unwell as a reason to get Georgine there. She sighed, turning back to look Blair in the eye. 'Sorry. I did accidentally lock you out. I'll let you in now and you can help yourself to new keys.'

With effort, she turned away from her car and crossed to give Blair a hug. 'Let's go home. I'm trashed.'

'OK,' murmured Blair, looking a bit happier.

When they'd finally made it home and Georgine had demonstrated how the new locks worked, glad to close her bedroom door and get into her night things, she fell into bed. She switched off the light and pulled the duvet up beneath her chin. *Ahhhhh . . .*

Half an hour later, she was still wide awake.

First, she wondered whether she should have slept in an armchair in Randall's flat in case he needed her.

Then, after realising that ship had sailed unless she wanted to wake her dad by returning, she tried to work out how close to the limit her credit card would be after paying the locksmith this morning. The bill had been over £130. That kind of unforeseen expense usually left a hole that was hard to fill. The rent from Blair had been helpful, but her supermarket bills had pretty much doubled and there were bound to be higher electricity and gas bills on the way.

Her heart missed a beat. In all the upset, she hadn't

asked Blair where she'd got the money to satisfy her debt and get rid of the bailiffs. She'd have to talk to her sister in case there were other debts that might bring bailiffs to her door. She hoped she could find a way to do it that wouldn't result in a repeat of this evening's atmosphere.

She turned over, trying to find that magic spot that would allow her body to relax and her dreams to carry her off. Instead, she saw a vision of Joe's expression when she'd been so lame as to introduce the 'what is this leading to?' conversation right when she had. For all she knew, he'd had no thoughts of anything more meaningful than a bit of afternoon delight.

Unaccountably, that thought made her feel particularly low.

Impatiently, she sat up and reached for her laptop. There was nothing she could do about Randall, Blair or Joe but she could look at her bank balance and work out how much she could pay off her credit card when it came due. She supposed she couldn't now get Blair to weigh in with a few quid for Christmas dinner, but maybe they could cook it together in their dad's flat. Even invite one or two of his neighbours – he often played cards with his friend Sol in the afternoons.

They could . . .

She stopped. Blinked. Gazed in shock at her bank balance.

That couldn't be right! Her eyes dropped automatically to the transactions itemised in neat rows below.

There was a £5010.32 credit from Patricia France.

Her eyes almost popped from her head. Her grandmother often put money in her account for birthday and Christmas presents but that was usually the equivalent of a hundred dollars. Georgine didn't think she'd had this much money in an account in her life. Tossing aside her duvet she flung open her door but when she saw no light around Blair's door she retreated under the duvet again. Her clock told her it was midnight; only early evening in Georgia.

She grabbed her phone and called Grandma Patty.

'Well, hello, dear,' Grandma Patty's voice said almost straight away. She sounded as if she was already smiling.

'There's over five thousand pounds in my bank account, Grandma. From you.'

'Well, good. I would've hated for it to get lost in space, or whatever happens to missing electronic transactions.' Grandma Patty gave a pleased laugh.

Georgine wished they'd Skyped so she could see her grandmother's face. 'But why?'

'Well, now.' A rustle came down the line as if Grandma Patty was getting herself comfortable. 'I went to this talk at my seniors club. It was called "giving with a warm hand". It made a lot of sense to me.'

Georgine floundered. 'Not to me. What does it mean?'

'It's a little more than I first meant to give, but when Blair rang me today—'

Georgine swore.

'I'm not sure that's a word you ought to say in the hearing of your grandmother, dear,' Grandma Patty protested. Then her voice softened. 'OK, before you go rushing off to pull Blair's pigtails, let me tell you the whole tale. "Giving with a warm hand" means passing some of your money to your dear ones while you're still alive, rather than making them hang on until you've passed. You get the pleasure of seeing them using it. I can give you fifteen thousand dollars a year without incurring gift tax, you know.' Grandma Patty paused as if expecting Georgine to

243

say something congratulatory. When Georgine didn't take the opportunity, she continued. 'So when Blair called me today to ask for a loan I realised she definitely could use help. I know you're always worried about money too, so I decided to give you each seven thousand dollars. How much did you say that came to in your money, dear?'

'£5010.32,' said Georgine faintly.

'And can you use it?'

'Of course I can *use* it—'

'Then use it, dear!' Grandma Patty's voice became stern. 'Georgine, I want you to have it. I want you and Blair not to have to scrimp. My, you're young to have the worries you've had! Grandpa Earl and I weren't in a position to help Randall when he had all his trouble because Randall was so positive that if we sent money it would go to his creditors instead of to him. When Grandpa died in 2010 I received a lump sum and a portion of his pension, so I'm well provided for. After I'd been to that talk I went and saw my accountant, taking along a lot of bonds and whatnot that Grandpa had bought over time. I guess I was told they were valuable when Grandpa died, but I was too upset to think straight. Now they've been sold and I was shocked at the size of the bottom line, I can tell you!'

Georgine had no idea what to say.

Grandma Patty's voice became gentle, coaxing. 'You have to understand that I've also given seven thousand dollars to each of my other grandchildren, your American cousins. And I will be *upset* if I hear any Tom-fool refusals from any one of you. You won't spoil my pleasure, will you? I've had a windfall, and now I want to share it.'

'Oh,' said Georgine, inadequately. She had to swallow a gigantic lump in her throat. 'Thank you so much,

Grandma. This will make a huge difference to me.' She could vanquish all the utility bills Aidan had stuck her with for a start. Be more relaxed about Christmas. Keep the rest for a rainy day, or think about changing her car.

They talked for a little longer, Grandma Patty asking for the usual update on Randall. 'My poor dear boy,' she sighed on hearing of her son's illness. 'Please, Georgine, will you try and bring him here at spring break? I'll fund the airline tickets.'

As her grandmother sounded so close to tears, Georgine promised to check with his doctors. 'If they're not worried then we'll come.' With the utility bills paid off and Grandma Patty providing air tickets, she wouldn't have to get casual work over the holidays.

When she eventually ended the call and lay down again she was able to drift off straight away.

Chapter Twenty-Four

Wednesday and Thursday vanished quicker than Christmas dinner set before a hungry family.

Tutors strove to keep students on track. Rehearsals and the Christmas party planned for Friday evening seemed the sole topics of conversation amongst Level 3 students. Although she saw Joe at rehearsal or in meetings, neither of them had mentioned their hot interlude, although Georgine sometimes thought the atmosphere would crackle if they became any more aware of one another. He'd given a rueful smile when he heard Randall's diagnosis and murmured, 'Glad it was nothing worse.'

Georgine cooked Randall's dinner on Wednesday evening. His antibiotics were having the desired results and he was already almost back to normal. Blair worked both of her jobs, day and evening, without complaint, though Georgine had half expected her to throw in the evening job now she'd received money from Grandma Patty. Blair, however, said she was trying to turn over a new leaf. Georgine had given her a huge hug and they'd put the bailiff episode behind them.

Relieved of financial worries, Georgine felt full of energy. The last couple of weeks before a show evaporated if you didn't keep up the enthusiasm and she fairly buzzed with it at Thursday's four o'clock production meeting.

'On the twelfth of December, less than a week away, we have the full run-through in the studio theatre. That's costumes, props, the lot. Sir John Browne Academy's last event is on the fourteenth so we'll get in to the Raised Curtain on the weekend of the fifteenth and sixteenth. Monday the seventeenth is dress and tech rehearsal.'

'And the last day of term,' Errol stuck in. 'It's a crap day for a dress rehearsal. The students will try to sneak off to the pub.'

Georgine fixed him with her hardest stare. 'We agreed that a Monday dress rehearsal for a Tuesday first night was the only sensible way to go. It gives non-tech crew students the weekend to relax and recharge, even if we staff are running around like silly buggers. With a show every evening from the eighteenth to the twenty-first, matinee and final show on the twenty-second, situating the dress rehearsal on Monday is vital. They won't hit the pub if they want to pass this module of their qualification.' She let her voice soften. 'Come on, Errol, you've done this often enough to know how to motivate your students.'

'They can rein themselves in until the after-show party on the final night,' Oggie added soothingly.

Georgine made a face of mock horror. 'We have to do the get-out first, because there's a carol concert at the venue the next day.'

Errol groaned and slapped down his pen as if Georgine had just confirmed his worst suspicions rather than simply mentioning something they all knew already. Georgine let it pass. Everybody reacted to stress in different ways.

The meeting wound up as soon as they'd agreed to concentrate efforts over the next few days on giving every scene at least one rehearsal. Georgine had emailed schedules already. 'And I'll be here at the weekend finalising props and costumes. Thank goodness we have all human characters in this show – no elves or Santas.'

'I'll be around at the weekend,' said Joe casually. 'Need a hand?'

'Yes, please, especially if you're any good at sticking sequins on with fabric glue,' Georgine said promptly. Her heart hopped as she remembered last time they'd been alone together. She hoped nobody would notice if her cheeks had gone pink.

'I may need training,' Joe joked. The smile in his eyes made Georgine suspect his mind had travelled in the same direction as hers.

Oggie took Joe off somewhere as the rest were filing out. Georgine crammed the production file and her laptop into her bag, slid into her coat and scarf and set off for home, trying to blow smoke rings with her breath in the frosty air and enjoying the memory of paying in full every single household bill she'd hitherto been so painfully catching up on.

Grandma Patty's money making her feel rich, and Thursday being the night the shops stayed open late in Bettsbrough in the run up to the festive season, she was soon changed out of her work clothes and in her car heading for town to do some Christmas shopping.

Almost all the shops had stayed open. The local Lions Club was towing a ho-ho-hoing Santa around on a sleigh (with wheels) collecting for presents for local children in bad situations. Georgine, with the memory of Joe confessing to stealing food fresh in her mind, gave a fiver.

Lights of all colours criss-crossed above the pedestrian area and the Salvation Army choir belted out 'Good King Wenceslas' and 'Once in Royal David's City' in the area facing the doors to the shopping mall. Georgine bought a cup of coffee and a hot turkey roll from a nearby stand and enjoyed both as she listened to the harmonies. They were a good choir and their voices seemed to imbue the air around them with Christmas spirit. When they began on 'Rudolf the Red-Nosed Reindeer' children tugged on the hands they held to get their parents to stop and listen too.

Finally, Georgine dropped all her change in the Salvation Army collection bucket and began Christmas shopping. Her dad was easy as he appreciated practical or edible presents. She bought him warm slippers and a chunky cardigan – easier to get into with a less able arm than a jumper – and the biggest box she could find of Ferrero Rocher chocolates.

She bought her mother a hand-painted silk scarf from a textiles student who had a stall – or a pop-up shop, as she called it. (It looked like a stall to Georgine.) The scarf was black with a riot of colourful flowers. Terrence was harder to buy for and eventually she went back to the textile student and bought him a silk tie bearing a subtle abstract pattern of blues and greens. She'd need to post their presents to their home in Northumberland at the weekend as they'd announced as early as September that they'd be spending Christmas in France this year.

Shame that their relationship was so distant, Georgine thought as she tucked the tie in the tote bag over her shoulder. It had been some years since Georgine felt close to a mother who'd divided the blame for the demise of Randall France Construction equally between Georgine and Randall.

She spent the most time trying to find a nice gift for Blair, something that said, 'You're my annoying little sister but I love you lots.' Eventually, she settled on a white marble and copper dressing table tidy from a shop that was usually too expensive for her to enter. It was pretty and individual, much like Blair herself.

She mentally glossed over the subject of buying a gift for Joe. Who knew where they'd be by Christmas? It was a whole nineteen days away.

Then, feeling almost sinful, she bought a new dress for the Acting Instrumental staff Christmas meal on Friday week. It was turquoise, which she knew would look dramatic with her hair, with a ladder of festive gold ribbon up the front. It was only £35 but it felt like a lot, given that she'd scarcely clothes shopped in the past few months, unless it was in charity shops.

Fired with the Christmas bug, she drove home, pulled down the loft ladder and scrambled up to drag out the box marked 'Christmas'.

Back downstairs, she found an *Only Fools and Horses* Christmas show rerun on TV for background entertainment and arranged the tree in the corner of her lounge diner. The same decorations came out every year, some dating back to her parents' collection. She set aside the tiny tree she put up in Randall's flat each year. She'd do that at the weekend, after she'd picked up his prescription meds from the pharmacy.

As she worked, she hummed one of the songs from the show – 'Some Kids Get Nothing for Christmas' – letting her mind drift over tomorrow's student Christmas party and Joe volunteering to help her finish the props at the weekend.

Joe.

Whenever she thought of him she felt as if a tiny firework went off inside. His confession about shoplifting to survive had squeezed her heart. She was glad that little of Rich Garrit remained except, thankfully, the old easy friendship he and Georgine had shared.

With a wriggle of pleasure, she thought of the way he'd kissed her. If Blair's phone call hadn't interrupted them . . .? They hadn't been holding back.

From a battered box she withdrew the tree-top ornament – a silver star with Mickey and Minnie Mouse in Santa hats waving from its centre, a relic from a Disneyland Christmas when she'd been thirteen and Blair eleven. Her parents had been together, Grandma Patty and Grandpa Earl had joined them at a Disneyland encrusted with decorations and lights. Life had been untarnished.

Gently, Georgine fixed the star to the top of the tree and stood back to admire it.

Maybe this would be a good Christmas. The show would be a success, Blair would be a bit happier, Randall would be as healthy as possible and Georgine would . . .

Was there a chance of making a Christmas memory or two with a complex, tall, brown-eyed man?

On Friday the programmes for *A Very Kerry Christmas* arrived from the printers, a giant box of white and silver gorgeousness that Georgine couldn't wait to wave about ahead of the students pouring back in for that evening's Christmas party.

'Congratulations, Georgine, you've done a lovely job,' Oggie said, giving her a hug.

'Looks as if the show's really happening.' Joe gave her a wink and a grin.

'You nearly took my eye out,' Errol complained as

251

Georgine tossed him a programme to examine. But even he grinned at her infectious excitement, and at Maddie and Keeley examining their thumbnail pictures to see how cool they looked in black and white.

And then it was time to get busy with the student party. Hannalee and Avril had volunteered to collect the party food order and carried long, flat boxes of finger food and cake into a small room off the studio theatre. The door was locked against hungry and over-excited students who might jump the gun while the staff rushed off to get ready in the staff area, threading silver tinsel through their hair or hanging baubles from their earrings.

'Thank goodness it ends at ten,' groaned Keeley, who always declared herself totally exhausted by the two-thirds mark of any term. But tonight nobody could be grumpy when students flooded in wearing anything from mini dresses or skinny jeans to light-up hats and Santa suits.

Georgine was kept busy selling bottles of Pepsi or Fanta. Joe was having fun with a whirling light show while a student called Kane played DJ on a small portable stage and the walls shook to Kanye West, Little Mix and Dua Lipa. The food came out after eight and was fallen upon as if by ravening wolves; students queuing from both ends of the table, meeting in the middle and eating the first plateful while queuing again for seconds.

Almost every box of food had been carried through and opened before the students showed any sign of slowing up. Georgine snaffled a plateful for herself and sought out a space on the bottom tiers of the retractable seating at the back of the room.

She wasn't alone for long. Joe appeared through the students, most of whom were dancing again now they'd taken on fuel, guarding the contents of his plate with a crooked arm.

He settled beside her. 'One samosa and two blueberry muffins is all I managed to get. Nice to see the kids enjoying themselves.' He nodded in the direction of the heaving dance floor. Then his voice changed. 'Hello . . . what are they up to?'

Georgine swung round in time to see four students carrying in drums and cymbals. 'Interesting. I wonder if someone ought to find out what they're doing?' She bit the end off a cannoli.

Joe peeled the paper case from a muffin. 'Someone probably should.'

Minutes later, the students returned with guitar cases and a mic stand. 'Nobody's stopping them,' Georgine observed, polishing off a chocolate brownie. A glance around showed her that Oggie and other members of staff were observing but not interfering. Not even Errol.

'Probably intrigued to see what they're up to.' Joe wiped his hands on his jeans. All the paper napkins seemed to have ended up on the floor.

Nolan, the bass player in Band One, got up onto the DJ's platform. Kane pulled one of his earphones aside to listen. Then he nodded and, over the fading final bars of 'Shout Out to My Ex' spoke in his DJ's growl into the microphone. 'Okaaaaaay, Nolan has something to say, so listen to my man here.'

Slightly out of breath, Nolan took the mic. 'So, um, yeah, right. Some of the other students want to know what our show's like. Shall we do a bit?'

The applause, whistles and hoots he was greeted with painted a big grin on his face. He shouted, 'Yeah!' and suddenly almost every Level 3 student was making his or her way to what had evidently been designated the stage, the musicians pulling out amps from behind the DJ's deck.

'So this was obviously prearranged. The entire cast's taking up their opening positions,' Georgine observed, climbing up to stand on her seat in order to see, something she would have taken a dim view of if a student tried it.

Joe climbed up beside her.

'Move back, move back! We need a space!' Nolan was shouting, waving his arms at the students on the dance floor. 'Bit further . . . OK, there's good.' He looked around at his fellow performers, seeming in a rush to get started before an adult felt the need to spoil the fun. 'Ready? From the top – two, three, FOUR!'

In the opening number of 'Everyone Loves Uncle Jones' both bands crashed in with what could only be described as glee. The vocalists clustered around the mics, not having quite enough to go around. '*We love you, Uncle Jones, the man who makes Christmas joy, for every girl and boy and boy and BOY*,' rang out.

Both dance troupes came on, hop-hop, step across, kick, kick, hip thrust.

The audience began to dance, to clap along, to whoop.

Georgine turned to Joe, laughing out loud. He put out an arm to steady her when the fold-away seat she was standing on wobbled, grinning all over his face, switching his gaze back to the students who so obviously wanted to perform just for the hell of it.

From 'Everyone Loves Uncle Jones' they moved straight into 'A Very Kerry Christmas', where female lead Kerry introduced the rest of the family, and the chorus and dancers came on and off.

Before long, they'd performed the whole of scene one. Then Oggie took over the mic before anybody could decide to count them into scene two. 'Thank you all very much. That was fantastic! I'm always proud of the students of Acting Instrumental, and you've just shown me why. We'll leave it there, I think, because we want most of this audience at the Raised Curtain, so let's not give the whole show away.'

A huge cheer went up, punctuated with raucous whistles. After waiting, grinning, for the hubbub to die down, he went on, 'And I'm afraid that concludes tonight's festivities as it's past ten o'clock and I should imagine our car park's heaving with impatient parents. Thanks to Hannalee and Avril for organising the party. Have a safe journey home. And Merry Christmas.'

Another round of applause and the room began to clear. Instruments were hurriedly stowed in cases and the laughing, chattering students milled towards the doors and funnelled out. Soon there was only a handful of staff members left and the kind of ear-popping silence that follows loud music.

Hannalee and Avril yawned and said they'd return in the morning to sweep up and collect empty bottles for recycling. Oggie declared he'd be joining Georgine and Joe for Saturday morning in the props room, which was news to Georgine, but it probably wasn't a good career move to say to her boss, 'But I was looking forward to being by myself with my assistant.'

As if life were offering her a consolation prize though, Joe caught her alone when she went to collect her coat. 'Will imaginary mistletoe work for you? I think the students snaffled all the real stuff.' He held his empty hand above her head.

Georgine giggled. 'Imagination is a wonderful thing.' She stood on tiptoes, slipped her hands onto his shoulders and touched her lips to his.

Joe caught her up and deepened the kiss until Georgine's imagination was firing on all cylinders indeed. 'Come up to my place,' he murmured against her mouth.

Heat low in her belly, Georgine began to agree, then groaned. 'I don't want my car to be here at such an odd time. It's not discreet. You could come to mine though—'

'Joe?' came Oggie's voice from the corridor outside.

Georgine jumped out of the clinch, face burning. 'Whoops! We're not being very discreet on college premises.'

A lot less jumpy but making an exaggeratedly frustrated face and muttering something about being the landlord, actually, Joe began pulling on his coat. 'In here, Oggie.'

Oggie pushed open the door and came in with an arm around his eldest daughter, who Georgine had met several times before. 'Martha's come home from university and wants to say hi.'

Martha, tiny and slender, didn't look as if she should be descended from big, strapping Oggie. 'Joe!' she cried, launching herself at him. 'Haven't seen you for ages! I'm dying to catch up. Can I introduce you to my new boyfriend? He's doing music at Bristol. I know it's a bit late but Mum's cooking pasta because we're starving. When she sent me to pick Dad up she said to see if I could persuade you to come too. So you will, won't you? Pleeeeease?' Then she seemed to realise there was someone else in the room. 'Oh, hello, Georgine. You didn't have plans with Joe, did you?'

Georgine didn't feel she could say yes, in view of what those plans were. 'Hi, Martha! Me? I'm just on my way home. Enjoy your pasta.'

She said her goodnights, Joe sent her a rueful look, and

in moments she was unlocking her car and driving home alone. And wishing she wasn't.

The frustrating close to Friday evening set the tone for the weekend. Saturday was spent finalising props for *A Very Kerry Christmas* and completing the inventory for those they'd recently inherited. By the end of the day they had the black starry backdrop, oversized baubles and polystyrene snowflakes galore neatly packed up, ready for the get-in at the Raised Curtain on the fifteenth, a week's time.

'I can't believe that's taken all day,' Oggie said, stretching out his back. 'We'd better do the costumes tomorrow, hadn't we?'

Georgine rubbed her aching shoulders. 'I hope we can get it done in the morning. I've Christmas presents to bake in the afternoon. Hang on.' From her jeans pocket, her phone had begun to burble. Her stomach sank to see the caller was the manager of the complex where her dad lived. 'Sorry, got to take this.' She retreated to the far end of the room, heart beginning to pitter pat unpleasantly.

'Georgine France?' asked the voice on the other end of the phone. 'This is Leena, scheme manager. Don't worry too much, but I'm ringing to say your dad's had a bit of a fall. Luckily, he was able to pull his red cord in the bathroom. The paramedics are with him but they think he's broken his arm so they're taking him to hospital.'

'Oh, no.' Georgine began to move in the direction of the door. 'Should I go to his flat? Or straight to hospital?'

'They're taking him to Peterborough District Hospital, so go there.' Leena sounded calm and collected. It was obviously all in a day's work for her. Georgine ended the call, made breathless explanations to Oggie and Joe, and shot off, phone to her ear, calling Blair as she raced into a late afternoon with the scent of frost on the air and jumped in her car.

The evening passed in a tedium of hospital waiting rooms, Blair flicking through magazines and sighing. Randall's arm was not broken, to everyone's relief, but bruised. He was given a sling to keep him comfortable. 'Bad arm anyway,' he slurred.

'Thank goodness it wasn't your good one,' Georgine agreed, giving him a gentle hug. 'But look at your poor face as well. You're getting such a bruise.' Randall's left cheek and eye were purpling impressively.

A nurse came to establish whether Randall could look after himself if discharged. She looked at him keenly, but Randall was adamant that he was no worse off than usual. When Georgine offered to stay at his flat he got quite testy. 'I yust ont to ho to bed! No'hing's changed.'

By the time Georgine and Blair got him home it was past one a.m. The only concession Randall made to his injury was to have a pillow under his bad arm. Then he thanked them and told them to go home.

Georgine wanted to protest, 'But you look more vulnerable than usual. Let me stay.' She knew he'd hate to hear it so said, 'I'll come back in the morning,' instead.

'Why?' he demanded. 'You're busy. 'Ight, unny.'

Georgine and Blair had little choice but to leave him to sleep.

When Georgine, after a restless night, texted Oggie and Joe to give them an update and then called to see her dad regardless of what he'd said last night, she found him eating porridge and reading the Sunday paper as if nothing had happened, apart from his left eye being swollen nearly shut.

He pointed to his arm and admitted, 'Bit stiff,' and took a couple of paracetamol. Georgine used putting his tiny Christmas tree up as her excuse for hanging around while he showered and dressed, which he seemed to manage with no more than a little extra huffing and puffing. He shuffled into the sitting room and nodded at the bijou silver tree twinkling with multi-coloured baubles. 'Pretty.' He smiled with the right side of his face.

When he announced Sol was coming round to play whist, Georgine knew she was no longer needed and drove back to Middledip to join Joe and Oggie for the last couple of hours on the costumes. By one o'clock, flagging and hungry, they decided any additional gluing of sequins to costumes could be fitted in somewhere in the week.

Oggie walked her out to her car, talking about the show. She waved farewell to Joe, who was watching, and drove home. Blair was out so Georgine fell onto the sofa for a combat nap.

Waking refreshed, she'd eaten a quick lunch and begun on the baking planned as Christmas gifts to Fern, the caterers at work and some for Randall to give to the scheme managers where he lived, when her phone buzzed.

Joe: *I seem to remember you saying something about baking this afternoon. Can you use a kitchen porter?*

She didn't have to think twice. Her lips curled in a smile as she replied.

Georgine: *If you're any good at washing up.*

Joe: *On my way.*

In minutes he was at the door, drawing in a big, appreciative breath as he stepped over the threshold. 'Mm. Something smells gorgeous.' He took off his glasses, which had darkened in the daylight, and stuck them in his pocket before he threw his coat over the newel post and followed her into the kitchen. 'Wow. Those look amazing,' he said when he saw the first batch of brownies cooling.

Georgine motioned towards the mixing bowl and other baking things. 'There's the washing up. If you do a good job, I might let you have a brownie with a cup of coffee when I've mixed up the final batch.'

'Slavedriver.' He heaved an exaggerated sigh, but then grinned and dropped a kiss on her hair before throwing off the shirt he'd worn over a charcoal-grey T-shirt, ready to begin.

While they worked, they talked about the party and the show, Georgine melting chocolate and butter together, Joe placing what he'd washed and dried within her reach on the counter. Whenever she glanced his way his eyes seemed to be on her. Despite their mundane tasks and idle chatter, she felt as if she could reach out and touch the tension.

The flexing of Joe's soapy arms kept capturing her attention. The edges of the tattoo she'd noticed in the past peeped from beneath a sleeve. She imagined something tribal, or a snake or eagle's wings. Maybe when the last batch of brownies were baked she'd ask him to show her . . .

She must have made her distraction obvious because suddenly she realised that he'd stopped speaking. Stopped working. She lifted her eyes to find his intent gaze trained on her face. Slowly, he stepped closer, hands dripping soap suds on the floor. He tilted his head to press hot lips to her neck, tasting her skin with the tip of his tongue.

Her eyes closed.

Ting! Ting! Ting!

'The second batch of brownies is ready,' she breathed.

He laughed against her skin. 'Georgine, I swear, the universe conspires against us.'

But he stepped back and they returned to baking, cutting into rectangles each slab of moist brownie. The short daylight hours of winter had passed already and it was dark outside now. She felt cosy and warm in the kitchen with him.

It was when she'd just poured the final batch of mixture into the baking tins that the lights of the kitchen flickered once, twice, and went out. She squeaked in alarm, looking at where she thought the kitchen window would be. There were no lights from nearby houses or the street lights she could usually see peeping between roofs. 'Power cut. I hope it doesn't last long.'

Carefully feeling her way along the counter, she giggled. 'I'm disorientated already. Where's the sink? I want to wash this cake mixture off my hands before I get it everywhere.'

A warm, bare arm brushed hers. Then a hand found hers and carried it to his mouth. 'Oh!' she breathed at the incredible sensation of him nibbling and licking the cake mix from her skin as the darkness pressed in on them.

'You were already driving me mad,' he murmured. 'And now you taste of chocolate. I'm not sure I can stand much more.'

She laughed, then sighed as his tongue found the sensitive webbing between her fingers and sent a dart of pleasure through her.

'With any luck, this power outage will last for hours.' He searched for her other hand and began licking the cake mix from that too. 'Because I would like to spend those hours—'

'Yes,' she gasped, closing whatever small distance remained between them. Proximity made the darkness unimportant as their mouths found each other, sweet with the cake mixture he'd sucked from her fingers.

She wasn't sure if any remained on her hands but he'd certainly need a change of clothes if so, she thought, as she stroked over his chest, his shoulders, his arms, the bare skin making her shiver as her fingers sneaked up the sleeves of his T-shirt to enjoy the most powerful part of his arms.

He made a deep noise in his throat.

Then common sense asserted itself. 'Blair might come home. Maybe we should go—'

'Upstairs,' he finished for her. 'Oh, yeah.'

Taking his hand, she felt her way to the kitchen door and out into the hall, letting out an 'ouch!' as she tripped over what she thought was probably one of Blair's shoes. Up the stairs, using the bannister for guidance, then she pulled him into her bedroom and closed the door.

'Pitch darkness isn't what I'd anticipated for our first time,' he murmured. 'But it's kind of hot.' He began to pull her top slowly up, the fabric shivering over her skin. It caught on her ponytail and she untangled it, pulling the elastic from her hair. Opportunistically, he unfastened her bra while she was occupied with that, and soon her top half was naked, her hair slithering over her shoulders.

She pulled at his T-shirt and he helped her drag it off. When her breasts came into contact with his skin they both drew breath as if air was in short supply. Each touch, each sensation felt magnified by the absence of sight. Georgine's skin almost burned as he unpeeled her from her clothes, lingering to explore along the way.

When she felt as if her legs wouldn't support her much longer she murmured, 'There's a bed around here somewhere . . .'

His low chuckle seemed to surround her like the darkness as she located the edge of the mattress, drawing him along.

He hung back for an instant. 'Hang on . . . need my jeans.'

'Now?'

'Wallet in jeans; condom in wallet,' he explained breathlessly. 'Though where the hell to stow the condom until the right moment in a dark room I've never been in before is going to be an initiative test.'

Her laughter was cut off as his mouth found hers again and desire blasted through her, making her hot and heavy as they slowed the pace, investigating each other's bodies with hands and mouths. And when 'the right moment' arrived, Georgine shook with laughter while Joe swore his way through locating, opening and rolling on the condom in pitch darkness.

Then the laughter stopped as he pulled her hungrily against his flesh and slid slooooooowly inside her. She made a noise that sounded like 'unghf'. He groaned. Groaned louder as he began to move inside her and she felt as if she'd never been wanted, needed, desired so much by any man.

Ever.

Chapter Twenty-Five

Georgine woke to a hand caressing the nape of her neck. Her alarm clock was flashing 00:00 but light showed around the edges of her door.

Joe's voice murmured in her ear. 'The power's back on and it's past seven. There's someone in your bathroom, so I'm assuming it's your sister. I don't know if you have a boyfriend policy, but it seems a good time for me to leave. I need to get home and shower anyway.'

Realisation flooding in, Georgine rolled over and sat up. 'Past seven? And I never finished making the brownies.'

Fully dressed, he was sitting on the edge of her bed, needing a shave. He smothered a laugh. 'That's the first thing in your head this morning? Good to be able to see you, by the way, however dimly.'

She blushed as she realised the duvet had fallen away and his gaze was on her breasts. He dropped a kiss on her temple and one on her right breast before easing away, with regretful sigh. 'See you later.'

She listened to the slight sounds he made treading downstairs and leaving. It was nice of him to consider whether she'd be embarrassed if Blair knew she had a man in her room and nicer still that he hadn't rushed off without waking her and saying a proper goodbye.

What he'd said about it being past seven o'clock clanged suddenly to the forefront of her mind. She leapt out of bed and into her dressing gown almost in one movement and went to knock on the bathroom door. 'Blair? Don't be too long. I've overslept.'

The door swung open and Blair stood there, ready for work, one eyebrow raised. 'Is this Monday morning in an alternative universe? All the clocks are flashing, the kitchen looks like a bomb in a bakery and I saw a man's coat and shirt downstairs.'

'Power cut while I was making brownies,' Georgine breezed, trying to wriggle past Blair into the bathroom.

'So you passed the time with a man in your bedroom? Enterprising.' Blair laughed as Georgine shut the door on her. 'Am I allowed to know who he was?'

Georgine shoved her hair up into a scrunchie, threw her dressing gown off and jumped into the shower, debating whether to reply. But, you never knew, Joe might be around for a while and Blair lived here. 'Joe Blackthorn,' she called out. It gave her an odd feeling – but nice-odd – to hear his name ringing on the air.

'Not all that shocked,' Blair called as her voice moved away from the door. 'At least he's not likely to draw you into bad financial crap if he owns Acting Instrumental. See you later!'

Georgine switched off the shower and hurriedly dried herself, humming happily as she replayed last night in her mind like a cross between *Great British Bake Off* and *9½ Weeks*.

*

Success! Georgine made it to work at eight thirty by the skin of her teeth, speeding along to her room as she unfastened her coat. She'd had to bundle everything she'd left out in the kitchen last night into either the fridge, the sink or the dishwasher and promise herself that she'd finish the brownie baking tonight.

In half an hour she needed to be in the studio theatre. Errol was leading act one, scene three – Kerry Christmas agonising over whether to inform the authorities that her uncle was a gangster. It came just before the interval and everyone agreed it needed to be punchier.

The light was already on in her room so she wasn't shocked to find Joe there, studying something on his laptop. He glanced up as she dashed in. 'Mawnin', Mizz Jaw-Jean.'

The warmth in his gaze made her want to fan herself. Or maybe it was the warmth in her cheeks. She'd shared her bed with this man. Her tummy did a cartwheel. Though they'd made love in total darkness it had been so intimate that she felt as if she'd shown him every part of herself.

'Morning.' Her voice emerged halfway between a breath and a squeak as she tried to make the mental leap from lover to colleague.

His eyes laughed, and then he returned to his task, the model of professional discretion.

Despite her initial jumpiness, she became absorbed in allocating performance night tasks to parent volunteers. When her phone alerted her to the fact that rehearsal began in ten minutes she saved her work and snapped her laptop shut. 'Can you work your way through the "own clothes" students and create a list of those who don't mind having sequins glued to them? Then we can start looking for opportunities to do the gluing. If we get too tight for time I know a couple of parents I could ask to help.'

'Sure thing.' He closed his laptop and tucked it under his arm, letting her precede him out of the room.

'Things are really coming together,' she said as they strode up to the foyer.

Then she heard Fern's voice say, 'There he is! Joe? Visitor for you.'

Joe turned to look across to the front desk, where a tall woman was gazing at him with an uncertain smile, and stopped suddenly.

Georgine had turned too. Pleasure flooded through her as she saw who the visitor was. She opened her mouth to say, 'Chrissy, you've finally turned up!' Then decided she was not a very important person at this meeting of ex-nearly-stepsiblings.

'Chrissy?' Joe's voice was tight with emotion.

'Hello, Johnjoe,' Chrissy said shyly.

Joe strode towards her, Chrissy opened her arms and they met in the middle of the foyer, laughing, hugging, launching questions at each other.

'So you did get Georgine's Facebook message?'

'I did, but only just. We've been away on a trip. Now we're here in the UK till after Christmas.'

'Georgine said you're married,' Joe said.

'That's right. My husband, Polo, is in the US Air Force. He's based at Rammstein.' Chrissy stopped to wipe tears from her eyes. 'We have two daughters, so I have a whole family now. Polo loves living in Europe. He drives us all over the place in our SUV. But how about you? What are you doing *here*? I could hardly believe my eyes when I saw Georgine's message.'

Georgine checked her watch and cleared her throat. 'Hi, Chrissy!' she beamed, when they noticed her. 'I have to get to something but maybe we could say hello properly over lunch?' She turned to Joe. 'You stay with Chrissy.'

His eyes were brimming with emotion but he looked torn. 'Sure?'

'Positive! Have a lovely morning together.' She hurried away to the rehearsal feeling so happy for Joe that she found herself singing snatches of 'Everyone Loves Uncle Jones' as she skipped along. Soon she was in the studio theatre, putting her head together with Maddie and Errol to decide how best the dancers could do the 'oohs and ahhs' as backing while Kerry Christmas sang out her turmoil at the front of the stage.

For once the morning seemed to drag. Georgine caught herself checking her watch, willing the hands around to noon, mind constantly returning to how Chrissy and Joe were getting on. Joe's face had looked like a kid's on Christmas morning. One who actually had some presents.

Although she intended to make a speedy exit at the end of rehearsal, she got caught up in a discussion about the student playing Casper Christmas, who'd been off all week with flu. As a result, Georgine found herself on the tail end of the lunch queue. She helped herself to Moroccan lamb tagine with salad and bread. Joe waved so she could see he'd bagged one end of a long table with Chrissy. As soon as she could, she headed over to join them.

Joe looked happy but shell-shocked. Chrissy was popping with excitement. 'I've seen all around this wonderful facility! Isn't it amazing? Puts Bettsbrough Comp to shame. Thank you for putting us in touch, Georgine. I never knew before whether Johnjoe would want to hear from me.'

'Why on earth wouldn't I?' Joe returned indignantly, twisting off the top of a bottle of fruit juice.

She shrugged. 'Because we never heard from you again once your rich uncle came and spirited you away?'

His face fell. 'I'm so sorry, Chrissy. I was so young and so glad to get—'

'Away, I know.' Chrissy managed a tremulous smile. 'I might have done the same in your shoes but it was hard for me. Then Dad had us out of that house in case your uncle turned up and asked for his money back, and I had to face the fact it didn't matter whether you came back or not because you wouldn't find us.' She gazed at him for a moment, while he gazed wordlessly back.

Then he swallowed. 'I'm sorry,' he repeated eventually. 'It wasn't because I didn't want to see you.'

Chrissy sighed. 'Dad was a shit to you. Worse than to me, even.' She took a big breath before adding in a rush, 'But that was why when I saw you in the music press I didn't try to get in touch. And then your band gigged in Kaiserslautern, near our base. K-Town's jam-packed with US military so Polo and me, we went along. It was amazing. You were amazing.'

Georgine felt her eyebrows shoot up. Drum techs got in the music press? And how did Chrissy know which band Joe was with?

Joe stared at Chrissy. 'You recognised me? Why the hell didn't you send a message backstage?'

'Of course I recognised you. I wouldn't know where to begin in sending a message backstage—'

They were interrupted by a commotion in the corridor. A young excited male voice shouted, 'It is! It's them! And they're asking for Joe. Oggie's sent me to get him.'

Expression arrested, Joe turned in the direction of the door. A tall, red-faced student flew through it, his gaze searching out Joe. 'Oggie said to get you. The Hungries are here! Here in our foyer. Man, how do you know them? C'mon!' He beckoned energetically.

Students jumped from their seats as if there had been a fire alarm, shoving to get through the doorway. 'The Hungry Years? Seriously?'

More slowly, Joe climbed to his feet. 'That's . . . unexpected,' he said, almost to himself.

Georgine glanced at him, bewildered. 'Is The Hungry Years the band you worked for? They're pretty big!'

'Pretty big,' he agreed briefly.

Chrissy looked at Georgine and laughed. 'You don't know?' Then, not waiting for a reply, she abandoned the remains of her meal and hurried to join Joe in the tide of bodies quitting the room.

After a surprised moment, Georgine leapt up and followed too, battling through an excited crowd of students. It was all she could do to make her 'excuse mes' loud and authoritative enough to persuade the excited teens to make way for her. Eventually, she got into a position where she could see Oggie with a group of men who all seemed to be giving Joe hugs and backslaps. Joe's grin looked bemused but he returned the affection, demanding, 'What are you guys doing here?'

The very blond one wearing thick black shades boomed, 'We wanted to see what was taking up all your time. See this place you're so proud of, JJ.'

'It *is*!' a girl next to Georgine squealed. 'Joe's JJ Blacker! I think I'm going to faint. JJ Blacker's been here for weeks.'

'I kept thinking I recognised him behind those glasses,' her companion began. 'But without his red hair—'

'Bull*shit*,' retorted the first. 'If you thought he was JJ Blacker you would have been on him like a suntan.'

Excitement buffeted Georgine from all sides. Raised

270

voices, pushing and shoving. She felt numb. Anyone who was even halfway interested in music knew of The Hungry Years, the British rock band. And here they were, currently being introduced to a beaming Chrissy. Fingers shaking, Georgine took out her phone and found her way to a picture of the band, glancing from it to the laughing men clustered around Joe. Liam Willson with the geeky specs; Nathan O'Brien wearing guyliner that ended with tiny circles beside his eyes; Rafal Radkov sporting so much hair gel you could turn him upside down and use him to scrape frost from your windscreen; Billy Langridge, the platinum-blond front man.

And JJ Blacker. Shorn of his wild red hair, shaved of the trademark pointed sideburns, the self-possessed man she now knew as Joe Blackthorn. Shot after shot of him, drumsticks a blur, a huge tattoo circling one shoulder. He looked so different as part of the band, buying into the group image.

Joe was JJ Blacker. The floor seemed to rock beneath her feet.

'Yeah, do it, JJ!' a girl shouted, and Georgine wrenched her attention back to what was happening.

The rest of the band was teasing Joe, stealing his glasses while shouting, 'Fake specs!' and calling to the kids, 'We know you love him, but we don't want him to leave the band. He said he's going to decide after Christmas but, tell you what, if you get him to stay we'll do you a free gig!'

'Don't leave The Hungries, JJ,' students began to shout, clapping, whistling.

After a minute, Oggie raised his hands for quiet. When the band members too made 'keep it down' gestures the students gradually calmed. Oggie lifted his voice. 'If health and safety could see you blocking the corridors they'd get me the sack. Make your way to the studio theatre and we'll see what we can do to persuade the members of The Hungry Years to talk to us there. Including –' he grinned at Joe '– our own Joe Blackthorn, more widely known as drummer and vocalist JJ Blacker.'

Georgine stared at Oggie and felt sick. He wasn't surprised. He'd known.

Students began to jostle in the direction of the studio theatre, the volume rising again, tutors joining the throng. Chrissy popped up to grab Georgine's hand. 'Come on! Maybe they'll play.'

Feet working automatically, Georgine traversed the corridors in a daze. By the time they reached the studio theatre, students had helped themselves to the portable staging. Errol, probably seeing the futility of trying to stop them, was directing operations to make risers and decks into a small stage. Students milled across the floor, exclaiming and laughing. Chrissy plunged in to join them.

As events director, Georgine ought to be doing the same. Assuming a role.

Instead, she drifted to the open tiers of seating and took up station at the back. From there, she was able to watch the members of The Hungry Years arrive, Oggie making a path for them up to the stage where Errol and Hannalee were hastily hooking up mics and stands.

The drum kit was ferried from its rehearsal position at the side of the room and hoisted onto the stage by willing hands. Guitars and a bass were offered up to laughing band members. Billy, grinning, said something to Oggie, who shrugged and turned to Joe. Joe, looking both bemused and amused, lifted his hands in an 'I don't know' gesture.

Billy moved up to the mic. 'Do you wanna coupla songs?'

All the air in the room seemed to disappear as eighty-odd students took in enough breath to yell, 'YEAHHHHHHHH!'

Billy grinned. 'JJ's not sure—'

'YEAHHHHHHHH!'

A little more conferring to background shouts of, 'C'mon, JJ, do it!' and, 'We love you, Hungries!' Then Joe nodded, shucked off his sweatshirt, leaving a T-shirt beneath, and picked up the drumsticks to a roar of applause.

The one with glasses, Liam, took a mic stand over to the drums and angled it down for Joe.

Whistles and shouts rose to fever pitch, almost drowning out the experimental strumming from Liam and Nathan on guitars, Raf on bass. Billy held on to a mic stand as if staking his claim at the front of the band.

Then, as if they were a few teenagers getting together to jam in someone's garage, the band members nodded at one another. Joe flexed his shoulders, lifted both sticks and brought them down into a *chadda-chadda-chadda-boom*, and the guitars *kerranged* into vibrant, noisy life, Billy shifting from foot to foot until it was time for him to come in.

Georgine felt like a tiny island on the horizon of a sea of people as the explosion of noise hit her like a physical force. She watched the man she'd slept with last night drumming with a major band. He looked radiant. His whole body moved in time with his flying sticks and he sang without, literally, missing a beat. This was why Chrissy had been able to see Joe in Germany without him being aware. He'd been on stage. Not a roadie or a tech. Up there, with an audience going wild.

Students held up swaying phones, intent on their cameras catching the moment. Georgine was the only one who seemed immune to the excitement. Alone, standing on a seat in the back row, wanting Joe to see her above the craziness. Could he meet her eye?

But Joe was doing his thing. He looked alive. At home. When they moved into another song, he sang the lead. It was a song she knew: 'Why is Winter so Cold?' A student band had covered it last year. The fact she'd liked the song seemed to mock her. She'd listened to the original on her phone without the least idea that the voice of the vocalist belonged to the boy she'd known as Rich Garrit.

Joe Blackthorn the man.

And now JJ Blacker the rock star.

Just how many times was she going to find out he wasn't who she thought he was?

That he'd been hiding something?

She understood him not wanting to dwell on his past and wanting people to know him as he was rather than as he had been – but being a famous drummer in a famous band? No. She didn't get why he'd hide that, and it made her feel as if the memories of last night were laughing at her. *He only made his move on you when you couldn't see and recognise his tattoo – get it now? Being hidden is his natural preference.*

She felt stupidly let down.

Slowly, she climbed from the seat, trailed to the end of the row and trudged down the steps to floor level. She skirted the bouncing, whistling, joyous students and let herself out of the studio theatre, leaving the noise behind. She detoured to the cafeteria to find hers and Joe's laptops still abandoned on the table, then sought the sanctuary of her own room.

There, she stared at her computer screen, trying to summon one of the hundreds of jobs she knew to be waiting. She couldn't think. The cogs of her brain felt as if they were turning through treacle.

She shifted her cursor over an app at random. Twitter. OK. She'd schedule tweets. Trying to come up with a dozen different ways to say 'buy a ticket for our show!' without seeming to say it, that was a job.

Instead, she found herself googling 'JJ Blacker' again; scrolling through image after image of him. Moody poses where his tattoo figured boldly. Candid shots of him frowning in concentration, singing, laughing, grinning. On stage, he truly did wear guyliner and mascara, as he'd once told her – and she'd laughed. It had seemed so unlike the Joe Blackthorn she thought she'd known.

People bothered snapping him doing his grocery shopping or asked him for selfies. She read interviews with him, about his life with The Hungry Years.

He never said a thing about an underprivileged childhood or Acting Instrumental.

He could really compartmentalise.

Chapter Twenty-Six

Joe felt as if he were surfing a giant, glittering wave of emotion, and something was making him reluctant to jump off the surfboard.

Being on stage with the guys again – even a thrown-together, tiny, portable stage for a thrown-together, tiny gig with the bass too loud – felt so right. It warmed him deep inside that they'd come to show him how much they wanted him. Even Billy.

They'd ended on a bit of a Q&A for the students, fielding serious questions about the music industry with a fair sprinkling of, 'Will you sign my guitar?' or, 'How did you get so awesome?' He'd attracted a lot of questions about what he was doing at Acting Instrumental, to which he'd put his finger to his lips and said, 'I'm relying on you guys to keep it quiet,' realising belatedly that there was no chance.

His euphoria had dimmed.

Word getting out – he didn't want to think about that right now. Instead he responded to a call to 'show us your tatt!' by laughing, 'You don't want me to lose my DBS, do you?'

276

When three o'clock arrived, Oggie cleared the room. Many students had buses or lifts to catch. Chrissy ran up to give him a hug with a quick, 'Polo's waiting for me outside. You have my contact details so I hope I can introduce my family to you before I go home to Germany. It's up to you.'

He felt a swirl of regret. 'I'll be in touch. I wish we could have spent more time together.' The band turning up had messed with his reunion with Chrissy as well as with his head.

'Wouldn't have missed meeting the rest of the band,' she cried, giving him another hug before dashing out of the door.

Several tutors – not Georgine, he'd caught her leaving partway through the second song – hung on long enough to be able to say they'd talked to the band, then Oggie sent them on their way too and locked the door. The band and Oggie perched on the edge of the stage to chat while they gave the building a chance to clear.

The mood was upbeat. The guys seemed enthused about Acting Instrumental, comparing it to to their more mainstream college they'd left in 2005. When they talked about doing a benefit gig Joe put in, 'That would be best directed towards the community courses in the holidays. I've already wondered about making transport available to bring kids here from Bettsbrough for those.' Then he left it to Oggie to explain the intricacies of funding.

Joe was able to sit back, to wonder where he'd have to go to track Georgine down. He wasn't stupid. He'd read her expression.

Pissed-off woman.

He sure as hell wished he'd told her about JJ Blacker.

*

277

It was well after five when he finally saw the guys into the car that had been waiting in the car park all afternoon. One last wave and he turned to hurry in to Georgine's room. When he stepped into the room and shut the door she was sitting at her computer, face pale and green eyes enormous.

She was waiting for him to show up, judging from how promptly she closed her laptop and met his gaze. 'I want to make it clear how little I appreciate your constant dissembling,' she began. 'It's not just once you've hidden an identity from me, but twice. I understand you have trust issues, and why, but it makes me uncomfortable. Even insulted.'

He didn't make the mistake of moving into her personal space but sat down across the table. 'It wasn't that I didn't trust you. Being Joe Blackthorn . . . you've no idea how healing it's been. And to be here. When I came, I'd had a big bust-up with the band that knocked me for six.'

She stowed her laptop in her bag and zipped it. 'You're the only one in the band to use a stage name, aren't you?'

'Yes, but don't read too much into it. Originally I became JJ Blacker because I didn't want to be perceived as hanging on the coattails of my uncle. Then, as we began to find success it was also so Garrit wouldn't know I was making money.'

She pulled her scarf from the back of her chair and wound it around her neck. 'Would you have ever told me?'

'I nearly did tell you a couple of times.'

'But?' She picked up her coat.

'But –' he tried to remember '– but I just liked being with you as me.'

'Which you?' She slid her arms into her coat.

Joe felt a sudden surge of irritation at the unsmiling way she was questioning him, all the while getting ready to leave as if this wasn't important enough to command her entire concentration. 'They're *all* me, Georgine! That's the trouble.' He yanked off his sweatshirt and T-shirt in one movement, turning his left shoulder so she couldn't help but see his tattoo. 'See this? It's all my faces. My identities. Bewildering, isn't it? That's what it's like being me. All I wanted was to be Joe for a while.'

She nodded slowly, studying the tattoo, mind almost visibly working. Finally, she raised her eyes to his. '*For a while*. A while that'll soon be over. The students are sharing pictures from this afternoon all over Instagram and Snapchat already. We'll have the press at the gates and you and Oggie will agree that it's best for Acting Instrumental if you return to your real life.' She smiled without warmth. 'Conservative as it sounds, I'm really not your brief-fling type. You've got a hell of a career. I'm sincerely proud of you and what you've achieved but there's no place in your life – lives – for me. Let's just let this thing between us fade away.'

She zipped her coat, swung her bag onto her back and brushed past him.

He wished he'd said 'now' instead of 'for a while'. 'For a while' told her he was keeping his options open. He wanted to go after her and assure her he was sticking around, that he was worth investing emotions in.

But his feet stuck to the floor. He couldn't, because he didn't know.

He'd loved it here, taking a breather from the craziness of tours and song-writing and studio time, away from the relationship with Billy that had hit a patch so toxic it affected the whole band. But things had just changed. He'd

279

felt part of it again up there, playing, the kids bouncing. Live performance really had it.

Yes, he wanted Georgine too! Somehow, he'd have to make her see that. He'd have to show her that just because the parts of his life were pretty separate at this moment, that didn't mean they had to continue to be.

Chapter Twenty-Seven

To hell with Instagram, forget Snapchat, yesterday's music-euphoria notwithstanding, Joe turned up at Acting Instrumental on Tuesday morning.

By the time Georgine arrived he was already taking a call from Ian at the Raised Curtain about the get-in on Saturday. 'Will your resident tech come in to do a handover? Or will they be happy for me and the crew to find our way around?' Joe asked, trying to ground himself in *A Very Kerry Christmas*. From the corner of his eye he saw Georgine enter the room and hesitate. He put his hand over the phone and murmured, 'Morning.'

After an instant she muttered, 'Morning,' and shucked off her coat.

In Joe's ear Ian said, 'That's why I'm ringing. Yvette, our technician, thinks a familiarisation session is essential but she doesn't work on Saturdays.'

Joe watched Georgine leafing through the production file with a frown of concentration. 'I think I can bring the crew down. Hang on.' He covered the mouthpiece again.

'How do I get permission to take the tech crew down to the theatre for a familiarisation session?'

She didn't look up. 'Talk to Oggie. You'll need someone else with you because there are too many for one car, and you'll have to do a trip-planning risk assessment first.'

'How about this afternoon?' Ian asked down the phone. 'Sorry for the short notice but Yvette's been flat out with our productions and she's struggling to find a window.'

'I'll find out whether the theatre-tech students are already tied up this afternoon and get back to you ASAP.' Joe was only giving about twenty per cent of his attention to Ian. The rest was all on Georgine, noting the small lines of tension, the set lips, the unwillingness to meet his gaze.

When he'd ended the call, he leant his forearms on the table. 'The atmosphere in here's colder than outside. Don't let's be like this, Georgine.'

With a meaningful look at the doorway, which he took as a reminder that they could be overheard, she shrugged. 'Don't worry. After the impromptu The Hungry Years appearance yesterday, you won't be here much longer.'

Stung, he rose. 'I don't see any press storming the gates.'

She turned a page of the production file. 'Give it time. And it's not just the press. The students are agog at having a real, live rock star among us. You're going to find it hard to do the job you're supposedly here to do. In fact –' she gave a little sigh '– we all are.'

The exchange set the tone for the morning: wintry. Joe moved on with arranging the trip to the Raised Curtain and every time he called into Georgine's room he found she wasn't in it, though her timetable said planning and admin this morning. It created a weight in his stomach.

However, he wasn't here to worry about his love life, or its hitches. Oggie offered to be the other car driver for the afternoon visit to the theatre and it only remained for Joe to free up the students in question from their planned activities.

Unfortunately, whenever he appeared in the corridors or stuck his head into practice rooms he couldn't help but be aware of a buzz and it wasn't just because he'd abandoned his glasses, there now being no point to wearing them for the purposes of disguise. He was no stranger to the attention but it felt odd here, at Acting Instrumental. He set his sights on carrying on exactly as before and hoped the students would soon get over it.

At lunchtime he sat with a singing tutor, Vix, who he hadn't had much to do with as her work lay largely with Level 1 and 2 students, but she was certainly prepared to make up for lost time now. 'I can't believe I didn't recognise you! I love The Hungry Years. When's your next album out?'

As she hadn't bothered to keep her voice down, a host of students from nearby tables jumped up and crowded round to hear the answer. Joe, who'd been looking forward to the gammon with spicy wedges on his plate, smiled. 'I'm Joe Blackthorn here. And Joe has only just got enough time to wolf this lot down before he has to gather up the tech crew and get to the theatre.' To add emphasis, he took his first mouthful and gave the students a little wave goodbye.

Although they moved back it wasn't long before the first piece of paper landed beside him. 'But do you mind giving me an autograph?' a slight, dark-haired girl demanded. 'You can do it while you're chewing,' she added helpfully.

Joe glanced at her hopeful face from the corner of his eye. Others were gathering behind her. One autograph would lead to dozens, then someone would ask for a selfie. He glanced at Vix, hoping she'd jump in and shoo everyone away, but Vix was looking through her bag as if she was searching for paper and a pen too.

Then a voice came from behind Joe. Georgine's. 'Let's leave Joe to eat his lunch, shall we? He'd need permission from Oggie to sign autographs anyway, and put your phones away because nobody's said it's OK to take photos. Off you go!'

Grateful, Joe turned in his seat to thank her, but Georgine was vanishing along with the disconsolately dispersing students. Though he liked her back view, he wasn't keen on it being turned on him.

After lunch he took three members of the crew in his car, Robby, Guy and Tristan. They were boiling over with questions about The Hungry Years but, 'I'm not here in that capacity,' he said firmly, and that quieted them down so much that he stowed the phrase for future use.

But not all that far in the future, because when he got to the theatre he found that one of the girls from Oggie's car had told the technician, Yvette, who instantly turned more starry eyed than seemed appropriate for her forty-plus years. 'JJ Blacker's *here*? Must get a selfie!' She fumbled her phone out of her pocket.

The students all looked hopeful, hands moving as if preparing to pull their phones out too.

'I'm not here in that capacity,' Joe all but shouted.

'Not appropriate,' Oggie snapped at the same time, sounding as sharp as Joe had ever heard him.

Yvette shot off a couple of shots of Joe anyway, and Oggie took her aside for a private conversation. Joe was incredibly embarrassed to see her get her phone out again and delete the photos like a sulky kid. The students giggled. A few Sir John Browne Academy students loitered, recognisable by their black sweatshirts, grinning as they listened in. Joe turned his back in case they caught on to what was happening and whipped out their phones too.

It wasn't an auspicious beginning, though Yvette soon bounced back, taking every opportunity to brush against Joe as she gave him a tour of the box. Oggie stayed close, and at least she didn't get her phone out again.

After a thorough, if awkward, familiarisation with the sound and lighting decks, Joe and Oggie got the crew back to Acting Instrumental for three o'clock, relief and anxiety warring in Joe. Oggie was frowning. Without being asked, he followed Oggie to his room and shut the door.

'That was unexpectedly tricky,' he admitted wearily, to save Oggie the bother.

'Indeed.' Oggie's frown hadn't disappeared. 'I didn't appreciate quite what a genie was being let out of its bottle when your friends showed up yesterday.'

'Possibilities dawned on me, but I didn't realise it would be quite like this.'

They talked about the situation for a few more minutes. Oggie was reticent about where they went from here, saying he needed time to think.

Joe left him, more conflicted than he'd been at any point in the past five weeks. The rift in the band looked on its way to being healed.

But he'd apparently paid a price.

Had they shown up without notice hoping that exactly this would happen? He didn't think so, but he couldn't deny that if his position here was made untenable then there would be one less thing preventing him from returning to the band.

Not one to give up easily though, he headed to Georgine's room to report on events at the Raised Curtain. Just as he reached the doorway, he realised she was speaking on the phone. When he heard her say 'Aidan', his feet paused mid-step.

'I'm glad you've got another job and the debt charity was useful,' she continued. 'But I haven't rung to get on your case. I just want you to know that I've had a wind-fall and cleared the arrears with the household bills.' She paused, presumably letting Aidan reply.

When she spoke again her voice was full of outrage. 'It's none of your business how much! If I do have any left over it's going on a car or a holiday, not to help you out.'

Joe shouldn't be eavesdropping on a conversation between Georgine and her ex-boyfriend about money. He turned and walked silently away. He'd award himself an early finish and spend a bit of one-on-one time with his laptop – his own MacBook Pro rather than the heap Acting Instrumental loaned him – mulling over The Hungry Years' schedule next year.

He'd promised them a decision after Christmas, and that was only two weeks away.

Chapter Twenty-Eight

The next day, Wednesday, catapulted Joe straight into hell.

It wasn't even eight thirty when his phone buzzed and *Pete the Beat* showed on the screen. About to leave his apartment, he answered the call with one hand while opening his front door with the other. 'Can I ring you back, Pete? On my way to work.'

'You might want to hold on.' Pete sounded grave. 'The *Daily Snoop* has done a piece on you and you're not going to like it.'

Blood turning slowly to ice, Joe closed his front door. 'What?'

Pete sighed gustily. 'Best you read it for yourself. I've emailed you the link to the online version.'

It took only moments for Joe to drop down on the sofa and wake up his MacBook Pro, open Pete's email and click.

CINDER-ROCKER – Punk-star victim of 'wicked' step-father in sink-estate childhood, roared the headline, bigger and bolder than that of the snowmageddon the paper was predicting for the UK next week. Joe's stomach plummeted into his boots as he read the words that sat alongside a picture of him sweating over a drum kit, sticks a blur.

Drummer JJ Blacker, of pop-punk band sensation The Hungry Years, *spent most of his young life in the care of an alcoholic mother and her 'aggressive' partner, the* Daily Snoop *can reveal.*

In a shocking exposé, a source close to the tattooed drummer tells of the true extent of abuse dealt out to Blacker by Deborah Leonard, 56, and her single-named partner, Garrit, 58, on the Shetland estate in Bettsbrough, Cambridgeshire.

'Garrit was a nasty piece of work,' says the source. 'The whole family was scared of him and he and JJ's mum drank whatever money they got. Schoolmates gave JJ the nickname "Rich" as a joke because he was brought up so poor.'

JJ – real name John Joseph Blackthorn, aka Johnjoe or "Rich" Garrit – was rescued by his music-producer uncle, Shaun Blackthorn, 58, in December 1998. Full story pages 6&7.

Hands shaking, Joe clicked the link to take him to the more in-depth piece, eyes flicking over a selection of picture-library shots of him on stage, at awards evenings or out shopping.

Almost too shocked to take it all in he read every painful detail about *Timothy Blackthorn, JJ's natural father* hiding his toddler son from the affluent Blackthorn family and that *Timothy drowned, swept out to sea in the strong currents off England's east coast. A post-mortem showed Timothy to have had almost three times the recommended level of alcohol in his blood.*

'The source' was quoted liberally, talking about hunger and deprivation; that *Deborah and Garrit bothered more about where their next can of lager would come from than ensuring JJ, along with Garrit's daughter from a previous relationship, Chrissy, had food.*

The piece seemed to go on and on, a lurid portrait of Rich Garrit that made Joe shiver, though he still wore his coat. Everything he'd least wanted in the public domain was there. He felt invaded. Exposed. Dirtied.

The final blow was struck by a paragraph about Joe's current whereabouts at Acting Instrumental, *a further education college for the performing arts in which he has a philanthropic interest. Young people attend this college, the premises of which JJ owns on the outskirts of Middledip village in Cambridgeshire, a few miles from the Shetland estate where, according to our source, he grew up a member of a gang where crime was the norm.*

'Oh, shit,' Joe breathed, dumping the computer on the sofa. He rubbed his hand over his face, brain racing. Who'd talked? He stared at the wall, forgetting all about Acting Instrumental and the scheduled complete run-through of *A Very Kerry Christmas*.

Finally, heavily, he rang Pete back. 'This is shit. Do you know where it came from?' His phone began to buzz with incoming messages and the beep-beep of a call waiting sounded in his ear.

'No idea, mate.' Pete sounded sympathetic. 'I suppose you can get Jerome onto it but although it's sensational-ised—'

'It's fundamentally true,' Joe finished, feeling sick.

Pete cleared his throat. 'The journalist's emailed me. He's asking if you'll give your side of the story.'

'Tell him to fuck himself.'

'I think a firm "no" is sufficient.'

Joe managed a hoarse laugh. 'And ask him what shit-eating lowlife gave him the story.'

'And we'll get a firm "no" in return,' Pete replied. He hesitated. 'You've no idea?'

'I suppose there are quite a few people it could be, but they're mainly close to me, which makes it doubly shitty.' Joe groaned, closing his eyes and letting his head flop back. The phone continued to buzz alerts intermittently. He'd get to the messages later. He let his mind run for a few seconds.

'Billy keeps coming into my head,' Pete said tentatively. 'But, no, we can't think that!' And, as if trying to convince himself, 'Can we?'

Joe groaned. 'I'm trying not to.' His heart sank like a stone.

'Until the past few weeks it wouldn't even have crossed my mind, but his last little stunt was about money. Tabloids sometimes pay for stories like this.' Pete let the thought hang in the air, then sighed gustily. 'I'm not sure how you'll find out. Anybody –' he paused, as if to say *naming no names* '– you challenge is unlikely to admit it.'

'Yeah.' Joe said goodbye and disconnected. He scrolled through the notifications on his phone screen. Raf, Nathan, Liam and Billy – but he'd have to get in touch, even if it was him, wouldn't he? – had all texted *Have you seen???* type messages, as had Chrissy.

Raf, Liam, Chrissy and Georgine had all tried to call him. With the sensation of sticking a pin in a list, he returned the call to Georgine.

'You OK?' she asked quickly. Like Pete, she sounded apprehensive.

'You've seen it then?' he asked wearily.

She hesitated. 'Seen what?'

'The reason I might not be OK.'

'Is this a new game? Random answers to reasonable questions?' She sounded puzzled.

He took a deep breath, realising people might want to talk about topics other than what had just happened to him. 'Sorry. Can I help you with something?'

Another pause. 'Wellllll . . . it's nine twenty and the run-through starts at ten o'clock. I appreciate you're not exactly contracted staff, but if you're not able to make it I need to get someone else to give everyone their calls when they're due on.'

Abruptly, the day he'd expected before reading the horrible newspaper article came into focus. 'Shit. I'm sorry. I'll be there by nine forty-five latest. I've got to make a call first.'

'Whenever you're ready,' she said briefly.

He could imagine her immediately turning her attention to the job at hand, preparing to find alternatives if he didn't turn up after all.

Quickly, he returned Chrissy's call.

'There's this article about you—' She sounded flustered.

'I've read it,' he cut in. 'Bastards. No idea where the story's come from, but sorry your name was dragged in.'

He heard her blow out a big, shaky breath. 'It was really freaky. Someone from my year at school put it on Facebook and tagged me. Everyone's going bonkers in the comments section, asking me if it's true that you're JJ Blacker.'

'Just ignore it,' he said quickly. 'Log out of Facebook till it's forgotten. Then even if some journalist tracks down the Facebook thread they won't be able to reach out to you.' He rubbed his hand over his head as if to encourage his brain to work under his unaccustomed soft, conservative hairstyle, then tacked on, 'Unless you *want* to reply to the comments or talk to the press, I suppose.'

Chrissy sounded shocked. 'I thought you wouldn't want me to.'

'I absolutely, totally don't,' he said frankly. 'I've never talked about the bad stuff for fear of exactly this sensationalism.'

She laughed. 'I won't talk, Johnjoe. I remember who was on my side when Dad and Debs were as they were; and who got me food when my belly was empty. We come from the same boat. I wouldn't do anything to screw you over. Ever.'

For a moment his eyes burned with the poignancy of the shared memory of rock bottom. 'Thanks, Chrissy.'

He rang off and, glancing at his watch and despite promising Georgine he'd make only one call, made another as he got up to leave. 'Mari?' he said, when his mother's companion picked up. 'Have you or Mum been approached by anyone?'

Mari sounded as confused as Georgine had. 'Anyone?'

'You haven't seen the article about me today?' He let himself out of the outside door and began to jog down the steps to ground level in freezing rain, debating how much to say. It wasn't absolutely beyond his wildest imaginings that Debs had succumbed to a journalist's chequebook if the craving for alcohol had gripped her strongly enough. But then, she'd had years to do that, and hadn't. And she'd appear in the article in a much better light if she had.

Quickly, he filled Mari in, rounding the jut of the big rehearsal room and heading directly for the studio theatre. 'I suppose Mum might want to read it for herself, but try to keep her calm if she does, because she doesn't come out of it well. Actually . . .' He paused outside the door, huddling into his coat. 'You'd better put Mum on and I'll speak to her myself.'

It took him several more minutes to brief his mother, asking her not to get involved, whatever the temptation. 'It's not what I wanted, and the story's really sensational-ised. What the journo didn't know, he's made up,' he said, which wasn't true but he didn't want Debs getting upset or defensive about the past. Things were bad enough without something sending her off on a bender.

By the time he'd finished reassuring her and trying to find ways to suggest she didn't read the article, he was outside the studio theatre, it was nine forty-six and he was late. 'Got to go, Mum. Ping me a text if you want to talk later, but best thing is just to ignore the whole thing. Particularly any approaches from journalists,' he added. Then he ended the call and went inside, already saying a breathless, 'Sorry!' to Georgine and 'Sorry, sorry!' to every-body, throwing his coat off and grabbing up Georgine's production file because he'd completely forgotten his own. He knew she kept a spare running order in the back . . . yep, there it was. He was all set.

Georgine was looking at him as if he was slightly mad, but that he could cope with.

Many of the students were staring at him too but whether that was because of The Hungry Years or because they'd read the *Daily Snoop*, he neither knew nor cared. At this second, submerging himself in his role at Acting Instrumental was all he wanted in the world. Something to make him feel normal.

Georgine tried to ignore how weirdly Joe was behaving. She hadn't ever known him to be late, or seen him look so spaced out.

She followed him as he made his way to the other side of the studio theatre staring at the running order as if he'd never seen it before. Errol, Keeley and Maddie were casting him puzzled glances too as they checked the positioning of the props for the first set, the opulent lounge of Uncle Jones signified by the lavish Christmas tree and a side table with a big, shiny lamp. Joe jumped and swung around when Georgine laid a hand on his arm.

'Sorry.' She ushered him a few steps away from the three extended rows of seating, where all the students were waiting to get underway. 'Are you sure you're OK to work today?' She even checked that the size of his pupils was normal, as, though it would seem out of character so far as he was concerned, drug use wasn't unheard of in the music industry.

He gave what she assumed was meant to be a reassuring smile, though it was a bit . . . haunted. 'Something's happened, but I'll get over it.'

'Do you need anything?'

'Nope. Ready to roll.' He frowned down at the paperwork in his hand.

Georgine could only wonder what was engraving the lines at the bridge of his nose. She turned away to take up station in the middle of the room and fix her mind on the job at hand. 'OK everybody! Are you ready?'

She grinned at the cheers and calls of 'Go for it!', letting the energy in the room tingle within her.

'As you all know, the aim's to run straight through, except for an extended lunch interval. Scene one, act one should take around twenty minutes, scene two half an hour, and scene three fifteen minutes. Bear with our lovely Level 2 student scene shifters as this is their first real opportunity to rehearse. Fern –' she flashed a smile at

Fern, who was clutching her script as if frightened it would run off '– will be prompting us if we need it. Joe will be supervising light and sound once we move into the Raised Curtain, but today he's acting as backstage manager, making sure everyone's where they should be and when. We're not stopping or doing over, so if something goes awry just make the best of it. We'll learn from today, ready for Monday's dress rehearsal. Any questions? No? Then let's go!'

Joe called out, 'Band One and Band Two, to the music stage, please. Troupe One, off stage left; Troupe Two off stage right, upstage. Kerry Christmas and Uncle Jones off stage left; Auntie Jones, Mum, Dad and Casper Christmas, off stage right, downstage.'

As one, the students got to their feet, taking up positions, picking up instruments. Then silence. Georgine felt an unexpected lump in her throat at all the pairs of eyes trained intently on her. Swallowing, she lifted her voice. 'Whenever you're ready, Musical Director.'

Errol turned to the band. 'Ready? Everybody? Yes? Here we go!' In the air he beat out *one-two-three*. On *four*, the upbeat, drumsticks lifted, the drums and bass came in *dadda dadda* for *five-six* for the introduction to 'Everybody Loves Uncle Jones'. Troupe One hip-hopped onto the stage at the beginning of the third bar as they sang: *We love you, we love you, Uncle Jones, it's true*. Troupe Two came on high stepping, *It's true, we all do*.

Georgine became instantly absorbed. She didn't want to miss a moment, but she clutched a pad and pen to record timings and note any issues. A few nerves showed in a shaky step here, a warbled note there. Uncle Jones dropped his plastic beaker, which would be a brandy balloon of cold tea on performance nights, but he finished his solo lines before casually retrieving it. She gave Trent a smile and an approving nod.

Though her attention was on the stage, a movement caught the corner of her eye. She glanced over to see Joe scowling fiercely at his phone, doing something to it and stuffing it roughly back into his pocket. Then he refocused on the students, his head moving slightly to the beat.

Scene one, act one whizzed by energetically, full of faces shining at the prospect of an extended family Christmas, and ended with enthusiastic applause from everyone not currently on stage. The scene change took at least twice as long as hoped, but that was OK, they had a spare three quarters of an hour at the end of act one before lunch. In this scene, Kerry Christmas watched through her mock TV as the gangster scene took place stage left. The Christmas tree had to vanish and covering it with a black cloth like a budgie in its cage didn't work well, so the whole tree had to be carried off, shedding baubles. *Check if the Raised Curtain has a screen to lend us*, she wrote on her pad. If not, she'd have to find time to adapt something. Much easier just to shove a screen in front of the tree.

She settled down to enjoy the much quieter scene two, carried by Kerry Christmas, Uncle Jones and his gang, who, on performance nights, would be dressed in black suits and trilbies, just in case the audience was in doubt that these were gangsters achieving wealth by stealth.

Scenes two and three went fairly smoothly, though the Christmas tree proved just as awkward to move on as it had to move off.

Finally, it was time to applaud the end of the first act. 'Well done, everybody! That was *awesome*,' Georgine called, adding a few whoops for good measure. 'I think that went brilliantly, don't you? We've earned a nice long break. We overran by ten minutes but each scene change took ten minutes instead of five. We've got Saturday and Sunday to refine scene shifting—'

To her surprise, Oggie walked in and uncharacteristically ignoring the fact that Georgine was speaking, headed straight for Joe and whispered something in his ear.

Horror swept over Joe's face, and he and Oggie, looking neither left nor right, marched across the studio and out of the doors.

'Oh-kay.' Georgine scrabbled to re-establish her train of thought. 'Why don't you guys tell us how you think it went?' This meant all she had to do was nod and make notes while others fed back. It left spare mental capacity for her to wonder what the hell was going on with Joe this time.

She wasn't left wondering for long. While all connected with *A Very Kerry Christmas* had been closeted in the studio theatre, the rest of the college had been set abuzz. Students arrived in the cafeteria whispering, checking phones and making exaggeratedly agog faces. Georgine frowned as she tried to listen in. It was definitely something to do with Joe. Surely these eddies of excitement weren't still over the members of The Hungry Years turning up on Monday and outing him as JJ Blacker? Her heart gave an uncomfortable thump at the unhappy memory of the chasm it had opened between her and Joe on the very day they'd woken in the same bed.

Avril and Vix had their heads together over a phone, so Georgine made a beeline for their table without even pausing to collect her lunch. Disregarding good manners, she craned to read over their shoulders. Phrases such as *victim of neglect* and *hunger and deprivation*, then *member of a gang* jumped out at her. And *JJ Blacker*.

'Oh, no,' she breathed, plucking the phone from Avril's

grasp and scrolling furiously back to the beginning of the article.

'Help yourself, don't mind us,' Vix said, exchanging arched-eyebrow looks with Avril.

Through numb lips Georgine muttered, 'Sorry.'

As she read in horrified silence, Avril said more sympathetically, 'It's awful, isn't it? Talk about from rags to riches. Poor Joe.'

'Or rich Joe,' put in Vix. 'Or even Rich Joe.' She drew a capital R in the air. 'Did you get the bit that said he owns these premises?'

Numbly, Georgine passed the phone back. Repelled by the nudging and gossiping that was going on everywhere she looked, she bought a large coffee and an omelette and retired to the currently empty studio theatre to search out the article on her own phone and read it all again. Knowing of his desire to put the past behind him, she could only imagine how Joe must be feeling

Errol, Keeley and Maddie returned ahead of the students, all obviously discussing the article that had exposed Joe's past to the world. 'Poor guy,' Maddie said, shaking her head. Keeley sighed.

Errol looked grave. 'But when the police have to get involved it can't look good for Acting Instrumental.'

'The *police*?' Georgine scrambled to her feet, catching her plate so it spun round and tipped her remaining half omelette onto the floor.

The students began to trickle back in as Errol muttered, 'Journalists wanting to come into our grounds, apparently. Not easily dissuaded until a patrol car hove into view.'

Then Fern came in and handed Georgine Joe's runthrough. 'Oggie says to tell you no Joe this afternoon.' Her thin eyebrows waggled up to her hairline.

'Right.' Georgine took the sheets of paper. The level of noise was rising with every student who arrived. She glanced around and saw the tutors had their heads together too, probably discussing what Joe's landlord status might mean for the college, and anger bubbled up inside her.

Impulsively, she marched into the middle of the room and clapped her hands like a school marm. '*Right*!' she called. 'Phones away, please, and let's concentrate—' She was about to say 'on the show' but somehow, 'On our own business!' came out of her mouth instead.

Surprised looks flashed around the room while she waited with folded arms and her deepest frown for phones to be stowed. 'Well done,' she said, as if the students were in infant school. Then she remembered herself and collected her manners from wherever she seemed to have left them. She consulted the running order. 'Band Two on the music stage, please. Kerry Christmas, off stage left. Uncle Jones and gang, off stage right. We don't have the luxury of correct lighting today so we'll have to imagine the lights going down to show the audience that it's late at night. Musical Director, bring the band in, please.'

And the opportunity for gossip was lost, at least for the moment, as they plunged back into the show.

At the end of the afternoon the run-through was declared a success. The students went home beaming; Georgine worked through her notes with Errol, Maddie and Keeley.

At five thirty Acting Instrumental was quiet apart from cleaning staff somewhere nearby. She gathered up her things and broached a winter evening that sparkled with frost beneath the campus lights. She threw her bag in her car, then stood at the open door in thought. A prickly, unsettled feeling had plagued her all afternoon, the kind that comes with the knowledge of a wrong.

She glanced at the gates from which, apparently, the police had moved journalists. Quiet and calm.

She took out her phone. No messages. Though she'd been advised by Fern that Joe wouldn't be around for act two, if someone was reporting to Georgine she had a right to expect direct communication. Matters were complicated, however, by Joe being a volunteer, as well as his owning the very ground she stood upon. And because they'd been to bed together.

She weighed the phone in her hand.

A voice came across the freezing air. 'Everything all right?'

Georgine turned to find Don, the site supervisor, regarding her quizzically, hair and moustache as silver as the frost. 'I'm fine.' She closed the car door. 'Just deciding what to do.'

'Too much to think of at this time of the year.' Don began to move off. 'Me and the missus bought tickets for the Christmas show. Tuesday, I think it is.'

Automatically, Georgine thanked him for his support. 'The students have been working really hard so I'm sure you'll enjoy it.'

Don waved as he headed for the main building, his breath a cloud in the air.

Making up her mind, Georgine put away her phone and turned on her heel. When she left the tarmac the grass felt crisp beneath her feet and, carefully mounting the ungritted steps, she was soon standing at the outer door to the upstairs apartments, pressing the button on the entry system. A beeping acknowledged her action. The sound stopped, but nobody spoke via the intercom.

Did that mean Joe was home but choosing not to respond? She took an uncertain step back. But then the door opened and Joe stood in the light, pale and solemn, and she realised she hadn't rehearsed what to say.

For several seconds they gazed at each other. Then Joe stood back to let her down the corridor to his apartment.

It was much warmer indoors, but Georgine didn't feel welcome enough to take off her coat. Joe waited silently for her to speak, his hands stuffed in his pockets. She cleared her throat. 'I just came to check . . .' She found she wasn't sure what she came to check on, but her words seemed sufficient to relax his expression slightly.

He beckoned her through into the sitting area, throwing himself on the sofa. Reluctant to get too close, Georgine perched on the edge of a chair, unzipping her coat but still not taking it off. 'I saw the article. It's horrible. Exactly what you didn't want.'

His bitter laugh suggested she didn't know the half of it. 'Yeah. Your prediction about the press at the gates came true.'

'But I'm sorry it did.' She glanced at a pad and pen lying on the coffee table.

He leant forward and snatched up the pad. 'I was writing a list. I can't get over the thought that the story must've been leaked by someone who knows me well.'

'Oh! How the story got to be in the *Daily Snoop* hadn't even occurred to me.'

He gave her a sardonic look. 'You can't be betrayed by someone who doesn't know the story, can you? I thought that it might be Billy, our lead singer. He might have done it for the money because he has a certain lifestyle to uphold. Or for revenge because we fell out. Or for publicity for The Hungry Years that doesn't hurt him. But we've been together since college. I just can't believe he'd do it, and we've talked through our difficulties, he came with the rest of the band on Monday . . . Though I've still had the phone in my hand about twenty times, ready to ask him.

'Could it be Mum?' he went on. 'That doesn't fit with the content of the article. Mum's cousin who lives with her? Why would she bite the hand that feeds, or at least houses, her? Garrit doesn't know about the band, I'm pretty sure. It has to be someone who knows me past *and* present, or I'd think it was one of the students. Oggie or Chrissy? No way.' He tossed the pad back on the table. It bounced off an empty coffee cup, altering its trajectory. And it landed at Georgine's feet.

She picked it up to return it.

And that's when she saw her own name. *Georgine. Suddenly got money. Pissed with me about the band*. Stupefied, she stared at the sprawling, loopy writing. She was on his list! When she eventually lifted her gaze she saw dismay written all over his face. 'You suspect me?' she asked blankly.

His head tipped wearily. 'I don't want to but, frankly, I had to consider it. The day after you had your hands and mouth on me you cut me dead for choosing not to confide in you, without even asking my reasons.'

Stung, she tossed the pad back across the table. 'I didn't – still don't – understand why you'd hide it.'

'Because I deal with things my own way,' he snapped. 'You didn't tell me about what happened with your dad's company until it was forced on you, but I didn't take it as a personal insult.'

'But that was something I was ashamed of! It's different.'

Again, the bitter laugh. 'How come you get to set the

benchmark of what has to be shared before a couple sleep together?'

Georgine climbed to her feet. 'How come you do?'

That at least gave him pause. Surprise gleamed in his eyes. 'Fair point,' he acknowledged.

She glanced again at his pad. 'What makes you think I have money?'

'I came to speak to you yesterday and you were on the phone, telling your ex about it. I made myself scarce when I realised I was eavesdropping.'

She felt her cheeks heat up. 'My grandmother gave me some money. I've used it to pay off the bills.'

'Right.' He screwed his eyes up and rubbed them. 'Sorry.'

'No problem,' she said stiffly, and left without saying goodbye. As she all but ran to her car, she shivered, but not entirely with cold. Joe had been so bleak. And some of that unhappiness had come from disappointment in her.

She unlocked the car and jumped in, starting up the engine, letting the blowers slowly clear the frost on the windscreen. It did nothing for the chunk of ice that had settled in her gut, though.

Until now she'd been pretty confident it was Joe in the wrong for keeping from her something she saw as important. But now . . . well, he was right about one thing. She'd never asked for his reasons.

Chapter Twenty-Nine

Joe rose early on Friday, focused on Saturday's get-in at the Raised Curtain, which was going to be crazy. Today every prop, costume, instrument and lead had to be assembled ready to be driven to the theatre in the morning, or consigned to the appropriate student.

Georgine was on his mind too, and had been all night. He'd never expected her to see his list and he'd only added her name when he'd been beating up his brain to consider every possibility, no matter how unlikely. Now he was ashamed of the way he'd talked to her and couldn't stop reliving the shock and hurt he'd seen in her face.

Maybe he'd be left alone by the outside world today to pick up the threads of the peaceful existence he'd enjoyed since early November and he could apologise to Georgine. There was her car in the car park as he hurried through a wind with an arctic edge to it.

He was frustrated in his plan to head straight for her room, however, by Oggie catching him in the foyer. 'Got a minute, Joe?' He turned and headed to his room without giving Joe much chance to object.

Joe found himself tutting like a thwarted kid. 'Busy day,' he pointed out from just inside Oggie's door.

'Must be if you can't even sit down.' Oggie busied himself at his coffee machine.

Faced with playing things Oggie's way or walking out on the conversation, Joe dragged off his coat and flopped into a chair while Oggie made two cups of coffee and placed one on Joe's side of the desk.

Oggie's eyes twinkled as he took his own seat as if Joe's petulance amused him. 'So. Fill me in on your intentions.'

'Today?' Joe picked up the coffee cup and inhaled the fragrant steam.

'For the near future,' Oggie suggested.

'Today: assembling everything for the weekend's get-in, dress rehearsal and show. Weekend: get-in and tech rehearsal. Monday: dress rehearsal—'

'In short, you're going to stick it out here until the show's over. And then?'

Joe sniffed the coffee. 'I don't know,' he admitted honestly.

'OK.' Oggie warmed his hands around his coffee cup, frowning. 'Despite you being the owner of these premises, my first duty is to this educational institution, its students and staff.'

'Yeah.' Joe drank a little more coffee. It was strong with not much sugar, just as he liked it, yet it was turning to ashes on his tongue. 'Want me to leave?' He managed to sound as if it was no big deal but, inside, his stomach had turned to stone.

Oggie pursed his lips. 'I wonder if the decision will make itself?'

Joe saw the compassion in his friend's eyes and his stone stomach began to sink. Oggie was warning him.

Joe had to drink again before he could reply. 'I won't do anything to harm Acting Instrumental.' At the idea that he, who'd helped bring life to this pocket-sized further education college, might unwittingly bring it trouble dimmed his enthusiasm for the day. He rose. 'Let's see how things pan out. I'll keep as low a profile as possible. If it doesn't look as if it's working . . .' What? He wasn't sure.

Oggie gave a nod, but sweetened it with a smile. 'Thank you.'

When Joe finally reached Georgine's room, it was empty. He toured the props and costumes rooms and saw signs of recent activity in open boxes, so headed for the big rehearsal room where all was to be assembled. There he found her with a fist full of lists.

'Hey,' he said, stepping into the room, cavernous without its usual complement of students.

She regarded him warily. 'I wasn't sure if I'd see you today.' She didn't smile.

He threw his coat on a chair. 'I thought you'd appreciate another pair of hands.'

'Yes.' But she hesitated. 'On the other hand, you've already broken the back of this job by packing and labelling the boxes ready to be checked today, so if you want personal time . . .'

'I've never wanted it less. But if you don't feel you can work with me . . .'

Her eyebrow quirked. 'As if I'd be so wussy. If you could bring prop boxes one to six through, that would be great.'

'Right.' He glanced around the room just to double-check they were alone. 'After I apologise. I was out of order last night and unnecessarily rude. I don't want things to be any more difficult between us than they have to be.'

306

She regarded him levelly. 'Thank you. There's lots to do, so let's get going.'

He refused to be dismissed. 'I'm sorry you found it disconcerting not to know about The Hungry Years. In fact, perhaps if I'd been less secretive the impact of the past few days would have been less awful.' He recounted his conversation with Oggie. 'JJ Blacker's in danger of spoiling things for Joe Blackthorn, yet I'm both people.'

She smiled faintly. 'I suppose that once you've been Superman you're never a hundred per cent Clark Kent.'

He moved closer, letting his voice drop. 'Clark Kent had it easy. Everybody seemed to understand that he must have his reasons for keeping his other identity separate.' Then, before he gave in to a sudden compulsion to plead for her understanding, he left for the props room to collect boxes.

They worked steadily all morning, with students and staff helping out or popping in to collect a slip that would remind them what they'd signed up to bring in the way of instruments or clothes. There was a lot of laughter, a definite buzz, and Joe began to relax and enjoy it, especially when not a single person asked him a question about being a rock star. But then, over lunch in the noisy cafeteria, he checked his phone to find a text from his mother.

Debs: *Garrit came to the door!!! He thinks I have dosh, now he knows who you are. He says he's coming back this afternoon 'to remind me' to get money for him.* :-(

'Shit!' Joe shoved his chair back and many eyes, including Georgine's, swivelled his way. Not wanting to draw attention to yet something else going wrong he looked at her and gestured with his head in the direction of the exit. Georgine caught up with him in the corridor.

He showed her the text. 'I'm so sorry. I have to go.'

'Of course.' She frowned, not seeming to realise she was rubbing his arm comfortingly. 'How's he found her?'

'That's what I'd like to know.' He said goodbye and drove to Bettsbrough, thinking grimly just how much he didn't need a run in with Garrit after all this time.

He parked behind Whispering Court and ran lightly up the stairs, using his key and walking into the apartment, dreading finding his mother had turned to alcohol at the threat of Garrit's return. Bernie the Jack Russell flew to meet him in a volley of yaps. Behind him Debs paced the floor, white-faced, and to his relief, appearing sober.

'He came to the door!' she cried as soon as she saw Joe. 'He seemed to think he was dead funny, didn't he, Mari?' she demanded of her cousin, who was seated on the sofa. 'He – he tried to give me a bottle of vodka, but I pushed it away, didn't I, Mari?' Tears trembled on her lashes.

Mari, looking as perturbed as Debs, nodded and said, 'He did, the rat.'

Joe relaxed slightly, acknowledging how hard that must have been. 'You were strong, Mum. Did he try to come in?'

His mother shook her head wildly. 'But he kept putting one foot over the threshold and laughing as if warning me he could get in any time. Bernie was barking himself hoarse, but Mari kept hold of him in case Garrit kicked him.' A tear escaped her eye and she wiped it with the side of her hand. 'I'm frightened.'

A fist grabbed Joe's gut and twisted. He'd never hesitated to blame his mother for their situation in the bad old days. Yet, though he'd known Garrit had treated her roughly, somehow it had never dawned on him that she'd lived in fear. A tiny seed of affection blossomed inside him. 'I'm here now. Did you tell him you'd be contacting me?'

Her chin tilted. 'I didn't tell him anything except to go away.'

Hiding a smile, because he was pretty sure the term would've been more Anglo Saxon than 'go away', Joe did something he could barely remember ever doing in his life. He gave his mother a hug. He'd just registered hesitant arms closing around him in return when a loud knock sounded at the door and she sprang away. Bernie flew at the door and bounced off, thoroughly enjoying the opportunity to air his best barking crescendo, if his beating tail was any indicator.

'Is it him?' Debs whispered.

'Let's find out. Hold the dog.' Joe marched to the front door and flung it open.

And there was Garrit. Older, hair and stubble grey but unusually short and neat, the sharp features the same. No surprise flickered in his eyes when it was Joe who opened the door. Instead, he smiled the sly, malicious smile Joe remembered only too well, because it had often preceded a slap around the head. 'Johnjoe,' he murmured. 'How lovely to see you. Flying high these days, I understand.' The smile became ingratiating. 'Congratulations! When I saw that article in the paper I said to my friends, "That's my boy, that is".'

His heart galloping at being so close to the man who'd made his childhood a misery, Joe leant on the doorframe and folded his arms in case his hands flew out and administered a slap of their own. How tempting it was to demonstrate how it felt to be at the mercy of someone bigger and stronger. To be trapped against a wall, to absorb a hail of stinging blows and kicks. Held on tiptoes in a chokehold. He had vivid memories . . .

Rather than allowing himself the luxury of revenge, he went for a cold, emotionless pursuit of information. 'How did you trace my mother?'

Garrit shrugged. 'Moved back here meself a while back. Seen her around.'

Joe tried not to let any surprise show, but the news didn't make him happy. He envisaged Garrit spotting Debs in town and following her home; asking around neighbours until somebody told him the number of her apartment. It made his skin crawl.

'Going to invite me in?' Garrit suggested hopefully.

Joe kept his face impassive. 'No. Did you come here for a reason?'

Abruptly, Garrit abandoned his pretence at friendliness. 'I came for money, Mr Rock Star. You owe me for twelve years' bed and board and now you can afford to pay.'

Red mist threatened the periphery of Joe's vision. It was only the memory of how he'd hated himself for hitting Billy that kept him from flinging Garrit over the bannisters. 'Leave, or I'll call the police,' he said through his teeth. 'Don't come back. Don't come near my mother or me. You don't want to push me, Garrit, because I'm no longer the half-starved kid you used to shove around.'

Garrit sneered. 'I'm not going anywhere.'

Joe didn't even raise his voice. 'Phone the police, Mum.'

'The police won't come out to someone calling on an old friend,' Garrit said, but he sounded less sure.

Joe made his voice soft. 'I'm overjoyed that you want to find out. If you're living locally again the cops probably have a few enquiries you can help them with.'

Garrit, scowling, turned on his heel and began to saunter

310

down the stairs, though he speeded up when Joe followed him. In the foyer, Garrit slammed out of the front door so hard it bounced off the outside wall before swinging closed with an injured groan and a click.

After testing that the door had fastened, Joe ran back upstairs, adrenalin still burning its way around his body. In his mother's apartment, he found Mari making coffee while Debs watched the street in front of the building. 'He headed off towards town,' she said, glancing at Joe. 'Thanks for getting rid of him.'

'My pleasure,' Joe said, meaning it. He tried to calm himself. He didn't want Garrit to affect him this much. He was a shit, one of life's losers, and had no right to make Joe shake with rage. 'Sit down a minute, Mum. When's the last time you saw him before today?'

Debs blinked as she joined him on the sofa. 'Just before he and Chrissy took off.' Bernie galloped up, looking as if he were thoroughly enjoying the exciting afternoon, and jumped up beside Debs.

Chrissy. Joe made a mental note to call her. Warn her. 'I presume you heard him say he's living locally?'

Debs pulled Bernie onto her lap. 'He's been following me, hasn't he?'

'Sounds like it. And he appeared so quickly after I arrived that I suspect he was out there to see me come in and barged past someone coming out,' Joe agreed sombrely, watching his mother shudder before taking the cup of hot, strong tea Mari brought in.

Mari gave Joe a direct look. 'I think Debs was brave to stand up to Garrit, particularly to not take that vodka.'

'So do I.' Joe smiled at Debs. 'Very brave. Well done. That was a particularly horrible trick from him. I'll bet he was astounded that you resisted.'

Debs flushed, eyes sparkling for an instant before she dropped her gaze.

Joe's heart squeezed. He'd been focused on Debs' problems with alcohol, and how they'd affected *him*. Maybe he hadn't given her credit for the clean life she was presently living and how hard it must be. Though he'd tried to create the best environment for her, it was impossible to remove temptation from daily life. She'd travelled Sobriety Road with Mari beside her, but little in the way of emotional back-up from her son. He'd even looked cynically upon the affection she lavished on the little dog currently gazing up at her from her lap.

'We can always move you, Mum,' Joe found himself saying. 'A hotel or rental property, until we find you somewhere else permanent. There are apartments at Acting Instrumental,' he added. 'But you couldn't be there during term time because of the students and I don't know how you'd find living in a village.'

Debs was already shaking her head, although she looked pleased at his offer. 'If I leave Bettsbrough it needs to be for far away, or he'll find me. Anyway, I don't want to leave Whispering Court. We're all going out for Christmas lunch tomorrow.'

His heart squeezed some more. 'Then I'll get a camera put up on the landing so you won't ever have to answer the door without knowing who's there. I'll try to get agreement from the other residents to beef up security at the front and back doors too.' He glanced at Bernie and joked, 'Maybe you need to get a bigger dog.'

Mari joined the conversation. 'Or you should just have let this one bite him. Bernie knows how to stay out of range of a kicking foot, I'll bet.' She leant over to fondle one of Bernie's black ears.

Joe restrained himself from saying, 'You soon learn to do that around Garrit.' Debs was upset enough already.

He stayed a while, burying his emotions in practical tasks. First he located a security firm on the internet and arranged for a representative to call on Tuesday morning, December nineteenth, when Joe hoped to be around before the opening of *A Very Kerry Christmas*. Then he jogged down to apartment 8, where the current co-ordinator of the residents' management committee lived, to plant the ideas of increasing security and encouraging residents to raise an alarm if someone slipped past them in the doorway.

Then his phone alerted him that he was supposed to be at The Three Fishes at seven for the Acting Instrumental staff Christmas dinner. Exhausted by the unpleasantness of the day, he almost rang Oggie to give his excuses. Then an image of Georgine swam into his mind and, after reassuring himself Debs was OK to be left and that she wouldn't open the apartment door without knowing who was on the other side of it, he drove back to Middledip.

He called Chrissy hands-free as he drove. 'Hi, Johnjoe!' She sounded out of breath and happy. 'We're in Oxford Street on the open deck of a tour bus in the middle of the mad Christmas shopping crowds. Polo and I are frozen but the kids love it!'

Joe pictured her beneath the bright lights that had bedecked every major street in London since September, trying to paint in the faces of her kids and husband, so far seen only on her phone. 'Don't want to sour the mood,' he said, trying to sound cheerful. 'But Garrit's turned up in Bettsbrough again.' He summed up the events of the afternoon.

'Oh, hell,' she sighed, when he'd finished. 'Did you – did you tell him you'd seen me?'

He was quick to reassure her. 'Of course not. I just thought you ought to know.'

'Yeah. Well.' She sighed again. 'I guess he's not on my Christmas visit list. There are . . . important people in my life.' *He's not coming near my kids* was the subtext Joe heard.

Joe disconnected as he drew up in the car park of The Three Fishes, wondering if there was anyone alive who'd willingly offer Garrit a place around their Christmas table. What he remembered of Christmases spent with Garrit was more about booze and the TV than family and food.

He pulled a black beanie hat and his glasses from his coat pocket and put them on, feeling, as he had ever since The Hungry Years began to hit the album charts, simultaneously surprised how easy it was to alter your appearance and faintly pretentious for doing it. But many an encounter on the tube or in restaurants had convinced him of how many people would invite themselves to chat, and bearing in mind the exposure he'd just received in the *Daily Snoop*, he wasn't taking any chances.

On entering the pub, vaguely registering his usual distaste for the smell of alcohol, he swung left towards the restaurant section. He found his party easily. Everyone was wearing jolly red Santa hats. He was the last to arrive, which placed him in a seat next to Errol and across from Don the site supervisor and, conveniently for someone not trying to attract attention, in a corner with his back to the bar. As greetings were exchanged, his gaze quickly located Georgine at the other end of the table.

Something in his chest misstepped at the expression of relief that flickered in her eyes. Had she been wondering how he'd fared after the SOS text from Debs? The thought warmed him.

314

She looked amazing tonight. Her turquoise dress made her hair gleam where it hung below the white fluff around her Santa hat, a string of Christmas lights above bathing her in a golden glow. The dress clung to the rounded swells of her breasts, its wide neckline displaying the hollows above her collarbones. It made him regret that darkness had cloaked their night together, cheating him of images to carry in his memory – apart from the glimpse of her body in the meagre light that had filtered around her bedroom door in the morning. More, he felt cheated of dinners in restaurants or lunches in wine bars. They'd had no chance to date. Everything had blown up in his face within hours of waking next to her, pressed against the satin of her skin.

He sent her a smile and tried not to think how much things had changed and yet stayed the same since they were kids. He had money now, a choice of comfortable homes, he could holiday in sun or snow . . . but he still didn't get the girl.

Errol broke into his thoughts. 'Wearing the wrong hat?' His smile was warm enough but, as usual, he couldn't help nitpicking.

'I forgot to buy a Santa hat for tonight.' Joe offered him one end of the gold Christmas cracker lying beside his fork. 'Let's find me another.' Though Errol won the pull, Joe swooped on the purple tissue Christmas hat that fell out and exchanged it for the beanie. 'Better?' It hung drunkenly over his eye, making Vix and Avril, who were sitting nearby, giggle.

Errol had the grace to laugh, and crackers began their sharp reports all down the table as others joined the fun.

They'd chosen their meals in advance. Joe's was soup and then turkey. It was a homely meal, well cooked and substantial.

He listened to the chatter, joining in occasionally. It was a warm, undemanding social occasion. Vix loved the cracker puns and mottoes, gathering them all up to read aloud. Keeley told funny stories, putting on all the right accents, as befitted a drama teacher. Several times when Joe's gaze flicked to Georgine's end of the table he found her looking at him. A lot of people had arranged not to be driving this evening and their glasses emptied and filled with noticeable regularity, faces flushing and laughs growing louder, but the level of red wine in Georgine's glass was slow to sink.

He didn't have a problem with drinking per se, but he suppressed a sigh when the main course was removed and Vix, whose glass had been refilled frequently, leant across Don – who looked as if he didn't mind – to gaze flirtatiously at Joe. 'So, Mr Rock Star, got lotsa groupie stories?'

Joe edged back, careful not to let his gaze stray to Vix's jostling cleavage. 'A gentleman never tells.' Because it provided ammunition to the likes of the *Daily Snoop*.

'Aw, c'mon!' Vix wheedled. 'Do you really select girls from the audience and send roadies to bring them to you?'

Joe raised his eyebrows to express astonishment at the very idea and tried not to think of Billy, who did that virtually every gig. Vix propped her chin on her hand and studied him owlishly. 'Was all that stuff about your early years real? Or a publicity stunt?'

Before Joe could decide on a reaction, Oggie rose, tinging his fork on a glass. 'Time to swap seats for the dessert! Joe, change with me. Vix swap with Errol, Avril with Keeley.'

Relief washing through him at this opportunity to avoid Vix's probing, Joe grabbed his cranberry juice and hopped up, muttering, 'Excuse me.' He cast Oggie a grateful smile as they passed in the space between tables. In moments, he was seated beside Fern, diagonal to Avril and opposite Georgine, with only the wall on his right. Some of the others grumbled at being switched around, but he was just relieved Oggie had found a way to head Vix off at the pass.

His Christmas pudding arrived, rich and fruity, swimming in custard, and he blew on the first delicious mouthful as he glanced at Georgine under the edge of his purple Christmas cracker hat.

She began to tuck into her crème brûlée. 'Is everything OK with your mum?' she murmured. 'Did she really see . . . him?'

Those nearby – Fern, Avril and Keeley – were deep in conversation, so he could probably reply without being overheard, but now he was with Georgine Joe just didn't even want to think what it meant that Garrit had crawled out of his hole. Waggling his eyebrows, he managed to make his Christmas hat descend almost over his eyes.

As he'd hoped, Georgine's eyes began to dance. Then the smile faded, and she leant closer. 'You still do it,' she murmured.

He paused, spoon halfway to his mouth. 'What?'

'Play the clown when under fire.'

Slowly, he returned his spoon to his dish. 'Shit. You're right. I see Garrit again and become an emotional teenager.'

Shock flickered in her eyes. 'You *saw* him? Are you OK? How about your mum?'

He nodded. The movement made his party hat slip. He snatched it off and crumpled it into a ball beside his plate. 'She's anxious, but OK, thanks. Garrit showed up as soon as I got there so I was able to see him off the premises and suggest he keep away. I doubt it had much effect on the shitty little ferret.' He found his hands had curled into fists and made himself unclench them. 'Seeing him again made me so angry I could hardly see straight.'

Georgine stopped eating. The Christmas lights reflected in her eyes. 'Not frightened?'

'Only that I'd grab the bastard by the throat and prove myself as bad as him.'

'You're *so* not like him!' She leant across the table as if it was important to her to stress the point. 'I'm glad you resisted. He'd be delighted to file charges of assault, wouldn't he?'

He stared at her, looking both sexy and cute in her Santa hat. 'That didn't even occur to me. Holy hell, would he have milked that cash cow!'

She picked up her spoon. 'I can see you're not enjoying this conversation. Let's talk about something else. The forecast's for snow next week. I hope it stays away until we have the show wrapped up.'

They fell to talking about the show and about tomorrow's get-in, which was safe territory. Safer than saying the words that formed in Joe's mind more and more clearly the longer he listened to her speak and watched her laugh and smile. *You've always been so good and kind, you've made me want to be a better person. I feel as if I've loved you half my life.*

That couldn't possibly be right. Could it?

Chapter Thirty

Awake ridiculously early on Saturday, the day of the get-in, as if this were Christmas morning and she was ten years old, Georgine poked her nose into Blair's room.

'What?' Blair grumbled from beneath the duvet.

'You'll remember to see Dad, won't you?'

'And cook him a nice lunch,' Blair agreed in the voice of one who'd been coached in this already. 'Sod off, sis. Enjoy working all weekend.'

'Too much fun to feel like work.' Georgine grinned as she withdrew. After eating breakfast as if it were a time trial, she jumped into her car and headed for Bettsbrough.

She pulled her car up to the door of the Raised Curtain for ease of access to her share of the boxes they'd divided between members of the get-in team, which was made up of tutors and the tech crew. Joe had been attending to his latest crisis on Friday so it hadn't been possible to allocate props or costumes to him, which at least meant she didn't have to feel anxious about whether he'd turn up. That's what she told the fluttery feeling in her stomach anyway.

Ian waved through the glass on which snowflakes and

Christmas trees had been stencilled with spray snow before unlocking the door. 'Want a hand?'

'That would be great.' Georgine beamed. She chatted happily with Ian as they brought in her boxes, excitement bubbling inside her. It was happening! Two days to set up and then dress rehearsal on Monday.

Then . . . showtime!

Ian had agreed to let her into the theatre at eight, two hours earlier than she'd asked the others to convene. She liked time to tour every area Acting Instrumental would occupy, making last-minute decisions, checking the props and costume area wasn't cluttered with someone else's stuff, going over her lists of boxes and their contents. One of her boxes contained tea, coffee and milk, all the mugs out of her cupboard and ten packs of biscuits. She set them out in the utility area where Ian had put an urn that was hissing quietly as it heated.

Everybody, including Joe, showed up promptly and she doled out hot drinks before walking everybody through the theatre, flagging up things like reminding the cast not to clutter up the cross over – the corridor that allowed people to cross behind the stage out of sight of the audience.

Then she set them to bringing in their share of things as allocated or, in the case of the tech crew, having a play with the decks in the box to complete their familiarisation.

'You've organised the hell out of this get-in, Georgine,' Maddie congratulated her when they sat down to eat the lunchtime sandwiches they'd brought. Even Errol couldn't think of anything to criticise. Teamwork was the order of the weekend.

The backdrop went up, the Christmas tree was erected at the back of the stage, the band stage platform put together and amps, mics and foot pedals assembled. And the double drum kit, of course.

All day Saturday and Sunday they worked, the tech rehearsal going on at the same time, voices suddenly booming out over the PA and lights rising and falling. Georgine slept like a baby both nights, content that they were as prepared as humanly possible for after lunch Monday and the dress rehearsal.

And there was no reason that it shouldn't go just as smoothly as the get-in had.

Chapter Thirty-One

The next morning, Joe's phone rang when he was eating breakfast. 'Hey, Pete,' he said, through a mouthful of granola.

'The stepfather's revenge,' Pete sighed sadly.

'What?' Joe glanced at his watch. He didn't have to be at the theatre until nine so he'd awarded himself an extra hour in bed. If he'd known Pete was going to ring he would have made it half an hour.

'The *Daily Snoop*. They've given your erstwhile stepfather a couple of pages to pour shit over you.'

Joe almost choked. 'That *fuckface*!'

'Yeah. It's bad news, JJ. I've sent the link. Ring me back when you've read it?'

'Yeah.' Joe dumped his phone on the breakfast bar and snatched up his laptop.

STEPFATHER: THE TRUTH ABOUT BLACKER screamed the headline, though this time the story was a feature in the inside pages.

> *'Yeah, black indeed,' says the man who for 12 years gave a home to John Joseph Blackthorn, the boy who*

grew up to be JJ Blacker, drummer of one of the UK's foremost rock bands, The Hungry Years. 'He was Johnjoe Garrit in those days,' continues Eric Garrit (58). 'Yes, I even shared my name with him. All the thanks I got for bringing him up was to be left behind and ignored. He's never bought me so much as a pint of beer out of his rock-star earnings.'

Joe paused. Garrit's first name was Eric? He scanned down the piece, his eye drawn by:

Eric adds bitterly, 'He was a little thug, running round with the Shetland estate gang. I never knew what he was up to except he was mixed up in crime as a "runner", delivering mysterious envelopes for the local hoodlums. His shady past's the reason he took a stage name, I suppose. And to think that now he works with young, impressionable people.'

The article went on in the same vein, assassinating Joe's character, painting Garrit as a hero breadwinner for Debs and Joe as well as Chrissy. A recent picture of Garrit looking rueful took up a quarter page. It explained the uncharacteristic neatness of hair and beard on Friday, Joe thought savagely.

He finished reading, sick to his stomach. At least there was no doubt about the source of the story this time.

By the time they'd clashed on Friday afternoon Garrit had probably already talked to the journalist and been gloating that this shit storm was scheduled to break. The greedy bastard, realising he'd have to go to ground when his story was published, evidently hadn't been able to resist trying to leech money from Debs or Joe first.

Blood pounding, he rang Pete back. 'I have no idea what to say. He's just a shit.'

Pete sighed. 'Maybe it's time for you to talk to the journo yourself.'

'No!' Joe, astounded by Pete's words, clenched his fingers around the phone. 'We treat the piece with the contempt it deserves. Talking to the press just provides fuel for their fires.'

A pause. 'If it wasn't for the accusations of crime and the fact that the band's fan-base includes a lot of teenagers . . .' Pete said heavily.

'But he was the one sending me round with the fucking envelopes!' Joe stormed.

Pete groaned. 'Oh, shit. There's that much truth in it, is there?' Then his voice became clipped. 'Can you get down to London, JJ? This affects the whole band so I don't think we can do nothing. You can't hide away from this and hope it'll go away. Not this time. I'm afraid that the decision about whether to leave the band might be made for you.'

After several seconds of tense silence while Joe raged around inside his head looking for a convincing counter-argument, he snapped reluctantly, 'OK, I'll come.' He disconnected the call and, muttering a stream of obscenities, rang Oggie to relate the latest chapter in what was becoming a horror story.

'So that's the picture,' he growled, when he'd laid it all out.

It was Oggie's turn to sigh. 'This is all very unfortunate—'

Joe didn't wait for him to finish. 'You don't have to tell me that.' And then he told Oggie what was going to happen next.

*

Georgine clutched her phone in disbelief as she listened to Oggie relating Joe's latest disaster.

'The new article is scurrilous,' he said sombrely. 'Parents are beginning to contact me. I'm explaining that I've known Joe since he was fourteen and see no truth in Garrit's story, but Joe doesn't believe Acting Instrumental won't be affected. He's given permission for me to make it public that he's no longer with us and he's left for London.'

'Poor Joe,' she said numbly. Unable to process the consequences of what Oggie was telling her, except to feel outrage at Joe's suffering at the hands of the press, she took refuge in pragmatism. 'So, who's to supervise the tech at the dress rehearsal?'

'For the rehearsal, I suggest we take a leap of faith and let the students do it alone. I'll supervise performances.'

Georgine's stomach plummeted at the finality in his voice and she didn't even thank him for stepping into the breach. 'So that's it then? He's gone?'

'For the foreseeable,' Oggie agreed gently.

'Thanks for telling me,' she said automatically. She'd begun to say goodbye when Oggie cut in again.

'Don't worry too much. He's resilient.'

'I know.' But then words sprang to her lips. 'If he ever did anything wrong, it was out of desperation, so he and his stepsister could survive.'

Oggie's voice suddenly rang with anger. 'Do you think I don't know? He's one of my best and oldest friends!'

Georgine came off the phone with a lot of lead in her belly, but warmth in her heart that Oggie was on Joe's side. Once more burying her emotions in practical tasks, she went off to break the news to the tech crew.

By the time the dress rehearsal was over, Georgine felt like she'd been wrung out in hot water. Nerves had set in and the students had become snappy. Samantha, who played Kerry Christmas, pronounced gloomily that she thought she had a sore throat coming. A dancer twisted an ankle. People forgot their words – prompted calmly by Fern each time – and missed cues. In fact, the tech crew were the only ones to really get everything right, as they pointed out. Smugly.

Georgine pinned on a smile and kept on coaching and encouraging. At least it gave her plenty to think about other than how Joe must have felt when he read Garitt's mischief-making hatchet job.

It wasn't until that evening, crashed out in front of the TV with a ready meal, spilling her woes to Blair, that she voiced the thought that had been hovering like a spectre all day. 'I don't know if I'll see Joe again.' The words ended on a squeak and any further words stuck in her throat.

Blair shifted both half-eaten dinners onto the floor and pulled Georgine into a hug. 'Oh, Georgine, I am so sorry! Shit on the *Daily Snoop*!' And then, when Georgine just cried harder she heaved a huge, dramatic sigh. 'No men for either of us this Christmas, it looks like. But we'll be fine. We will.'

As promised, Oggie assumed Joe's role in the box on opening night, although the nervous but professional students, as he reported to Georgine, left him little to do but take video evidence of them working the decks. After the show had finished its run, Georgine would upload a folder of video clips to the college intranet for students to download and make part of their assignments.

In line with the adage that a bad dress rehearsal meant a good show, the first night went *beautifully*.

Georgine went front of stage and gave the most inspiring

introduction she could conjure up, then, despite a hundred and eighty pairs of eyes gazing down into the stage area, the students flung themselves into the show as if they'd never get the chance to do it again.

And the audience lost their hearts. They clapped every dance, every song and even the scene-shifters with single-minded fervour that was not totally accounted for by the first night audience including a lot of parents.

In the wings, in the cross over, in the props room and in the changing rooms where Errol, Keeley and Maddie made certain everyone hit their cues, Georgine had nothing to do but look on and burst with pride.

It really was a fantastic show. She wasn't needed until the encores. Then she found that the students, gobsmacked by the applause, whistles and calls for more, truly needed someone to lead them back on to line up for their bows.

She held them there for her wrap-up speech, gazing up at the rows of attentive faces. 'Wasn't that amazing? Aren't these students something else? I know many of you in the audience tonight are family and friends and you must be very, very proud. They have worked so hard!' She led a fresh burst of clapping. 'Now you know what a fabulous show this is I hope you'll spread the word as we still have a few tickets available for Wednesday, Thursday and Friday. Both performances on Saturday, like this one, are sell-outs. Ladies and gentlemen – the Level 3 students of Acting Instrumental! Let's give them another round of applause!'

Backstage, when they'd finally filed off the stage and the audience could be heard shuffling out, the students were as high as kites, laughing, wiping tears, chatter-chatter-chattering, hugging. Before long they were shouting goodnight and going out into a sleety darkness to catch their lifts.

After making sure everyone was out, including the volunteers who'd run the bar, torn tickets and sold programmes, Georgine thanked the site supervisor, who'd turned out to lock up, and went home with the applause still ringing in her ears.

But when she reached home and saw Blair's expectant face and heard her eager, 'So? How did the first night go?' Georgine burst into tears again.

'It was so brilliant,' she wailed. 'These must be happy tears.'

For nothing would she admit she was crying because Joe truly had stayed away.

Show week was passing speedily. Wednesday, the second night, although not a sell out, had pulled in a good crowd, and now it was Thursday and the audience was gathering in the foyer again, chattering about the dusting of snow they'd had this afternoon and hoping no more would fall to make getting home difficult.

No amount of snow was going to stop Georgine. Dressed in stage black in case she had to sort something out during a scene change, she hurried around producing a needle and thread or a replacement shoelace from her backpack as needed.

'I love you and your magic backpack,' leading lady Samantha sniffed when Georgine had sewn a vital, right-on-the-boobline button back on for her. Samantha was feeling the strain of carrying so much of the show and Georgine had been watching her swing from highs to lows. Luckily, her lows tended to come before shows, but then she was fine. After shows she boinged about like a power-ball, high on success, then couldn't sleep.

Maybe this show had too much reliance on two char-

328

acters, Kerry Christmas and Uncle Jones, Georgine mused, checking one of the tech kids was setting up a video camera. She liked to take video on the first and last shows and one in the middle.

Randall and Blair were in the front row tonight. They'd arrived early as Randall moved slowly, and Georgine had arranged for them to be let in so he wasn't kept standing. Peeping from the wings, Georgine could see him watching everything intently as the scenery for the first scene was checked and rechecked and lights rose and fell. She was glad to see his bruises had faded already and his left eye had opened again. She slipped out to hug him. 'Hi, Dad!'

'Hi, honey.' Randall smiled his lop-sided smile. His hair was neatly combed and his air of being a child out for a treat made Georgine's heart ache.

Blair waved her programme. 'Great pic of you, sis.' She turned the booklet around to exhibit the page.

Georgine grinned, although her eyes were drawn to the picture of Joe as Assistant Events Director rather than her own. 'Fame at last!'

Then she hurried backstage. Keeley was on duty in the girl's changing room this evening and Georgine slipped through the door and mouthed, 'OK?' at her.

Keeley gave her a thumbs-up.

Just as Georgine was turning to leave, she heard one of the students say, 'Shame Joe's not here. He did loads towards the show.'

Georgine kept walking, knowing that she'd be combing the audience later just in case Joe had sneaked in.

She did, twice, but he hadn't.

It was totally unfair that the *Daily Snoop* had outed and then vilified Joe, and now other tabloids had picked up the story too. He should be here to enjoy the success of getting such fab attendance across the whole run. Georgine had texted him this morning.

Georgine: *You'd be fine in the box if you want to turn up. Nobody would know you were there. Oggie had a few emails about you on the last day of term, but it died out quickly. Come back if you want to.*

There had been no reply. Either he was busy being a rock star or he thought it would be easiest to make a clean break. Or both.

Oggie supervised the tech as he had on Tuesday and Wednesday and, it seemed, would on Friday and Saturday. Georgine left the backstage area and ran up the stairs to the box.

'OK?' she asked, finding Oggie and three students looking out through glass at the backs of still-mostly-empty seats and an empty stage.

'All I have to do is watch these guys work,' Oggie reported.

The students grinned, looking pleased.

'Great!' Georgine left, but halted when she realised Oggie had followed her.

'I don't suppose you've heard from Joe?' he asked.

Georgine shook her head. 'I texted him. No reply.'

'Same here.' Oggie shook his head, lips tightening. 'That journalist! Joe's not only our landlord but our benefactor, personally funding all kinds of extras to give our students a fantastic grounding in the performing arts. He funds the scholarship that Jasmine won this year to write and compose our Christmas show and he's looking at funding transport from Bettsbrough to get kids here for holiday activities. He could spend all his money on travel and fast

330

cars, but he chooses to try and help young people! And here's some awful bloody journalist from some awful bloody rag trying to bury all that in a lot of muck-raking. I doubt we'd even be in this theatre if not for Joe's philanthropy, and I don't know of any other further education college locally that has its own events director.'

The floor rocked beneath Georgine's feet. 'Wow. Do you mean he *funds my role*?'

Oggie looked as if he wished he hadn't shared quite so much. 'Well . . . if not for his funding, I'm not sure how . . .' Leaving the thought hanging, he rejoined the students in the box.

Georgine trod back downstairs. She hadn't known who funded the scholarship or the extras. And Joe had effectively been paying her wages for the past few years in this fantastic job she loved? It was like finding out that Santa was real. And that if Santa withdrew his support, she could lose her job.

She shoved that thought aside. The show must go on, as it had throughout the history of theatre. For now, she had a job to do, no matter who funded it or how unjustly that person had been treated by the tabloids.

Much later, when all the bows had been taken and the audience gone, she shivered as she brushed snow from her car with stinging hands and drove back to Middledip, snowflakes dancing in her headlights, snow on the roofs of houses as if someone had gone over them with a huge roll of cotton wool.

She arrived to find Blair had already taken their dad back to his flat and was waiting to excitedly tell Georgine it was the best Christmas show *ever* and Randall had absolutely loved it.

'That's fantastic,' Georgine said, taking refuge for a few

moments in a big congratulatory hug from her sister that might also have held elements of understanding and consolation too. 'I'm shattered and we're only halfway through the run.' She freed herself and, yawning, carried a mug of hot chocolate to bed and fired up her laptop.

She looked up the articles in the *Daily Snoop* online and read every word again. The reporter's name was Sy Calderwell. Next to his byline was a link: *Send Sy an email.* 'Don't mind if I do,' Georgine murmured. And began to type.

Chapter Thirty-Two

Joe spent the week in London feeling as if he were existing in a black cave of unhappiness.

He had several meetings with Pete and the band. Pete counselled calling a press conference for 'damage limitation'. Raf, Liam and Nathan, like Joe, were inclined to let the negative stories die on their own. Billy was conflicted. 'I'm not being shitty, JJ,' he said. 'I want to do the best for the band. I just don't know what it is. We need advice. What about Jerome?'

Pete pulled a doubtful face. 'Is Jerome, as he represents JJ, the right source of that advice?'

'Yeah, yeah, we all trust him.' Billy clapped Joe on the shoulder as if to say that they trusted Joe too, so Joe set a meeting up with Jerome, but they had to wait until Friday because he was advising in court until then.

In the meantime, Joe tried to write, but the song came out so freakin' sad. He'd never written mushy 'miss you so much it hurts' songs, but he *was* missing Georgine so much it hurt. He tried to practise banging fills on the drums, but then he'd drift over to the piano to play sad

333

songs like 'Running on Empty'. Except now it wasn't food he was hungry for.

He couldn't remember feeling like this. Adrift. Hollow. Alone. He told himself there was no way it could be over.

Then that there was no way it could carry on. His past was going to keep turning on him like a wild animal. Journalists would drag out his 'Cinder-rocker' past and pronounce judgement. He refused to drag Georgine into that.

To distract himself, he invited the guys around to jam, as he'd done so many times before. Half expecting a refusal, he made sure to include Billy in the invitation but the blond front man seemed eager to turn up. He looked Joe in the eye and appeared so completely normal that Joe doubted Pete had guessed correctly when he'd tentatively linked Billy to the *Daily Snoop* article.

Billy even joined in quizzing Joe about musicians he might use if he truly did go solo, and he realised he couldn't think of anyone he wanted to work with more than Raf, Nathan, Liam and Billy. 'Don't make me cry,' he joked, without entirely joking. He got over his writing slump when he and Billy express-wrote a song called 'This is Bullshit!' aimed at journalists. They played it for the rest of the band and talked about releasing it on an album. He shoved any lingering doubts about Billy to one side and was just glad that the boys were working together again. It hadn't really taken much. A chat, honesty, and pulling together in adversity.

Continuing with The Hungry Years had never seemed more possible.

But it would take him further from Georgine.

On Thursday, Joe met up with Chrissy and her family, as they were flying back to their US Air Force base in

Rammstein, Germany on Saturday. He liked her teenage girls, Zoe and Celine, and found her husband wasn't really called Polo, but Paolo, an über-cool American air navigator of Hispanic descent. Gladder than he could say that Chrissy invited him, Joe agreed to visit the family on the base later in the year. Zoe and Celine bounced about and declared it cool, pronounced as two syllables: 'coo-wul'.

He rang Debs to check whether Garrit had been around. He hadn't, but Debs had read the second *Daily Snoop* article and was mad enough to phone the police if Garrit so much as showed his nose in her building.

Friday, he awoke feeling that his black cave was in danger of closing in on him. Everything on the radio and TV was about Christmas, and he hadn't planned one. Still, he thought as he drove to the meeting with Jerome, Pete and the band, he'd spent days alone in his small house in Camden before. Who cared if one of them was December 25th?

He arrived at Pete's house almost at the point of not caring what came next.

As it turned out, the meeting was over in no time, though Pete struck a sour note at first, referring to the 'emergency' in the hushed tones of one mentioning a recently deceased friend. It made Joe feel terrible, as if he were responsible for dragging The Hungry Years into his horrible past.

Jerome, black brows drawn into sharp diagonals like charcoal strokes, listened to Pete's worries attentively.

Then he listened to Joe offering to definitely leave the band and immediately go public on it to spare The Hungry Years contamination from words like *gang* and *thug*.

And Billy's, 'Won't that cause "did he jump or was he pushed" speculation?'

Lastly, he listened to Nathan, Liam and Raf declare that the whole thing should just be ignored. 'It's Christmas in five days. People will be more interested in whether it snows and what the Queen has to say than JJ's shit.'

Then, when Pete began again, 'We can't ignore it. In an emergency—'

Jerome visibly lost patience. 'It's not a fucking emergency; stop calling it one,' he snapped, brows knitting. 'Is this what's had you running around like headless chickens? The press is not the law of the land and you can perfectly legitimately do nothing! If the police ever contact JJ about his conduct at age fourteen, that will be the time to prepare a defence.' He glared at Pete, who'd opened his mouth again. 'Get over yourself. Are you new to the music industry or something?'

Pete looked offended. 'I have a reputation to think of.'

'Really?' Jerome drew out the word as if there was a lot more he could say.

Ignoring Pete's spluttering, Joe gazed at Jerome in shock. 'Seriously? That's it?'

Jerome put away his pen and zipped up his document case. 'It is so far as I'm concerned. Come and talk to me if you want to try and sue the *Daily Snoop*. Or if you make your decision about the other matter and would like my help.'

'What other matter?' demanded Raf, who didn't worry too much about privacy.

Jerome's mouth closed as if zipped like his document case. It was left to Joe to say, 'Whether I stay with the band.' After this week, there being a decision had kind of got away from him.

Nathan, who'd been balancing his chair on its two back legs, clunked it to the floor. '*Still*? I thought we were going to start on another album in January, like we planned all along. Shit, JJ, you and Billy wrote a song for it.'

Raf and Liam treated Joe to matching gimlet stares.

Joe glanced at Billy. Billy held up both hands as if to show he had no tricks up his sleeves. 'I want you to stay, JJ.'

'OK,' Joe agreed, dazed at this light dawning so suddenly in his cave of unhappiness. 'Then I'll stay.' A wave of warmth crashed into his chest. It felt like coming home, or when Shaun had taken him in and given him back his family.

Jerome's white teeth flashed. 'Jeez. You musicians. No wonder you keep the likes of me busy. Expect a note of my fees.'

He hurried off back to whatever was awaiting his august attention and as the front door clicked behind him, the place erupted into cheers and whoops. Joe found himself under fire from fist bumps, hugs, shoulder slaps and nipple tweaks, with a few four-lettered friendly insults thrown in.

He was back with the band.

Chapter Thirty-Three

It was the Saturday before Christmas and Georgine had tired of hoping for Joe to return.

She was tired full stop. Everyone was. Some students even groused about doing the 'Satdee Matnee' as they called the matinée show. The snow had begun with soft slow-falling flakes and they wanted to have snowball fights instead.

Much of the matinée audience consisted of guides, scouts or youth clubs and they treated *A Very Kerry Christmas* as a pantomime, laughing at Kerry's most impassioned songs and booing and hissing Uncle Jones' gang. They cheered and clapped a lot too though, so the beaming cast had that energy to take into the last night.

The snow continued through the day like feathers from a gigantic burst pillow and forming a carpet to crunch softly underfoot. The students got their snowball fights out of their systems and the audience still turned up, even though they had to fight their way through a whole two inches of snow to get there. The radio was forecasting at least one more inch overnight, gloomily, as if their sole intent was to panic the countryside into either buying up everything in the supermarket and risk being stuck in a snowdrift, or holing up indoors to starve.

The students were excited by the *Bettsbrough Bugle* covering the evening performance. Georgine shoved aside surly thoughts about bastard journalists, because it wasn't the fault of the young female reporter from the *Bugle* that Joe didn't get to see the show he'd given so much to; nor that the very bastard Sy Calderwell of the *Daily Snoop* hadn't printed anything of the nice-side-of-JJ-Blacker stuff she'd emailed to him.

The Mayor of Bettsbrough attended and made a speech praising the Raised Curtain and Acting Instrumental and the extraordinary standard of the shows each put on. The students cheered and took up their starting positions as if they could do two shows a day for the rest of their lives.

Georgine stopped feeling like throwing it all in and began driving enthusiasm instead, giving everyone silent double thumbs-up in the wings and waiting for the audience to settle before going out front of stage to give one last, rousing introduction, including congratulating the composer, Jasmine, who had a place in the front row, and ending, 'Whenever you're ready, Musical Director!'

Band One and Band Two transferred their gazes to Errol on the other side of the stage. He air-counted *one, two, three, four* and bass and drums crashed in on *five, six*. The company swung into *A Very Kerry Christmas, Uncle Jones* for the final time.

Georgine watched the whole thing with a rock in her throat. Every single student sang or played or danced or acted – some of them all four – their hearts out. When they'd taken three bows on their own, she floated on the stage to give her final speech with a bottle of water in one hand and a tissue in the other, truly scared that she might not be able to speak.

'These students are amazing,' she said, voice trembling. 'This has been our most ambitious show and longest run to date, and they've worked so professionally to bring you this fantastic piece of musical theatre.' She waited for a fresh round of applause to die away before bringing on every non-cast person to receive their own accolades: Errol, Maddie, Keeley, Fern, Oggie and the parent volunteers. She thanked the tech crew, who flashed the lights in acknowledgement, and she thanked the audience too.

Then Samantha went off and skipped back on with a bouquet for Georgine, and she pretended to be overcome – which wasn't hard in her current rocky emotional state – though she got flowers after every run, because Oggie arranged it.

Finally, the audience filed out with great smiles on their faces. The cast went to the changing rooms for the after-show party, as you seriously could not take forty-plus teenagers to a pub. Avril, Vix and Hannalee put out soft drinks and sausage rolls, and everybody hung up costumes that were to return to Acting Instrumental. The tutors exchanged Christmas gifts – token only, was the rule – and, touchingly, a few of the kids presented boxes of Roses and pots of Christmas cacti to the staff too.

Then Georgine, the directors, Oggie and the tech crew got straight on with the get-out, conscious that the Raised Curtain would be used by others tomorrow. Props were dismantled and packed. Equipment disassembled and checked off.

Georgine grinned and chatted with everybody. Inside, the rock had dropped from her throat to her stomach because even to the very last second she'd harboured some forlorn hope that Joe was there somewhere. That maybe he'd be the one to walk on with the bouquet.

But he hadn't.

So it looked like that was that.

Chapter Thirty-Four

Sunday was the day before Christmas Eve. After a lengthy and well-deserved lie-in, Georgine was roused by Blair at her bedroom door. 'Are you awake?' Blair whispered. 'Something's happened.'

In a heartbeat, Georgine was very awake indeed. 'What? Is it Dad? He hasn't gone out in the snow and fallen, has he?' She reached out and dragged back a curtain to give her enough winter light to see her sister, who was dressed to go out.

Blair came into the room, giving her 'a look'. 'Don't be so pessimistic. It's something good.' She coloured prettily. 'I have a date.'

Georgine collapsed back on her pillows, clutching her heart. 'FFS, Blair! Don't frighten me. I'm just surprised you haven't had loads of dates already. Where did you meet—'

'It's Warren,' Blair stuck in, as if it ought to be obvious. 'Isn't that amazing? He says he wants to talk.'

'Oh!' Georgine digested this unexpected turn of events. 'That's great! Isn't it?'

'Hope so.' Blair bent down and gave Georgine a hug. 'So, don't worry if I don't make it home tonight.' A grin and a wink and she was gone.

Left alone to shower and dress, Georgine tried to decide how to fill her day. If Blair and Warren made up – which would be *lovely* – she'd have to get used to a silent house again. She was glad about the absence of debt collectors and bailiffs, but no little sister to chat to or spat with? That she was going to miss.

It only took her an hour to realise that doing nothing gave her too much time to think about the sadness in her heart, and so she pulled on her boots and coat and drove to Acting Instrumental, which looked pretty in its Christmas clothes of snow. She let Don the site supervisor know she was there and set to restoring the *Kerry Christmas* props to the props room. Then she jumped back into her car and drove to Bettsbrough, where the snow was rapidly turning brown, and called on Randall, bright and enthusiastic about how well the show had gone. She made up for neglecting him for the past couple of weeks by cooking a full English breakfast for an early supper.

The next day was Christmas Eve. Georgine went grocery shopping at six a.m. to beat the hordes and shopped as if Blair would be with them for Christmas dinner, and possibly Warren too as Blair, true to her suspicions, hadn't come home last night. Whatever had been happening in Blair's life while Georgine had been immersed in the show, it seemed to have put a reconciliation very much on the cards. If it turned out to be just Randall and Georgine on Christmas Day, they'd eat their fill and then she'd make meals to freeze for later in the holiday. She still had two weeks off to look forward to.

But she wasn't feeling time-offy yet and time off was rarely completely time off for those involved in education so, once back home with the festive shopping put away, she downloaded video clips and photos amassed during show week and organised them, along with those from rehearsals, and began to think about the Level 2 students' show in April, which would be a musical revue: much more straightforward.

When she'd edited the footage of the final show, she stared at its icon for a long time . . . then sent a link to Joe's phone. However he'd left things, and however abruptly he'd left them, he deserved the opportunity to see the show he'd done so much work towards.

Then she shut down her laptop.

As Randall was engaged in the residents' lounge that evening, playing bingo and singing carols – he wasn't too good at the latter, but was happy to listen to those who were – Georgine wrapped up warm and wandered down to The Three Fishes to join the village Christmas Eve merrymaking. En route, she paused to help some giggling village kids make a slide on the pavement, hoping, belatedly, that it didn't send any poor pensioner off to casualty for a plaster cast.

When she reached the pub she found it warm and cheery. Coloured lights flickered and 'Merry Christmas Everybody' and 'I Wish it Could be Christmas Every Day' played in the background. There were BOGOF deals for Christmas punch and mulled wine. Tubb had very sensibly taken down the dartboard.

Georgine bought raffle tickets from Janice and laughed when what she won was having her car valeted by the men at the village garage. 'But it's only held together by the dirt!' she joked. Then, with a lovely warm feeling, she remembered Grandma Patty's money and thought she might spend part of her Christmas holiday looking for a newer car.

She drank four large glasses of mulled wine while she chattered to everyone she knew in the village – which equalled a whole bottle to herself, but it wouldn't hurt, just for once. Then Blair and Warren turned up looking starry eyed and happy and bought prosecco because they were on their way to Georgine's to gather some of Blair's things. She was moving back in with Warren.

'I was too miserable without her to let money come between us,' he said, his eyes glowing as he looked at Blair.

'That's fantastic!' Georgine cried, hugging them, tears prickling hotly in her eyes. 'What a fantastic Christmas present for us all!' She'd always liked good-looking Warren, who worked in the travel industry and was always smartly dressed. She gave him a big hug. 'Merry Christmas! Great to see you guys back together,' she said as she waved them off with a beaming smile.

After giving them an hour to finish up at her house she called, 'Merry Christmas!' to everybody in The Three Fishes, receiving a chorus of, 'Merry Christmas!' in reply, and walked a slightly wobbly line home, slipping over on the very slide she'd helped make and lying on her back, laughing with unladylike snorts, before climbing cautiously to her feet, relieved she hadn't cracked open her head.

The alcohol hadn't made her sleepy, so, once home, she went onto YouTube and watched The Hungry Years gig videos and their segment of a music documentary, watching, wide-eyed, a JJ Blacker with tousled red hair and pointed sideburns. He looked so happy, as if playing with the band was everything he needed.

Good. She was glad.

Chapter Thirty-Five

Joe had decided on a quiet Christmas Eve in Camden – if your idea of quiet was drum practice. But his plans were overset by an early phone call from Pete.

'What now?' he asked apprehensively. The last couple of calls from Pete had not led to anything good and he'd thought Pete and his wife, Luanne, would be Christmassing at a chalet in the Alps by now. He should have known Pete never totally unplugged from his news feeds.

'You got a direct line to Santa or something?' Pete demanded. 'Early Christmas gift, anyway!'

Joe twirled a drumstick with his free hand. Through the window he could see a sprinkling of tiny snowflakes. He'd heard on the news that there was a lot more of it to the north of London. 'What are you on about?'

'Sending a link,' Pete said shortly, and rang off.

The link came through right away. Apprehensively, Joe clicked and was taken, with sinking dismay, to the *Daily Snoop* online.

JJ BLACKER PAINTED WHITER shrieked the headline. Underneath was a picture of him grinning, his arms around the big Christmas tree prop at Acting Instrumental, captioned *A Christmas Eve good news story – Benefactor Blacker.*

According to a new source close to JJ Blacker, he has spent the last weeks working as a volunteer, giving something back to the music industry.

The piece, short and jolly as befitted its seasonal-good-news status, briskly refuted Garrit's allegations.

Our source goes on, 'I knew him from age eleven to fourteen. He was a neglected child. His stepfather, Garrit, was the one with dodgy connections.'

The article ran on, redefining Joe as a poor kid at the mercy of an unscrupulous stepfather figure.

Shaken, Joe tried to absorb this unexpected bounty from the *Daily Snoop*. Why had Pete been so off when he'd telephoned? To be the subject of a good news story was, well, good news. Great news! Slowly, picking up his sticks to twirl to help him think, he cast his mind back over everything that had happened in the past couple of months. The more he thought about it, the larger a hitherto unsuspected spectre rose above him. He stood gazing unseeingly at the winter's day beyond his sitting room window and tried to order events in his mind.

Eventually, he realised he'd have to act, and took up his phone again with a heavy heart and a shaking hand to ring Pete back. Before Pete could utter a word, Joe gambled on his hunch. 'Why did you do it, Pete?'

A long, pregnant pause. Then Pete snorted, 'Don't know what you're talking about.'

'You gave the original story to the *Daily Snoop* and then tried to inflame the situation with the others.'

'Are you *absolutely* raving *mad*, JJ?' thundered Pete. But his voice, however outraged, wavered, and the sinking feeling inside Joe intensified. He'd heard that tone whenever Pete knew himself not to have the high ground. The band even had a jokey name for the vociferous lying, 'the act of great indignation', which Pete put on when trying to trick a venue into providing over and above what had been agreed, or a record-label minion into putting their boss on the phone.

'There aren't many people who know everything the *Daily Snoop* printed.' Joe interrupted Pete's blustering denials. 'I'll tell you how I know you're the leak. When you rang this morning you were angry where you should have been happy. Pissed off where you should have been delighted. The only reason I can think of for that is that good news for me equals bad news for you. You hinted that Billy was the leak to lead to more bad feeling between him and me, didn't you?'

Silence. Joe could almost feel Pete squirm on the other end of the phone.

'You *want* me out of the band,' Joe went on. 'You tried setting Billy and me against one another and when that didn't work you created bad publicity and pretended it was me bringing it down on the band. You want the band on your books – but not me.' Joe could hardly believe what he was saying. Pete! He'd been their manager for years, steering them to bigger and better venues, bigger and better record deals, bigger audiences. He'd shaped their image, nurtured and polished. *And he wanted Joe out of the band*.

More silence. Then a long, deep sigh. 'I'm not admitting

responsibility,' Pete muttered, his voice shaking. 'But I do think you're holding the band back.'

It felt as if Pete had reached through the phone and punched Joe in the pit of his stomach. 'Because of my background?' he said numbly.

Pete gave a snort of derision. 'Don't be ridiculous! Don't you think I could spin that into a positive if I felt like it? No, it's your attitude.' Then when Joe made no reply he expanded, 'Your bleeding-heart act, wanting to select songs for their sincerity instead of making commercial decisions! Jeez, JJ, the kids love songs full of obscenities and jokes. You can stuff anthems about society's ills; give them plenty of the F word instead.'

Joe could feel a layer of sweat forming between his hand and the phone. 'Billy's songs.'

'Billy's songs,' Pete repeated, as if he were congratulating Joe on working it out. 'Look,' he went on magnanimously, although Joe detected desperation lacing his voice. 'We could get together in the New Year and find a way forward. Now you and I have been able to clear the air maybe we can find a few compromises—'

Joe disconnected on a wave of bitter anger. Then, as best he could with hands that shook with emotion, he began to set up a conference call. Before too much longer he, Raf, Nathan, Liam and Billy were all hooked up. 'I've got shit news,' Joe began, and set about unravelling Pete's machinations as best he could, heartened by the outrage of his fellow band members and stout declarations of having been completely in the dark.

It was only much later in the day, when he was exhausted after hours of debate, that he allowed himself to return to the JJ Blacker painted whiter piece in the *Daily Snoop* and reread it from beginning to end.

Only one person could be the 'new source'. Georgine. Could she possibly be signalling that she accepted everything and everyone he was? For much of the day a text from her had waited on his phone but he hadn't let himself look at it until he'd dealt with the fallout from what Pete had done. Heart beating loudly as he dared to hope, he opened the text and followed the link it contained to video of the students putting on their show.

His eyes misted over to see the joy shining out of them. That was what the performance business ought to be about. Not backstabbing and questionable methods but positive role models . . . like Georgine France.

Chapter Thirty-Six

Georgine's Christmas Day dawned with no hangover, but heaps of expensive presents and a Christmas kitchen fairy cooking a mouth-watering turkey dinner.

Not.

In fact, she awoke to silence banging on her eardrums and a *Merry Christmas!* text from Blair to say she'd bring Georgine's present to Randall's later. Outside, fresh snow had fallen, enough to make Georgine's hungover eyes flinch from its brightness.

After going downstairs to make a large mug of coffee and pick up her parcels she'd stowed beneath the tree, she returned to bed to rip through wrapping paper bearing sparkly Santas or perky robins. Her haul, mainly from her colleagues, amounted to: a box of different-coloured Papermate pens, a red leak-proof travel mug with a blue G on the side, shower gel, Christmas socks, a small brown bear who did handstands when wound up, and a shopping list pad with a music stave across the top. Shopping list was spelt 'Chopin Liszt'.

She screwed up the paper and checked her phone in

case anybody else – like Joe – had texted her. Nope. She answered Blair's festive greetings, then rang Randall to say Merry Christmas and that she'd be at his place at noon. Phone conversations with her dad tended to be a bit one-sided and short, but he managed, 'May-ee Kissmas', which made Georgine's eyes burn.

Her mum phoned from France: 'Because Terrence has invited simply *everybody* for lunch, and I won't have time later. Did you open your email, yet? My gift should have arrived at nine UK time.'

'Not yet.' She opened her inbox while her mother waited. When she found the email she could hardly believe her eyes. 'A weekend at a spa? That's an amazing present!' she squeaked.

Barbara sounded pleased. 'I've sent Blair the same. I thought we could all go together.'

Georgine grinned. Aha! So that was how her mother had justified such a massive expenditure. 'That will be wonderful,' she said.

When Barbara had rung off, Georgine lay back down and wondered whether to text Joe. She could say something light like, *Hope you have a good Christmas*. But he hadn't replied to her last text and the age of instant communication made it pretty pointed when someone didn't communicate. Especially a someone you'd slept with.

She decided to wait and see if he texted her.

She got up for a long shower with the new shower gel, a big glass of water and two paracetamol. By the time she'd dried her hair her headache had lifted and it was time to drive to her dad's, occasional snowflakes whirling down around the car from a pale grey sky.

Christmas afternoon proved quite jolly. Randall loved his new cardigan and put it straight on, his bruised arm much better now. He was even happier when he discovered Blair and Warren had patched up their differences as they turned up together, hauling a black bin liner of gifts.

Georgine almost cried to see Randall wearing a smile that could power every light on the Christmas tree. He used his good arm to hug Blair hard. 'Am vey peased, Bear. Vey peased i'deed.'

Warren kept beaming at Blair and winking.

Randall had invited his friend Sol to dinner, a fact that had passed Georgine by, so she prepared every last vegetable she'd brought and hoped for the best, rotating veg madly between microwave and oven to get everything hot at once. They ate squashed around Randall's tiny folding table with just enough elbow room to pull the crackers. The mottoes, which seemed to have been translated from another language, caused both mystification and hilarity.

'Man no a isla?' Sol read. 'Isla's a girl's name, isn't it? Obviously man's not an isla.'

'Man is not an island?' Georgine suggested. 'But I'm stumped by "be necessary woman and invent it"?'

They puzzled over that until Blair consulted her phone and came up with 'Necessity is the mother of invention.'

It was as she laid her phone back down on the table that Georgine spotted something glittering on Blair's finger – something that definitely hadn't come out of a cracker. She was so shocked that a morsel of spicy stuffing caught in her throat and shot up behind her nose, making her eyes stream, not helped by Sol treating her to several hearty thumps on the back.

'Blair! Are you engaged?' she demanded when she could speak again.

Randall dropped his fork messily down his new cardigan. 'Bear?'

Blair blushed, her eyes sparkling. 'Warren asked me yesterday and we went shopping for the ring. We were going to announce it at the toast after dinner if nobody spotted it before.'

'Toast?' Georgine said guiltily. 'Was I supposed to be buying prosecco?'

Blair beamed. 'We brought champagne. It's hidden in the sack of Christmas gifts.'

Warren produced a cool bag harbouring a bottle of champagne and four glasses – obviously he hadn't known about Sol coming, either, but Georgine happily went with a wine glass instead. 'Only half a glass. I'm driving.' And she'd probably got some of last night's booze still sloshing about inside her.

Over the last of the turkey, they toasted and congratulated Blair and Warren about five times. Randall kept saying, '*Vey* ha-hee, *vey* ha-hee,' and Blair gave him a long, intense hug whispering, 'We're very happy too, Dad.'

What a special Christmas for them, Georgine thought mistily, as everybody cleaned their plates of Christmas ice cream dessert with lots of *mmms*, flopping back and rubbing their bellies, quite unable to eat another thing.

'But I could squeeze in a cup of coffee,' said Warren, getting up to make it.

'And let's open the chocolates while we exchange gifts,' Blair cried, and they all discovered they could fit a little more in after all.

The washing up was abandoned in piles on every surface. Georgine received a top she'd wanted from Blair and jeans from Randall. She didn't bring up Barbara and Terrence's munificent spa gift in front of him in case it made him feel bad, and Blair must have felt the same as she didn't mention it either.

Then they Skyped Grandma Patty, who was dressed in a red shiny sweater that made her silver hair glow.

'Ha, Mom! May-ee Kissmas!' beamed Randall, making Grandma Patty get all tearful. 'Bear's engaged!'

'Oh, *Blair*, honey!' cried Grandma Patty, clapping her hands. 'Now you definitely have to come to the States for spring break!'

Georgine saw the hope on Randall's face and promised rashly, 'We will. We'll talk to your doctor and make sure it's OK, Dad.'

'We'll manage between us,' Blair added.

Overcome, Randall blew kisses at his daughters and his mom. Even Warren got one, which made him laugh.

Then Grandma Patty had to catch her lift to Randall's brother's household for Christmas dinner. Georgine washed up and Blair and Warren dried, taking up the entire kitchenette.

When Blair was ready to leave, Georgine elected to depart too. Randall and Sol were deep in a game of solo whist, which Georgine had no intention of ever learning to play, so she dropped a kiss on each of their heads with one last, 'Merry Christmas!'

Outside, it had begun to snow properly again. 'Do you have plans now?' Blair asked uncertainly, flicking Warren a look that Georgine interpreted as 'if my sister's going to be alone I'm going to invite her to our place'.

'Yes,' she said promptly, because this morning's sadness was threatening to return and being a gooseberry would definitely not be a cure. 'Enjoy the rest of Christmas and congratulations again!' She hopped quickly into her car before Blair could press her on what her supposed plans were. She circled the car park, waving gaily and making fresh tyre tracks in the snow. Once out of sight, she relaxed, driving home in silence because one jolly Christmas tune on the radio would have her in tears.

Snow blew from the bodywork of the few cars she saw, as if they were bursting out of Christmas cards. Avoiding passing beneath Bettsbrough's jolly Christmas lights, she headed for the safety of the little village of Middledip and a solitary evening drinking wine and eating chocolate.

She'd treat herself to a couple of new books for her Kindle, and then Christmas would be over so far as she was concerned.

Chapter Thirty-Seven

Once safely parked outside her house, she gathered her Christmas gifts and the leftover turkey to make into a curry to share between her freezer and Randall's.

Juggling everything, she fumbled for her key, trying not to drop it in the snow. As she unlocked the door, a car door slammed nearby. She glanced around to see a man coming towards her, snowflakes landing on his black beanie hat and big black coat.

Frozen in more ways than one, she watched his feet sliding in the snow as he approached the point where her garden met the pavement. He glanced down at the single row of footprints she'd made. Then, carefully, he began to make a set of his own footprints alongside.

When he stood beside her, he smiled. 'Well, Mizz Jaw-Jean. Happy holidays.'

She stared at him. 'Joe. Where did you come from?'

His dark eyes regarded her. 'I've been waiting in my car for you to come home and I think I've turned into a snowman. Any chance of you inviting me in?'

''Course.' Georgine was beginning to shiver herself. She

pushed open the front door and he kicked the snow from his boots then followed her in.

In the small hallway, she removed her own boots and stood them on the doormat. Her heart was fluttering but she kept her voice even. 'You wouldn't have had to wait if you'd phoned. Anytime over the past eight days, in fact.'

He nodded. 'But some things are better said face to face.'

'Right.' Good things or bad, she thought. Slowly, she took off her coat and scarf and hung them on the newel. She ought to offer him coffee or something, but if he'd come to say goodbye then she'd rather not delay his actual exit while a drink was consumed.

Dumping his coat and hat, he followed her into the lounge. Not giving her a chance to choose the armchair, he caught hold of her hand and drew her to sit with him on the sofa.

'Thanks for getting that article in the *Daily Snoop*,' he began softly.

'Was it in?' she said, surprised. 'I looked for it for days.'

'Christmas Eve. It was their Christmas cheer story. I felt like my heart would burst when I read it.' His hand, despite his claims of feeling like a snowman, was hot on hers.

'My pleasure.' Her voice was flat. 'I only told the truth.'

'But you didn't have to bother and it means a lot to me that you did. I've found out the person who leaked the original article was Pete, our manager. I spent most of yesterday talking to him and the guys. It seems Pete had decided that if he got me out of the band he could manipulate the others better. Billy proved particularly malleable so Pete had begun to set us against one another in pursuit of feathering his own nest.'

Despite her stomach feeling hollow with apprehension,

she was intrigued. 'Oh?' She pondered for a moment. 'How? What did he hope would happen?'

'What almost did happen – me leaving! The Hungry Years is a successful band and Pete wanted more of our pie. He knows I'm too fly to agree to anything like that so he began stabbing me in the back and trying to set the others against me. Whether he genuinely thinks Billy's songs are more commercial than mine I don't know, but that's what he gave as his excuse for trying to oust me. He'd told Billy too, who was flattered into believing everything Pete said from that point on. Pete had even sent Billy a new management agreement to look over, thinking that if he could get our front man onside it would be easier to persuade the rest. I've seen the agreement now and it contains a totally unethical clause to allow Pete to play something on every recording made by The Hungry Years.'

So Joe was staying with the band. Her throat felt stiff and unnatural. She had to fight to speak. 'What would be the point of that?'

He gave a harsh laugh. 'It gets Pete a share of all our recording royalties! Another reason to dump me, I suppose, as he's a drummer so could have taken my place in the studio. Giving that shitty article to the *Daily Snoop* was inspired, playing on all my insecurities and making me look in the wrong direction for the danger. It was completely destabilising. But I'm afraid he's gone too far. The band members have agreed to sack him; including Billy, who feels a complete prat at the way he's been used.'

'Wow.' She tried to put herself in his shoes and comprehend the scale of the treachery. 'You must feel so betrayed, but I'm glad you know exactly who the leak was.'

He seemed to understand what she didn't say. 'I never

360

really thought it was you. That day, I was just listing every possibility, however unlikely.' His fingers tightened around hers. 'Thanks for sending me the show reel. The students were awesome. You must have been mega-proud. I got emotional watching it.'

She nodded, accepting the change of subject and glad, despite everything, that she'd let him see the fruits of all their labour. 'Yes,' she said, then, remembering how she'd looked for him at show after show, 'You should have been there.'

His gaze dropped. 'Oggie said the same. I didn't want to . . . I knew if I saw you . . . And what if people had realised and started looking at me instead of the students? Taking photos.'

'I hadn't thought of that,' she replied honestly, immediately able to see how it would have stolen the show – literally.

He looked straight into her eyes. 'Georgine, I'm back with the band. We're starting work on a new album and this year's tour's going ahead. I'll have side projects, maybe a couple of solo singles, but I'll be with The Hungry Years.'

Her heart began a slow, heavy slide towards her feet, yet there was happiness within her sadness. Happiness for him. 'That's fantastic. The band means so much to you and you've earned every moment of your success. I wish you a wonderful future.' And she did, despite the ominous tingling behind her eyes.

'Thank you.' But he didn't sound particularly thrilled. 'Being in a band . . . it's a commitment.' He frowned. 'I know you're deeply dedicated to your job, which makes you brilliant at it, but being in a band's even more intense. We're dependent on each other and the band's more important than any one of us. Does that make sense?'

361

''Course.' Her eyes were so full of tears now that if she moved even one eyelash the drops would spill. She smiled, as if it would somehow make her tear ducts absorb the fluid again.

He stroked her hand. 'You're upset. I'm trying to be honest. The recent friction in the band, the uncertainty, it could happen again. More than one person wants to be on top, same as in business. Or a gang.'

The tears gave in to gravity and began to trickle over the curve of her cheek. 'I want what's best for you. You deserve to be happy.'

Frowning, he began to squeegee the tears off her face with his thumb. 'I'm not sure whether you're getting what I'm saying here.'

She nodded, which sent more of the traitorous tears slipping over her skin. 'I think I am. I'm genuinely happy for you. I'm just not altogether happy for me. Not right this second.'

She pulled away and made a dash for the kitchen roll, knocking the whole thing over so that it spilled across the floor. She rescued it and blew her nose several times, pausing only when she realised he'd followed her and was hovering close.

'I should have spoken to you before I made the decision.' His voice was hoarse.

She laughed between nose blows. 'Why? It's your career! Joe, you've made such a success of your life. That success is a two-fingered salute to every horrible person who was mean to you when Garrit gave you and Chrissy a bad life. I honestly couldn't be more pleased.'

His eyebrows flipped up. 'It's a funny-looking pleased.' He tore off a fresh sheet of kitchen roll and gently helped dry her cheeks. 'Musicians make crap boyfriends. Always

362

off somewhere: in a studio, in a plane, in a different time zone, a long way from home.'

She bit her lip so as not to cry harder.

'But I'm still going to ask if you think you could try it,' he added.

Georgine paused, just as she'd been going to blow her nose again. 'Try it?'

He slipped his hands around her waist, then let them drift south until they rested on the curves of her buttocks. 'At first I thought cutting ties would be best for you. Those articles made me feel unclean, like I used to: a damaged nobody. I thought if I went back to my life with the band the feelings of wanting to be with you every minute might fade.'

'But what about what I felt?' she demanded croakily.

He stroked her bottom. 'Initially, I didn't think too clearly about that. I just felt as if I would infect you with all my horrible baggage.' He smiled suddenly. 'Then I remembered Mizz Jaw-Jean being my friend when I was a raggedy-arse waif and she was the prettiest girl in the school. And once that got in my head, I couldn't get rid of the idea that she might be there for me whatever happened. So I came back to see if you'd be more than my friend this time.

'In fact,' he added, 'I've actually told the band that if me going back doesn't work for you, then I'm leaving after all. They told me to get up here and be really freakin' convincing.'

Her heart whooshed up into her throat. 'Don't leave the band. It's part of you.'

'Only if I'm always coming home to you.'

Her laugh was almost a sob as she threw her arms around his neck. 'That's a deal, JJ Blacker.'

'Joe,' he reminded her, holding her so tightly she could scarcely breathe.

'I don't know,' she gasped, with mock solemnity. 'Johnjoe.' She kissed his jaw. 'Rich.' She kissed his cheek. 'JJ.' The corner of his mouth. 'And Joe. Sleeping with someone who's four different people could be kinda fun.'

He threw his head back and laughed aloud. 'I've loved you since I was about twelve. Loving you four times over will be easy.'

'Me too,' she breathed. 'Loving you times four, I mean! Shall we go upstairs and start now? My feet are like blocks of ice and we could begin with a long, hot shower—'

He groaned, leaning his forehead against hers. 'I would so love to. Trouble is . . . my mum.'

She giggled. 'Won't she let you stay out on a school night?'

He laughed back, swinging her right up off the floor. 'Believe it or not, we're spending Christmas together. Garrit making a pest of himself at her place has unsettled her and I didn't want her to feel that way over Christmas. She's been sober for several years and I respect her for that. We've come to a better understanding recently – another case of me stopping my constant looking back, I suppose – and so I invited her and Mari to join me at Acting Instrumental. I don't absolutely have to go back and spend Christmas evening with them but it might be hurtful not to. I've been with them since yesterday evening and it's been . . . an experience.'

'Wow.' Georgine hardly knew what to say. To spend Christmas evening with Debs Leonard, the woman she remembered seeing so often with lager cans for company? But she saw the plea in Joe's eyes and tightened her arms around him, heart soaring with happiness. 'That's really going forward. Let's go and spend an evening with your family.'

'Mm,' he breathed, between kisses. 'Mum and Mari are sleeping in one of the other apartments so, sooner or later, they'll leave . . . *Then* I'm holding you to that promise of making out in the shower. And, by the way, the forecast's for snow for a fortnight, so pack enough clothes.'

She pulled back to look at him. 'It's not. It's set to thaw.'

He ran his tongue down her neck. 'Not my snow.'

Epilogue

One year later

'I don't see why I should talk to you ever again,' Oggie groused as he fidgeted from foot to foot in the freezing cold. Georgine could see and hear Oggie and Joe as she organised two rows of teenagers, making sure everybody had streamers to throw and helium balloons to release.

Joe grinned at Oggie. 'Because you're one of my best and oldest friends?'

Oggie, pointedly, did not grin back. 'Best and oldest friends do *not* poach staff from other best and oldest friends!'

Georgine turned around to chime in, 'Strictly speaking, he didn't poach me. I demanded to be given the job.'

A young man approached Georgine shyly. 'Good afternoon. Miss France? I'm Jamie from the *Bettsbrough Bugle*. Do you want to go ahead with the grand opening and we'll do the interview after? Then the photographer can get his shots and go.' He cast a glance at where Joe was looking suitably bad-boy rock star, hair grown out on top

366

but blond these days. 'Will Mr Blacker give an interview, do you think?'

The change to Joe's expression was so subtle that anyone else would probably miss that he was thinking 'Ohhhhhhhh noooooooo . . .' Even after the smash hit of the last album, *Into the Future* by The Hungry Years, he wasn't best buddies with the press. Georgine sent him a special smile. 'I hope he will,' she said clearly, so he couldn't help but hear. 'But record his speech in case he doesn't have time.'

'What speech?' Joe demanded.

With a skip, she propelled herself to his side. 'You are going to give a speech, aren't you?'

Joe put his lips close to her ear. 'Only because you won't sleep with me if I don't.'

'Shhhhhh!' She felt her cheeks burn. 'I'll sleep with you twice if you give an interview to that nice young journalist as well.'

He laughed, abandoning his bad-boy rock star persona and planting a big kiss on her mouth. 'OK. Let's get this party started.'

Georgine had borrowed a couple of tech students from Acting Instrumental to set up the public-address system. She looked across at them and they gave her a thumbs-up, so she stepped up to the microphone, beaming at the crowd of people who were swinging their arms and stamping their feet as they waited in the raw December afternoon not because they wanted to see the opening of the centre Georgine had been slaving to bring to reality, but because JJ Blacker was involved. But, hey. You used what you had.

'Thank you very much for coming, everybody. In a moment I'm going to ask our guest of honour, Mr JJ Blacker –' she paused for applause and a few girlish

367

whoops '– to officially open this youth centre, here on the Shetland estate.

'But before I do,' she went on, 'I want to tell you a little about our fabulous new facility. We've worked with Bettsbrough Council to erect this building on the edge of the estate, close enough for young people to reach, but not so close that they disturb the neighbourhood.' Buoyed by laughter, she grinned. 'We plan to have a programme of activities and events, both drop-in and scheduled, encompassing just about everything we can think of. No teen from the Shetland estate ever need say there's nothing here for them. Students from Acting Instrumental will offer short workshops in music, drama and dance, and we're getting help from the A Level PE students of the Sir John Browne Academy to implement a sports programme.' She waited out a ripple of applause. 'JJ' – she always felt self-conscious when the occasion called for her to call him that – 'is going to say something about funding in a moment. What he probably won't mention, so I will, is that he's donated all the royalties of his recent solo hit "Running on Empty" to this project.'

Joe lowered his brows at her as the audience cheered. Georgine grinned, unrepentant. 'So, with no further delay, let me hand over to our guest of honour – JJ Blacker, drummer and vocalist of famous pop-punk band, The Hungry Years!' She never quite got over the dream-worldliness of this man, who spent a whole lot of time helping her out of her clothes, being a rock star.

The applause was louder this time. A girl shouted, 'Got your sticks, JJ?'

Joe smiled and dispensed with formality. 'I'm only making a speech because my girlfriend says I have to.' Again, laughter. Then he became serious. 'It's no secret that some of my formative years were not the best. The Shetland estate then was known as Shitland.' Louder laughter, mainly from teenagers. 'I spent twelve years here. And for most of it I was scared, hungry, cold and wondering if it was the best life had to offer.' No laughter at all. Georgine had to swallow a lump in her throat.

'For me,' Joe went on, 'things got a whole lot better when I went to live somewhere else. I don't want you guys to feel like that. I want you to be glad to stay here in Bettsbrough, to grow up with something to do other than run around with a gang or get drawn into bad stuff that will wreck your life. For that reason, when the other Hungries offered to play benefit gigs for Acting Instrumental, the performing arts college in Middledip I'm also involved with, I got together with Mr Ogden here' – he gestured towards Oggie – 'one of my best and oldest friends. We decided that Acting Instrumental is doing very well already. So, we'd like to do something right here, instead.'

He reached out and took Georgine's hand. 'This is my other best and oldest friend, Georgine France. She'll be heading up the team at the youth centre.' He looked around the audience, gazing directly at the photographer from the *Bugle* while he got his shots. 'I thought for a long time about the name of the centre. When I lived here I was known as Rich Garrit, but I didn't want to use that. I could have used my stage name, JJ Blacker, but that seemed a bit up myself.'

Jamie the journalist moved a little closer with his voice recorder. The photographer inched in beside him.

'So,' Joe concluded, 'it's my pleasure to declare open Blackthorn's, the youth centre of the Shetland estate.' Just as Georgine had coached him, he flung his arms in the air and the double rank of teenagers, many of them students of Acting Instrumental, past and present, released the red and gold balloons they'd been holding and joyfully threw their streamers to float on the breeze.

Under cover of the applause, Joe stepped back from the mic and caught Georgine round the waist. 'OK?'

She gave him a great hug as people, organised into a queue by Oggie and his family, who had come to help, passed by. 'It was perfect,' she whispered. 'You've done a good thing.'

He took her hand and joined the flow of people heading inside for the free hot chocolate they'd laid on. 'Do I get my reward now?' His eyes laughed.

'Soon,' she promised. 'When you've been nice to the journalist and signed a few hundred autographs at 50p each to add to Blackthorn's funds.' She began to steer him to the hovering young journalist, who was obviously eager not to lose what was no doubt the scoop of his career so far.

'Bargain.' Joe gave her hand a parting squeeze. 'So long as I'm coming home to you.'

Acknowledgements

Every time I write acknowledgements for a book I'm humbled anew by how many people give up their time and expertise to help me create the most authentic story I can.

Heartfelt thanks to:

Jacqueline Barron (www.jacquelinebarron.com), who talked to me for hours about working in the world of music, drama and dance, and pointed me towards wonderful resources, including further education colleges for the performing arts. She also created the idea for the scholarship that resulted in *A Very Kerry Christmas, Uncle Jones*. Jackie is an accomplished performer and tutor, appearing all over the world. As I said to her, we haven't done too badly for two girls from an ordinary comprehensive school.

Jackie introduced me to Jack Savidge of the band Friendly Fires (http://friendlyfires.co.uk), who seemed not one bit fazed by being asked to help someone he didn't know. Jack greatly influenced all band-related stuff, including pointing out when I'd got my facts wrong, even though he knew I didn't want to hear it because it messed with my plot. I'm indebted to both he and Jackie for explaining the music royalty system to me.

Wayne Parkin of The Lace Market Theatre, Nottingham helped me create the show and advised on everything theatre-led. That he drove to meet me in Leicester each of the many times we talked made things super-easy for me. I'm sure our fellow diners were entertained when he jumped up to act things out.

Someone else who didn't know me, this time introduced by Wayne, is Alex Wrampling, head of drama at Landau Forte College. Alex answered a shoal of questions about education and subjects such as video evidence for qualifications. Both Wayne and Alex were kind enough to beta-read an early draft of the manuscript to keep me on track.

Paul Matthews first told me about the further education colleges springing up now that people have to stay in education or in an apprenticeship until the age of eighteen, and helped me create the whole idea of Joe being involved with Acting Instrumental. He's answered a lot of questions about musicians, students and education, and provided me with terminology.

Paul also introduced me to his colleague JJ Sims who was in the process of implementing a small further education college himself: a girl's football academy. I was so impressed by his 'can-do' attitude and vision, and I love the idea that you don't have to be one of the big cogs in our education system to make things happen. The fact that JJ is known by the same initials as my hero Joe is absolute coincidence!

The *Daily Snoop* articles were only possible because Rachel Henry put her fantastic journalistic skills to work on my behalf and signposted me to the resources I needed.

And though it was inadvertent, Ashley Panter gave me the title of the students' Christmas show by texting a typo when she texted me 'A very kerry Christmas, Auntie Sue'. Trevor Moorcroft aided my memory of the pub in Brighton called The Hungry Years.

As always, loads of social media friends answered questions or gave me insight. If ever I need opinions or experiences I just go onto Facebook or Twitter and ask!

My friend and good writing buddy Mark West (www.markwest.org.uk) has beta-read just about every book I've ever written and entertains me with his pithy comments. I was delighted to be able to return the compliment this year and write 'And . . . breathe!' next to one of his long sentences, as he so often has with mine.

Team Sue Moorcroft continues to support me and celebrate with me and I could not be more grateful. Thanks to every single one of you, especially Mick Arnold for 'Whispering Court' and Sue McDonagh/Jayne Curtis for 'the *Daily Snoop*'.

And thanks to the person from my own school days who inspired this book. I doubt you'll ever know that you did, or why I looked back after so many years and began to suspect what your situation had been. I've heard you have a happy life now, and I'm sincerely glad.

For Ava Blissham, it's going to be a
Christmas to remember . . .

Countdown to Christmas
as you step into the wonderful
world of Sue Moorcroft.

Available now.

It's time to deck the halls . . .

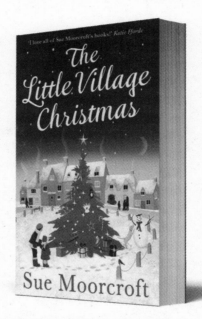

Return to the little village of Middledip with this
Sunday Times bestselling Christmas read . . .